ADVANCE PRAISE FOR

Drug Lord

"*Drug Lord* should come with a warning sticker: CAUTION, THE TRUTH WILL SET YOU FREE."

— **Paul Rosenberg, author of**
The Breaking Dawn and Free-Man's Perspective

"Hunt and Casey do a great job describing in creative story telling what happens behind the scenes in the pharmaceutical industry while critiquing the drug war. Head to head comparisons of big pharma to black markets, and of FDA to the DEA, illustrate what every American should know."

— **Ralph Weber, CEO, MediBid Inc., author of *Rigged:***
How Insurance Ruined Healthcare

"Ayn Rand's *Atlas Shrugged* was the novel that sparked a free market revolution in the 20th century. *Drug Lord* could be the novel that ignites that spark into an inferno in the 21st century. And I can't think of a better person to pen it with than Doug Casey."

— **Jeff Berwick, *The Dollar Vigilante***

"In *Speculator*, we met Charles Knight who balanced contempt for bureaucracy with personal ambition. His next adventure takes him into the heart of the two-headed beast: drug wars and the pharmaceutical business. As a physician entrepreneur I loved this book, and cannot wait for the next installment!"

— **Jonathan M. Sackier, MB, ChB, FRCS, FACS, Hon DSc,**
Visiting Professor of Surgery, Oxford University

"*Drug Lord* is as equally entertaining as it is edifying. I read it over the course of three days and was totally absorbed. Knight's adventures were much more fun than my usual day-to-day, to say the least."

— **Ross Ulbricht**

"Karl Marx was right that economics determines history. But he didn't realize governments could distort economies so badly that only the intrepid might survive. And only after they reaped generous rewards could the 'meek (proletariat) inherit the earth.' *Drug Lord*'s intrepid hero, Charles Knight, is the representation of this ultimate reality. Engaging and enlightening".

— **Barry Reid, author of *The Paper Trip***

"Charles Knight hits his stride, stepping on from his smashing role in *Speculator*, to gather steam in *Drug Lord*. *Speculator* was great and successful, but *Drug Lord* is possibly better: it's different; it's smoother, and Charles Knight is smarter now. The dialogue and settings teach life lessons."

— **Bo Keeley, executive hobo, racquetball champion, global vagabond, and prolific author**

"Charles Knight is back—a little older, a little wiser, and trying to get a whole lot richer. This time he's learning how to sell legal drugs at an illegal discount through an even less legal market. Casey and Hunt manage to entertain and inform at the same time, revealing the often fatal, though unintended, consequences of regulation by the FDA, the DEA, the IRS, and a cornucopia of bureaucracies. *Drug Lord* is another stylishly written paean to free markets and free minds."

— **Jo Ann Skousen, Professor, Chapman University**

"Through a cleverly crafted plot, Hunt and Casey sound the alarm on paternalistic laws, over-legislation, and the growing police state. The story reads like historical nonfiction as government officials morally justify evil acts for a perceived greater good, letting the reader ponder serious philosophical issues while enjoying a thoroughly good yarn."
— **Jeffrey James Higgins, retired DEA supervisory special agent**

"*Drug Lord* is *Chicken Soup for the Ancap Soul.*"
— **Albert Lu, CEO, Sprott US Media**
and host of *The Power & Market Report*

"*Drug Lord*—it's Ayn Rand with guns and drugs! But that doesn't do John Hunt and Doug Casey justice. They've written a thriller that's whatever the opposite of 'escapism' is. Call it 'right-here-and-right-now-ism.' It's an adventure in rationalism with a heartening lesson. Reason is not only the source of liberty, it's the source of virtue."
— **P.J. O'Rourke, Editor, *American Consequences* magazine**
and author of *How the Hell Did This Happen?*
The Presidential Campaign of 2016

Books by Doug Casey:

The International Man

Crisis Investing

Strategic Investing

Crisis Investing for the '90s

Totally Incorrect

Right on the Money

Books by John Hunt:

Higher Cause

Assume the Physician

Your Child's Asthma

Books by Doug Casey and John Hunt:

Speculator

DRUG LORD

Doug Casey
and
John Hunt

Book 2 of the High Ground Novels

Drug Lord

Published by High Ground Books, LLC

ISBN-10: 1-947449-02-8

ISBN-13: 978-1-947449-02-2

Cover design by Jim Ross

Edited by Harry David (HD Editorial Services)

Dedication

THIS book is dedicated to Julian Assange, Edward Snowden, and Ross Ulbricht. All unjustly persecuted, much in the mold of Charles Knight. The real criminals are those behind the government's efforts to take away the freedom of those who most vigorously promote liberty.

Acknowledgments

WE are grateful to Harry David, Paul Woodward, and Nathalie Marcus for their wise and efficient editing and guidance; Jim Ross for his artistic perseverance. We individually gained intellectual stimulation from Cameron Clay, Dick Hanley, Ancha Casey, Matthew, Kimberly Johnson, John Slovensky, Jeffrey James Higgins, Jo Ann Skousen, and our families, friends, colleagues, and growing number of readers.

Contents

Prologue 1

1   Return to the Front 5

2   Field Marketing 13

3   Planning Stages 21

4   The Snake Pit 31

5   Morlocks in Mordor 38

6   The Legal Business 56

7   Getting Snuffed 67

8   The Ground Force 81

9   Dirty vs. Clean 92

10   First Impressions 101

11   Illegal Expansion 112

12   Bootlegging Gondwana 119

13   Legal Permits and Permissions 127

14   Evils and Expletives of Competition 135

15   A Parolee and an Enemy of the State 147

16   Truth and Consequences 160

17 Home Is Where the Beast Waits 170

18 Devil's Brew 176

19 Maximum ProPG Pathways 190

20 Two for the Price of One 197

21 A Piano at War 204

22 The Lesser of Two Evils 209

23 Awakening 215

24 Kabuki Theater 224

25 After-Action Report 243

26 Burning Down the House 249

27 Building the Dark Side 261

28 The President Learns a Lesson 268

29 Small-Small Time 285

30 Enemies of America 297

31 Fieldwork 305

32 A Most-Flexible Wood 311

33 Import-Export 316

34 Everybody Likes Bamboo Desks, Don't They? 322

35 Who's in Charge Here? 327

36 Executive Action 334

37 Chinks in the Armor. 338

38 El Gordo Spills the Frijoles 343

39 Quality Control 351

40 Field Trip 358

41 Black PR 364

42 Evil among Us 369

43 Rogue Scientist 376

44 False Flag 381

45 Who Needs Killing? 394

46 Getting to Know You… 408

47 Praetorians 418

48 A Good Deed Unpunished 429

Epilogue 436

If the words, "life, liberty, and the pursuit of happiness" don't include the right to experiment with your own consciousness, then the Declaration of Independence isn't worth the hemp it was written on.

— *Terrence McKenna*

Prologue

STEPHAN Liggett's brain lingered in test pattern and needed coffee. Coffee is an addictive drug. Life is full of addictive substances—some good, some bad, some irrelevant.

Like many addictive drugs, his coffee offered some proven health benefits, but could also cause harm. No government currently outlawed his coffee, so he didn't need to rob a bank to pay for it.

His caffeine-depleted brain concluded, falsely, that it would take less time to wait in the long line at a coffee shop with the other morning zombies than it would to load, grind, and brew it at home. And so his first important action of this morning was to consume a drug—bought on the free market at a Starbuck's—in order to make his brain function better.

After a week relaxing at the beach with his significant other, work held less appeal than usual, so Stephan made no effort to rush. The facility's head veterinarian would sometimes show up early, but Stephan usually opened the place up. The dogs weren't going anywhere. If the poor things were even still alive. Faint hints of the morning sun illuminated a newly installed security card reader that tracked everyone's comings and goings. Stephan lazily fumbled with his ID card, and the door to the laboratory building opened.

The building smelled like work. Chemicals from the labs on the stories above, old paint, new floor wax, printer ink, mold from the forced-air ducts, fiberglass from the drop-down ceiling panels, all mixed with the evanescent hints of the animal lab—a veterinary facility—in the basement. The scents

1

of the kennel ascended along with the elevators, and squeezed through available cracks in concrete, and leaked through the laminate floor.

The kennel area itself smelled a bit like bamboo because the current drug undergoing testing was made from the plant. They sprayed an aerosol version of it into the dogs' lungs.

The elevator moved at a pace best described as *imperceptible*, as usual. "Sure, you can save money on the elevators. No problem." Stephan mimicked the imaginary voice of the building's architect, adding an effeminate lilt that came naturally to him. "We'll simply adjust the factory speed settings to *permanently retarded*."

It's not like the university's administrators gave a damn about the efficiency of the people in these buildings. As long as the occupants brought in grant money, nothing else really mattered here.

Stephan had grown close to many of the people at Visioryme, the company that contracted for this current study. Visioryme's CEO was his favorite. Unlike the CEOs of so many other small pharmaceutical companies with whom he had interacted, Tristana Debocher was kind and empathic. But also somehow broken, as if she were buried under debris, or bearing the weight of some unspoken personal tragedy.

They had met many times during the planning and contracting for this study. Stephan did all sorts of work, from applying for approval from the Institutional Animal Care and Use Committee, to biohazard-inspection preparation, to FDA filings. He took on these tasks—far outside the scope of his official role as a vet tech—because he succeeded at navigating the administrative landscape where others failed. His unthreatening persona and gentle manner disarmed the defensive department secretaries. Instead of reflexively erecting barricades, minions of the administrative swamp were inclined to help him. Adequately stoked with a medium-sized café latte, Stephan could conquer academic malaise. Tristana Debocher saw it. She complimented him on his thinking and his work ethic. His lack of a college degree didn't seem to matter to her.

Her invitation to join the company as a sort of Man Friday both flattered and intrigued him. Working for a startup pharmaceutical company had never entered his mind. But then neither had working in a university animal lab. He would have preferred traipsing about the world, scuba diving and hunting for treasure. Alas, while he possessed extensive skills, he lacked extensive money. Her proposal offered him the chance to acquire more of both, while removing even the faintest shadow of job security.

He would respond to her today. One way or the other.

He heard the dogs barking before the elevator sluggishly settled on the first subfloor, where the windowless veterinary labs lay concealed from prowling animal-rights activists. The door remained closed for what felt like minutes after the elevator had stopped. The delay served as the passive-aggressive retribution of the construction contractors against the university budget hounds. Through the elevator door, the dogs barked louder.

Not normal.

The doors pulled apart, so slowly.

Immediately a black nose peeked through. Stephan slid against the back wall of the elevator in a surge of fear.

The rest of the black dog followed the black nose into the elevator as the door made way.

The dog leaped toward his face.

He didn't have time to scream.

But he didn't need to scream. The dog, a female collie, put her paws on his chest and licked his chin and nose, while dancing around on her hind feet, wagging her tail in greeting.

Stephan gently lowered the animal back down onto all fours, and scratched behind her ear while peering out of the elevator. Dogs, freed from their cages, barked and played and rollicked, engaged in a canine party.

The black collie stayed by his side. With curiosity tempered by timidity, Stephan stepped into the corridor. Some of these animals weren't habituated to normal human contact. There was no guarantee they would be fond of humans. He'd seen dogs in the lab lash out unpredictably at vet techs. If he were locked in a cage all day with needles running experimental drugs through his veins, he might bite whoever came near him too.

Why were they out of their cages?

Not all of the sixteen dogs were out. He counted just eight at large, having their heyday in the lab. The other eight remained caged, but added to the bedlam with their own excited voices.

Stephan started by corralling one of the dogs, comparing his collar to cage tags. The collie helped. Her breed rounded up strays, after all.

The head veterinarian emerged from the elevator.

"Stephan, what's going on?" the veterinarian asked.

"No idea. They were like this when I got here."

The vet studied the reoccupied cage, jiggled the door's simple lever latch up and down, and didn't say a word.

The two men looked at each other. Each had the same thought.

PETA.

It seemed obvious that animal-rights activists had intruded and let the animals out. Just to mess up their experiments. Everyone knew it might happen sooner or later.

The helpful collie brushed up against Stephan's leg and barked repeatedly in the manner of dogs frustrated at human stupidity. She jumped up on her hind legs and clawed at one of the empty cages. Maybe she wanted to go into *her* cage too.

A red card on the cage and a red collar declared the collie to be in the active treatment group—those subjected to Visioryme's drug. The dogs with the blue cards and collars had received only placebo.

Stephan studied the empty cages. All of them had red cards.

He rounded up the dogs one at a time, and returned each to its cage.

Every dog running free wore a red collar.

Stephan muttered to himself uncertainly. "Damn PETA."

1

Return to the Front

CHARLES Knight swayed on the bow of his fifty-four-foot sloop to the syncopated rhythms of metal drums playing through the sound system at top volume. Jimmy Buffett shared his love of island culture. The sloop ran large through Atlantic swells propelled by an eighteen-knot early-autumn easterly breeze. He grinned as the wind tossed a sheet of salt spray through his long hair.

Six miles up ahead lay Charleston, where he would enter the United States for the first time in seven years. How would he feel when he arrived? Would it feel like home?

He wiped salt crust from around his eyes and squinted into the late-afternoon sun as it reflected off the ocean. In the distance, a powerboat crashed through waves, sending spray to either side.

It was coming his way.

Charles moved aft to the cockpit, deactivated the autopilot, lowered the music volume, and turned his boat closer into the wind, away from the distant vessel. He tightened up the mainsheet and the genoa. His straight left knee and bent right knee together braced him upright while his boat heeled hard over. He felt the rush as water lashed over the gunwale. It never failed to elevate his energy. He couldn't help but grin. He and his boat headed back out to sea, cutting through the water at 8.5 knots.

Unfortunately, the powerboat turned to intercept him, traveling at more than twenty knots. The reality of impending trouble diminished his enjoyment of the moment.

A few minutes later, the twenty-six-foot-long Defender Class Response Boat with obscenely oversized twin outboards approached his yacht. A machine gun mounted toward its bow suggested this was no friendly vessel welcoming him home to his native shores after so many years abroad.

A life-jacketed man on the bow aimed his weapon directly toward him. It was an aggressive display of power—all the rage in Washington and embraced by predisposed government employees at all levels.

The Coast Guard had hailed him on the radio three times as they approached. Of course, he had ignored them, impatient buggers. But it wasn't as if his sailboat could outrun them. The boat came up close and the officer in charge hollered through his loudspeaker.

"This is the United States Coast Guard. Head into the wind, and prepare to be boarded."

Damn. Charles had hoped to avoid this.

His concern arose from the small issue of having a hundred thousand doses of illicit drugs stashed onboard his boat.

He waved to the Coast Guard as if seeing the boat for the first time, and fired up the 125 HP Yanmar diesel that would keep him heading straight into the wind. He rounded up. His mainsail luffed while he furled the genoa, which he accomplished simply by freeing a sheet and pressing a button. Modern technology allowed him to sail the ocean alone in his boat, which he had christened *Caroline.*

Her mainsail made a horrendous racket, and the boom struck about, angry at having to face the wind head-on.

He glanced at the armed vessel as it came nearer. The testosterone-fueled man who stood at the M240 machine gun had his finger on the trigger. The wrong wave might lift the Coast Guard boat's bow and, combined with that misplaced finger, lead to a barrage of 7.62 mm rounds shooting through his hull. Or through him. Was the threat of a sailboat approaching the U.S. shore now sufficient to induce the Coast Guard to keep its guns locked and loaded and aimed at him?

The Defender came alongside. The sailor manning the machine gun sported expensive sunglasses under the brim of his Coast Guard hat. The buoyancy of the sailor's orange PFD would partially counteract the density of the bullet-retarding vest that lay underneath, and just might keep him afloat if he were to find himself in the water. The man still aimed his gun directly at Charles, who stood in the cockpit of his sailboat—unthreatening and with a bright and welcoming smile.

"Sir," a voice said through a loudspeaker from inside the partially enclosed Defender. Through the glare on the glass, Charles could see the man holding the microphone. "Sir, you are in United States waters. We are boarding your vessel."

Over the last several years, Charles had learned that if one had the intention of defying authority, then *questioning* that authority was best done quietly. He had acquired the ability to seethe on the inside and smile on the outside, a facade he never could have maintained in his youth. The muscles around his mouth tightened as adrenaline surged throughout his body. Psychiatrists might call this anxiety, but the term *anxiety* applied only when this process occurred inappropriately. The fight-or-flight response that now suffused Charles provided his mind and his body with the neurotransmitters it needed when facing imminent danger. His senses sharpened with the pending incursion of threatening interlopers.

Although Charles had followed the excesses of recent political administrations in the news during his long absence, he had not personally experienced the cultural transformation that had occurred in the nation of his birth. He attempted to restrain a foolish urge to peel back the Kafkaesque layers of the Homeland Security onion. He did not succeed. He yelled to be heard over the panoply of sail, engine, and wind noise. "Why do you wish to board my boat?"

"Sir, you have no choice in this matter. You are being boarded." The officer nodded to three men who tossed lines around available cleats and safety rails and pulled the Defender tight aboard. The two vessels now bobbed side by side, the red polyethylene of the Defender rubbing against the navy blue gelcoat of the *Caroline*. One man aimed his M16A2 at Charles; the machine gunner on the bow kept his weapon trained on him as well. The officer had his pistol drawn, but at least *that* weapon was not aimed directly at Charles's chest.

"You made it clear I have no choice, but *why* are you boarding my boat?" Charles pushed back sun-bleached hair—lightly caked with salt—that tickled his equally salty shoulder.

"Sir, you failed to respond to multiple radio hails. You failed to respond to amplified voice hailing. You failed to respond to standard visuals, and you are approaching the U.S. shore. Sir, you *will* be boarded."

Adding the word *sir* supposedly made the armed threats, property invasion, and warrantless search respectable. Protected by their government-issued uniforms, two of the men jumped aboard Charles's boat. An objective observer might recognize this as the behavior of pirates. Should Charles exercise his right to repel boarders? Best not.

"Sir, are you armed?" one of them asked. They were trained to ask as a matter of course. But this time the question sounded blatantly silly. Charles wore only a bathing suit.

Charles held his arms over his head. "Where do you think I could stash a gun on me?" He turned around, revealing his deeply tanned back. No gun lay strapped by duct tape adjacent to his spine. There was no place he could possibly conceal a weapon on his person. Might as well frisk the exposed forearms of a man in a short-sleeved shirt, as commonly occurred at TSA checkpoints. To be entirely forthcoming, he would need to moon them. He refrained from doing so, for now.

Training to follow rigid protocol tends to reduce a man's ability to think for himself. An unexercised brain atrophies. This provided one explanation for why the IQ of government employees was statistically below average. Their innate intelligence was not necessarily subnormal. But the organizations in which they worked encouraged obedience, not independent thought, as the path to success. Stupidity can be a learned trait.

"Sir, do you have a weapon?"

Charles struggled internally. "I have a paring knife on the table here. For apples. Want an apple?"

His exasperation apparent, the officer snapped, "Do you have any weapons on your boat, sir?"

Just then, one of the men opened up a hatch under a cockpit cushion and loudly called, "Guns here!" He reached down and pulled up an AR-15, magazine in place, safety engaged. He held it gingerly, as if it were a dead animal.

The officer said angrily, "*Sir*, you said there were no weapons on your boat!"

"*Sir*," Charles replied with even more emphasis, "I didn't have time to respond."

The officer sneered and called to his two men: "Search the vessel."

The officer turned back to Charles. "We will examine this boat, sir, and will remove all contraband and impound your vessel as necessary. You have an assault weapon on board."

"You mean I have a semi-automatic rifle."

"An AR-15 is an assault weapon, sir."

Charles's tendency to question authority overtook him.

"Why do you believe that?" he said before he could stop himself. "Because it *looks* like an automatic weapon? Like that M240 machine gun your man is, rather impolitely, pointing at me? Calling a civilian semi-automatic rifle an *assault weapon* doesn't make it one. Someone in *your* position should *know* that."

Was the officer an ignorant victim of propaganda and doublespeak? Or a purveyor of it? Most people were both.

The most effective and destructive lies are the lies one tells oneself.

"It *is* an assault weapon," the man repeated.

Hear or say anything enough times, with enough certainty, and it becomes the truth. Brainwashing was the *real* assault weapon.

Attempting to counteract brainwashing with logic usually proved quixotic. But right now it served to distract the man from fully supervising his underlings. So Charles asked, "What makes you think it's an assault weapon?"

"As a matter of law, the pistol grip and the flash suppressor are the most relevant criteria … sir."

"The ever-dangerous pistol grip," Charles said. "Without that pistol grip, I suppose there's no way I could assault anyone with it. Is that what they teach at Homeland Security School?"

The officer kept his cool, despite his evident desire to punch Charles in the face. His training helped him maintain a pretense to the moral high ground, however robotically.

"What was your departure port?" the officer demanded.

"I've been traveling the world."

"Answer the question, sir. What was your port of departure?"

"I'm coming in straight from the Bahamas—Nassau, most recently."

"You possessed that weapon in the Bahamas?"

The weapon was illegal on shore in most places he had visited, but he hadn't carried *that particular weapon* on shore. Charles saw no need to answer the question.

"Sir, what is your citizenship?"

More of Don Quixote emerged. "I'm an American, but I carry a U.S. passport."

The officer glared at him as he climbed aboard the sailboat. "Clarify. Are you a U.S. citizen?"

"As I said, I am American. I'm also a U.S. citizen."

"My name is Petty Officer Chittingham. One of my men will go below with you to retrieve your passport and your manifest. Do not attempt to reach for anything that might conceivably be a weapon."

"Petty Officer Chittingham, why do you believe you have the authority to order me around on my own boat?"

"We are the Department of Homeland Security. Do as you are told!" The man's trained demeanor faltered.

"Of course."

Charles felt himself tip toward flinging sardonic insults. Doing so would be a departure from both his upbringing and his usual friendly approach to dealing with others. His father, had he overheard the remarks that Charles so far avoided saying out loud, would be horrified, and as angry as he ever became.

Not to mention, sardonic insults might lead to Charles getting handcuffed.

Charles went below and obtained his documents. He watched the men as they searched the boat, opening each compartment, squeezing every life jacket. They found a pump-action shotgun and a 9 mm Glock pistol, and carried them up on deck. But they hadn't found the drugs. Not yet.

"Why do you carry all these weapons on board?" Petty Officer Chittingham demanded.

Charles answered truthfully. "In case I run into people who insist on boarding my boat against my will and want to take my stuff."

"You're worried about piracy?"

"Exactly. *Pirates*." Charles watched the petty officer for a response, but the man didn't seem amenable to incisive introspection. "These guns are my last resort. After cooperation, hospitality, and friendly smiles have failed."

"What is your intent with these weapons once you land?"

"They're not for sale or transfer."

"Do you have any contraband on board?"

"You would have found it, don't you think?"

"Perhaps a small amount of illegal drugs?"

"There are no narcotics on this boat."

Chittingham flipped through Charles's passport and mentioned quietly, "This expires next year." He flipped some more. "You're very well traveled, Mr. Knight. When was the last time you were in the United States?"

"Seven years ago."

The officer stared at Charles for far too long, and then asked, "You're heading into Charleston?"

"That's right."

"Check in with the port authority immediately upon entrance into the harbor."

"I will."

"Welcome back to America," the man said with an edge of spite.

Charles replied, "I'm hoping there's still some left."

"What's that?" the man spat back.

Charles didn't clarify. There was no percentage in tilting at that particular windmill.

The Coast Guard men jumped back aboard their Defender. For good measure the man on the bow aimed the muzzle of his mounted machine straight at Charles again. Charles smiled at them as they accelerated and sped away.

His heart pounded. He took a few deep breaths in an attempt to calm himself. But the clamor of the luffing mainsail triggered a Pavlovian urge to reassert control, and until he did, the tension would persist. He turned the wheel to port, bringing the boat off the wind until the boom fell to leeward and the mainsail filled, silencing the fretful noise. He kept turning until his boat aimed back toward Charleston. He pressed the button that shut down the engine. The peacefulness of the downwind sailing blessed him with needed serenity, and his heart began to calm.

Sourced from the far side of the world, his drugs remained well hidden behind a tightly bolted, corroded, and salt-caked aluminum fitting at the base of the mast, in the deepest part of his bilge, down near where it mounted onto the keel. Charles knew from painful personal experience that it was a miserable place for a man to crouch to work. And no dog had ever been trained to sniff out the particular drugs he had chosen as his first foray into his new career.

He looked toward the entrance to Charleston Harbor several miles away. He hoped to make it in before the sun set.

11

The winds blew well for what would be the last brief leg of his long voyage. He hauled out the genoa. It filled, and the boat leapt forward two knots faster.

Charles stared up past his mainsail at the erect but slightly curved mast. He laughed aloud at a joke, one that the sloop's namesake, the human Caroline—so lovely, so kind, so honest—would have appreciated. Actually, she would have hit him. Playfully, of course.

Caroline's family duties had carried her away from him, probably forever. All he had of her now were fond memories of their past together. That, and this lovely boat that bore her name and carried him toward a destiny he could not conceive.

2

Field Marketing

CHARLES entered the United States with minimal hassle from Immigration or Customs, and soon discovered that he felt no sense of place. It didn't feel like home. He'd arrived on another planet, immersed in a seemingly familiar landscape, but with strange people, off-tenor voices, confusing demeanors, unpredictable motivations. Why had he expected to feel at ease here?

Charles went to scout out what would soon be his biggest competitor in the drug trade: Walmart.

The visit provided a veritable cornucopia of competitive intelligence.

The line to the Walmart pharmacy backed up beyond the common-cold remedy section and intruded into the main aisle. It was as if the line was intended to aid in selling the conveniently positioned Dr. Scholl's foot products: the customers had to stand for so long on the concrete floor that heel and arch pain was certain to result. A silver-haired man of about sixty stood in front of him. His bearing, demeanor, and dress distinguished him from the rest of those in line.

Waiting for so long while moving so little, the neighbors in line began to converse. Almost everyone here seemed to have time on their hands. Their conversation took the form of complaints.

He listened for insights into the market.

First came a Southern accent. "I 'member when ya just gave ya *prescrip*tion to the phahmacist—in those days he knew ya name—and he'd fill it right then and theah and give it to ya. Jus' like that."

Another turned her head to say, "Now it takes them an hour just to process the prescription."

"Yep, and half the time the *in*surance rejects it."

"And they send you back to the doctor to get a different prescription."

"And it takes two months to get an appointment with the doctor."

"Mine won't do it over the phone. They always make you go see them to get your prescriptions rewritten."

"And of course the doctor charges you just to write a prescription for a medication you've taken for years."

"I have Medicaid," a man proclaimed in a superior tone. "They pay for everything. I don't have to worry about any of that."

Long gone were the days when pride would prohibit any admission to being on the dole. Now people bragged about it. Charles stood in this line for an education, and he was getting one.

A woman two people up, plump and colorfully dressed and with caring and perceptive eyes, spoke in a pleasantly lilting, musical accent that attested to either West African or Caribbean roots. "This country is so strange. I feel like a circus doggy. Gotta jump through all these hoops to get what I need. Where I come from, you don't need prescriptions. If you know what you need, you just go to the pharmacy and buy it."

"That doesn't sound safe at all," a well-kempt and well-kept brunette in an expensive overcoat said, confident that she always did things the right way. She took her children to the doctor for regular well-child visits and vaccinations, and paraded them to the dentist every six months; to do otherwise amounted to nothing short of neglect. She was frustrated because all these people in line were making her late for her daughter's soccer practice. She was in charge of the orange slices today.

The plump customer shrugged.

Charles almost chimed in to help that wise lady teach the soccer mom. In almost every country he'd visited—and he'd been to most of them over the last seven years—a pharmacist was the first source of inquiry for medical problems that might be solved with a pill, a lotion, or a bandage. A pharmacist could provide quick and practical solutions, and didn't require an appointment or ask for a fee. The U.S. system, mandating doctors' appointments and prescriptions, was slow, bureaucratic, expensive, and served little useful purpose—except to place doctors as a liability wall between the pharmaceutical companies and the lawyers.

An impatient woman immediately in front of the silver-haired man said, "This is ridiculous. There should be a *law*."

Nods of agreement followed, along with a hum of approbation of the rightness of the observation, although the woman hadn't specified what kind of law she had in mind. Even the seemingly wiser fat lady nodded.

But the silver-haired man in front of Charles didn't. Instead, he lowered his shoulders and ever-so-subtly shook his head from side to side. Charles noticed that. He had shaken his own head too and he felt … what was it? Either dejection or disgust.

He pushed the feelings aside. Why judge chickens for seeking the security of their coops?

The line moved haltingly forward. Three pharmacy staff worked the computers and phones, communicating digitally with insurance companies and by phone with doctors' offices, engaging in constant battle. Two pharmacists filled the prescriptions, a process that consisted only of counting pills and assuring regulatory compliance. Despite six or eight years of undergraduate and graduate education to get a PharmD, and considerable practical training as well, they were not allowed to provide medications without a doctor's order, nor give any meaningful advice. Clearly, the American Medical Association—the self-styled doctors' union that only a small minority of physicians actually supported—had more pull with the legislators than did the pharmacists' union.

Only one staff member was dedicated to shortening the long line of customers. No wonder it kept stretching back farther, now reaching the cosmetics section.

Charles's hair remained long, but unlike on the open ocean, it now stayed calmly still. In contrast, his mind moved, analyzed, and problem-solved. He said nothing, but heard everything.

What these people in line lacked was an understanding of *why* the line was so long, *why* it moved so slowly, *why* there was only one staff member working the line.

But they didn't ask why. They weren't sufficiently interested in why. They had their lives to lead after all, and their lives stayed busy. So they just complained.

Most of them probably used the same strategy when voting.

Charles always asked why.

The layers of the problem went deep; Charles had peeled them away in his travels and his experiences. To him, the underlying causes of the long, slow line for medications were obvious.

He had returned to the United States with the intent to do something about it.

The silver-haired man finally made it to the pharmacy register. His eyes met those of the hurried but not unsympathetic staffer whose job was to face the customers.

"Name?" she said.

"Thomason. Warren Thomason. But I'm here visiting my son, Jeremiah. I'm picking up his prescription for him."

The man spoke in a dignified voice accustomed to being heeded. It was a voice that would become important to Charles.

The pharmacy tech turned and fished among the hanging plastic prescription bags. Her efforts fruitless, she walked behind the counter and consulted in a whisper with a white-coated pharmacist. It wasn't hard to see that Mr. Thomason would not obtain what he had waited so long for.

The clerk returned to the register. "I'm sorry, Mr. Thomason, but the insurance company doesn't cover the medication the doctor prescribed for your son. You will need to contact the doctor and get him to prescribe something else."

Mr. Thomason spoke with measured words. "Insurance never covers this. We pay cash for it."

"Oh, really? Um. I'm sorry. We didn't understand."

The pharmacist called over from behind the tall bench, where he stood to count pills. "The price is a lot higher now, Mr. Thomason."

"Why's that?"

"FDA gave a U.S. company approval to market it here. Because of that, the U.K. company we used to get it from isn't allowed to ship it to us anymore. The U.S. company that got approval hiked the price through the roof. We checked with your insurance, and they aren't paying. I'm sorry."

"How much would it cost if I had to pay for it myself?" His jaw tightened, but his voice remained controlled.

The pharmacist nodded to the clerk, whose face initially went blank, followed by a trace of … what was it? Panic? Embarrassment? She recovered and transitioned through a dozen or so screens on her computer as the line behind Charles extended further toward the flat-panel televisions. "It's … um … $7,416 for one month."

Thomason said nothing for several moments.

Charles wished he could see the man's face.

Finally, Thomason said, "I see," and walked away.

Charles stepped out of line. He had learned what he needed to. In his years abroad, he had been afflicted by various tropical diseases. But few were as destructive as the injury caused by the concurrent diseases of medical insurance and regulatory tyranny.

Why would people pay an insurance company each month to invade their privacy, make decisions for them, and block their choices? Why would they pay taxes each month to a government that did the same?

He followed Mr. Thomason. Mr. Thomason was just the right sort of market to research. He caught up to him as the man leafed through a magazine at the end of a checkout line, mumbling to himself. Charles picked up another magazine. It was called *People* magazine, but he had no idea who any of the people in it were.

"Pissants," Mr. Thomason muttered under his breath.

Charles took the opening. "That's what I think." He pointed at the cover of the magazine.

Thomason looked over at the stranger, whom he hadn't noticed until now.

"Pardon? Oh no, I'm thinking of something else."

"Oh, sorry. I thought the Kardashians were an extraterrestrial species in *Star Trek*."

Thomason laughed. "That's the *Cardassians*, but they look alike."

"Wouldn't it be nice if these magazines started celebrating people who actually do something worthwhile?"

"Yes, but then no one in the line would buy them."

Now Charles started feeling a sense of place, a faint connection with a person he might understand. He held out his hand. "I've been out of the country for many years. Just got back yesterday."

Thomason turned to study Charles then. His perceptive eyes took in every superficial clue available. Those clues would never be sufficient to judge a man comprehensively, and certainly not a complex man like Charles. Well-attired and well-spoken could add up to either an honest friend or a conman.

Thomason reached out his hand in return. "Welcome back. It's not the same place you left."

Perhaps Thomason needed to let off steam. Or perhaps he had some other motivation for telling Charles of his frustration.

"My son's prescription medicine is now unaffordable. It's a forty-year-old drug for muscular dystrophy that he's been on for years. Patents are long expired. It used to cost $100 a month at most, and *that* was high. Now they want to charge us an obscene sum."

Charles said, "Eighty-nine thousand dollars per year." He raised an eyebrow in faint apology before explaining, "I overheard the pharmacist and did the math."

Thomason looked into his eyes for several long seconds. "It's horrifying."

Charles spoke professionally yet conspiratorially. "Would you be interested in getting your son's medication much more cheaply?" His eyebrows both lifted then, and the glint in his eyes spoke volumes. His expression conveyed not criminality, but the brilliance and motivation of the hacker mentality, those rebels who circumvent problems created unnecessarily by bureaucracy.

The silver-haired man read the expression well.

"You're talking to a desperate father. Not that I'm likely to trust you, but what are you proposing?"

"What if I could get it for about what you used to pay? Completely quality controlled and tested by top-flight laboratory analysis."

"I might kiss your feet and oil your hair. But only if I believed you, and if it wasn't stolen goods. And I'm not just going to believe you, young man."

"Nothing stolen. Always ethical. But it may not be legal. I'm not sure I can, but let me see what I can do." Charles handed him his card. It was blank other than the word *Paladin* and an email address.

Thomason looked at the card skeptically. "All right, young man. I'll put this in my file of strange business cards and interesting people."

Charles grinned. "Thank you. Perhaps we can do business. You impress me as a man who can think for himself. What do you do, by the way?"

Thomason slid a business card of his own out of his wallet, wrote the name of the medication on it, and gave it to Charles. His eyes conveyed deep amusement.

Charles glanced at the card and raised his eyebrows for the third time.

Thomason said, "I'm a federal district court judge. One who can think for himself. Don't tell anyone." Thomason held his finger to his lips. If he expected Charles to be fearful, he expected wrong.

Charles smiled back. "Perfect. I'll be in touch, Judge Thomason."

This man might become a client that even Walmart could not properly serve.

Because Walmart obeyed the law.

*　*　*

Charles called Maurice as soon as he got back to his boat. His eagerness to see his uncle added a spring to his step and energy to his mind. The country felt a little more like home.

One would not expect a man as financially successful as Maurice Templeton to answer the phone with a snore instead of a salutation. Charles imagined the scene: the phone connected but lying on the floor under the end table; Uncle Maurice stretched out with one very fat leg on the couch, the other unshod foot on the floor, head back on the armrest, mouth wide open, and eyes tightly closed. The man wasn't going to be any slimmer than the last time he had seen him.

"Uncle Maurice, are you asleep?"

A groan and cough came through the earpiece, followed by a mumbled "No. I'm dead. Leave the flowers and get out."

"Uncle Maurice, it's Charles."

No response.

He spoke louder. "It's Charles. Your nephew."

A loud and croaking voice replied, "How're you doing, m'boy? It's been a while…"

They had talked occasionally, but it had been seven years since Charles had last seen his uncle.

"I apologize, Uncle Maurice. A lot of water under the bridge, or over the dam, or wherever it flows. I'll catch you up."

"How are you now? At least still in one piece … physically?"

"I'm good. That which doesn't kill us makes us stronger. At least that's what Nietzsche thought." He threw the name out, unsure whether he sought to impress his uncle or to incite a rant. "But how are you, Uncle Maurice?"

"Well, to start, you can drop the honorific; I'm *Maurice* to grown-ups. Otherwise I'm OK. But Nietzsche and these extra two hundred pounds of fat I'm dragging around are trying to kill me. I can't see any of it making

19

me stronger. You think the Russians who survived the gulag came home stronger?"

"I love philosophizing with you … Maurice. But…"

"Or survivors of Japanese internment camps? Those who survived were *already* the strongest, since they didn't succumb to disease, hypothermia, and everything else that killed off the other prisoners. I guarantee you they had weaker constitutions on their way out."

"OK, Uncle, I get it."

"What about car-crash survivors who require multiple surgeries? You think they feel stronger?"

"Fine, Nietzsche was wrong."

"Damn right he was wrong. You can't be out there throwing around quotes willy-nilly."

"Maurice, *please*. I need to discuss something of a more practical nature."

"If it's practical, then the solution is usually the application of either lawyers, guns, or money. Sometimes all of them."

"I choose the money."

"I told you that you had to wait 'til you were legal before you could get it. They have more crap to nail you with all lined up. If they see you've got any assets they could lay their hands on, they'll take them."

"Statute of limitations has passed. I'm legal. They can't touch me."

"Really? Don't be so damn sure, m'boy. The law won't protect you if they want to go after you. But the money's all yours if you come to New York and get it." Charles heard the phone click as the conversation ended by unilateral decree.

He continued, ruefully, "OK, Uncle. I hope you're doing OK, old buddy."

3

Planning Stages

THE doorman at the Royal Major General greeted Charles with suspicion.

"I'm Charles Knight. Here to visit Maurice Templeton in 11B." Charles stood attired in a modestly priced but well-fitted gray pinstriped suit. He had transformed into a young New York City banker. But only in appearance.

"Good evening. May I see some identification?"

Charles provided his ragged library card from his hometown of Red Lodge, Montana. It had expired a decade ago.

The bellman accepted the library card as proof that Charles presented no danger to the residents of the building, and lazily waved him on toward the elevators.

"You're not going to accompany me?"

"No, Mr. Knight. I'll pretend I trust you, young man."

Young man. It was OK to be young, but the phrase could be at once patronizing, perfunctory, and judgmental. Some might use it as a form of endearment. The federal judge in the pharmacy yesterday used it innocently, for the most part. But this doorman or bellhop or concierge, or whatever he was, used it to denigrate. No matter. Charles didn't need to deal with this man in any other role than a doorman.

Charles knocked on the apartment door and waited. There never lived a man less inclined to exert his body than his Uncle Maurice.

"Who the hell is it!" Maurice bellowed, a threat more than a question.

"It's your nephew."

"Then I have to let you in, don't I."

21

"It would be nice if you would." Charles leaned his forehead against the door and sighed. He heard a grunt and the plodding of the man toward the door. At least he could still walk.

The door opened and Charles looked through it, not at his uncle's face, but at his already-retreating silk robe, which along with silk boxers comprised his uncle's business suit. He shuffled away toward the couch. Charles followed his formidable uncle's formidable backside, and closed the door behind.

Insulated wires crossed the carpet from the walls to the low tables that surrounded the couch, and then back to computer monitors a few feet further away. Reports and newspapers lay scattered about. Food wrappers overflowed from trash containers. It must be the day before the maid's biweekly visit.

After settling back in on his couch, Maurice at last looked at his nephew and said, "You look good, kid. Real good. Like a professional. I like your hair long."

"Thanks, Maurice. I dressed up for you. And shaved." Charles's smile broadened. He loved this man and wasn't afraid to admit it.

"What profession are you professing, by the way?"

"I wanted to discuss that with you, Maurice."

"Good. I'm glad to help." Then his head fell back against the armrest of the couch, and he snored.

Charles watched him sleep for a time. This was the man who respected him enough to challenge him by thrusting him into a complex world full of risks and opportunities. And who cared enough to supply him with backup, just in case.

Years ago, Uncle Maurice had sent him off on a quest for nothing less than the meaning of life.

Charles went around the corner to the kitchen and opened the refrigerator. He drank straight out of an orange juice container he found inside it.

"Don't you drink straight out of the orange juice container!"

Charles peeked back around the doorway from the kitchen. His uncle's eyes were shut.

"How did you know I was?"

Maurice opened his eyes. "I don't get paid the big bucks for being stupid. Now, remind me of where you've been for the past seven years, huh?"

Charles returned to the living room, slid some papers off the seat of an armchair, and sat close to his uncle.

"I've been traveling and working."

"Where?"

"Everywhere."

"Everywhere?"

"Pretty much." He recalled every place and every person he visited, not because of any unique gift of memory, but because excitement and adventure and newness trigger the biological processes of the brain that form permanent neural connections and therefore permanent recollections. "As you might recall, after Gondwana, Caroline and I sailed to India, and then Southeast Asia. A few years later, the world Caroline came from caught up with her. She retreated to her palace in Denmark. I retreated to everywhere else on the globe." The wistfulness on his face could not be mistaken. "I'm afraid she's not as happy as she could be."

"Seven years, and you barely stayed in touch with me."

"I did too! I checked in with you and Dad like clockwork every anniversary of Mom's death. And of course your birthdays, and International Pi Day too. You know I enjoy talking with you."

"And I appreciate that, kid. Throw in Guy Fawkes Day next time. But it wasn't enough to stop your old man and me from worrying. You have any idea what it's like to be a parent and not know if your child is alive or dead? Any idea at all, young man?"

There was that *young man* again. Thirty years old and still a young man. Well, it's all relative…

"I'm sorry, Maurice."

"You missed calling on my birthday a few years back."

"Yeah, sorry about that too. I crossed the International Date Line the wrong way and got confused."

"We almost sent Interpol to look for you."

Charles raised his eyebrows. "Interpol… Hardly my first choice."

"You're going to be getting the same lecture when you call your dad. He lost your mom; he couldn't bear the thought of losing you."

"I would have come home, but I wasn't welcome in the U.S. The government made that clear."

"Don't get me wrong, kid. We understand why you stayed away from this place."

"They stole my money, Maurice. And they threatened to lock me up."

Maurice nodded. "And you did what you had to do."

"I just got back to the U.S., and already I feel like a peasant."

"I expect your time in Africa with Xander was just the tip of the iceberg in making your personal world bigger."

"Bigger than a jail cell."

"All's well that ends well. That's what I'm saying. It was that trip to Gondwana that put you on the road to who you are today."

"It turned me into an international man. Otherwise I might have stayed a serf in the fiefdom."

Maurice said, "Every move you make can change your life. You walk outside, and turn left instead of right at the corner, and you could wind up living in an alternate reality."

"Perhaps we do that with every turn." Charles smiled. "I've had a good time wherever I've taken a turn, but you're right. Before Gondwana, my turns were small. There's a big difference between reading about the jungle and running through it with people shooting at you. You're living life to the fullest when you're about to fall off a cliff."

Charles felt remorse immediately. The words had rolled out fast, and his brain had only caught up a second later. His uncle rarely left his apartment. What he had just said sounded like a judgment.

He hoped Maurice would let it pass. Maurice had had far more than any normal man's share of adventure before a polo accident made getting around too hard. After that, he moved less, ate more, and after a few years had transformed his body into its present Temple Mount.

"You fell off a cliff into a lot of money, Charles."

"Not as much as I wish."

"Yeah? You running out of your gunrunning money, then?"

"That's not what I meant. And it's not gunrunning money, Maurice. And I didn't live off of it. I've hardly touched that money."

"If you haven't touched the money, how have you been living? Every country in the world has laws against foreign travelers working."

"Most laws are made to be ignored. I learned how to shake hands with the locals, figured out what they wanted, and got it for them. I'd hit the local art galleries. And of course the polo club, if there was one. Just like you taught me."

Charles saw Maurice's proud smile. His uncle had gone out of his way to influence him to take up the sport; it was a game—a whole world, really—that the average person had no clue about. It was the most fun you could have with your clothes on, sure, but as Winston Churchill pointed out, having a polo handicap was better than having a passport.

Charles added, "I'd set up appointments with lawyers and real estate brokers. They'll talk to anybody from out of town, and they know every-body. Some would take me home for dinner with the family, or invite me to parties and introduce me to their pals. One thing always led to another. I'd get immersed in some arbitrage or another, usually between old friends I had just left behind in one country and the new friends where I landed. You taught me to go where the action and the money are. So that's what I did. Sometimes, I went where the big legal money was, and sometimes I went to where the big illegal money was."

"Girls?"

"After Caroline? There's nothing like a long-haired dictionary to improve one's language skills…" This was part of Charles's job. Without lying, he would willfully exaggerate to aid Maurice's imagination. A good-looking young American on an adventure through developing nations never suffered for lack of attention. It made the occasionally necessary, usually enjoyable, and always complicated pursuit of female companionship sub-stantially easier. Uncle Maurice appreciated living a global life, vicariously, from the confines of his couch.

"How about friends?"

"Well, a lot more than if I'd stayed rooted in Montana like a garden vegetable." Charles's education differed from most: gained through experi-ence, active living, going places, and doing things. His cosmopolitan friends were far more interesting—and knowledgeable—than some professor paid to deliver the same stale lectures year after year to college students who com-mitted themselves to indentured servitude in exchange for four years of indoctrination.

"Everything I hoped you would do." Maurice's nod revealed pride in his sister's son.

They sat for a while in comfortable silence.

Then Maurice asked, "Have you still got a grudge against those people in D.C.?"

"That hasn't changed… Forgive and forget, some say. Others say forgive, but don't forget. For me there are some things you should neither forgive nor forget."

"What are you going to do about it?"

"That's one reason I'm here to talk with you. What liquidity, if any, do I have?"

"Other than your money from Smolderhof? May he rest in pieces."

"Smolderhof's dead?"

"Last month. Cancer finally ate away his esophagus and tore through his soulless heart."

Charles didn't waste any time thinking about him. He deleted Smolderhof from his mind. Dust to dust. A bad memory and a good riddance. "I've got no intention of bringing that money back here for the U.S. government to rob me again. I'm keeping it offshore."

"Well, then you've got to work with what's here. What the SEC and IRS failed to find and couldn't take." Maurice held his finger up. "And there *is* some."

"I'm glad for that. And that Springer and his partners dodged the bullet." He felt the familiar sensation in his belly of frustration combined with anger when he considered how his friends had almost been blown away—physically, legally, and financially—years ago.

"Your friends know you were framed, Charles."

"I know." But did they really believe it? He hadn't seen Elliot Springer face-to-face since he had last set foot in the United States. Charles had left San Diego in a hurry, after throwing his emptied weapon into the bay near the airport.

Charles cleared his head. "What have I got to work with?"

"You have gold. A lot of it. Silver too. More of that. If you had let me know you were coming, I could've told you how much."

It served no purpose to remind his uncle of his earlier telephone call.

The metals had proved invisible when the government had swooped in to confiscate essentially everything else he owned, and almost all of the $200 million he'd made short-selling the stock of Smolderhof's B-F Explorations. The purpose of the metals was to conserve capital, but Charles's absence coincided with a bull market in the precious metals. He now had twice his original capital, thanks to Maurice's ingrained habit of always taking some gains off the table and into gold. In effect, he'd been paid handsomely to see the world.

"I assume I own no equities?"

"Actually, you have a substantial stake in a small bioscience company in Virginia."

Charles pulled his head back and raised his eyebrows. "I do?"

"Yep. The SEC missed it when they confiscated the rest of your visible assets. I kept it in a separate account for you."

"What's the company?"

"Visioryme Pharmaceuticals."

Charles scanned back through time. "I remember, sort of. Wasn't that supposed to be a quick speculation on some FDA decision? Not much more than a day trade?"

"Yeah. It was one of the last trades we made before the axe fell. The government focused on rounding up your B-F Explorations booty, which was mostly cash and puts. They found all of that. As far as I know they've never connected you and me. I'm glad I'm your mother's brother and not your father's. The name Knight got way too much attention in the investor circles. They started calling you the 'Gordon Gekko of Gondwana' in the media."

"I would've liked to have seen that. Gekko was the only halfway decent character in the damn movie."

"I kept the articles. They're in the guestroom."

The guestroom stayed packed high with papers and magazines. Maurice hoarded financial publications. Maybe there was a bed in there somewhere.

"What happened with Visioryme?"

"The FDA came out against it. Stock fell to six cents. Bad bet."

High-tech, big wreck. Biotech stocks were almost as risky and volatile as mining-exploration stocks. But he had to push a little farther. Maurice wouldn't have mentioned the holding if Visioryme was dead.

"What happened then?"

"You got distracted by B-F Explorations, ducking bullets, blowing up armies, and lollygagging with royalty, and you never sold the position. I figured it wise to let sleeping dogs lie. You would have been diluted to homeopathic levels in subsequent stock issues except I ponied up some cash each time the price was in the tank. You ended up with a substantial percentage in Visioryme. I liked the fundamentals—the FDA be damned. It was my tout that got you into that dog, so I felt responsible."

"So you threw good money after bad?"

Maurice shrugged. "They got a new CEO, young chick, after the FDA dropped their bomb on them. She was a buyer too, and that got my attention. It turns out she's got an instinctive grasp of biochemistry—quite a competent scientist. And she's pretty good at this thing they call *regulatory science*, whatever the hell that is. Scientifically guessing how much crap the regulators will dump on you, I suppose. She gained some revenue through contract lab work to keep the doors open. She kept it alive. Visioryme looks like they could finally win now. They have an antidepressant that sailed through phase 3 studies. The FDA is poised to approve it. Share price has rebounded somewhat, but it's still pretty cheap. As you might imagine after years of losses and share dilution."

Maurice had imbued Charles with an affinity for small, highly volatile stocks in mining exploration and technology. Most investors stayed away from them because of their high risk. A speculator had to be conscientious, diligent—and often patient—to make money in them. Or else rely on blind luck.

On Charles's behalf, Maurice had been speculating on Visioryme.

Charles felt an instinctive distaste for the pharma industry. The subsidized and highly regulated industry hid behind a faint patina of free market rhetoric, while fully immersed in the *political* economy, where profit held little relationship to value produced.

"Another antidepressant on the market?" Charles asked. "How's that a good thing? This country already seems filled with zombies. With all the me-toos in the antidepressant sector, how are they gonna get market traction for another happy pill?"

"It's not a pill. It's inhaled."

Charles paused. "Does it work?"

"Yeah. The inhaled drug bypasses the liver. Goes straight to brain. Works faster than all the others. Takes minutes instead of weeks to kick in. Claims to have no side effects."

Neither man would readily accept that a drug lacked side effects, especially a drug designed to have effects on the brain.

Charles nodded slowly. "Inhaled, rapid, maybe no side effects. That's the marketing angle then. Might make the difference." He didn't feel an ounce of excitement about it.

Maurice waggled his hand back-and-forth in a universal symbol of equivocation. "But they don't have a deal with Big Pharma yet. That's bad.

I don't think Visioryme has any marketing strength among their personnel. They can't sell the drug if they can't market. In that business, they don't beat a path to your door if you have a better mousetrap. More likely the industry will try to shut you down, to keep you from breaking their rice bowl."

"Sounds like I should sell my stake after this next FDA news hits." Charles stood to go get more juice. Visioryme wasn't important. He considered how to describe his newly planned career to Maurice.

While drinking the orange juice—from a glass—he had an epiphany. He tossed it around in his mind for all of five seconds before calling to Maurice from the kitchen. "On the other hand, if I want to look like a solid citizen after years on the road, I need something that looks legit."

"You mean working with Visioryme?"

"Maybe I can bring something to their party."

Maurice croaked in the voice he reserved for harsh critique. "Why the hell would you want to get into the pharmaceutical business? It's a freakin' irrational minefield of bureaucrats exploding business plans at random."

Charles returned from the kitchen. "I have another reason altogether. For what I'm planning, there could be ... let's say ... *advantages* to working in a legit pharma business." Charles stared at the floor while he said it. But then he looked at Maurice conspiratorially. "But first, we need to talk about my plan A."

"Plan A?"

"Plan A is a bit illegal, Maurice. It could get me imprisoned. Or killed." Maurice yawned.

At any moment, Maurice might collapse into a slumbering stupor—the consequence of being chronically underslept from the sleep apnea he kept ignoring. So it was best to keep driving forward. As they had done when Charles was still a youth and Maurice weighed a hundred pounds less, the two men spoke intently. They wrote lists, scanned the Internet, and made phone calls for information, talked through the pros and cons of Charles's ideas, and molded an abstract into a series of concretes.

Charles had no intention of creating a vast enterprise. His financial aspirations were modest. Intellectual stimulation, psychological gratification, and spiritual enhancement were more important to him. But ideally, they flowed from efforts to earn an honest buck. Preferably as an entrepreneur. Legality was not a deciding factor. Laws were often arbitrary, or even irrational.

Contemplation of the new business—and planning its details—filled much of the next week, with breaks taken for chess, piano, and, of course, eating. Their lack of familiarity with the illicit drug business left them with many questions unanswered. Yet all the while, Uncle Maurice never tried to dissuade him from the undertaking. And to Charles, that was the best endorsement he could find for the value of his proposed endeavor.

In the process, Charles electronically found his way to a reputable manufacturer in India who could supply sufficient amounts of the drug for the son of the Honorable Judge Thomason and for as many other American patients with muscular dystrophy as might appear. The cost? Less than $50 per *year.*

He wished he could announce it to the country.

At Maurice's urging, he found a laboratory that could run mass-spectroscopy assays and several other standard analytical methods to determine the contents of any drug, any time. Trust—but verify—had to be standard operating procedure.

As the overall plans worked toward a semi-final shape, Charles wondered, "What will Dad think when I'm doing this?"

Maurice replied with a yawn. "He'll think you're a drug dealer."

Charles closed his eyes and rubbed them, resignedly. "Yeah, I suppose he will."

"Yes, he certainly will. But don't worry, kid, we'll disabuse him of that notion entirely. Because you're not talking about being a low-level *dealer* here. You're talking about being a *Drug Lord.*"

4

The Snake Pit

"WE need to talk."

Donald Debocher did not like the sound of that. They were words that could send a jolt of foreboding through any husband's psyche. He had no time, energy, or interest in the type of discussion implied by his wife's proclamation. He *never* had the energy or interest, but this morning his lack of time trumped other considerations. Hoping Tristana would think he hadn't heard her, he shut the front door firmly behind him and climbed into his car without catching even a single breath of the crisp autumn air.

Just as he started the car, his phone rang. The screen showed the number of a person he disliked intensely: Seth Fowler. Fowler was an ambitious asshole, and a conniving bastard. A blowhard, specializing in jingoistic diatribes, and a bully. He couldn't think of a single virtue when it came to Seth.

He shouldn't answer, but he did, even injecting a friendly lilt in his voice.

"Seth, how are you?"

The man's resonant voice provided him with an authority that Donald lacked. Not visible through the phone was Fowler's muscular build and short-cropped hair topping an equally meaty head. The man had a lukewarm IQ, but also an animal shrewdness barely disguised by a forthright social veneer.

Fowler replied, "Very well, Donald. I hear you're good also."

"Yes, FDA treats me well."

"Good for you. I can't think of a finer person to keep watch over our

31

nation's pharmaceuticals. You at the FDA deal with the legal ones, I deal with the illegal ones, huh?"

These calls were predictable. Same stupid comments.

Fowler wasn't in *the club*—a club consisting of FDA regulators, the pharma people who dealt with them, and anyone who wanted to sound in the know. Club members would say, "FDA demands…" or "FDA states…" Only outsiders would say, "*The* FDA demands…" A single word, *the*, provided the clue as to whether the speaker was enculturated sufficiently. Nobody at FDA would respect anyone who referred to them as "*the* FDA."

Donald sighed. "As always, Seth."

"Hey, haven't hardly seen you and Tristana since you moved out of the neighborhood. Kate wants to have you over."

The bastard had made moves on his wife several times before. Is that what was on his mind? Probably that too. But he knew what this call would *really* be about.

"Sounds good, Seth. Look forward to it. What's up?"

"I've come across some money. Never mind how. I need to know where to put it."

Whenever silver extorted from some drug dealer lined Fowler's pocket, he ended up calling Donald to try to double or triple down on his cash. The guy took down a lot of dealers, and so he called Donald a lot.

He had to give the man what he wanted. If he didn't… Damn, he couldn't contemplate the outcome.

One night, one bad night, an inebriated Donald had blundered into telling Fowler some tidbit of insider information. The DEA agent's reptilian brain had kicked in. He investigated it, got the goods, and used it against him ever since. If the authorities ever found out Donald's lapse, he'd be looking at a stretch in a federal pen.

"You know I always do right by you, Donald. I always let you piggyback on me. You've done well that way."

"You still have all my earnings, right?" Donald didn't know for sure. Seth showed him documents from time to time, but they were easy enough to fake. And he certainly had no legal recourse if Fowler decided to keep it himself. He should ask him for some fat stacks of $100 bills he was owed—but he was afraid to.

"Of course I have it," Fowler replied in the smarmy tone that he adopted when he lied. "I have to pay taxes on your capital gains, my friend, because it's all under my Social Security number."

There was no reason whatsoever to trust Seth Fowler. The guy was the only DEA agent Donald knew, and he had no idea whether the man was an exception or the norm. Fowler freely admitted he had killed a man out of spite. And that he'd put poison in batches of confiscated heroin and sent it back to the street "just to thin the herd." But whereas Fowler could prove Donald's malfeasance in a court of law, Donald had nothing on Fowler but some drunken braggadocio.

He sighed. "Look, Seth, I've got a couple for you. Two small pharma companies. One's going to get the nod; one's gonna get shut down. I'll make sure to give you plenty of time to take advantage of the moves."

"Make it soon, Donald. Does it make sense for me to be sitting on money when you're sitting on some of the best insider knowledge known to man?"

"Soon, Seth."

Donald hung up. If he gave the man what he wanted, Donald earned too—maybe. If he didn't, Donald would lose everything. In a way, it was comfortable to know that he had no choice in the matter.

Donald relied on the commute to energize him. He used the hour inbound to Silver Spring to swear vigorously at other drivers, construction workers, the weather, tourists, and the world at large. This got his adrenaline percolating. The commute was his coffee. By the time he reached his office building—the home of the United States Food and Drug Administration— he was fully torqued.

He passed through the building's security check, feeling three inches taller than his 5' 7" frame, and three times more powerful. Photos of prior commissioners and assorted dignitaries covered the wall opposite the elevators, their eyes gazing at him from the past. He, however, was the present and the future strength of the Administration, as evidenced by his promotion last week. It was the next step on his ascent to commissioner. So far, climbing the ladder had only entailed staying the course: following the unwritten rules, keeping out of trouble, not rocking the boat, playing the game, and, most importantly, not allowing anyone under his control to take any risks. Balancing all this took real skill, if only at backslapping and back-stabbing. It was hard work to accomplish so little so well, but he was good at it. He smiled with smug pride at his past successes. He was an ant that had climbed over the bodies of the others and could almost see the top of the heap.

Now, with this promotion, he would have to implement a new process. He would adopt an aggressive posture to protect and increase his newly assigned satrapy. He'd *have* to stand out and distinguish himself as being more than just another time-serving salaryman. From this point upward, he would have to win his gambles, and make damn sure that the bastards near him *lost* theirs.

For years, he shared a secretary with three other scientific reviewers. Next week, he would have his own. He displayed a thin smile and nodded as he walked past his current shared secretary. He didn't want her to think he was too friendly: sexual-harassment suits were practically an alternative currency, or an early-retirement plan, for the cubicle dwellers. The higher one rose in the bureaucracy, the bigger the target painted on one's back. Just look at what happens to cabinet appointees.

A stack of folders awaited him on his desk, just like every day for the past many years. It was the same stack as yesterday, but taller, and it had to be cleared this week, before he changed jobs. He picked up an enemy folder even before he sat down to begin the daily grind.

Each folder contained hundreds of pages, meticulously arranged in the specific order demanded by the Administration: document after document, prepared at huge expense by a pharmaceutical company's massive regulatory division, following every FDA dictum to the letter in an effort to get their paperwork over the initial bureaucratic hurdle so that their spectacular new medication, capable of saving a bazillion lives, could move on to scientific review. His secretary knew that a packet would rarely even get on his desk before twenty-five days had passed from receipt. The Food and Drug Administration had thirty days to respond, and Donald knew it was best—certainly for him and FDA—to use all those days. It wasn't as if anyone's life might be at stake.

Well, maybe some people's lives might be at stake. But life itself was a terminal disease. Why should his career suffer a negative hit to accelerate some product to market? Nobody gets out of here alive anyway.

The first rule of FDA was *Send It Back*. It was the easiest course of action, and it also served to test the mettle and sincerity of the filers. After a few such returns, the pharma execs would get testy, but what could they do about it? They certainly couldn't risk getting on the wrong side of an FDA scientific reviewer!

Donald smirked in satisfaction at the power he already held over so many wealthy pharma execs. He couldn't hold back a broader, crooked smile as he thought about the puppet strings he would hold beginning next week. He scribbled a note for his secretary on the top of the first folder. *Send It Back*. He checked off the box that said "Insufficient safety data on the precursor compound in pre-clinical animal models." He didn't have a clue what animal data might be appropriate; that was for *them* to figure out. But better safe than sorry. Safety first. *Send It Back*.

He spent the morning shuffling through the rest of the folders in much the same way, to much the same end, just as he had done for years. Nothing on his pile was going to make it to committee. Committee discussions were risky in that he would have to at least pretend to be knowledgeable on the minutiae of the file under discussion.

They should make a rubber stamp that said "*Send It Back.*"

Maybe he would put that phrase on his wife's tombstone. The woman had become a problem, with her intensifying harangues. The simple fact that he was married to her burdened his existence. It was her fault, not his fault, that she worked in the very industry that Donald regulated. He'd told her to seek other employment, but she was stubborn, and countered his demand by saying it was he who should be the one to get a different job. Hah! No chance. But now, in his new position, questions might be asked about her, and accusations made.

He picked up the next folder. He could neither focus on nor absorb the information it contained. Something about a new drug for HIV. It was this company's fifth attempt to get it right. That was *their* problem, and he wasn't going to let it become *his* problem. Their persistence angered him.

Send It Back.

*   *   *

Tristana had shaken her head when he slammed the door, knowing that Donald had heard her. Donald was always so stressed, so concerned about what his coworkers would think, what his boss might want. At the FDA, her husband lived in fear of lots of little bits of nothing.

She wanted him to quit his job. It was killing their relationship, and it wasn't doing his health any favors, which was ironic for an official in the agency that billed itself as regulating health. At least talking about it, and confronting the issue, might help things, but he wouldn't talk.

Bit by bit, she worked to change herself for the better, and she had success. Every year she felt a little healthier, a little bit closer to being normal. But Donald? Each year he became more of a jerk. She blinked rapidly to dry her eyes, and then sniffed.

She regained her composure by the time she arrived at the one-story headquarters of Visioryme. She put on her game face and smiled at her assistant.

"Hi, Stephan."

Stephan Liggett was fit, clean cut, well dressed, good looking, competent, effective, and gay. He sat in his chair, at once attentive and relaxed—a seated version of *parade rest* in the military. He smiled and looked her in the eyes.

"Hi, Tristana. How was your weekend?" The pitch of his voice rolled up and down, rising far too high at the end. His lilting speech provided one of the many indicators of that which was already abundantly clear.

"It's getting worse at home."

"Maybe you need to inhale some of your own company's antidepressant?"

"Or just avoid going home. I'm happier *here*."

Stephan winced in concern. "You'll be even happier today. Or not. Stock price is still rising. Three weeks straight."

"That's good."

"But the reason for our meteoric rise may kinda suck."

"It's hardly a meteoric rise, Stephan."

"You know that big shareholder we've never heard from?"

"You mean Paladin?"

"Yeah, Paladin. Now we've heard from him. Paladin is a one-member LLC."

"Yeah, I remember from the 13Ds. What's his name?"

"His name is Charles Knight. It looks like he's buying lots more of our stock too. He's why it's going up. He's filing new Schedule 13Ds almost daily. And he wants to meet."

Tristana shook her head. This was sudden. "How much of us does he own?"

"As of this morning, twenty-eight percent."

"What!" Anger and panic flooded her face. Anger at herself, for there could be no one else to blame. Panic because this might change her world. She knew nothing of the man who was buying her company. She gritted her teeth and suppressed it.

Stephan sensed her angst. He cocked his head, and said, "I'm pissed too."

"When does he want to meet?"

"The email requests a meeting this week; it's on your computer."

"We should take this head on. Set it up for as soon as he can come in. And get me everything you can on this guy."

Tristana closed the door to her office behind her, sat down, and laid her head back to gaze at the ceiling. There was change on the horizon, on all fronts. Good or bad, she had no idea. But one thing for sure was that the horizon was less than a week away.

Her life needed some whopping changes.

5

Morlocks in Mordor

THAT same day, Charles took a Northeast Regional train from New York's Penn Station and walked out of Washington's Union Station into the autumn air of a city defined by lost potential.

Like all American kids, he'd been steeped in noble foundation myths and fairy tales about *Our Nation's Capital,* as the place was referred to with reverence. From a distance, or from the point of view of a child, its power seemed awesome, exciting, and benevolent. But Charles had grown up, and the city, although awesome, was no more benevolent than a mass of intestinal worms that thrived by consuming most of a body's nutrition. Washington's power had grown exponentially. The denizens of the place had become more aggressive. It now presented an aura of decay and corruption no longer concealed by the marble facades. Once considered wonderful, it had morphed into a monster that had become the enemy of so much that still *was* wonderful. It emitted lies the way a hill of burning tires did acrid smoke. It pretended to be a cornucopia, the source of everything great and good. But its effect was that of a black hole, consuming anything that came near. It had become the Death Star.

Mordor.

The city sucked the integrity out of its inhabitants, whether they contributed to its power structure or suffered as its victims. There were some who, at least while feeling the increased courage and decreased inhibition alcohol offered, might say there was nothing wrong with the city that ten megatons on the Capitol wouldn't cure. And that might have worked years ago. But the place had metastasized to a degree that it would now take another forty megatons, spread in a quadrant going out ten miles in each direction. But few truly wanted that. After all, the city also contained the Smithsonian, the National Gallery, and the Library of Congress.

At least in theory, it was better to clean out the garbage than to burn down the house. But Charles had witnessed, during his travels, just how hard it can be to decontaminate an infected system. Scraping the dirt off of dirt just leaves dirt.

Even in Sodom there was one decent man. Charles knew for a fact that at least a few principled, sound, and mentally awake people lived in this vicinity. One such person had just arrived from the British Virgins two days earlier.

Charles walked for an hour along Washington's broad avenues. In the area around the Capitol, young people in suits hustled, going about their business of involving themselves in everyone else's business. Budding bureaucrats, political hacks, lawyers, and lobbyists, their lives in transition, fading from idealism into cynicism, from hope and momentum into despair and inertia. This early in their careers, they felt they accomplished good by performing the duties the system demanded of them. They proudly proclaimed to their family and friends all the good they did and how good they were. Here, in the Center of the World, surrounded by those who reinforced their delusions, they had neither time nor inclination to overcome them.

As Charles walked further south and east, the city blocks transitioned. Just twenty years ago, this area would have been off-limits for a white man, certainly at night. But as money flowed to the center of political power, gentrification followed. In the decades after World War II, poor black people had complained as middle-class whites moved out to the suburbs, leaving behind little but ghetto and combat zones. Now they complained as the political class moved in and bought up the properties, making even poverty unaffordable.

But the gentrification had yet to overtake the whole town. Soon, Charles was deep in Southeast Washington, D.C. Evening came early now, and the many broken streetlights were unable to ward it off. He kept walking into the dimness, but took a moment to make a phone call to provide his location to his recently arrived friend, whose help he hoped not to need.

The city competed with Baltimore, Chicago, and Detroit to be murder capital of the nation. From the Virginia side of the Potomac one could see the monuments and government buildings, but just behind these landmarks lay other buildings that most tried to ignore. Other than liquor and convenience stores, legal commerce faltered in the area. A few old row homes remained, left from the days when it was a middle-class area, but they'd mostly been replaced by low-rise projects modeled after garden apartments in the suburbs. Except here neither gardens nor grass could be found, just cheap construction giving way under hard use. Liquor-store parking lots served as the poor man's country club. Homeless people panhandled and hustled at every store exit. Junkies scurried around, working any angle they could to get the next fix.

The yuppies bustling around the Capitol might well think the people down here resembled H.G. Wells's cannibalistic cave dwellers, the Morlocks. But if they thought it, they'd never say something so politically incorrect. The locals, on the other hand, would think the yuppies were like the weak and passive Eloi, in the unlikely event they'd ever read *The Time Machine*, or even seen the movie.

It was therefore ironic that here in Washington the Eloi preyed on the Morlocks much more effectively than the reverse. The political-class Eloi and the underclass Morlocks did, however, share a basic worldview. In this city, whether it was in the shadow of the Capitol, or under the burnt-out streetlights of Southeast D.C., the ends *always* justified the means. The political class thrived only by being more grandiose in their ends, and more subtle in their means.

With some trepidation, Charles stepped into the shallow doorway of a closed store so he could observe the street. He made a second phone call. Leaning against the wall, he watched. He began to admire the spontaneous organization of the system before him: an ecology of individuals interacting to accomplish their goals—some worthy and some self-destructive, some legal and some illegal. Some of the worthy ones were illegal, and some of the self-destructive ones were legal; a perverse system of incentives was in operation. Some members of the ecosystem were just hanging out on corners. Some sat on steps. Others moved in and out of buildings.

He tried to identify the bosses, the lookouts, the muscle, and the runners. Some of the cultural clues here mirrored those he had discovered in Nairobi, in Minsk, or in Phnom Penh. But each culture presented its own specific and dangerous idiosyncrasies.

Here he couldn't be sure who held the stash and who held the cash.

One person never held both. He needed to find a lieutenant who oversaw the process to help him enculturate. That would be difficult. It would take far more than just distant observation over an hour or two to understand who was who. He had no expectation that he would be allowed the luxury of such time. This was no temporary trap house location that could operate only until the police just *had* to bust them for being too obvious or for causing too many problems. No, this commercial infrastructure permanently supported the local drug trade, and those who felt they owned it would protect their property and their privacy.

By now, anyone who had eyes knew Charles was lurking.

The drug trade in this area was well established and well organized. It had operated in this neighborhood for decades, in and among the abandominiums—empty row houses where users could find temporary shelter, or if they could cop no smack, where they suffered through the agonies of withdrawal.

The lack of traditional gangs, or organized-crime influence, made the D.C. drug trade unusual. Perhaps the presence of a dozen different police forces from the government—including thousands of FBI and DEA employees—discouraged large outfits like the Crips or the Bloods. But that didn't make it an open city.

Instead of such gangs, geographic loyalties prevailed. Southside D.C. stuck together, and uptown—the northwest side of D.C.—did likewise. Outsiders from New York and other cities tried to move in, but were always driven out with extreme force. Instead, the ecology consisted of individual players—an economist would call them entrepreneurs or perhaps franchisees—running their blocks with the efficiency of Walmart.

Charles needed to find a way in. But it would take days, and be dangerous. He'd already stayed here too long. Time to leave, for now. He stepped out of the recessed doorway.

"Got a dollar, light skin?" asked a stumblebum with a stringy gray beard who clung to the wall to Charles's left. Filthy and torn clothes hung obscenely off his emaciated body. Beyond him, on the other side of the street, a lanky teenager in a hoodie appeared from the dusk, like a moth attracted to a light. The kid watched closely.

This was it. Charles wanted this. But that didn't mean he was ready. His heart rate jumped just as it had when he provoked the Coast Guard. His muscles tightened.

41

Charles lifted his head slightly and replied. "No. But I'll give you *twenty* dollars if you take me to cop."

The guy looked first at Charles and then glanced around the neighborhood. Charles watched his eyes dart to every car, parked or moving, and each of the scattered people who could be seen walking. He said, "Give me the money and I'll get it for you."

"No way. You gotta take me to it. I didn't come all the way down here to get burnt."

The guy shrugged his shoulders. "If I ain't back in ten, I ain't comin'. If I got good news for you, you gotta split the bag with me."

Charles replied, "No split. But I'll give you twenty-five."

The guy sneered and staggered off. He was jittery, in need of a fix. But he seemed to have free roam through the neighborhood. He moved briskly down the block, turned between two buildings, and disappeared. Charles checked his watch: 7:05. No one who looked like him should be hanging out alone in this poorly lit area. A sole dope fiend presented little threat, but one of the hustlers or stick-up kids might sniff him out, gather some allies, and become courageous. In the face of the mob thinking that resulted, Charles would have little chance of talking his way out. Concern for safety should have prompted him to leave thirty minutes earlier.

But safety allows for existence, not for life.

A man emerged from a door just across the street. He wore a velour sweat suit, a Kangol hat, and a shining pair of Jordans. This new man looked at Charles, and then turned back inside.

This place felt nowhere near as dangerous as the back streets of Bangkok, the slums of Mumbai, or the sheet-metal-and-bamboo shanty towns of Lagos. This was safer than the surrounds of Moscow, or anywhere north of the Piazza Garibaldi in Naples. Charles had traveled through and lived in such places. The gradual death of his youthful naïveté had permitted the rest of him to survive and thrive. And so his guard was up, in Condition Red, but he wasn't panicky.

Two men approached him from the other direction now, starting across the street toward the shadowed wall on which Charles rested his back. Although they weren't coming from the direction the dope fiend had retreated in, that didn't exclude the possibility that these were the guy's dealers, responding by phone. They walked with easy, menacing confidence.

Whether the guy's source or not, it was clear these men were asserting property rights to their turf.

One man stood as tall as Charles, the other substantially smaller. Assessing their builds proved difficult. Their absurdly oversized leather coats obscured any sign of muscles or guns. They could each have a baseball bat concealed under that garb.

As they came toward him, Charles remained leaning against the wall. These men approached because they saw a man who did not belong, hanging out on a street they had decided belonged to them. Quite different from sub-Saharan Africa, where he would be greeted warmly as a potential source of funds. Or in Southeast Asia, where he was more likely to be ignored than hassled. An old street fighter's adage came to mind: be polite and respectful when you meet new people, but figure out exactly how you might need to kill them.

"Yo." The tall one stared at Charles, his head cocked to the side. "Fuck you doin' here, slim?" His shaved head complemented his intimidating tone.

Charles replied stonily and slowly, "Waiting on a friend."

"You makin' the block hot, white boy. Take yo' ass on!"

"Who are you?"

"Oh, my bad. I'm Smith, and this my man Wesson. Right now you dumbass is fuckin' our block." His mouth showed some gold teeth underneath his sneer.

"No disrespect intended," Charles replied.

The man pulled a Glock 40 from under his coat. "Fuck wrong wit you, light skin? Don' you know where you's at? Yo' dumbass gonna end up in a dumpster. Last chance, man, stay the fuck from 'round here. I see you ass again, it gonna end up face down. We clear?"

Charles compromised their business, and his presence would attract unwanted attention from law enforcement. He had to go another route. He had to take a chance.

Charles said, "OK. I'll move along. But first, I'll pay you three hundred dollars for some information."

"Yo, this mo'fo's Five-O man," said the smaller man in a soft voice. "Stop playin' with this dude, and drop him in that alley over there. Let the li'l niggaz handle him."

The stick-up kids had gathered across the street, watching this interaction intently. The teenagers made their living robbing dealers, the homeless, addicts, and anyone else who looked worth the trouble. But they made their *name* killing for cheap while they were still minors and could only get locked up in the juvenile system. There the apprentices would serve time as journeymen, picking up new skills and connections. When they got out, they'd have a guaranteed spot on somebody's team. The worst case was some hard time in a real prison, but even that would be as valuable to their resume as grad school would be for one of the yuppies a couple miles away on Capitol Hill.

"Ay Big Youngin, dude say he got three hunred on him!" hollered the tall one toward the group of teenage boys. They stirred, the adrenaline level rising; something would happen.

Racism exists mostly as a matter of class and culture, but has its biological roots as well. Most small primitive tribes called themselves "people" in their own language, while using a different word for outsiders—a word that made outsiders seem somewhat less than human. It made sense from an evolutionary point of view. Those outside your group had to be viewed as a potential threat—intent on stealing your property, or worse. Thus humans have been genetically programmed for hundreds of thousands of years to discriminate based on superficial indicators such as skin tone. Higher cognitive functioning was usually required to overcome such biological programming. Such higher functioning could be found in individuals, but not in groups. Racism still had some survival value, but its origins lay in group-think and collectivism.

When dealing with a mob, individuals didn't matter. The lowest common denominator took over. The brainwashed collective rules. Different race equals different group equals dangerous outsider.

Charles—a whitey, a cracker, a honkey—was naturally hated and feared. Their attitude was reflexive and programmed. And understandable, even if stupid and psychologically bent.

The locals had bad habits, and very bad manners. But the fact that their hostility was overt made them potentially safer companions than the typical government yuppie, whose days were spent running protection rackets under the cover of the law.

Washington has distinct characteristics, beyond its multicultural criminal mentality, its drug culture, its numerous police forces. Of course, every city has its own character that draws some types, and repels others. Because of that, its basic nature is reinforced over time. Las Vegas draws gamblers and grifters. L.A. draws hipsters and wannabe actors. Jacksonville and Colorado Springs nurture Jesus freaks; Seattle draws ecofreaks, San Jose techies, and San Francisco gays. Birds of a feather do flock together. People who crave power over others flock to Washington. The government provides the essence of the city, its raison d'être. The place has no other reason to exist. Detroit at least used to make cars and trucks; Chicago at least used to butcher cows and hogs. But Washington never in its history made *anything*. The people drawn to this city during its entire history were conspicuously *un*productive. Or, rather, counterproductive.

Sure, Washington was unrivaled in the creation of laws and regulations, but to Charles, that could never count as production.

Charles never sought power over other people. He had a hard time understanding those who sought such power. His was a charming, but dangerous, form of naïveté.

It was easy to see why black children in a white school, or white children in a black school, chose to sit together in the cafeteria. Charles could empathize. The kids felt they were in an alien realm, as did Charles in this city. Like them, he needed to be near his own kind. But skin color was irrelevant in determining who Charles's kind were. His kind crossed ethnic, national, religious, and color boundaries. His kind were simply people with whom he shared values.

Whether anyone native to this street would qualify as Charles's kind he had yet to determine.

"I'm not liking your smell, cracker."

The man signaled to the stick-up kids, who started to move.

A teenage girl appeared as if out of nowhere. Her dark camouflage had kept her hidden: a street punk dressed head to toe in black, complete with black fingernails and raven hair.

She bumped her hip hard into Charles, pushing him backward against the wall. "Hey, Tomo, I got him. *I* like the smell of three hundred dollars."

The teenage boys stopped and watched. The pack of coyotes had to decide whether the meal was worth fighting an uninvited predator for.

The bigger man looked over at the girl.

"What the fuck, Rainbow? You the boss now, bag bitch?"

"I ain't no bag bitch, Tomo! Never!"

"Yo' mama was. I know that for fact."

45

Rainbow's expression didn't change as her fist sprang up and hit Tomo in the front of his neck.

Tomo's eyes bulged and he stumbled back.

"Bitch!" He croaked, his hand grasping his throat. He worked his jaw up and down and coughed. His lips pursed as he worked to breathe. The girl had cracked him in the larynx.

Tomo recovered some, but he didn't take the assault lightly. He came forward fast and threw Rainbow aside with a quick move of his left arm. "Now fuck off, Rainbow. You interrupting business." He coughed and gagged.

He turned his anger and smacked his weapon against Charles's cheekbone. The Glock then lined up under Charles's chin. The cool muzzle pressed his neck backward.

"*That* ain't business, Tomo," the girl replied. "*Three hundred dollars* is business. I need the money."

"I told you, you be ho'in for the H!" With his free arm, Tomo slapped her back against the brick wall, and she went down hard. He glanced over at his partner and ordered, "Keep that bitch down."

He stepped back from Charles and held the gun sideways, aiming at Charles's belly. If he pulled the trigger, the ejected empty case would probably hit the guy in the face.

"And now, whitey, I'm gonna start you bleeding so the sharks can feast." He gestured toward the teenage boys with a shake of his head.

This city might be less dangerous than half of Bangkok, but this man wasn't, and neither were those boys.

The little man interrupted, shouting, "Tomo, yo' head bein' lit by a beam!" He pointed at a red laser dot reflecting off Tomo's scalp.

Charles knew it was coming. A few minutes earlier, his friend had pulled up in a parked car a few buildings away. And watched. And now acted.

Charles spoke with a calmness he didn't feel. "My friend is just knocking on your door. Knocking with his rifle. Let me make this abundantly clear to you, Mr. Smith—or should I call you Tomo? I don't give one fuck about your threats, or your disrespect bullshit. Right now, I care for one thing only, and that is making money."

Charles then looked at the smaller man. "Mr. Wesson, look down the empty alley there. Do you see the man leaning against the side of the car? Do you see his right arm on top of the car? Maybe you can see that he has a rifle aimed at Tomo's head? Or maybe soon at your eyeball? I've been next to that man as he took out a head just like yours from ten times as far away. There's no way he's gonna miss plastering your brains on the bricks. I'm just sayin'."

"You Five-O, dude." The short man winced as he looked down the street.

Charles replied with convincing assurance. "No. If I were a cop, you'd already be full of holes. I'm a businessman, with friends, here to make *very* good money working with good people. Apparently you won't be one of them. Now's the time to decide if shooting me is worth dying for. Because I guarantee you *will* die."

The teenage boys stayed still across the street and watched closely. They studied the man aiming the rifle from down the street. White man was going to get dead, or wasn't, but there was no percentage in their acting. At least not yet.

Tomo's gun wavered, and he said, "That dot still on my head?"

Wesson replied, "Yeah. It's not wigglin'."

Tomo lowered his Glock. He shoved his chin out and raised his shoulders, and, with blatantly feigned nonchalance, tucked his pistol into his belt. "You get fuck on outahere."

Charles nodded. "All I wanted was a meet. Maybe another day."

"We ain't puttin' you next to no one, Five-O. Instead, someday soon, I'm gonna hunt you down. Nobody shine a beam on my head and survive."

"Don't look for me too hard, Tomo. You don't want your brain tagging a brick wall."

"Fuck you, mofo."

The two men retreated back to where they had come from, strolling with as much cockiness as they could muster, staring down the street directly into the red laser.

Charles wasn't out of the woods yet. The teenage boys were every bit as dangerous, and not rational in any way he understood.

"They more of them than they is o' you." The girl's voice sounded weak. Charles kneeled down next to her. He could see her face in the dim light, but not the blood that meandered down through her hair.

"Let me help you up?" he asked in a gentle tone, seeking permission.

She looked at him with the cynical eyes of a dark life lived alone. But those eyes softened. She reached up a hand, and he took it. He put his other hand beside her shoulder and guided her upward as she rose on unsteady legs. Charles felt his own legs shaking too.

"Are you OK?"

"Nothing new." She felt the back of her head and winced. Blood soaked her fingertips.

"You're gonna need stitches."

"And you're gonna need this." She handed him his wallet.

Charles smiled as he took it. The girl had skills. "Why are you giving it back?"

"It's yours. I just lifted it before someone else did."

"Thanks for helping me."

The girl shrugged. She wiped her hand on her black leggings. "I didn't. I was trying to help *me*."

"Right."

She looked up in his eyes again. "What do you want for that three hundred dollars?"

He had an immediate need to get out of this place, but he took the time to reach into his wallet. His money was untouched. He pulled out a business card, this one with a phone number. "Will you call me tomorrow?"

She held the card to pick up enough light so that her young eyes could make out the words. "Paladin. That your name?"

"Close enough."

Rainbow padded her multiple pockets. "Darn, I must have given out my last business card at the drug dealer convention."

"You're called Rainbow?"

"Yeah. What of it?"

"Pretty name. Weird name. You Native American?"

"Yeah. One-third."

Charles laughed as he saw the girl's eyes glint in appreciation of her own joke. He watched her face soften, as her eyes had before. A shared sense of humor could be a good start.

She dropped her gaze. "Look. I'll call you. Or I won't."

Charles nodded. "Stay well, Rainbow. I hope you call."

"You better do as Tomo said and get your ass outahere. That man holds a grudge. And once you on his bad side, you never on his good. You watch your back, Paladin. He'll have plans for you now."

She strutted over to the teenagers, and they gathered around her, craving whatever knowledge she had about the white man against the wall. She was helping him get clear.

Charles stayed on his side of the street, moving quickly, without running. The boys noticed, but their mob mind hadn't yet decided on an appropriate action, and Rainbow distracted them from thinking about it.

As Charles approached his friend's car, the man packed up his rifle into the back while keeping a wary eye on the teenagers.

"Xander, your timing and your aim are impeccable."

The Dutchman's voice sounded heavy with chastisement. "You know, had I pulled that trigger I would only have killed one of those men. Then things might have gotten complicated for you."

"I was more worried about those kids rushing you. You have the wrong gun for that many."

Xander Winn smiled. "It's been said that sometimes you don't go to war with the army you want. You go to war with the army you have. Perhaps you'd like me to carry an antitank cannon in my trunk as well? Anyway, you're just lucky I was around, or you would have been in real trouble." He then reminded Charles that "Proper Planning Prevents Piss Poor Performance."

Xander climbed into the driver's seat. As soon as Charles had the passenger door halfway closed, Winn took off, squealing the tires partly because it was fun, and partly because his 1968 Mustang was capable of doing it. Lots of baby boomers were partial to vintage muscle cars. Their history and connection with a treasured youth compensated for their expense, lack of comfort, and poor handling compared to better-engineered modern counterparts.

"Xander, only a true friend would aim his gun at a complete stranger on my behalf."

Xander spoke five languages fluently, and a few others reasonably well. His Dutch accent had been modified by living internationally essentially forever, including considerable time in the U.S. But he still had quirks of grammar and syntax, as well as the occasional lapse of vocabulary, that would inform a listener that he wasn't a native. "It's not the first time I've done that for you. Today is relatively ... shall we say ... a cakewalk."

"Yes, it is. Still I'm grateful."

"I'm glad I was in town."

"For long?"

"No. I gotta fly back across the pond tomorrow."

Xander drove as if he had no fear of police cruisers or automated traffic cameras. Far into middle age but more fit than most men thirty years younger, Xander sported an appealingly scraggled look, the result of life in the outdoors. One thick rough hand lay on the steering wheel. The other rubbed one of his blue eyes. So he drove with one hand and one eye, at twice the speed limit. And he thought nothing of it.

"Should I ask what you were doing in that neighborhood, Charles?"

Charles reached up to hold the window edge to stabilize himself and said, "Let's talk at your place…"

Xander shot onto the interstate, and Charles sat firmly back in his seat. Though determined to feign indifference, he imagined what it would be like to merge with a cement wall at ninety miles per hour. His jaw muscles cramped, his elbows extended, and both legs stretched out to press the brake pedal that didn't exist on his side of the car. Adrenaline pumped into his circulation as it had when he first met Xander, seven years earlier, when Xander had saved him from plunging off a cliff to his death. Except now *Xander* was the threat to life and limb.

Ninety-five miles per hour.

"We have guns in this car that are totally illegal here," Charles said through his teeth. "Better not be pulled over for reckless driving. This place is overrun with cops…"

"You're worried that I may be pulled over for a traffic violation, but didn't mind if I got arrested for having a rifle braced on the roof of my car in the middle of D.C.?"

"The rifle kept me alive. The speed is going to make me dead. Or maybe put us both in the slammer."

"That's a good point, kid." Xander let the car coast down to an easy eighty, only slightly above the flow of traffic. "We'll be at my place in ten minutes."

Unless part of the president's motorcade, no one driving sanely can get anywhere around D.C. in ten minutes. Xander and Charles weren't part of the presidential motorcade, yet ten minutes later they were pulling into the driveway of a condominium complex directly overlooking the Potomac from its Virginia shore.

"I don't get here often," Xander said, "but it's nice to have this pad. A man needs a crib in a place or two. It's yours for as long as you need it."

From the top-floor balcony the two men sat sipping scotch while looking out over the river, the city lights reflecting on the water. Something about water—the sea, a lake, a river, even a stream—increased Charles's happiness quotient. Water was not just essential for life, but for comfort. Proximity to water raised his baseline enjoyment of life. He breathed a sigh of satisfaction.

"Charles, what are you doing back in this country? I thought you were through with it, and especially through with the kind of people in this … *particular* place." He waved his hand at the vast scene below, encompassing the whole of Washington. "These people lied to you, lied about you, and stole your money. They worked with the people who almost killed us both."

Charles smiled at Xander. "It's where the market is."

"Market for what?"

"I'm getting into the illegal-drug business."

Xander—Charles's accidental mentor in his erstwhile career as a speculator—was not one to judge anything based on illegality or legality. The qualifier *illegal* had little relation to morality, or to right or wrong. Laws crafted by politicians or regulators had at best an occasional and accidental relationship to morality. You could be sure only that the laws somehow benefited—directly or indirectly—the people who wrote them. Lawmakers were rarely Xander's friends.

"The standard illegal drugs?" Xander asked. No judgment.

"Not quite," Charles responded.

"Ha," Xander snorted. He stood and retrieved a cigar humidor from inside, and drew out a couple of Cohiba Esplendidos. "Excuse my poor manners. A good scotch is improved by a better cigar." He poured them each a couple of fingers of Pinch in short crystal glasses.

The whisky's ornate bottle caught Charles's eye.

"Reminds me of times in the Congo," Xander said, as he held the bottle up.

Charles preferred drugs other than tobacco. But a good cigar was hard to turn down, especially with a nice scotch. "I wonder how scotch would go with coca leaves? I chewed it a lot while in Peru. You start chewing a small handful of leaves. Then you pop in a good-sized pinch of bicarbonate of soda to release the active ingredients. After a few minutes you'll feel your mouth and lips getting a bit numb, like Novocain. It helps with altitude sickness. You get kinda pleasant and mellow, but alert too. Vendors sell it on street corners."

Xander nodded. "Similar to khat, in that way. In the days when I was hanging out in Somalia I used to chew khat to be social with the locals."

Unless one asked the right question, Xander rarely shared his vast reservoir of experiences. Charles had no idea Xander had been in Somalia. Probably during some critical period of civil unrest.

The men spun the globe of the drug world, poking fingers down on random places and reviewing that location's drug of choice, and occasionally its laws regarding them. It became a friendly game of *can-you-top-this*.

Charles said, "LSD and psilocybin are effective against a bunch of psychiatric ailments. Yet they were both banned in the U.S. because they helped unite the '60s counterculture—which Nixon hated. LSD treats post-traumatic stress and depression, and probably more. And in microdoses way below the amounts that send you on a trip, it increases both athletic and mental performance. Yet it stays banned."

"Even in the Netherlands," Xander sighed, as he took the reins. "There must be hundreds of little kava bars in Vanuatu. Dirt floors. You sit around on wood stools or beat-up old plastic chairs, and they give you half a coconut shell full of a drink mashed up from the kava plant's roots. At least on the out islands, young boys still chew the roots up for you. That part is a bit unappetizing. Then you sit around, everybody speaking in a low voice. It's called *nakamal talk*. Very mellow. The only violence in Vanuatu happens when visiting Aussies go there to get drunk."

Charles said, "Yeah, there's almost no violent crime in Vanuatu. I've heard the kava culture is one reason. Of course they say that cocaine and heroin *cause* crime, and are different. But that wasn't true when they were legal, before they passed the Harrison Act in 1914. Only the U.S. could create a violent war out of a nonviolent trade."

"Not just the U.S., kid. Although this place leads the world in that sort of foolishness. When I was a kid, same age you were when I met you in Gondwana, a Cuban friend—Victor Espinosa—and I figured we should get into the marijuana business. Our idea was to get our private pilot's licenses, then fly down to Mexico to set up a deal with local growers. Start with a fifty-pound bale. It was possible then, before the border became a veritable militarized zone. Fly back up and dump the bale in a field where a truck would pick it up. Repeat as needed."

"Ahh, the good old days."

"The penalties for getting caught were mild, and the chances of getting caught were nil. Buy a bale for five hundred dollars, sell it wholesale for ten thousand. Leave the retail dealing for those who weren't wise enough to stay clear of the low margin and the danger. It could have turned into a big business in a short time. But the problem is that by the time you know your way around, the bad guys on both sides of the law have figured out you exist."

"So did you do it?"

"You can't kiss all the girls," Xander replied wistfully. "So, Charles, why are you wanting to sell illegal drugs?"

"Because I want to kiss all the girls. I've always said I'll try most anything once. Twice if I like it. Plus, as you said, when drugs are illegal, they're highly profitable. And there's a void in the market that needs filling."

"In your cash flow predictive models, don't forget the money you'll have to spend to take on the Drug Enforcement Administration."

"Not likely an issue."

Xander raised an eyebrow. "I thought we cured you of cocky."

"No, I've thought about this quite a bit."

"How will you avoid falling victim to the DEA? There's thousands of *them*, and one of you."

"Because they won't care."

"How's that?"

"Because I'm focused on drugs that are illegal because the Food and Drug Administration blocks them, not because the DEA blocks them."

"So, you'll have to fight the FDA?"

"But they don't carry guns, and they don't have Hollywood making heroes out of them. Actually, the larger concern is Customs."

"So you're going to be a rum runner. Like JFK's father, Joe Kennedy? He made a fortune running booze to the U.S. from Canada and the Caribbean during Prohibition, competing with Al Capone and Meyer Lansky. What kind of rum are *you* gonna run, Charles?"

Charles smiled. "I'm interested in prescription drugs. Viagra to start with, and a few others. Viagra has high value for very low weight and volume, and it's not the object of armed assault by government bandits. I'm going into international prescription pharmaceutical arbitrage, Xander. Except without any prescriptions."

Xander didn't smile as often as Charles, but he smiled now. "Ha, Charles! That I like. It's a good market niche, and fits you."

"I'm not going to do it the way you might expect, either. We're going to innovate."

"Well, you don't want to get on a playing field where there are a bunch of dinosaurs thrashing around."

"No. But I'd like to be a little comet, crashing down to ruin their day."

"I worry about you, you know."

Charles looked over at him.

Xander reached and tapped the back of Charles's hand with two fingers. "Kid, you have a great outlook on the world. You're a glass-half-full guy. Hell, if the world were only a bit of foul backwash in the bottom of a beer mug, to you it would be partly filled with opportunity."

"I'm not sure I like the analogy…"

"Well, it's a gift, for sure. But your feelings about the nature of humanity are a double-edged sword. Your optimism minimizes—too much, I think—the less savory aspects of the human animal. You've seen those ugly faces. And you're moving into a field where you'll see more."

"I already have," Charles replied. The second person he had met in his new endeavor had pledged to seek him out and kill him. Was Tomo a bad omen? Or just a bad start?

Charles thought the future of humans was to travel on a road to the planets, the stars, and other galaxies. Humans needed only time, capital, and freedom to turn the impossible into reality. Time was infinite. Capital could be accumulated. Freedom, the third essential, remained the hardest to attain.

"I think anything that can be imagined can probably be done. Someday."

"Charles, you act as if you were free. But there are a lot of people who think they have a right to tell you what to do. If you complain, they'll claim that since you live in a democracy, they have a moral right to take whatever they want from you. Majority rule is like two wolves and a sheep voting on what to have for dinner. Somehow these nuts conflate democracy with socialism. I'm not crazy about either one. But they have the upper hand in this country. You should be on your guard, coming back here."

Charles reached into his pocket and pulled out a silver blister packet of ten blue pills and handed it to Xander. "Speaking of happiness, this is for you."

54

"What is it? " Xander asked.

"Fiagara, with an F. Same stuff as Viagra. I assume you're dating someone."

"Do you always keep this stuff with you?"

Charles responded, "Just a little candy to give to guys like you. Stuff like this is my product. I need to build a client base."

"Seems like a safe and harmless pursuit."

"Right. Now, how about you show me the guns you have for me. I'm gonna need them."

6

The Legal Business

STEPHAN entered Tristana's office. "Hey, Tristana. Charles Knight is here."

Tristana's heartbeat bumped up a notch. She asked, "What's he like?"

"He's hot, and he's wearing a suit. And a tie. Just my type."

Tristana raised her eyebrows.

Stephan scowled and grinned at the same time. "But he's more the kind of man you need than I need." He sighed. "He looks like a fighter."

Tristana grinned back. "Send him in, please, Stephan."

The man who came through the door smiled from a deeply suntanned face. His eyes, the slight grin, hair that fell to his shoulders, the purple bruise above his cheek, and his general demeanor together made a statement. The whole package raised a flood of emotions in Tristana, stemming not from her perspective as a beaten-down pharma entrepreneur so much as from her position as a beaten-down wife.

"Good morning. Very nice to meet you. I'm Charles Knight."

She liked the way he took her hand into his. The muscles in his hand and arm stayed taut. No threatening grip, but just a warm, dry palm and firm fingers. So unlike the limp imitation of a dead fish her husband used when he greeted someone. Or when he touched her.

She held on longer than she should have—and held his gaze longer than she thought seemly, before turning away. In reality, she was frozen. She had envisioned an older, tired, respectable-appearing man, but here was youth and vigor, and an attractive pinch of impertinence. The exact opposite of Donald. Definitely not a salary man.

She needed to suppress this intrusion of immature schoolgirl thinking, and do so immediately. "Mr. Knight. It's a pleasure."

He replied gently, "Tristana, please call me Charles."

She nodded quickly. "So, I finally meet the man behind Paladin."

"My holding company. I'm embarrassed to admit that for the last many years, I didn't even know I owned shares of Visioryme. Now I own a lot. And I'm glad for it."

"You're now our single largest shareholder."

"Yes."

Tristana prodded him. "What's your interest?"

"May I sit?" He said this while motioning her to take a seat at her own desk. Then he effortlessly moved a heavy metal chair to a position where he had an unencumbered view of her. He moved to sit down before she could consent.

He said, "My interest is making money, of course. But the fun part of making money is creating value—goods and services people need and want. And doing it well, so they're happy to pay you their hard-earned money."

"That sounds..." She searched for a word and came up with "... honorable. Are you planning on controlling?"

"Not alone. I have limited expertise in this field."

"I see. You're working with others." She had received no hints of any consortiums among the principal investors. She would likely have heard. "Can you tell me who?"

"Hopefully just you." He cocked his head to the side. It was cute, endearing, if cliché.

Relief flooded her, although she knew it was premature.

He continued. "But effective relationships are based on trust. First, we have to get to know each other."

She didn't know why she said it, but she did. "Sounds like lunch."

He replied smoothly, with a modest but hopeful tone, "... and dinner, and the afternoon in between, if you're available."

Dinner, breakfast, and all that might lay between. It was a phrase a college roommate had used regularly in response to a particularly good pickup line from an attractive boy.

She settled on the more conservative. "My day is your day."

What the hell did that mean? This was her company. But maybe not. Not anymore. This man could totally upend it. Have her fired by the week's end if he could get the directors together for an emergency board meeting and sway them. Failing that, he could conduct a proxy battle and replace all the directors, which might be the next item on his agenda.

But then she realized it was ridiculous to immediately play out the worst case. God, had she picked that trait up from Donald?

Knight said, "I'm grateful for any time you have. I've read all the annual reports and 10-Ks. I know what the reports say; I want you to tell me what they *don't* say. All the fears, all the concerns. I want reality. The reports are helpful, but they've been filtered by lawyers and spun for funding rounds and for the FDA. I'd like to go over everything again, but directly from your mouth." He was not smiling, but his eyes were interested, encouraging.

Tristana's professional brain kicked into gear then, as she refocused herself. "That will be easy, Charles. Visioryme is extremely well positioned."

"Well positioned, huh? Ten years without a dollar of profit. You want to try again?"

She sat back in her desk chair. "Sorry. I wasn't trying to give you a PR answer. Look, Charles. I really am being candid. The truth is that Visioryme is in pretty good shape for a small pharma company. Not financially—we've just got enough to cover our running costs. But, as you know, we do have a potential blockbuster drug just about to come out of the pipeline."

"Of course. Can you give me a verbal summary of where you are now, what challenges you think lie ahead?"

"Certainly." He said he'd read all Visioryme's public documents, but he also claimed he hadn't known, for years, that he even owned a big chunk of her company. So he was most likely just a lucky guy born to wealthy parents, and not a rocket scientist. Tristana decided to start with the standard pitch she gave to anyone with questions about Visioryme.

"As you know, Visioryme is a specialty pharmaceutical company, developing medications to correct cognitive and emotional disturbances that lead to varying states of depression and confusional symptomatology. We're focused on a specific pathway that is involved in neuronal connections that form during exposure to emotionally charged visual and auditory stimulation. Our founder, Tim McBride, is a neurochemist, and named this molecular pathway *ProPG*. He's a tenured professor now, and a radical thinker. Used to work with Shulgin and Nichols."

Knight's face suggested that he did not know the names. Few these days did.

So she explained. "The guys who designed a lot of psychedelics in the 1960s? LSD, Ecstasy, and the like? There are hundreds of designer drugs out there, with all kinds of effects, although very few have been properly investigated, for regulatory reasons. Well, anyway, the ProPG pathway is similar to the dimethyltryptamine pathway. It may be one and the same actually. You do know DMT, right? No? Well, the ProPG pathway is amenable to manipulation with a natural substance obtained from a fungus that grows on the woody part of certain types of bamboo."

"Only bamboo? No other source?"

"That's right. We process bamboo for the fungal material that lives on it, chemically modify it, and the resulting compound serves as an antidepressant. The compound is called VR-210, but we have chosen a marketing name, Sybillene, that will be used when FDA approves it. Unlike other antidepressants, Sybillene has a rapid onset, and unlike the competitors, it doesn't cause side effects." She felt her heart flutter slightly as she said this last. She had always been a lousy liar.

"Side effects like...?" He prompted her from across the desk.

"Most antidepressants cause sleep disturbance, nausea, sweating, anxiety, restlessness, constipation, diarrhea, headaches, weight gain, and dry mouth. They make some patients think rather unclearly, and act irrationally or violently under some circumstances."

"Why would anyone want any of those?"

"And sexual dysfunction."

Knight chuckled. "And definitely not that one."

"Sybillene doesn't cause these side effects."

"No side effects at all?"

"No."

This handsome man, more confident than many older men she had known, looked into her eyes intently. Was it that twinge of guilt that made it feel like he could see through her? Did he know she was not entirely forthright about the side effects of Sybillene?

But he didn't probe further. "Sybillene is your primary focus, then?"

This question put her back into her groove. "Laser-focused. We've finished phase 3 studies and submitted our NDA—New Drug Application—to FDA to obtain their permission to market Sybillene as an antidepressant."

Outsiders rarely knew the phases of drug studies, so she continued, "Phase 1 is safety testing in healthy people. Phase 2 is safety and efficacy in people with the target disease. Phase 3 is establishing efficacy in a larger group with the disease. We had to successfully complete phase 3 before the FDA would approve it. They used to just require proof of safety, but since the 1960s, they've required proof of effectiveness too."

"How have you kept this company going without sales?"

She replied. "Well, we've had to sell more stock in private placements…"

"Yes, and I bought into them."

"Yes, your timing wasn't bad. You bought the cheap ones, when we had to offer warrants as a sweetener. That was a good move."

"Maybe. You bought then too."

So maybe he knew that she too was a member of the lucky-sperm club. Maybe he knew she'd been the only child of a wealthy doting mother who was widowed young. She'd left Manhattan for upstate New York for a high-end education at a girls boarding school in Westchester, and on to Smith for four more years of gender segregation. She graduated the day after her mother died in a car accident on her way to celebrate with her.

"I did buy on each price dip. But most of our funding came from *non-dilutive equity*."

"Which is?"

"Government money. SBIR grants, NIH grants, DOD grants."

Knight's face flashed some unexpected expression. What was that? Pain? Tristana wasn't sure. She continued. "And foundation money too. We wrote a whole lot of grant requests. And enough of them got funded."

Usually people nodded at this point, providing some recognition and positive reinforcement for the hard work that went into successful grant-funding efforts. Knight, however, said nothing, and his face remained blank. Maybe he didn't understand.

She continued. "There have been challenges. The drug is best delivered through inhalation because, if swallowed, the liver chews it up. This is the first inhaled antidepressant, and FDA has caused us all sorts of aggravation about that: ensuring that dosing is consistent, that delivery from the inhaler device is appropriate, and the like. All that costs money and time. Plus, FDA is just slow." She thought of Donald with some distaste, and pitied any new drug application that crossed his desk.

"So you still have no revenue." Charles went straight to the crux of the matter.

So she would too. "Other than NIH grants, no. The NIH grants have kept us going for years, but that's all coming to an end."

Knight said, "Grant money tends to encourage bad habits. Companies start focusing on creating value for granting agencies instead of their real market. That leads to waste. What is your cash situation?"

She sighed. "Well, that's the bad news. At our current burn rate, we have three months to breathe. And only if we take very small breaths."

"When will the FDA approve?"

"They might decide any time in the next couple of months. We're desperately hoping they approve. They've put us through absolute hell getting this far."

"Assume they approve. Then what are your plans for monetization? Market it yourself? A deal with large pharma?"

Tristana shook her head and bit her lower lip, not cutely, but in anger. Anger at a convoluted and dysfunctional system that hurt everybody around it. "Big Pharma isn't about R & D anymore. Now they're just marketing powerhouses. Innovation comes from small, entrepreneurial outfits, like us. So you would think they'd jump all over a drug that's about to be approved by FDA, but they haven't."

"Why not?"

Tristana knew the answer. It wasn't a problem with Sybillene or the potential demand for their medication. Not at all. Usually she would never say aloud any of what she had figured out about the situation, but there was something about Knight's demeanor, or perhaps the fact that he owned much of the company, that prompted her to do so now.

"The entrepreneurs and hands-on scientists that founded the giant pharma companies are long dead. Now they're run by professional managers. These guys don't buy shares with their own money. They have ownership only through options provided as compensation. They get fat salaries and have great pension packages. But if they take risks, they might get fired and lose their perks and their pensions. So they play it extra safe. They get bonuses based on last year's profits; those come from marketing, not from developing some science project on the never-never plan. In this industry, mistakes are dealt with by firing a scapegoat. So none of the potential goats will touch any remotely hot potato. Sybillene is a hot potato. Sybillene is treating a brand-new biochemical pathway, and doing it through an entirely new delivery method—inhalation. It's just too much radical newness for the boys of Big Pharma to embrace."

"Say no more. I understand."

Tristana continued anyway. "Also, Big Pharma managements don't use much of their companies' free cash flow for research, development, or even acquisitions anymore. Those only bear fruit years after they've retired. Instead, they have their companies buy back shares in the open market, to boost the value of their options position. That also pleases their buddies in the banks and money-management outfits."

"Sounds like a great way for the corporate execs to get rich. Even though it will eventually run the company into the ground."

"Yeah. And it's all funded by marketing old drugs with new names. They can sell them at high margins because FDA keeps competitors out. Believe me, I know this firsthand."

Tristana wondered if this man with the reassuring grin would understand the interconnected net: FDA, Big Pharma, and the whole so-called health care system. It would take X-ray vision to see through all the layers of corruption. Maybe he was sharp enough to make sense of it all. Maybe those eyes were even perceptive enough to understand *her*.

Were some hormonal and chemical fluctuations suppressing her normal rationality? She swallowed and realized that, once again, she had been staring at him too intently. In return, his smile broadened, centering from his eyes, where some early crow's-feet appeared. *Disarming.* She liked him. She felt a long-forgotten warmth flow through her. Indeed she was disarmed. And thus defenseless.

She smiled back at him. He could see into her. So why not admit it?

He said then, "Yes, Tristana. Why not admit it? And then get past it?"

Was he still talking about the… What were they talking about…? The risk aversion of large pharma to acquire Visioryme? Or did he just read her mind?

A good carnival barker, a sideshow mentalist, or even a good poker player could pick up on curls of the mouth, shifts of the eyes, and subtle body language to provide clues as to what went on in the mind as it responded to the stimuli surrounding it. And if a mind could be cleared of the imprints and aberrations that it picked up over a lifetime of such environmental stimuli, then perhaps it could see things as they really were.

She responded with more resolve than she felt. "OK, let's get past it all."

He nodded.

So he was just thinking about Big Pharma after all. Not about her.

The fanciful notion that he could read her mind lingered, however.

"What, then, is our strategy for turning this science project into dollars?" Knight asked. "I presume, in the case of Sybillene, that it centers on marketing."

Yes, he was back to business. Or perhaps he'd never left the business topic at all.

She breathed easier. "We aren't anticipating a buyout. We expect we'll have to run this race ourselves. We'll need to use a contract marketing firm to sell Sybillene to the pharmacies, and convince the doctors. That's not easy."

"And the cash needed to keep the company going during this time?"

"We need ten million more. But that includes manufacturing build-out expenses, if our ramp-up analyses are correct."

"And the time frame to be cash flow positive?" His voice came in monotone as he performed necessary tasks, checking off his boxes. Just as she would do herself.

Tristana explained. "The deal we've set up with the marketing firm should have us cash flow positive in less than six months. They'll be paid commission only, and it's a slow ramp-up."

"What's in your drug pipeline?"

"After Sybillene starts bringing in cash, we have several preclinical compounds ready for clinical testing. Meaning ready for phase 1. We also have one that is in phase 2 clinical already. VR-315 is targeted at schizophrenia—it treats psychoses like hallucinations and paranoia. Possibly helpful in PTSD. Post-traumatic stress disorder. VR-315 also targets the ProPG pathway, but in a slightly different way."

"Time course for VR-315?"

"Three years if we work incredibly fast. The FDA process is insanely slow."

"How fast *could* you prove that it works and is safe? Let's say we ignored the FDA entirely."

"You can't ignore FDA."

"Humor me."

"We could prove VR-315's value in about nine months, assuming we had the money."

"The rest of the three years is tied up with FDA demands?"

"I'm afraid so. And time also amounts to money. That's the other problem. These trials can cost hundreds of millions."

"Those are mostly FDA-induced costs too, I presume?"

"Yes. Ninety percent of it."

"Did the same thing happen with Sybillene?"

"Yes. Worse. It has taken us years longer than it should have."

"Was that to ensure safety?"

"I wish. It's almost entirely risk aversion by FDA bureaucracy. They're the same type of people—psychologically—that run the pharma companies. Sometimes they're *actually* the same people. The revolving corporate regulatory door, you know."

"Doesn't that—pardon my French—piss you off?"

"That's all right; I speak French." She broke a wry smile. "But it does, and very much. My husband is an FDA scientific reviewer. Actually, he's been promoted, starting next week." She felt like she was supposed to mention her husband to this man, but doing so deflated her. She always lost energy when she thought of Donald. Especially so right now.

Knight offered no congratulations for her husband's recent promotion. This sort of man would not offer false praise. But neither did he reveal any evidence of dismay at her marital attachment. His apparent indifference triggered a flash of disappointment in her.

She drifted further toward a growing infatuation. "Who are you?" She knew it was bold even as she blurted out the question.

His smile warmed. "I'm a shareholder getting to know the people and the business I'm invested in. I'm fairly good at learning things about which I know too little but need to know more. In this case, that's the pharmaceutical industry."

She waited, tipping her head to the side to indicate that she wanted more information. It worked. She won a tiny battle. Or perhaps he let her win.

"I'm not trying to play the man of mystery. It's just that I was more interested in finding out a bit about … this." He looked around her office.

He then told her about his successful speculation as a younger man in Africa, and how the SEC and IRS had stolen his money without due process, demanding either his money or his freedom. They took his money, and he considered himself lucky. A distaste for them, borne of a lesson learned painfully, was evident on his face. As a result of the whole affair, he'd been living outside the country for years. He didn't specify where.

She did her analytical best to assess whom she was dealing with. Some of her impressions were tinged by imagination, maybe from childhood notions of what men were supposed to be. He was possessed of an easy self-confidence, perhaps like that of a young Taoist monk who recognized the enormity of the world, and knew his place in the cosmos. It was as if he treated the world as a playmate.

Her thoughts took her back to an entirely unrequited crush on a young professor as a freshman at Smith. The prof's ignorance of her designs on him led to a dejection that was relieved by Donald's timely arrival on a weekend visit from Brown. A chance meeting, both at loose ends, and one thing led to another. Several years of occasional weekends together led to their eventual marriage. Back then she didn't know that men weren't all like Donald. They weren't all soft, cowardly, manipulative, controlling, and passive-aggressive. They weren't all like the corporate drones and government employees that populated Washington and the pharma business. She had not, until this moment, realized that there were men in the world like Charles Knight.

It bothered her that she let her thoughts wander. She stood suddenly. "Will you please excuse me for a moment?" She strode out of the office and closed the door. She didn't look at Stephan as she went by, but walked quickly to the bathroom, locked the door, and breathed. She needed to get control of a situation in which a new force had entered the scene. She was in uncharted water.

Charles Knight was the exact opposite of Donald.

*　　*　　*

Charles's phone buzzed while he awaited Tristana's return.

"It's Rainbow." Her tentative voice came through the line.

Charles smiled. "Rainbow. I'm happy that you called."

The tentativeness decreased, and the teenage tone emerged. "Whatever." Then the hesitancy came back, and Charles noted that she could speak, when she chose to, with minimal ghetto slang. "I want to talk to you about three hundred dollars."

It was Charles's turn to hesitate. Rainbow's unknown history might include prostitution, her violent negation of Tomo's accusation notwithstanding.

He probed. "What do you think I'm asking for, Rainbow?"

"It better not be sex, or I'm hanging up right now."

Charles relaxed. "Nothing of the sort. I'm seeking contacts only. Some people who can help me start a business."

"Drug business?"

"Yes."

"You gonna compete with Tomo? If you compete, you gonna be dead."

"Not at all. Different drugs, different market."

"You gonna be dead anyway. You're too hot to come back here, Paladin. I come to you and you pay my ride?"

"I'm tied up today." Charles paused to prioritize his list. How important was this girl? He had no idea if she had any worthwhile connections. Meeting with her could be a waste from a business perspective. He'd already agreed to dine with Tristana so he could further understand Visioryme.

But the so-called *honest* pharma field disconcerted him at many levels. What would be the payoff? Another antidepressant on the market? Hardly an earth-shaking event. In fact, probably a negative.

He shouldn't prioritize Visioryme over his plan A.

But maybe he could pull off both. He'd start with a test.

"Let's meet in the city at six PM, Rainbow. Dress for a nice restaurant, OK? I'll call you with the address in a bit."

7

Getting Snuffed

CHARLES turned his attention back to a major purpose of his visit: assessing Visioryme's CEO. Tristana's eyes revealed a rare force of will, although clouded, obscured by something. She seemed preoccupied, and he was determined to find out by what. Possibly the husband—a drone at the FDA. Certain occupations attract certain types of people. Cops and soldiers were often guys with an extra Y chromosome. Accountants liked order and detail. Bartenders tended to the social and liked to party. Low-level government employees craved security, and preferred an established hierarchy. Some scientists would work for the FDA, NIH, NSA, or NASA simply because they had failed to get the same agencies to fund their pet projects while in academia.

But people who *stayed* in government with the intent of working up through the ranks amounted to a special breed. Maybe they were born to it, or maybe the system poured their unformed characters into a standard mold. They sought to control other people. In light of his recent promotion, perhaps Tristana's husband was that sort. If so, it boded poorly for Tristana.

So perhaps it was her husband, and his distorted values, that oppressed her spirit, sucking her life force away. On the other hand, and here Charles sharpened his focus, possibly it was Visioryme that was the problem: there might be some ruinous flaw in their new drug, Sybillene, that she knew about or suspected. Most people had the capacity to lie to themselves, immersed in the self-destructive optimism of false hope. Perhaps something else was broken here at this company, and she kept it concealed. A thousand things could destroy a small company overnight. One of them was a shortage of cash.

Charles calculated how much gold he might require to fund the company's needs. He would have to consider the situation carefully before letting more gold leave his coffers, whether the gold Maurice retained or the much larger amount he'd acquired with Smolderhof's money seven years ago. The metal was not only his working capital, but his savings for a rainy day. It was money in its most secure form, although over the last decade it had also proven to be a great speculation, as the dollar lost value and people around the world increasingly transferred their trust away from government currencies and into the yellow metal. He knew from gritty, painful, hot and sweaty personal experience just how much human labor it took to dig that gold from the ground in some of the most dangerous and nasty places on the planet. Anything he spent his energy on had damn well better garner him more gold than if he spent equivalent energy digging in the ground for it.

He thought even more carefully before sending good gold after bad. His first impression of Tristana left him uncertain. Of the nine critical factors Charles reflexively—and rigorously—looked at before making any financial commitment, the first, and most important, was People.

The other eight factors all began with P as well, for a simple mnemonic taught by Xander Winn: Product, Phinances, Paper, Promotion, Politics, Price, Push, and Pitfalls.

Tilting the odds in his favor required the alignment of all nine Ps. But the *People* element was the sine qua non for any success. Good people could turn a desert into a paradise; bad people would turn paradise into a wasteland. The fact Tristana was attractive and approachable naturally inclined Charles, like any man, toward her. But Passion wasn't one of the nine Ps. And neither was Pheromones.

Biotechnology stocks, like mining-exploration stocks, existed in the financial universe as black holes for capital. Money orbited around them until it veered too close, at which point it crossed the event horizon and winked out of existence. Sometimes the money reappeared in someone else's universe, but most of it disappeared, consumed by paying human beings to waste their lives undertaking useless work in support of bad ideas.

In the case of small pharma, funding flowed into uncertain, expensive, and never-ending science-fair projects. At this point, if Visioryme were to survive, it would need more money. That meant, in essence, selling more shares, since only a fool—or a clever predator—would lend money to a company with a big burn rate but no revenues. A company like Visioryme would be foolish to borrow since the lender could easily wind up owning everything, unless of course the government stepped in to rescue it. Visioryme had dipped its little snout into the trough of a few agencies in the past. But government inevitably proved a problematical partner. And at this point, Visioryme didn't have the political connections to fix a parking ticket, much less finagle a government bailout.

When Tristana had risen to leave, abandoning him abruptly in her office, he noted her distress but didn't know its source. Charles remembered a time, years ago, when he himself had exited an office in just such a manner. He had been flustered by the astounding beauty of a woman named Sabina, a beauty that activated his male biology in a way that diverted far too much blood flow from his rational mind. He had walked out to regain control of his brain function.

But he did not imagine that the parallel could be true right now with Tristana.

No, the woman was conflicted in many ways. But the conflict itself indicated the presence of some integrity. Sociopaths rarely have conflicts, partly because they don't perceive a difference between right and wrong, leaving them little to be conflicted about.

Apart from whatever promise its products might have, both Visioryme and its CEO interested him as an aspiring drug lord. They provided two more reasons to spend time in Mordor.

Charles studied her modest office, one befitting a company that was running on fumes. She wasn't trying to impress new investors with superficialities. No impressive artwork. No pictures of her husband, or children, if any. No certificates, awards, or diplomas hanging on the walls. Nor pictures of its occupant smiling and shaking hands with political celebrities, a staple of corporate offices everywhere, but especially anywhere near the Washington Beltway. Instead functional whiteboards and corkboards covered the walls with comments, charts, lists, and dates.

Tristana returned after several minutes, looking stronger and determined. So much the better. This company would need a woman of steel to see it through the next barriers to success that were endemic to this industry. The fact she'd persisted so far spoke well of her. It was ironic: an industry that was supposed to heal, but was itself so cancerous that it promoted death. It was also ironic that the characteristic most required for success—absolutely unstoppable persistence in the face of all those who discouraged you—was the very same characteristic that led to the most embarrassing failure.

Charles stood. "I've invaded your time and space on short notice. I appreciate any time you have to give me, in light of the other demands on you. It's lunch time. But only if you're still available."

She nodded.

"Then let's go!"

Charles walked with Tristana deep into the heart of hostile territory. The more fashionable addresses in Alexandria were inhabited by lawyers, lobbyists, and contractors vying for access to government resources and legal mandates. Much of the quaint *Old Town* had merged into a sprawling expanse of faceless buildings and clogged highways, making it indistinguishable from other areas of the Greater Washington megalopolis.

He glanced at Tristana again. Her long hair lay imperfectly maintained, as if she didn't really care how it looked. She wore little makeup. Fortunately, like most women in good health and physical condition, she had little need for it. She probably didn't consider time spent applying it to be worthwhile, except for rare and particularly important events. Apparently, this meeting with him today did not reach the level of a special event. She was trim and held herself well, but he had the impression that she had once stood with her shoulders further back, stronger.

Many men turned their heads to watch her walk by. Charles, as always, remained unaware of the women who watched *him* walk by.

Over lunch at an overpriced yet mediocre restaurant—the type that catered to people on expense accounts—Charles and Tristana talked about the FDA and drug development. The regulatory process and the machinations of its bureaucracy were so much less interesting, and less pressing, than Charles's need to find himself a marketing team across the river for an entirely different sort of pharmaceutical venture.

"I appreciate the education you're giving me, Tristana. But the whole drug regulatory process sounds like a distorted morass that needs to be abolished. Or perhaps just ignored. And not just for the benefit of the scientists and companies that develop the drugs, but for the people with conditions that need the drugs, who now receive them ten years too late, and at a hundred times the cost."

"I know," she said, with a tone of resignation. "But there is a way through it," she added with a hint of optimism.

"That's not for me. Now that I get the general gist of it, let's talk about real issues that would matter if we lived in a world that wasn't suffering from a bout of insanity."

She looked at him quizzically, but he could sense a spark of enthusiasm.

Tristana, her imagination constrained and suppressed by years of living within the Washington Beltway, and married to an FDA man of all things, needed to be led. But she seemed to like where Charles could take her. Between her experience and his idealism, together they created an image of a world that most would describe as naïve and unrealistic: a world that was efficient, honest, and fair, and in which things made sense. It was a pleasant fiction.

Lunch lasted two hours. It seemed like fifteen minutes. And every minute that passed as they talked about such things, Tristana grew more attractive.

* * *

Later that evening, Charles came out of the twilight into a restaurant named RIS, in the West End, one of Washington's best. It smelled somehow of his mother's kitchen, but with a sophisticated elegance—as if his mother had also been a gourmet chef. He wore a blue sports coat and khaki slacks—a comparatively casual look for a place that, although it billed itself as a neighborhood bistro, was mostly frequented by doctors, attorneys, and high-paid lobbyists.

He studied the tables nearby to no avail. For a moment, his heart fell as he considered that Rainbow might not come. But then she appeared, having slid quietly through the door right behind him.

Charles smiled instantly in unrestrained surprise. "Rainbow, you look great."

Rainbow's face flashed an uncontrolled blush, immediately followed by a scowl. Her transformation could not be described as complete, but compared to last night she appeared respectable. Not in the context of the hood, but respectable in terms of the society that would serve as Charles's intended market. She wore a dress that rode both a bit high at the thigh and a bit low at the neck. Perhaps a bit trampy, but it was cleaned and pressed and not manufactured from leather. The sneakers didn't add panache, but served a useful purpose. She had probably walked a ways from Foggy Bottom, the nearest metro stop. Her fingernails remained black, but she had toned down the black makeup a notch or two. As she now stood before Charles, she could fit in perfectly among the teenagers who *didn't* fit in at any of Washington's wealthier prep schools.

The clientele of the restaurant might wonder about the two of them together. Charles didn't care about that. He *did* care that Rainbow might feel out of place in this restaurant. He could have met her at a McDonald's. But he wanted her out of her comfort zone. He said quietly, "Let's eat."

Charles's hunger had been fully sated by his lunch with Tristana, and he had another dinner with her coming later. He ordered just steak tartare while Rainbow haltingly ordered a cheeseburger, well done—each undertaking their own rebellion against anything medium.

Charles said, "I wanted to thank you for helping me last night."

She fidgeted. "You didn't need me. Your man woulda taken out Tomo, wouldn't he?"

"Yes, he would have. Tomo didn't own the land I stood on, but he threatened me as if he did."

"Tomo owns that street."

"People lie to themselves all the time, Rainbow. It's one of the greatest problems I've encountered in the world."

"You've traveled the world?"

"Yes. Almost everywhere."

"What's your story, Paladin?"

Charles sipped at his water. "I'll tell you mine if you'll tell me yours."

"Nothin' to tell."

"I'd like to hear it anyway. As for me, I grew up on a ranch in Montana, the son of a small-town newspaper publisher. How old are you?"

"Fifteen."

"I was thirteen when my mother died."

Rainbow's eyes widened. From that moment on, she looked at him differently, her eyes focused on him as a person instead of glancing around the room, seeking threats, as they had been doing since she entered the restaurant.

She said, "I was thirteen when *my* mom died too."

Charles had found a fracture in her hard exterior. Faint, but no doubt a rupture that extended as deep as his own.

"Rainbow, I'm sorry." He need say no more. Uncompromised silence filled several minutes.

Rainbow looked up at him finally. "What did *you* do when your momma died, Paladin?"

It was seventeen years ago, and his throat still closed some when he thought back to that time. He'd spent the summer after her death with Uncle Maurice in Manhattan. His father focused on managing Charles's younger brother, while barely surviving his own grief. Charles's life changed that summer in ways that percolated through him to this day.

He bit the inside of his lip before he replied. "I struggled. Sometimes I cried. And I grew up fast. I didn't pay much attention to other people for a while. Not even to my own brother. I took a lot of risks. But I never got lazy. I worked hard, trying to turn myself into someone I wanted to be."

Rainbow nodded. "But it isn't *fair*."

Charles gently shook his head and frowned. "Nobody promised *fair*, Rainbow. But you and I have won the largest lottery in the history of the world, just by being alive. The chances against ever being born are astronomical, you know. Combining all the DNA from all the generations through your father's and mother's lineages, the chance meetings of your ancestors, the timing of selection of that one sperm from among hundreds of millions, on just the right day, to join with that one egg that also popped out on just the right day to create each of your ancestors. And finally you. And me."

"You said this meeting wasn't about sex."

Washington was full of jerks taking advantage of anyone they could. She'd likely been surrounded by them throughout her life. Maybe it was all she knew. "Excuse me," he said with a cough. "I was talking about our *luck*."

"Gotcha!" Rainbow flashed a satisfied smile and pointed at him. "By that look on yo' face, I *really* gotcha."

Charles recovered and grinned, meekly. "Yep, you did indeed."

Their meal arrived, and Rainbow dove into it. The burger, though well done, was still fat and juicy, unlike the fast food endemic to the ghetto.

"Rainbow, I know you were just joking, but I want to be entirely and absolutely clear that sex is not any part of this conversation."

"You gonna lecture me?"

"Nope."

"OK, Paladin."

She was a teenager, and a young teenager at that, but the girl's tone of voice revealed spunk and a degree of self-confidence that Charles respected.

He said, "Soon after my mother died, I quit school."

"Me too."

Charles nodded. "And I started educating myself instead of relying on classrooms."

"Me too."

"Really? How are you educating yourself, Rainbow?" Damn, that sounded too patronizing. He wished he could take it back.

But she just shrugged and replied, "School o' life."

Charles raised a brow. He studied her eyes, how she held her hands as she ate, and how she chewed. Maybe sometime in the future, he would have enough credibility that she would consider listening to advice from him. But that time was not now. Maybe sometime in the future he would have enough wisdom that he would feel comfortable *offering* her advice. But that time also was not now. They both had much to learn. And they lived in different worlds.

He said, "My school of life involved starting small businesses, and reading what the best people had learned before me, so I wouldn't have to reinvent the wheel. I worked hard, and had my profits stolen from me, twice."

She said, "*My* school o' life involves starting small businesses too, and learning from others, just like you. But my profits been stolen from me a lot more than just twice."

The girl possessed an unexpected quickness of intellect that Charles welcomed.

"I read books too. Lotsa books. My momma," she continued, "she was a addict. She loved me, but she loved her heroin more. That's the thing about heroin. You try it, and then you love it. And no one else matters to you." She swallowed, and her eyes moistened. "I didn't matter."

Was there anybody else who loved this child? He hoped she had someone.

He asked, "Do you have any other family?"

She didn't answer right away. But she didn't keep eating. Charles waited.

After a bit, with lowered eyes, she said, "I don't know my father. But then my momma, she didn't know who my father was either. Not for sure. She thought maybe he was some Navajo guy. Or Cherokee or something.

That's why she called me Rainbow. But it says *Quincy* on my birth certificate. That's my real name."

"You look like you might have some Native American in you. Your hair, your eyes, your cheekbones. Makes sense. You're a good-looking young lady."

Rainbow's eyes focused down at her plate. Then she looked up at Charles and said, "Thank you."

"Where do you live?"

She smiled grimly. "It'll shock you."

"That wouldn't be the first time tonight."

"Yeah? I move 'round a lot. But right now I live with the dealer who killed my mother."

What could he say to that? He chose "Wow. *Tomo?*"

"*No!* Not Tomo. Tomo's a beast. You watch out for Tomo, Paladin."

"Someone else?"

"Yeah. The closest thing I have to family."

"Again, wow."

They stayed silent at the table. Charles wondered what sort of relationship this girl had with her mother's killer. In the world she lived, it was likely abusive, with the man holding the power, and the girl losing herself. But maybe Rainbow defied the odds. Some did.

He ate his steak tartare slowly, a morsel at a time. It tasted delightful, but it would have been even better without the concern he felt about this girl's difficult life. He didn't know if she needed saving. And wasn't sure he'd know how to save her if she did.

But maybe he could create an opportunity for her.

"Can we talk about business now?" he asked.

"Three hundred dollars of business?" Rainbow prompted.

"For starters."

"Maybe enough to pay for stitchin' in my head."

"Did you get stitched?"

"No. My time's too valuable."

Charles nodded. "I need to make some connections."

"What kinda connections?"

Charles looked around the restaurant. The couple at the adjacent table had little to say to each other, which meant they were either absorbed by their own thoughts, or perhaps entertaining themselves by listening in to nearby conversations. Charles lowered his voice.

"I need a team. They need to be comfortable with selling product upmarket, in Northwest D.C. Look around you. This is the type of neighborhood my products will sell in. I need people who can sell product, take risk, but look respectable up here too. Like you do now, but not like you did last night. You understand?"

"Yeah. Clothes make the man."

"I suspect you know better, Rainbow. But people in this city *think* they do. My team will need to blend in, will need to be worthy of trust. Tomo's definitely not the type. Do you know anybody who might be?"

Rainbow took another bite of her burger. Then she looked up at Charles and nodded. She spoke while she chewed. "Trustworthy. Yeah. Maybe." She chewed more. "Probably could blend in, with a little effort."

"Who?"

"I need to talk to them first. What products you selling? Meth? Heroin? I won't help if it's heroin."

"Neither. None of the drugs you're expecting. Most people wouldn't consider my products illegal. But they are."

Rainbow squinted and frowned at the same time. "'Nuf mystery. What's the product?"

"The first drug I'm going to be moving is Viagra."

She snorted. "You funny."

"Funny, yes. But also true. The list goes on from there."

"You serious?"

"Dead serious."

They consumed the rest of their meal in silence, just like the bored couple adjacent to them. Charles and Rainbow had much more to talk about. It's just that now was not the time.

* * *

For Charles's second dinner, he rushed back to Virginia to a restaurant known as Chez Philippe. Tristana wore makeup.

Charles noticed another difference. It had nothing to do with the makeup, but Tristana's eyes now glowed sharp and bright, reflecting that her mind, as well as her body, had become engaged. Energy flowed, and it affected Charles. The chemicals and thoughts that create the feeling of *eros* were lively in both of them.

"How did you get reservations here? It's almost impossible to get in…" She laughed lightly, after they were seated at their table in the most appreciated restaurant of the D.C. suburbs.

"I bribed the maître d'."

She arched an eyebrow. "How much did *that* cost?"

"Ten."

Tristana's eyes widened and she blurted back, "That's all?"

"Not dollars."

She turned her head slightly to the side, narrowed her eyes again, and asked, "Ten *what*?"

"Ten of what he wanted. The maître d' is a gay gentleman in his late fifties. It seemed likely that he might be a fan of Viagra. I gave him ten generic Viagra pills, equivalent to more than forty bucks a pill. It was a bribe worth over $400. Plus he got to avoid seeing a doctor."

"He accepted random pills from a stranger?" she stated, shaking her head in disbelief.

"Lots of people accept drugs from some of the most disreputable-looking types imaginable, and always have. The man didn't even blink."

"It's not legal."

"No, it's not."

Charles studied Tristana's face. Her darkness had returned. He said, "I suppose it's possible the guy might get arrested for having an erection without a doctor's prescription. *Oh, the humanity!*"

She lightened up slightly.

"The man had a desire for the Viagra. His taking it isn't going to hurt anyone. He had something I wanted, and I had something he wanted. It was a fair trade. I gave him an instruction and warning sheet with it, and a certificate of analysis, and a description of the company that manufactures it, which is a well-respected multibillion-dollar pharmaceutical giant in India. I get it very cheaply, and I have a lot of it."

She lightened up further. "Really? You keep a lot of Viagra around?"

"I do."

"Do you use it frequently yourself?" She dug at him clumsily, like a tease who'd had no opportunity to practice the art for years.

He grinned mischievously. "That day has yet to arrive."

"How do you get it, exactly?"

"I buy it overseas and bring it back with me."

"How much does it cost you?"

"Eight cents a pill."

"And you say it's forty *bucks* here? A five-hundredfold markup then? That's amazing. Even in this business…"

"This isn't Pfizer's pill, of course. Knockoffs certainly, but chemically and functionally identical. It's just a generic made outside the U.S."

"I'm still amazed at the price differential. And I thought I knew about these things."

"The huge amounts Pfizer spent to get its Viagra patents extended in the U.S. paid off for them."

She nodded knowingly.

"Viagra prices have risen every year since it was released in the United States. All their branded competitors wanted Viagra to stay on patent too, because the introduction of any cheap generic erection drugs would force *all* their prices down. An erection is an erection, after all. Only the generic manufacturers—and of course all men using Viagra—wanted to see the patent expire as it should have by law. The generic companies and the American individual male just don't have the pull with the system that the large pharma companies have. So Pfizer and the other large pharma get the laws reinterpreted for their benefit."

Tristana would be a fan of pharmaceutical patents. At this point in her drug-company career, the central necessity of government-established patent protection had been carved in stone in her brain. Charles would not enter that discussion with her. Years ago his friend, Elliot Springer, had tried to change the hardwired psychology of the beautiful and sociopathic Sabina Heidel. Elliot had failed to cure her, and that woman went on to convince the man who now occupied the White House to steal Charles's money. Trying to change people's worldviews was a fool's errand.

Tristana sipped at her wine. Charles looked at her eyes over her glass. She scrutinized him. She seemed calm, considered. She had temporarily flicked off her sexual light switch. But now the switch came on again. He could see it in her eyes.

In direct challenge to the message that her eyes conveyed, Charles said, with no warning and in a low monotone, "Tell me about your husband."

He watched her eyes as he asked. He watched the sparks disappear, the glistening sheen become dull, the green of her irises fade to a dull earthy tone, their color diluted by an unpleasant thought.

"He's at home by now, I suppose." Her response came in monotone.

"I see. How do you work around the conflicts of interest with his position at the FDA?"

She shrugged. "Until now, it hasn't been an issue. He's been working within FDA's regulatory-review framework, and he recuses himself from anything Visioryme submits. But that's changing, obviously."

"How?"

"He's been promoted to be the director of the Office of Regulatory Enforcement. That's part of the Division of Regulatory Affairs."

"Ah. I see." He visualized a bigger cog in a slow-turning wheel. A primitive, medieval wheel that blocked the entrance to a pristine hi-tech factory.

"I know he had some meeting today to work out some of the conflicts of interest regarding me. He was pretty uptight about it. I don't know how that went."

"From what you've told me, the FDA is one enormous conflict of interest! Scientists and bureaucrats game the system to get jobs with Big Pharma later. Big Pharma uses the FDA to set up stumbling blocks for small companies, either because it wants to quash any competition, or because it wants to buy them out on the cheap when they're near bankruptcy."

She said, with resignation, "They really should rename it the Federal Death Authority. I don't doubt that they kill more people every year than the Defense Department does in a typical decade."

Charles broadened his usual smile for a flash. They were on the same wavelength. "I read that 7,800 lives have been saved by the FDA's expanded regulatory authority that began in the 1960s. But then those very same regulations caused the early deaths of 4.5 million people, deaths that could have been prevented by drugs that the FDA only approved after years of delay. That's 4.5 million deaths compared to 7,800 lives saved. They have about the worst safety record imaginable. The FDA should ban themselves."

"You would not like my husband."

That statement would prove prescient.

"Compared to all the big pharmaceutical companies, I can't imagine that your small company represents a major conflict of interest…"

"*Our* small company." Tristana corrected him.

"Right. And I appreciate your saying that. What does his new position involve? I'm not looking for trouble with either your husband or his employer."

"He'll head the office that sends the U.S. Marshals out to confiscate products that are misbranded, adulterated, or in some other way not within the bounds of their regulations."

"Oh. I love him already."

Tristana creased her lips and shook her head. "I'm sure."

"You know, of course, that I'm entirely unlike your husband."

She replied, slowly, after too long a pause. "Charles, I'm acutely aware of that."

*   *   *

Charles's parting with Tristana thirty minutes later had been awkward; both knew what they wanted next, and yet both made it clear that their desires would not be fulfilled. She was beautiful and interesting, and her spark of life was not completely extinguished, although the ember seemed to be fading. Perhaps it could be stoked; maybe she would again light up. But whether a one-night stand or something more, it wasn't a complication they needed. Besides, after a late lunch and two dinners, he was stuffed.

He awoke the next morning content to be alone in his bed in Xander's apartment.

8

The Ground Force

RAINBOW guided Charles through the back alleys of the D.C. ghetto.

He proceeded without the protection of Xander and his rifle, trusting his security to the judgment of a fifteen-year-old girl. He studied her fingerless gloves, overly large coat, and baggy pants. It was a haphazard-looking fashion statement, but a theme of black and burgundy gave it none-too-subtle hints of gangster and Goth.

"Are you wearing steel-toed boots?"

"I sleep with them."

"Why?"

She responded with teenage exasperation. "*Because*, there's not always time to find my knife."

"Why are you taking this risk, Rainbow?"

"Two reasons: money and money. And it's more a risk to you than to me," she said flatly, nodding to two disheveled prostitutes leaning against an unlit lamp post. "Callin' it a night, ladies?"

"After-hours clubs always be open, honey," one responded with comfortable familiarity. "Woman's work ain't never done!"

Rainbow laughed, shaking her head.

The other hooker pointed to her. "Rainbow, you should be in school."

"I *am* in school, China. White boy here my teacher."

Charles smiled at China. Tall and thin, she possessed an uncommon beauty. Her choice of attire was all that differentiated her from the $2,000-per-night escorts who frequented Capitol Hill. The prostitutes earned their money through hard work and risk, much the way Charles earned his. He respected China far more than he respected the power brokers and political hangers-on that might pay for her services.

They walked past. "Rainbow, are you sure your contacts will be open to distributing *my* type of drugs?"

"Do you like money?" she responded.

"Yes."

"So do they."

Charles chuckled. "I'm looking forward to meeting them."

But Charles felt a fleeting sensation of dread. A dangerous reality intruded into his usual state of cautious optimism.

"Couple of things, Paladin. This is an introduction, nothing more. I'll let you die if you end up being stupid again. Save you once is all."

"Sounds reasonable."

Rainbow gave him a meaningful look through a disheveled mess of dark purple strands that emerged from under the toque into which she had stuffed her hair. "These guys are clean, meaning they don't use, but it doesn't mean they sit at home watching Discovery Channel."

"I like people who take action."

She continued, "For the introduction, I want five percent of your selling price," she continued.

"No."

Rainbow stopped and turned, fire in her eyes. "What do you mean *no*?"

Charles stopped too. "I mean *no*. I offered you three hundred dollars. That's what you get for the introduction. If you want five percent of the business, you need to be a business partner. That means we have to trust each other first, and then you have to both invest money and work hard. I doubt you have the money. So the question is: are you able and willing to work hard enough, and smart enough, to earn five percent of a business like this? Keep in mind, five percent is based on profits and risk, not revenues. I'm not about to pay you a sales tax. If you're willing to pull your weight, I'm looking to hire. But be real, Rainbow, five percent takes a ton of work and a lot of time."

Rainbow sniffed. "You could get *shot* before the day's over, homey, so you best give me the three hundred dollars now. We'll talk about partnership later, if you can still talk."

The girl continued to grow on Charles. She had chutzpah.

She took out a small notebook from her pants pocket, used a well-sharpened pencil to note the transaction in a ledger, and then put out her hand.

Charles reached into an inside zipped pocket and pulled out three bills.

"There's more where these came from. If I'm not dead."

"No promises, Paladin. A guy got rolled right there," she pointed to a well-lit and open section of the sidewalk, "for nothing but a ten-dollar phone card."

"Killed?"

"Nah. He didn't put up a fight, so I let him go."

"You mean *you* rolled him?"

Rainbow glared at him. "I was young, OK? You should gimme whatever other money you have on you. It's safer with me."

Charles laughed. "You could just lift my wallet again."

Rainbow responded, "Hey, I *gave it back*. Figured you'd want to keep your credit cards and license."

"I don't have either of those things."

Con artists win their victims' trust. It's what they do. Charles looked at the girl. She'd come to his aid. She indeed had given him back his wallet. She'd opened up to him, or he assumed she had. She'd elicited his sympathy, and dug up an empathic connection. Everything a good con would do to gain his confidence.

She said, "Seriously, hand it over. No one's going to look for money on me."

Maybe the girl felt immune to the inherent risk of violence and theft that intertwined with street life. Teens assumed immortality, after all, even when they saw death all around them. He handed over his wad of bills. If she were a street con, it was enough money that she would disappear around the next corner. Two thousand dollars would be a small price to test the girl's character.

Rainbow lifted her eyebrows at the money. She inserted the cash in a small hole in the lining of her jacket instead of one of the fifteen pockets that it sported on the outside.

In answer to a question he chose not to ask, Rainbow said, "Don't worry about it. You got my word. I'll give it back. This cash is a ten-dollar phone card compared to what we could make together. If you don't screw it up."

She led him into a run-down five-story building. The elevator didn't work. Water dripped from decayed ceilings in the foyer. Tenants here didn't complain to a landlord, because nobody paid any rent.

They walked up four flights of urine-soaked stairs to emerge in a dingy hallway. She pointed him toward a door coated with peeling paint. She stepped around him and knocked. Five knocks. Then four more. A moment later, darkness obscured the glow through the peep sight. Then the door opened, and Charles found himself faced with a gun muzzle.

The owner of the gun stood six inches taller than Charles, and substantially wider. How did the man get his thick finger inside that trigger guard?

Rainbow said to the man, "He's good." The man lowered the weapon halfway.

Charles glanced around the room while being patted down. It possessed the furniture for, but lacked the trappings of, an active office. No paperwork lay in heaps. No yellow stickies. And only one laptop computer. It seemed a temporary facility designed to minimize discovery by the law. Two windows, and two additional doors leading who knows where—to safety or to death.

The man found the small .380 pistol inside Charles's waistband.

"There's a round in the chamber," Charles said. "I'll want that back after we chat. It belongs to a friend."

The man shrugged, released the magazine, and ejected the round into Charles's hand. He wiped the weapon with a rag and set it on a desk.

Another man came through a side door.

According to Rainbow's assurances, this was not a group of dope fiends and two-bit peddlers. These men worked some of the higher-rent districts, and didn't use what they sold. Four more men, dressed in stereotypical garb complete with color-coordinated accessories, followed. The team consisted of six men, each one a distinct mix of features. Tall, small, thin, fat, strong, gaunt, older, younger.

Two of the men gave Charles the once-over, silently taking in his Levi's jeans, gray T-shirt, and lined leather jacket, and then settled down into well-worn cloth chairs, giving the man in the middle a knowing glance. Charles nodded at each in turn, picking up on the apparent hierarchy, but pretending to ignore it.

Rainbow nodded respectfully to the man in the middle, and then broke eye contact and looked at the floor. "Alpha, this is the guy I told you about." Suddenly, she seemed unsure that this was a good idea. She had fallen into the biological role of the weaker. Alpha was the alpha.

Alpha nodded, then turned to Charles and spoke in a distinct ghetto accent. "Let me be clear: we start by not liking you."

The others nodded or sneered, their silent agreement acknowledging that Alpha spoke for them all.

Charles didn't hesitate. "Alpha, I can work through that prejudice if you can." And prejudice it was. They had no reason to *not* like Charles. Alpha assumed Charles belonged to a group he didn't like. Little did Alpha know that Charles wasn't much of a joiner.

Charles didn't plan on changing the world. But maybe he could change Alpha's mind.

Rainbow took her backpack through a door to the right, into a tiny adjacent room. Charles watched her place her jacket and backpack on a yellowed mattress before returning.

Alpha continued, "Rainbow here ain't native to our hood, but she's been with us for a time and pass' a few tests." Rainbow swallowed and shifted her stance. "So I said I'd give you some of my precious time to impress me. You got five minutes."

Three men leaned against the wall on Charles's left. A wooden chair lay unused to Charles's right. He spun it around and sat down.

"I'm a businessman," Charles began, his smile faintly perceptible. His expression informed those around him that he was of good will. And that he either *had* no fear or *showed* no fear. Both characteristics gained him some respect. "And I need business partners."

"Fo' what?" Alpha asked.

"I want to know how to move product in this town," he stated.

Alpha sneered, "It be a steep learnin' curve that you ain't ready to be navigatin'…"

Charles took in his comments.

"I hear you had a friend gonna blow out Tomo's brains. Convince me you're not a cop."

"I'm not a cop, but that will take some time to convince you. I'm the opposite of the police." Charles's face held steady, insistent. Alpha stayed silent, so he continued, "What you know has value to me. If you can teach me what I need, we might move on to make some serious money together. I have a few questions."

"You go 'head and aks yo' questions."

"I'd like to know if you want to sell better product and aim for a wealthier life."

Alpha cut him off. "Rainbow, you did your homework on this dude?"

Rainbow said, "There's margin in this, Alpha."

Alpha shook his head. "Trust you better be right, chicklet." His glance conveyed an unveiled threat. He turned his attention back to Charles.

"My name is Paladin."

Alpha quickly said, "Paladin, huh?" He laughed derisively and gestured to Rainbow. "Where'd you find this guy?" Then to Charles, "Why don't we skip our names, like you skippin' yours? You call us like this: I'm Alpha." He stabbed his chest with his fingertip. Then he pointed around the circle. "This here is Beta, Gamma, Delta, Epsilon, and that guy there is Mr. … uhh … Zeta."

"Yeah, that's me. I'm Zeta," the youngest man in the room said with a chuckle.

Charles smiled. It was clear how Alpha became the alpha of the group. Charles had no interest in a stereotypical drug gang. He needed extraordinary. Here he had his first hint of special.

"Excellent, Mr. Alpha," replied Charles. "It's more than excellent. It's scholarly. The Greek Alphabet Men."

The man recently named Gamma spoke up. "Yeah, that's us. We're Street Scholars." He seemed the oldest of the men, maybe fifty years or more.

Epsilon—a man Charles guessed was about his own age—chimed in, "The Alphabet Men. Sounds like fuckin' 'Sesame Street.'"

A state commission in Mississippi voted to ban *Sesame Street* in the early 1970s. The white-run state government believed that the peaceful interracial interactions of the children on *Sesame Street* might spark unrest among the South's unprepared and "harmoniously segregated" population. They needn't have feared. Shockingly little had changed since then, despite two generations of American children having watched the show. Politicians, and the law itself, encouraged prejudice and systemic racial discrimination, in everything from census forms to special agencies. A handful of sociopaths made their fame and their wealth stoking those flames, and the media followed like sheep.

To Charles, government and academia treated men such as those who stood in front of him as if they were incapable of caring for themselves and those they loved. The attitude—encoded into law—just patronized the people it claimed to help. Talk about disrespect! No weakness here. No victims stood in *this* room.

"Ask your questions." Alpha's face stayed stern. Charles couldn't sense a crack in his outer shell. No humor evident. From Alpha's left cheek to his shaved scalp a scar sliced from a wound that had not received the benefit of timely or carefully performed suturing. The pale scar stretched wide, distorting the curve of his face and the wrinkles around his eyes. This man would not give his trust lightly.

"Is selling drugs the biggest part of your business?" Charles asked.

Alpha narrowed his eyes. "Next question."

"How much money do you get to keep at the end of each day?"

"Next question."

Charles then asked, "Where do you live?"

Epsilon said, "You wanna know what we like to eat too?"

Gamma followed with, "You writin' a book?"

Charles replied, "No. I'm filling in the blanks on a business plan."

"You aren't afraid that we gonna kill you and take whatever you got?"

"Why would I be afraid of that?"

Alpha took over. "No more questions." The others reflexively put their hands closer to their barely concealed weapons in case Alpha signaled a bad end to this meeting.

Rainbow spoke up earnestly. "Paladin, best we get to the point." She turned to Alpha. "Alpha, he wants you to sell pharmacy products."

"Ya, ya, we know—Viagra."

Charles interjected, "Not only Viagra. But that's the first."

Alpha crossed his arms.

Charles continued. "My drugs are illegal, so the gross margins are high. And there's no one enforcing the law, so risks are low and the costs of doing business are low. It's a different clientele, with more money, and an easier game."

Rainbow raised her head. "There's good money in this, Alpha. And no one else has to die." She looked around the room at the six men.

Charles watched closely. Rainbow's eyes reflected a bit more light from the window, moisture accumulating but not enough for a tear. The girl cared about these men. And as he took in their faces, he began to suspect that these men cared about her too. Maybe *this* was her family?

Alpha quietly stared at Rainbow for several tense moments, until finally taking a deep breath. He'd made a decision.

"Go on." Alpha leaned in with his arms crossed on the table, and refocused on Charles.

"I need a sales team willing to sell cholesterol-lowering drugs, diabetes medications, antidepressants, asthma meds, and expensive drugs for rare diseases. And as you mentioned, Viagra."

The guy now named Zeta asked, "All pharmacy shit?"

"Correct, all pharmacy shit. But this stuff isn't legally imported. We bypass Customs, and some medications haven't been approved by the U.S. government. It's contraband. But you gotta be completely honest with the clients. I don't mean you need to stay within the law. I do mean honest. The clients have to trust you. They have to look forward to your return. This is an untapped and very real business, waiting for us. I have good product at good prices. Just illegal. And outside the purview of the DEA. Even the D.C. police won't care."

"You walkin' in here with your *purview*-talkin' ass, tellin' us we don't already run an honest biz, cracker?" Alpha glowered.

"As I said, just because your business is outside the law doesn't make it dishonest."

Zeta shook his head. "Man, people ain't gonna buy that shit. Drugs from Canada? Drugs from India? Drugs from China? People know that shit ain't real."

"We can change that perception. My drugs *are* real, and there's a huge and fully proven market for them, black market or otherwise. Every batch I get in will be tested by mass or Raman spectroscopy at a top laboratory to ensure it is what it's supposed to be. High-technology stuff. I'm even working on an assay device cheap enough to let people assay their imported drugs themselves, just so they can be completely confident of what they're buying. They shouldn't be relying on the FDA to ensure they're getting the right stuff. That's like relying on the Department of Agriculture for your food. My device will work for heroin, meth, and coke too. The drug manufacturers I import from are multibillion-dollar corporations in India. They serve huge legal markets in their own country. They produce real product and lots of it. They just don't have approval of the FDA to sell it here in the U.S."

"So, we make money cuz the G doesn't want that stuff in the country?"

"Not exactly. We make money cuz lots of people want these drugs. We make money because the big pharmaceutical companies don't want competition, and they get the G to block the imports. The FDA protects Big Pharma's turf and scares away any company trying to bring in cheaper product."

"Sounds like what I do," Delta said with a deep voice every bit as big as his bulk.

Charles turned to Delta, a man whose muscled arms bulged even through his thick coat. "That's exactly what I'm saying. The FDA is even bigger than you, Delta. Their enforcers have kept out the competition, because the competition is foreign corporations who've got to play it legal. I don't feel that urge. So this gives us an opportunity." Charles smiled. "And I have imported, and I will continue to import, right past the FDA and anyone else who tries to stop me."

Epsilon asked the key question. "How much money do *we* get?"

Charles looked at Epsilon and replied, "That's the right question. You buy from me at wholesale price, and sell it at whatever your clients are willing to pay. You keep what you make."

"What's the catch?"

"You mean, other than it's still illegal and you can still go to jail?"

"Yeah."

"Then there's no catch. This is black market, but I run an honest business. When I make agreements I stick to them, as you'll see with time. My hope is that we develop an honest business together. Simple."

"Is that what you frat boys talk about at parties: honest business?" Epsilon retorted.

Charles smiled. "You're the ones named after the Greeks, Epsilon. Not me."

Epsilon frowned and said dejectedly, "We ain't no goatbangers."

"Why us?" Gamma, perhaps the calmest of the lot, asked.

Charles indicated the girl. "Because Rainbow here said you could be trusted. And I'm starting to trust *her*. Trust is essential. I've been out of the country for many years, and I don't know any distributors here. You know how to sell product, you're not afraid of breaking the law. If you have a bona fide business that has room for expansion, we could team up. Make some money together. Honestly and fairly."

"Let's talk margins," Epsilon stated. Charles liked him. Epsilon, the shortest by far, might have the tallest intellect. At least he asked the sharpest questions.

"Sure. Let's start with Viagra since I have an abundant supply at the moment."

"What's the usual price?"

"In the pharmacies right now it's up to fifty dollars. Per pill. Sometimes it's a bit cheaper. No matter what, you can offer a great deal."

"How much wholesale?" interjected Alpha.

"I can sell you five thousand pills for four dollars per," said Charles.

"Holy shit."

"Fuck me…"

Charles held his hands out, palms up. "Rainbow told you the margins were big. She wasn't lying."

Alpha said, "Don't want five thousand. Not yet. Need to test the market on our turf first."

Charles considered this. There was market for knock-off Viagra everywhere, not just in Northwest D.C. "All right, how about five hundred, same price."

Alpha nodded. "Deal," he said, and stood up and shook Charles's hand, ending this first meeting. He turned to the girl. "Rainbow. You growin' up. You meet up with … um … Paladin here. We don't need to be seein' him in this part of town. And we don't need him gettin' whacked here either. Dude already made enemies. There's those that want him dead. So you watch out for him."

"Yes, Alpha."

Charles looked at each of the men in turn. He had no sense he could trust these men. Nor could they trust him. Trust had to be earned. Time to start earning.

Charles picked up his gun. Delta tossed him his magazine, and he and the girl quietly left, leaving the Alphabet Men making jokes about Viagra. Charles took shallow breaths as they went down the stench-filled stairs and left via the fire escape exit into the alley.

"Alpha trusts you, Rainbow. Letting you be the go-between."

"He's just using me. Moving money and mulin' drugs is the part of this business everybody likes to avoid."

They walked together more than a mile to the nearest entrance for the metro, at which point Rainbow reached into her jacket lining and handed Charles back his roll of hundreds. She asked, "Where do you live?"

"I'm staying at a friend's place. Across the river." He stuffed the money securely in a pocket.

"Where can I pick up those five hundred tablets?"

"How about the entrance to the original Smithsonian. Tomorrow, eight AM?"

"I'll see you there."

*　　*　　*

The next morning, Rainbow handed him $2,000. Instead of the promised five hundred pills, Charles gave her a thousand. He could get paid for the additional later, if the Alphabet Men's honor held. Small offers of trust might lead to loss of a few bucks, or to huge gains. It seemed a worthwhile—if incompletely analyzed—speculation.

9

Dirty vs. Clean

CHARLES spent the day reading everything he could about the FDA and its structure. He already understood the essence of the beast, both its publicly stated purpose and what it in fact wound up doing. He'd explained a lot of his views to Tristana already, but he still needed details on how the bureaucracy worked: their standard operating procedures. He studied some of their court cases and hearings before administrative judges, and read the sections of the Code of Federal Regulations that applied to the FDA in its myriad regulatory and enforcement functions. Although his mind wasn't wired to think like a … *functionary* … he started to see how the FDA dealt with the many gray areas that existed in the law. One thing became clear: they were proficient at using gray areas to expand their own authority. As with almost every agency in Washington, both the FDA's budget and its workforce grew significantly faster than the country's. If the FDA ever let some company off easy, it made sure that its mercy was acknowledged.

The FDA made no effort to hide the reality that it effectively owned any drug that it approved for marketing. It ruled as the unquestioned tyrant in an entire sector of the economy, a regent that required the loyalty and cooperation of its nobility—the pharmaceutical companies. It lived in an inbred symbiosis with its clients, again the same large pharmaceutical companies. On the one hand, the agency raised the costs of doing business by an order of magnitude, with its endless delays, often-pointless and repetitive testing, and massive paperwork burden. But on the other hand, the agency made it exceedingly difficult for competition to enter the market, thus ensuring drug prices stayed very high for a very long time. And when there were only two entrants—two drugs for a given disease—it would not take long for the FDA to find cause to shut down the manufacturing facility for one of them, triggering a fiftyfold price increase by the preferred competitor. These price spikes, for one drug or another, happened all the time. The media and activist college students inevitably blamed the free market.

Everybody decried the high prices, but few recognized the real cause. The pharma business was just as high tech as the computer business, but every year prices went up for the newest medications, while dropping for the newest computers. Some thought it an excellent reason for creating a new agency to regulate computers—so as to increase profit margins for certain well-connected companies. That would have to be sold as something to protect the public, of course. Maybe the socialists would conjure up a *right to computers.*

Rainbow called him late in the afternoon. Her voice came as a welcome reprieve from Charles's foray into the regulatory quagmire.

"Alpha's guys already moved your product. All of it. Easy. I've got another two thousand dollars for the extra you provided. And Alpha wants 5,000 more pills. Tonight."

Charles had brought 100,000 Indian-manufactured generic Viagra pills into the country in his boat, hidden in the mast, undiscovered by the Coast Guard. Mass spectroscopy proved the pills were exactly as they were billed: unadulterated, full potency. The pills had cost him $8,000, plus a 3,000-mile solo sailing trek across the Atlantic from West Africa, where he had loaded them on board during a long, sweaty day, deep in a hot bilge.

Arranging the meeting with Rainbow's pals had cost him some money, some time, and some promises. But he now appeared to have a low-end, but highly experienced, sales team.

Perfect.

That evening, Charles drove back to D.C. to meet up with Mr. Alpha and Rainbow at a diner. He needed to discuss something that just might induce the man to walk away. Better that happen now rather than later.

Charles saw them chatting together in the dim light of a corner booth. Alpha smiled at Rainbow and patted her on the head. He pulled his hand away though, as he caught sight of Charles, and his face went flat. Rainbow waved him over.

He slid into the circular booth. "Rainbow. Alpha. How're things?"

Alpha nodded and spoke quietly. "I think we're in. But we need to talk about what other … medications … you plan on sellin'."

"OK. But I need to talk about something else first. Before I share the details of the business with you, we have to establish some fundamentals."

"Establish away, Paladin."

Charles nodded. "I'll be in charge of what I do. You're each in charge of what you do. I supply. You sell. I don't care how you sell, up to a point. You can build a multilevel organization, and pyramid market. You can spread your offerings by word of mouth. You can print sales literature. Just don't get caught."

"We not in the business of gettin' caught."

"And I think we should let the online pharmacies keep the online market for themselves, at least for now. We have our own niche."

"I don't got programming skills, Paladin."

Charles nodded. "And each of us is responsible for his own protection and safety."

"Fair enough."

"We need to come up with an inventive way to move the money. The government can follow money. Moving money is getting tougher all the time. They're trying to get rid of cash so that everything will be done by check, or credit card, or bank wire. At that point they'll know everything about everybody. Their ability to follow the money is their biggest ally and our biggest concern."

"Smart man, you. You know what we known for years."

"The good news is we have some time before anyone will even start looking at us."

"Yeah, Five-O don't care about this. You can take that to the bank."

As fear of terrorism grew and the War on Drugs expanded, it had become harder and more dangerous for anyone to deposit or withdraw cash from banks. Questions to answer and forms to fill out amounted to more than just a nuisance; they were a threat. Bankers were obligated to report clients to the feds if they even *suspected* any illegality, including tax evasion. Avoiding banks proved that one knew which way the wind was blowing, but it took more than avoiding banks to make it in the drug trade. Money flowed uphill, which, if the feds ever started caring about this little venture, is just where they would aim their bullets. Charles would be sitting at the top of this hill. Best not to sit still up there.

"I'm taking some serious financial risk—in addition to some other obvious risks. Please be clear about that."

Alpha nodded impatiently, and said, "Here's what we want. We want those mass-spec analysis sheets printed up sufficient to provide to each customer for each medication. Some customers think that paperwork makes the stuff more real, and that makes our job easy. And we need to never be short of product. We can see how this can get real big, real fast. So we got no interest in small time. If we make promises to deliver, we gotta deliver. That means we gotta trust you. And you gotta trust us."

Charles hesitated sufficiently long to consider the demands before responding. "Alpha, I can promise to do everything within my power to never leave you short. Hurricanes, bureaucracies, and customs inspectors are my nemeses, and they're hard to predict. But I'll take on extra expense and risk to manage a larger inventory."

Alpha nodded.

There was trust among the Alphabet Men, trust that he hoped to earn. He came from outside their race and culture. But over the years and the miles and the countries, he had learned that race, religion, and social status were relative trivialities. A person's character, however, wasn't just important. It was critical.

One of the many permutations of Pareto's law, the 80-20 rule, posited that if it weren't for the mob mentality that takes over when too many people get together, eighty percent of them would live basically peaceful and productive lives. That percentage—if even roughly accurate—gave Charles some optimism for the human race.

The other twenty percent were potential problems, however. They would blow with the prevailing social and political winds. In stable, prosperous times they weren't much of a problem. But they didn't have a moral compass, and couldn't be relied on to do the right thing.

The real problem, however, arose with the twenty percent of *that* twenty percent: the sociopaths. That meant about four percent of the population were congenital criminals, frauds, liars, cheats, and power-hungry narcissists: all that is evil wrapped up into one package, even though they looked like everyone else.

The population's character formed a bell-shaped curve. On the other side of the spectrum, twenty percent were people you'd like to associate with, and twenty percent of that twenty percent, a vastly different four percent, were stand-up guys—with no regard to accidents of birth like sex, race, or nationality. So only one in five people were consistently honorable, and only one in twenty-five could be trusted under almost any circumstance. The decent people tried to cluster—as did the bad guys. There was a lot of truth to the old cliché about birds of a feather.

Were the Alphabet Men birds of his feather?

"I have one more important item to discuss before we extend our business arrangement. One rule that needs to be followed."

"What's that rule?"

"Throughout this business, we have to be the good guys."

"Meaning…"

"We need to be the ones providing our customers what they want."

"Sure."

"And do it honorably."

"Meaning…"

Rainbow shook her head in frustration. "*Meaning*, he don't want you to lie, cheat, or steal, Alpha."

"That right, Paladin?" Alpha prompted, an eyebrow raised.

Charles hesitated. His words had gotten ahead of his brain.

"So you think we gonna steal from you, cracker?"

Charles shook his head and frowned. "No. If I thought that, we wouldn't be sitting here right now. I just don't want us stealing from *others*. I don't want us using violence unless it's in self-defense. We don't own our clients, and we don't own the streets. If someone does business better than us, then we respect them and learn from them. We don't kill 'em."

"You wanna stay clean? That it?"

"More than clean. I want to stay *right*."

It was Alpha's turn to shake his head. "This business *ain't* clean. Blood flows in this world."

Charles knew that. "Drawing blood doesn't bother me. Drawing *first blood*, unprovoked, *does* bother me. In my own life, I don't *initiate* force or fraud against anyone. I've found if I live by that, and work with people who do the same, then things go well for me. If I cheat on it, things go bad. So it's my one overarching rule."

"So we don't draw first blood."

"We don't draw first blood *unprovoked*." There was no point in giving a course in ethics at a diner, over a soda. Keep it simple.

"Paladin, I don't care how safe you think this deal is. You had best be ready to have your blood drawn. Some people just like that sort of thing."

"About four percent of people."

"Maybe, Paladin. Maybe…"

Charles patted a bulge under his waistband.

"Those four percent are why I carry this."

"You do know how to use that problem solver, right?"

"I do. And I'm assuming that you do too. All of you."

Alpha nodded. "We no strangers to cannons, Paladin." Alpha lifted his shirt slightly to reveal that he too was strapped.

"And Rainbow?"

She looked down under the table. "In my steel-toed boot."

Charles smiled. "The one you wear all night?"

"Very same. Alpha insists."

Alpha nodded. "That I do."

"You're gonna need to expand the Alphabet Men, Mr. Alpha. If things go as I expect, you'll have to expand a lot. Do you know men like yourself in other cities?"

"Some. Not many."

"Good people make for good business; bad people make for bad business. If you can trust them, then deal with them, bring them close, hold onto them. If they break our rule, then part ways. Blame yourself for having made a bad judgment. Then try not to make the same mistake again."

Alpha held Charles's gaze for several seconds. "That ain't how it works on the street, my man. In the hood, we pay back twice over. You saying if they fuck us, we just let 'em skate?"

"If you're damn sure they stole from us, that counts as first blood. Respond as you see fit. But protect yourself, Alpha. Make sure nobody has anything they can hold against you. Anyone who turns to the G should only have their word and a few pills to back them up. Oh. And, even though none of our drugs are even on Schedule III, watch your back. Keep an eye out. We're under the cops' radar for now, and I hope that lasts a long time. But there will be other teams working against us as soon as they figure out what's happening. Competitors."

"Competitors not gonna obey your rules. They like drawing blood."

Charles closed his eyes. "We can live like animals, or we can live like men. I choose men."

"A'right, we'll give it a shot, Paladin." Alpha stuck out his sizable hand to shake. "But I'm not waiting for the other guy to kill me. We clear?" Alpha seemed pleased with himself.

"Clear. Hopefully people aren't going to be shedding blood for Viagra."

Alpha replied, "But they'll spill blood for money. Time for a beer?"

"On me."

"You play pool?"

Charles replied, "I do. I do indeed."

Alpha nodded to Rainbow. "You best split, kid. You don't be drinking, or I hide yo' backside, girl."

"'K, I'm out." She stood up and nodded to the two in turn. "Wouldn't want to embarrass you at the pool hall." She flashed a sassy smile and turned on her heel.

Four hours later the two men split $600 of winnings from their night partnering in the pool hall attached to the bar. Charles didn't learn all the specifics of Alpha's life story while playing pool. But little bits came out here and there. Alpha not only had street smarts, but a high IQ. Had he two parents instead of none, he might have graduated from high school, gone to college and become an attorney, and joined conventional society. But his parents disappeared almost before he knew them, and his life followed a different path. His attitudes were more important for understanding who the man was now than the specifics of how he got there. All evening, Alpha remained pleasant, and self-controlled. He never cut corners or tried to welch.

They walked out of the pool hall together into an empty street. Charles started to offer a ride to Alpha, but Alpha spoke first.

"About my girl, Rainbow." Alpha allowed another small glimpse into his private life. "I kinda inherited her. She thinks she's more than a kid, but she's not."

"That's the way I was at her age, Alpha. I suspect you were too."

"What she is, though, is smart. She's too smart to be sacrificed as a youngin."

The world sacrificed young people all the time. The young got sent to foreign wars as cannon fodder. The young got sent to the drug war as target practice.

"If I start liking you, Paladin, maybe you can introduce her around in your world some? Your uptown world. She don't have many who think like you 'round her. It might do her good. She don't need school. She learns better without the school. But she needs an education in the world outside. Maybe give her some alternatives to what I can offer."

In some ways, Rainbow was starting far behind where Charles was at her age. In other ways, she stood far ahead of him, even now.

"You want me to get her a job in 'burbs? Something off the street?"

"Maybe. That'd be good."

"I can pull some strings. She cleans up nice."

Alpha sighed, every bit like a father might when thinking about a daughter. "Yeah. She don't want any of her homeys to know it."

They sat in quiet for a few minutes. Charles began to wonder if this man might have developed some sort of instinctive trust in him. Or whether the evening's beer consumption had softened both his exterior and his judgment.

"Alpha, Rainbow is a connection from me to you. It could put us all at risk, if we don't do this carefully."

"I value the kid, Paladin. Want no harm to come to her…"

"She'll need to keep secrets. Let me think about what I can do. Can you tell me more about her? Some background."

Alpha sighed. "You want the long or short story?"

"Long, short, whatever. Just tell me what's going on."

"Short story. She needed a place to stay. Long story: her mamma was a smackhead. Bad addiction. One time, I supplied her with drug I didn't know was laced. Cops found her living on her own with her mamma four days dead. Autopsy said cyanide." Alpha shook his head, and anger flashed across his face. "They threw Rainbow into the system, and tore down the house. After a bit, Rainbow paid me a little visit. The girl's good with knives and such."

"She was going to kill you?"

Alpha responded with a barely perceptible shrug. "I convinced her it wasn't me. Anyway, that's past. I'm responsible for her now, because her mom got a bad batch and Rainbow got no daddy. For a while, I kept one eye open and I locked my door at night so I could get some rest. But we good now. She's a good kid, just got no family."

Charles remained quiet. He didn't know what to say. But before he could pawn her off, or recommend her to a contact in some employee position, he would have to work with her himself more.

99

"Go a long way to advancing our business, Paladin, if you elevate her personal lifestyle."

"Let me spend some more time with her. I'll see what I can do. Did you find the source of the bad batch?"

"Rainbow ain't stopped looking." Alpha gestured that he no longer wanted to discuss that topic. "She's a good runner, but won't sling dope, cuz it fucked up her mamma. She don't want me distributing that shit no more either."

"Maybe we were meant to meet," Charles said.

Alpha shrugged. "Me the candyman. You the anarchopharmacist. What a team we'll make."

First Impressions

CHARLES called Tristana's assistant the next day. "Stephan, good morning. Charles Knight here. A colleague and I would like to host a late lunch with Ms. Debocher and her husband, and perhaps you? And anyone else she would like to bring."

"Please allow me to check her schedule."

A few minutes later and Charles had the date. His pulse quickened. It was just flirtation, an opportunity to elevate her self-esteem. He cautioned himself about where it might end.

Stephan would join them. If the husband showed, he would get to know the new lead enforcer at the FDA. It was smart to get the measure of someone he likely couldn't avoid either professionally or personally.

Maurice had compiled a thorough dossier: Donald Debocher—graduate of Brown University. In his first and only round of applications, he had failed to get into medical school. His college transcript proved reasonably solid, with grades that should have gotten him in, so he must have failed the interviews. Luck always played a part in these things, but perhaps the interviewing professors and doctors had sensed something not quite right about young Donald.

Debocher had climbed through the levels at FDA faster than most. His fitness reports revealed good numerical scores, while the written evaluations were devoid of depth. It was as if his supervisors couldn't find any particular merit, but neither could they find a reason to hold him back. He seemed to rise through the ranks in part by the luck that had failed him earlier. He was in the right place at the right times.

But repeated luck usually means that the recipient has positioned himself to leverage lucky breaks. So Donald must have been doing something right. Or perhaps someone was helping him. He was about to become the youngest-ever FDA director of enforcement. He was either very good at his job, or an expert at backslapping and backstabbing, as the occasion dictated. Most likely, he was just an obsequious bootlicker who always did what he was told, but also took compromising pictures of his boss at conventions.

Charles spent the rest of the morning at three different banks in Maryland. He pretended to be the same man for all three—a physician by the name of James Sandridge. The doctor held a junior faculty position at Johns Hopkins. Sandridge not only maintained an excellent credit score but conveniently looked a bit like Charles. Rainbow had served as intermediary for obtaining a false driver's license. It wouldn't work if it was run through a computer system, but it was fine as visual ID. There was a big demand and a commensurate supply. Illegal aliens were buyers, as were those who needed something "official" for one scam or another.

The managers at all three locations were eager to provide credit to a young doctor. Testing their procedures, he opened checking and money market accounts with modest cash deposits, and applied for a signature line of credit, purportedly as startup funds for a new private practice. He used the street address of a post office as his business address, without the *PO Box* in front of the number. The post office allowed this now in order to make it more likely that FedEx would leave packages. For Charles, it made his pretense at a street address a bit more realistic. After three hours of pretending to be a doctor, he felt he needed only a white lab coat and a stethoscope around his neck to open a practice.

He arrived fifteen minutes early for the lunch with Tristana, Stephan, and Donald, and was surprised to find Rainbow waiting for him. She wore the same respectable outfit as earlier, but she had further toned down her rebellious makeup. He couldn't help but smile. The girl was smart enough to blend in when she shouldn't want to stick out. He chose a table with care, setting his back to a brightly lit window, with Rainbow next to him.

Donald arrived next, alone, in a wrinkled business suit. Older than Charles, but still a young man, Donald didn't look like someone Charles would even associate with, much less hire, much less invite to his home.

It didn't take a mystic to read his aura. His asymmetric face hosted lips in a permanent sneer. His eyes darted around like those of a hunted animal, squinting more on the left than the right, accentuating the message that his mouth conveyed. The man resembled his dossier picture, but the live version standing in the restaurant's entrance appealed even less. His features and expression, combined with his occupational choice, convinced Charles that Donald Debocher's defining characteristic was disdain for the world. And a fear of it.

Charles chose not to jump up to greet him. If love at first sight existed, this feeling was the opposite. The antipathy he had felt on reading the man's dossier, and seeing him obliquely through his wife's dimmed eyes, now settled into disgust. It took Charles some effort to check his negative reaction. But he did so in a manner that would please both a yogi in India and a tai chi master in Hong Kong. He needed his training from both to compensate for the severity of his visceral distaste for Donald Debocher.

He caught Donald's attention, and waved him over.

Different cultures train a person to react in different ways. A Zen monk, a yogi, and a Western philosopher might meditate together. In response to a loud noise, the monk and the philosopher would each startle, while the yogi would be unaffected. If the same loud sound then went off predictably every sixty seconds, the monk would startle the same way each time, because he's living in the moment, and each moment is new. The philosopher would adjust to the noise, and react less each time, as it became part of his reality. The yogi would have no reaction ever, because the loud noise is outside of his reality.

Being adept at all three approaches was as useful as knowing how to drive a car, fly a plane, and sail a boat, allowing one to travel on land, air, and sea.

Charles thought that a man from any culture would react the way he reacted to Debocher, because the man inflicted a continuous unwelcome disharmony, the very nature of which forced its way into one's reality. What had Tristana seen in him, and why had she married him? It gave him pause: her bad judgment might spill over into business decisions.

"Donald. I'm Charles Knight. Thank you for coming. I believe your lovely wife and Stephan will arrive shortly." Charles smiled more thinly and less warmly than was his usual way with new introductions. "This is

Rainbow. She's a student—a young associate of mine interested in business. Rainbow, this is Donald Debocher."

Donald ignored Rainbow more than he ignored Charles. He sat opposite, his face directly illuminated by the early afternoon autumn sun, his eyes squinting, and somehow accentuating his baseline sneer. He couldn't see Charles's facial expressions against the intense background, while Charles could note his every tick and grimace. He made no effort to alleviate Donald's awkwardness.

But Rainbow, sizing him up as a *mark*, engaged him with a neutral comment. "Nice weather," she said.

Donald replied without looking at her, "Not really."

The tone was thus set for the remainder of their relationship.

"What do you do, Mr. Debocher?" Rainbow asked.

Donald glanced up, and then returned his gaze to a menu that might as well have been upside-down. "I work at FDA."

"The FDA?"

He lifted his eyes, and said, "FDA. Right." But something about Rainbow seemed to lift him out of his self-absorption. "What do *you* do, Rainbow?"

She lifted her head with pride and said, "I assist Mr. Knight."

"I see. What sort of work is that?"

"Whatever he needs. If he needs drugs, I get him drugs. Guns? I got those too. Fake ID's. Whatever."

Donald lifted his eyes back up and kept them up, now staring, first at Rainbow, and then at Charles.

Charles's face didn't change.

Rainbow smiled then, jiggled her head back-and-forth, and pointed. "Hah! Gotcha, Mr. Debocher! Just kidding."

Donald's face cracked into what was more grimace than grin.

Then she added, "Mr. Knight doesn't need drugs and guns from me. He's already got all he needs." She waited for a response, and got none.

Charles raised an eyebrow at Rainbow. She shrugged back. A couple more minutes passed before Donald broke the silence.

"Mr. Knight, what's your story?"

"My story is long and dull, Donald. It's like 'War and Peace,' but without the war, the peace, or the romance."

"Oh, I'm sure there's a lot more than that. You're, what, about thirty?"

"I am."

"Yet wealthy enough to invest heavily in Visioryme."

"Some might say I'm not sufficiently diversified, and don't watch my portfolio as closely as I should."

"Is pharma your core interest?" Donald looked at his menu as he asked this. The man had a hard time with eye contact, and not just because of the difficult lighting.

"It hasn't been. Going forward, it might be. At least for a time."

Charles experienced a physical sensation in his abdomen, burning and twisting, knotted and hot, as two destructive emotions battled within him.

"Would you excuse me for a moment?" Charles got up, found the bathroom, walked in, looked into the reflection of his eyes, washed his hands, and left. Rainbow stood waiting outside the door, hands on hips.

"What's with that guy?"

Charles replied. "I don't know yet. Let's learn more about him. You may like his wife."

When he returned to the table, Donald had moved around to take Charles's seat, out of the sun.

"Well done, Donald." Charles said, genuinely amused as he contemplated whether it was a political power play, or simply bad manners.

"What's that? Oh, the seat? Yes, it was too bright over there." Still Donald did not look up toward his eyes. Charles walked past, reached over another table while apologizing to its occupants, and adjusted a set of blinds to block the sunlight. He then sat down opposite Donald and looked at his face.

Donald looked up, and then back down at the menu. Fidgeting, he mumbled in the way a controlling husband does to apologize for his spouse. "Where's my wife. She should be here by now."

"I hear you have a promotion coming?"

"Yes. You shouldn't know that though. Not announced yet."

"I've got the benefit of insider knowledge."

The man looked up.

Charles added, "Don't worry, I won't trade on it."

Donald did not appear amused. If anything, he looked ill. Or perhaps frightened.

"What's your new position?"

"I'll be Director of Regulatory Enforcement." His voice and his demeanor revealed his hubris.

"Wow. That sounds like something. What does that job entail?"

"We track companies that are out of compliance, both in this country and overseas, and ensure that they either become compliant or that they're closed down."

"In compliance with what?"

"With FDA rules, procedures, quality programs, GMP, etc."

"What's GMP?" Rainbow asked.

Donald looked like he shouldn't have to answer that question. But after a moment, he flashed an insincere smile and said, "good manufacturing practice."

"I see. You're like the drug police. A narco squad." Charles made extra effort in his face to convey that the comment was a joke.

"Not illicit drugs, if that's what you mean." No humor in this man.

Charles tried another tact. "What do you do if you suspect a company is not ... what did you say ... not *in compliance?*"

Donald replied with boredom, as if he were wasting his time. "We drop in on them and inspect them. If there are troubles, we might provide a warning to resolve the issues, and then re-inspect."

"And if the company disagrees with what you say they need to do? If they think they're doing it the best way already? If they think they know more about their business than you do?"

Now Donald became more animated, although he still kept his eyes low. "Hah! Then we close down the cocky bastards. And I assure you they don't know better than FDA does. We have a better grip on what's important than all the pharma companies put together. We certainly have a better overview than the little players—many of whom don't have a clue, no offense—and better than the large ones too. We can see the big picture."

Rainbow asked, "How do you close them down?"

"Among other things, we use U.S. marshals to confiscate the misbranded or adulterated drugs."

Charles shrugged and shook his head. "I'm sorry, Donald. I'm not sure I understand those terms. *Misbranded?*"

Donald glanced up for a flash, his eyes catching Charles's, then quickly darting away, this time toward the door.

"Yes, misbranded. It means that they've labeled their drug in a way not acceptable to FDA, or are advertising it in an unapproved manner."

Rainbow said, "So you decide what drugs are available for people to take?"

Donald deigned to look at the girl for a moment. "That's right."

"And if a company or a drug doesn't follow your rules," she added, "you close them down?"

"More or less. Pretty much right."

"Can you help get me a job at the FDA?"

Charles thought about kicking her, but held off for now. Let her follow her instincts.

Donald wasn't equipped to gauge innuendo and sarcasm, so he smiled at the compliment.

"Well, I worked very hard to get where I am. And, unfortunately," he added, "we don't hire your ... age group."

"That *is* unfortunate," she replied.

Donald readjusted himself in his chair, a subconscious display of internal discomfort that Charles noticed, but that Donald himself might not have perceived.

Charles redirected. "You mentioned you blocked unapproved advertising. Unapproved by whom?"

Donald pulled his head back, his chin almost disappearing into his neck, making him look like a turtle. His eyes still darted from side to side like those of a cornered rodent, reflecting how his brain worked.

"FDA has to approve all literature that accompanies medications, and all phrases and images used in any method of marketing and advertising drugs and medical devices: print, radio, television, sales calls, you name it."

Charles asked, "You found a way around the First Amendment?"

"It doesn't apply."

That was true; it took nothing more than a policy letter from an agency to obviate freedom of speech.

"Oh. And what does *adulterated* mean, Donald?" Given what had almost happened between Charles and Tristana already, the word, so close in sound, might rub a nerve.

Rainbow looked up at Charles and squinted her eyes slightly, but didn't say anything.

His wording, however, didn't get a rise out of Donald. Perhaps he was sufficiently enamored with his government agency that he allowed its lingo to supersede common language.

"*Adulterated* is FDA terminology for a drug that is not formulated as approved, is packaged in a manner not deemed by us acceptable or safe, is manufactured without compliance with official standards, and the like." It sounded as if he were quoting a handbook of regulations.

"Sounds ominous."

"Not really." Donald looked at his watch. "Sometimes the companies complain, but we're there for the common good. Doctors don't know what we know, and the scientists developing these drugs are motivated by money. The public doesn't have a clue about anything; they need a watchdog."

Rainbow nodded. "I'm really glad you're there, protecting us all."

Now Charles did tap her under the table. Not to chastise, but to acknowledge a barb that her target would fail to note.

Donald shrugged. "We don't think about that much, actually, you know, when we're on the ground, in the trenches."

Charles jumped on that, a bit too harshly. "You don't think about protecting the people?"

"Yes, of course we do. But day-to-day, it's more concrete. It's all about enforcing the rules. That's how they're protected…"

"Do you ever run across rules that are wrong? Rules that don't apply in a certain situation?" Charles was not trying to be Socratic by asking questions. The chances that Donald would have an epiphany were close to zero. He dug into Donald's mind to see how it worked, and what lay hidden away in its unwholesome nooks and crannies.

"I don't understand."

This impressed Charles as a sincere response. A man like Donald would be incapable of understanding.

"Hmm." It might be like asking a prison guard such a question. He rephrased it in more explicit terms. "Is the FDA always right?"

Donald glanced back at Charles, his face wrinkled and his sneer exaggerated; perhaps the man had had a mild stroke that caused the contortion. He shrugged slightly, and said, "Right? It's the rules. Sometimes the details have to be sorted out by a panel of administrative-law judges who know the rules. Very rarely in a courtroom. But, yes, as a matter of fact, FDA is always right. After all, we wrote the rules." He looked at Charles quizzically.

Tristana approached the table, and Donald turned to her, snapping, "You're late."

Tristana apologized to her husband with a nod. But Charles saw the restrained anger underneath.

Rainbow stood politely and introduced herself before Charles had a chance.

"I'm Rainbow. I work with Mr. Knight." She spoke to Tristana without accent in perfect King's English, with no trace of Ebonics. The girl could play to her audience.

Charles stood up, while taking in the couple's dynamics. His welcome was quite distinct from her husband's—which consisted of a barely audible grunt and a false smile. Tristana smiled at Charles. If Donald noticed any of their unspoken communication, his face didn't reveal it.

She settled in next to Donald. "Stephan's parking the car." She ignored Donald. "What sort of work do you do with Mr. Knight, Rainbow?"

"Help him acquire drugs and guns mostly."

Tristana had a markedly different reaction to Rainbow's presence than Donald had. "That's fantastic." She laughed. "No doubt Charles could use some guns and drugs."

Rainbow smiled, and Donald frowned.

Stephan overheard the comments as he came up to the table, took a seat next to Rainbow, and gave her a hug. "I've never met you, girl, but I like you already."

It was Stephan's way. To Rainbow's credit, she took it well. This time Charles played his appropriate role and introduced her to Stephan.

"What sort of work you do for him, Rainbow? Really."

"Well, it's not just guns and drugs. I mainly try to keep him away from bad people."

"Good for you, girl. That makes for good business." Stephan squeezed her shoulder conspiratorially.

Donald mostly stayed quiet during the meal. From time to time he would appear to be praying as he read his smartphone screen under the table, answering emails.

In contrast, Stephan remained animated, if a bit boisterous. He turned his gay stereotyping on and off with ease and, as a natural performer, was eager that his companions notice. Debocher's nonpresence helped everyone enjoy themselves. Stephan came off as insightful, cynical, and sometimes caustic. He was a good-natured parody of himself.

"Charles, Charles, you're *just* my type of *man*. I can help you be gay if you want."

Donald laughed far longer than he should have at Stephan's silly statement.

Charles drily commented, "Perhaps another time," while shaking his head vigorously.

Stephan laughed and ordered a pitcher of beer for the table, claiming that he would get Charles drunk enough to change his mind.

"Donald has to go back to work, so he can't party at lunch like we can. Ahh, the suffering of the public servant." Tristana patted her husband's shoulder. It was the first evidence of any affection between them. Donald pulled back.

Charles, sitting across from Tristana, watched her closely. Her eyes changed between life and death, or perhaps love and boredom, as rapidly as Stephan could switch his gay persona on and off. They dimmed when Donald came into the conversation, imposing his existence on her consciousness.

Visioryme's CEO stood on the verge of implosion, or on the verge of coming alive. Neither would be optimal for his investment. Charles placed his hands on the table, indicating that his time was up. "I'm grateful for the company and the amusement. Stephan, you're awesome. Donald, I have a private call soon, but wish I could stay longer."

Rainbow and Charles stood up.

Charles looked at Tristana, but paid close attention to Donald. "Tristana," he said, "I can see you at the office in an hour or so." It was a statement, not a request, and Donald's face turned ashen, and his lips tightened. He made no eye contact. "Would you mind if Rainbow joined you until then?"

Tristana looked up at Rainbow. "Sure, glad to have you. I'll show you around Visioryme."

* * *

Charles took no pleasure in observing the demise of a marriage. But it was doomed to fail from the start. He also realized he was setting himself up for retribution by the government. Donald and his cronies could throw enormous barriers in the way of his success in any pharmaceutical undertaking.

Well, not *any* undertaking.

They could only stop the ones they knew about…

11

Illegal Expansion

THE trees fell bare as November trickled by. Charles had never spent so much time in and around Washington, D.C. The place oppressed him, as if the city and its environs took on the negative psychic energy of its parasitic inhabitants. Walking beside Rainbow lightened it. She regaled him with bizarre, intimidating stories of her experiences living among these buildings and the people in them.

Steering clear of this part of town would be wiser, perhaps. But he needed to keep an eye on things, and that entailed some risk.

The approach to Alpha's office remained as grungy as before. But he found it changed inside. Two computers, papers, a new mattress with sheets for Rainbow. And general cleanliness.

"Hi, Mr. Alpha. Rainbow said you wanted to see me?"

"Yes, we're running low on supply already."

"Fantastic. I've got a bit more on hand, and will send some more down tomorrow with Rainbow."

"We got no shortage of interest."

"Your guys doing OK?"

"Sure they are. Buy from you for four, sell for sixteen. Clients love it. No brainer. Room for some pyramid too. Especially if you lower your price. We can expand."

"It's all about volume; we'll talk. I've got another easy product for you. And then one that's harder, but very good."

"Yeah? What d'ya got that's easy?"

112

"What else, besides six inches of blue steel, do men want?"

"Women. God knows why, but women."

"Right, and how do they get women?"

"Money."

"Right. What else?"

"Power."

"Sadly I agree. What else?"

"OK, what you getting at?"

Charles patted his head. "Hair. Women like either a full head of hair on their man, or a shaved head. To them, half bald is half flaccid."

"You wanna sell hair-growing pills?"

"You bet. Much of your market will overlap. All of them will be return customers, every month needing more."

"Addicts without addiction," Rainbow said.

Charles showed Alpha a two-inch hinged clear plastic device. "I picked up this pill cutter."

"I know what a pill cutter is." Alpha shook his head. "Recall this sabbatical of yours is my daily biz, cracka." Whereas he had in the past used the term to denigrate Charles, now he used it in a comradely way, much as one black might address another as *niggah*.

"Of course." Charles continued, "The leading hair-growth medication is called finasteride. Merck makes it. They use one-milligram pills, once per day. Its brand name is Propecia, and they sell it for about a buck a pill. But the same exact drug, finasteride, is used in five-milligram pills to shrink prostates, but they call it Proscar. It's off patent and generic now, and costs thirty cents a pill at Walmart. It's the same drug, made by the same company, in the same facility. But if you buy the Proscar you get five times the drug for one-third the price per pill. It's a fifteenfold savings. You sell it to bald people along with a pill cutter to cut it up. They can grow hair for cheap, and we profit from the exchange. And it's easy to find your market. Just look for people who are balding. Every one of them is a potential upsell to Fiagara, too. At least, once they grow their hair."

"OK, Paladin. Why don't people do that already, on their own?"

"Doctors are stuck in boxes, afraid to take risks, that's why. Docs won't tell the patients about it. There's no percentage in it for them, just risk. What if a man can't cut the pill right? He might get more or less than a milligram, from one day to the next."

"Does that matter?"

"Not in the least."

"Why do patients have to get doctors to prescribe hair-growth drugs anyway?"

"Ahh, they shouldn't. Prescriptions are a way for Merck to make more money, FDA to have more power, and a doctor to pick up a fee for an appointment. As an insane bonus, the population feels that this unholy trinity is needed; they've been brought up to believe everything is dangerous. They feel safer when they can shunt responsibility away from themselves to some self-appointed priesthood."

"Well, I'm runnin' wid ya. Needing prescriptions always seemed like bullshit to me. I got a nose for bullshit."

"It's only because the system is so stupid that there is even a profit opportunity here for us. I'd like to get rid of the system, but that's not possible. So we do the next best thing: we build our own system, and run it in parallel."

"What if they make a mistake and buy a drug that isn't right for them? You know what they say on TV—'see your doctor to make sure this shit is right for you'." Alpha did an excellent imitation of a black comedian doing an imitation of a serious white actor pretending to be a dignified doctor.

"What if they make a mistake and buy a car that isn't right for them? Shouldn't we make them see a mandatory car counselor before they buy a car? Look, we aren't stopping people from seeing their doctor. That's up to them. We're just making it possible for them to have a choice. This stuff is over-the-counter everywhere else in the world. There aren't people dropping like flies from wrong medications all over the world. And people can research whatever they want to know. It never hurts for people to take a little personal responsibility for what they put in their bodies."

"If you're comfortable, I am. Hell, I used to sell any kind of shit that I didn't know what was in it…"

Charles saw Alpha's face go dark. He had no doubt what Alpha was thinking about. Alpha didn't look at Rainbow, but Charles did.

After a moment Charles answered, "I'm completely comfortable. In fact, I'm fighting for Americans against the biggest enemy they have."

"Who's that?"

"Those people up there." Charles pointed towards the Capitol off in the distance.

"I'm working with a fuckin' revolutionary, ain't I?"

"You still in?"

"Sure."

"Good. As the Alphabet Men do their rounds, maybe have 'em do some market research. Ask the clients, or anybody they talk to, what else they'd like us to sell. Keep track of who wants what, and give me the info. I'll see what I can do about getting supplies." Charles paused. "And see if they'll give us referrals to friends."

"We already working that angle, yo. This is *our* business you keep trying to re-teach me."

"What are you doing tomorrow, Alpha? Up for tix to the 'Skins tomorrow night?"

"I gotta see my boy tomorrow."

"What's your son's name?"

"Jayden."

"What do you have planned?"

"He'll be all wanting to play video games. 'Call of Duty.' Loves that. Sometimes goes all night. He can shoot faster than his old man."

"Does he die a lot when he's playing?"

"Oh yeah, all the time."

Charles nodded. "The game is programming your kid to run suicide charges, jump in front of bullets, numbing his mind to self-preservation. You know they're brainwashing him to be cannon fodder for their next war."

Rainbow took this all in and said to Charles, "You can't help yourself, can you?"

"What do you mean, Rainbow?"

"You're takin' on the feds and pharmaceutical companies. You planning on taking on the video gamers too?"

Charles chuckled, embarrassed. "No. You're right. I won't live long enough."

Rainbow poked at him with her finger. "We'll both be dead before this is all over. Nobody gets out of here alive."

Alpha scratched his shaved head. "So you got a spare ticket to the 'Skins for my boy?"

"I want one, if Jayden's coming," Rainbow interjected. "Are you going to bring Tristana? She said she was a fan," she added.

Charles shrugged. "Maybe next time."

Alpha's eyebrows lifted. "Who's this Tristana you talkin' about, Rainbow?"

"It's Paladin's booty call."

Charles shook his head, and Alpha and Rainbow grinned.

Rainbow punched Charles's arm. "Really, Alpha, this lady Tristana runs a company in Virginia. Could be a good boss for me. Teach me a new set of skills, you know."

Alpha nodded almost imperceptibly to Charles. Out of the sight of Rainbow, Charles nodded back, with a grin.

*　　*　　*

"That wise guy is still in town?" Donald Debocher demanded of his wife.

"Yes, Charles is still in town. We have another meeting tomorrow."

"I'll check into him at work. The guy is bad news. I've got a nose for these things." He sat on their bed, fiddling to button his cuffs.

Tristana didn't reply at first, instead retreating into her dressing room and closing the door. She stood there for a few minutes.

"We're gonna be late!" he called through the door.

She clenched her teeth, stood up, and came back into the bedroom. "Charles Knight seems to have the money we need to keep Visioryme going. He's low-hanging fruit. We need his money."

"Yeah, so maybe he has the money. Maybe." He stood by the door. "But you don't have to whore yourself."

"Fuck you, Donald." It was the only appropriate response, and she found it came easily to her. She pushed past him, not too gently, and retreated downstairs to the family room, where she flipped on the television. She slid her shoes off and put her feet up on the coffee table. He hated it when her feet were up on the table. She bent down and put her shoes on the table too. A minute later he appeared.

"Don't make me late." He said it while shaking his head.

"I'm not going, Donald. You go hang out with your parents by yourself. Give them my best regards." He had already turned and walked into the next room. How could his parents have raised a man like that? She couldn't understand it. Why would *anyone* marry him?

She muttered, "I hate being Catholic."

116

"What's that?" Donald called back from outside the room.

"Nothing."

"What do you hate about being Catholic?"

"Nothing at all, Donald."

He stuck his head back into the living room. "Visioryme may not be able to afford to keep going without Knight. But it sure as hell can't move forward *with* him." He moved out of the room and toward the front door.

"What do you mean by that, Donald?"

He didn't answer.

"What do you *mean* by that statement, Donald." She spoke precisely, through parted lips and clenched teeth. It was not a question, but a threat response. One of her nostrils even flared. He couldn't see her appearance, but her intonation should have been very clear to anyone.

"Don't get in bed with people who make FDA anxious," Donald called back to her. "I *mean* that."

She had no chance to respond because he had turned to leave. A moment later he climbed into his car and slammed its door.

The opposite of attraction is repulsion. The further he drove away, the less pressure she felt.

*   *   *

"How much can you get me?"

Email would have been better than the weak phone connection, even though Internet connection speeds were very slow in West Africa. But there were other advantages to a conversation.

Charles heard back through the line, "How much is it that you are needing?" Chandra spoke accented English with Indian idiosyncrasy, intentionally exaggerated. He ran a wholesale pharmacy in Gondwana, where Charles had first learned about the huge price disparities for pharmaceuticals. Soon after meeting Chandra, Charles formulated this business plan that had become a reality within a few months.

"Got a pen?"

"Yes."

Charles recited his list. "One million tablets of finasteride five-milligram pills. Same number of hundred-milligram Viagra tabs. Generic equivalents."

"Chipkali ke gaand ke pasine."

117

Charles didn't understand the Hindi words spoken under the man's breath, but it was an expletive of some type.

"This is very certainly a very big order," the pharmacy wholesaler intoned from across the Atlantic.

"It's not done yet." Charles went on to list eight more medications that he wanted, albeit in much lower quantities.

"When is it that you need them?"

"How fast can you get them?"

"Three weeks."

"Will you bring them in by camel train?"

"Will you be taking them out hidden in umbrellas?"

Charles laughed and was about to hang up when he remembered. "Oh, Chandra. No Nigerian product. It has to come from known entities in India or another respectable source country, all with well-edited English-language labeling. And to make sure, I'll have all the drug lots tested here. There can be no counterfeit stuff. No mistakes about that, right?"

"Understanding you completely, Charles."

"For these deals, I need you to forget my real name and call me Paladin."

"Paladin? Like the old television show I have once been listening to?"

Charles's tone revealed his surprise. "You know 'Have Gun—Will Travel'?"

"Yes. My daddy and I were happy to be watching it before the war. All my friends would be coming over because we were having the television."

"Of course." It happened that people outside the United States often knew the most truly *American* television series ever made. Yet people in the U.S. under the age of sixty had rarely heard of it.

"Charles." He paused. "Sorry, I am meaning *Paladin*. It's not like I'm not wanting your business. Lord Krishna knows I do. But why are you not buying this direct from India yourself?"

"Chandra, those companies in India are just as susceptible to threats as any other company. They don't want to get on the wrong side of the U.S. government by selling for black market import here. Plus, they sell you this stuff in Gondwana at a tenth of the price that they'd sell it to me, because I'm American. Plain and simple. This is pharmaceutical arbitrage, and Gondwana gets the lowest wholesale price for these drugs of anywhere on the planet."

"It's good to be poor."

"Hey, Chandra, I'll see you in three weeks."

12

Bootlegging Gondwana

THREE weeks later, the West African coast began to emerge from the rainy season. In mid-December, the still-moist air kept the dust down. It rained intermittently through the day in Gondwana, but the raindrops fell pleasant and soft, quite unlike the pelting assault of water from thick, dark clouds during the height of the season.

Mud-soaked cars awaited inbound travelers at the airport. Broken men, using broken buckets filled with muddy water, scratched out a living washing the cars. On the streets nearest to the beaches they used ocean water to get the job done. Salt plus mud proved tough on Gondwana's vehicles.

Charles knew his friend TJ would be waiting for him to emerge from the hot, crowded, and decrepit room where first the immigration officials, and then the customs agents, aggravated tired travelers in hopes that some money might be discreetly placed in a passport to speed the process.

After a full day and night of traveling, and then passing the immigration gauntlet, he found himself in no mood for additional frustrations with Customs. He hated their boldness in practicing extortion. So he walked through with his suitcase, entirely ignoring the agent's frantic shouts as he slipped out the door and around the corner to find his waiting friend. The two men smiled broadly, shook hands as a ritual, and then hugged.

Nobody bothered to chase after him. He had just labeled himself too tough a target for graft.

T.J. Wandeah stood five feet nine and two hundred pounds. His was a muscular build, but he also had the paunch common to well-to-do men in Gondwana. And, like many of them, he also had Type II diabetes. He very much needed to drop at least thirty pounds. But a diet of beer, supplemented by lots of imported processed foods, and then more beer, was not conducive to good health. Nor were overgenerous portions of the local baked chicken and rice.

They stopped on the way to the city for some of that baked chicken, rice, and beer.

When he first came to this country seven years earlier, Charles often needed TJ to translate from African English to his own, American version of the language. Charles's inability to understand plain English always amused—and often frustrated—the locals. Americans' inability to understand simple language proved to the children of Gondwana that Americans, although rich, were somewhat stupid.

"So, what have you come up with to help us improve Gondwana's export numbers?" TJ asked with a smile. "It is easy to sneak things into the country, but harder to them get out. We produce very little that anybody else wants, so ships often leave the country empty. Filling them up with drugs will be conspicuous. It's easy to search an empty ship."

Charles looked around the restaurant. The staff congregated near the noisy, old air conditioning unit, which conveniently blocked their ability to overhear the conspiring men. "It can't be an empty ship."

"Do dogs smell these drugs?"

"They aren't trained to do that. No reason to."

TJ chewed his way around a chicken bone. "I maybe have an idea that can help my brother too. If we can find a ship, I may be able to find something to stick your drugs into."

Charles grinned. "TJ, I think I might have the ship."

*   *   *

The capital city's port was walled, gated, and fenced off from the main road that headed northwest along the coast. The adjacent highway's traffic flow was interrupted whenever a vehicle broke down. That was pretty much an hourly event.

They sat, hot and sweating, in the stationary line of muddy vehicles. Their truck's weak air conditioner provided little more than a warm rasping wheeze to fight the oppression.

"Hey, Kollie, why do they leave their broken-down cars in the middle of the road while they repair them?"

Kollie was TJ's friend, whom they had picked up on the far side of the city. Old and grayed and with the fogged eyes of someone exposed to sun for far too long, he seemed barely competent to drive. Charles knew how Kollie would answer the question. But he loved hearing the answer, which was the same, always, anywhere in Gondwana.

"What else *would* they do?" Kollie responded in the lilting English that brought pleasant memories flooding back.

It never crossed anyone's mind to push the cars to the side of the road. There was a certain logic to this. Pushing a car involved work. And the gravel roadside was a less inviting surface for repairs than the pavement.

Charles liked to envision a fantastic future for this place, essentially the poorest region on the planet. But it would take more than capital and experience. Cultural inertia had to be overcome. It might happen someday.

The port area came into view, but it took them another thirty minutes to maneuver through the chaotic traffic. It was like a chaotic zoo. The trucks, minibuses, and cars were the elephants, wildebeest, and zebras, constantly swarmed by thousands of motorcycles, their unhelmeted riders—sometimes numbering four per motorbike—skittering through traffic like mosquitos and flies. Unlike in a zoo, however, no formal organization ruled this place. Gondwana's capital city was more aptly considered a jungle. Charles smiled subtly with the realization that he far preferred a jungle to a zoo. A zoo was a prison camp for animals. And a prison camp was like a zoo for humans.

Kollie worked at the port, so the gate attendant allowed them access with no formalities. Here, who you knew mattered more than what you knew.

Historic events had occurred in this port, the economic crux of the country, over the years: events that changed the course of wars. The West African peacekeeping forces entered through here, and later, those of the United Nations. This was where one of the former presidents was lured, trapped, and brutally killed. Now it served as the entry site for the supplies of low-quality goods from China and Lebanon and Western NGOs that dominated the import consumer market.

"Bastards."

"What is it, TJ?"

"See those containers there? They are filled with furniture donated to the Gondwanan people by an NGO. It was a huge campaign. Made the newspapers here."

"I bet it did."

"My brother last year started a furniture-manufacturing business, out in Djenne County. Provides about a hundred jobs, makes some money, manufactures stuff people need, right? How is he supposed to compete with stuff that is *given* away, huh? This stuff will suppress demand, and drop the market price for months. How is my brother supposed to stay in business? So I say, *bastards!*"TJ shook his head vigorously.

Charles said, "Good-hearted people being stupid. It's no wonder Africans distrust the whites. In the U.S., if a company was doing this, the government would label it *dumping*, and the Commerce Department would block the trade or stick a punitive tariff on it. But destroying the local economy *here* is celebrated as charity."

TJ replied, "If it was actual competition, my brother would have to suck it up, find a way to reduce costs, and stay profitable. But how do you compete with free stuff? This is just stupid."

"He's still going to need to suck it up, TJ."

"First, colonizers came in and took over the place, and replaced tribal territories with maps drawn up in Europe. Then you send in missionaries to convince people our old gods were devils. Then you take the minerals and timber. When your colonialism failed, you pulled out your governments and militaries but left your Marxism here. You whites turned our land into a giant snake pit where all the worst people vie to control our government. So then we have decades of civil wars. Now some whites feel guilty for all the damage. So after sending us brutal soldiers, Middle Eastern gods, and stupid ideas, now you send us container ships full of cast-off junk and free food. Maybe that makes all the white men feel like saints. But all you do is destroy small businesses that would make these things, and the farmers who grow crops."

Charles's usual smile had disappeared.

TJ looked at Charles.

"Charles, what's wrong?"

Charles rarely got angry, but it did happen. "TJ, you know better than to lay any of that crap on me. My whiteness doesn't mean I had anything to do with it."

TJ did know better, but, like many people, he needed an occasional booster shot to immunize him against collectivist thinking. He'd allowed himself to lump Charles—who happened to have white skin—into a group of colonizers from a century earlier, who shared a skin tone with Charles, but little else.

"Look, TJ, I can't apologize for all the crap that happened here, because I didn't have anything to do with it. So my apologies would be not only pointless, but fraudulent. But I do empathize, and I do care. And I'll fight alongside you, my good friend."

TJ sheepishly replied, "Charles, I like it when you are around. You call me to the mat."

They drove on through the port. Two Panamax container ships and three midsized feeder ships stood alongside the piers. Another small feeder lay tucked in at the end, loading some containers probably bound for the furthest-eastern port city by the border, to which overland traffic remained impossible. This was no highly automated port with massive robot-enhanced cranes. Manual labor dominated here. The port was a throwback to the 1950s in most ways. When it came to loading and unloading the small coastal freighters, it was a throwback to the 1930s.

Kollie directed TJ toward a dark red ship and pulled alongside near the stern, away from where a crane and men unloaded containers. Kollie spoke on his phone as he led the way up the ship's gangway.

From the top, Charles took a moment to look out over the walls of the port. Little had changed since this place was the focus of an adventure that had changed his life. The scattered sprawl of dilapidated buildings and containers lay interspersed with new construction. The city itself was slowly recovering after years of destruction, desolation and decay. It was a cyclical phenomenon that had occurred several times since the place went independent.

He looked toward the ship on the next pier, still fully loaded with its containers. The name of its Chinese owner covered over half its hull. The Chicoms, as some unreconstructed conservatives in the U.S. still liked to call them, were communists in name only. The Chinese knew Mao had been no more than another in a series of emperors stretching back over two thousand years. The key to getting along with the powers-that-be, in China as in the U.S., was to go along. So they paid lip service to whatever political notions the current imperial thugs might promote, but paid much more attention to their bank accounts than to any dictates from on high.

The Chinese, who sold cheaply made goods here at a profit, at market prices, had done more to overcome African poverty than all the Western international aid given away for free. Much of the Western aid first went to salaries, benefits, and expense accounts of officials at various charities and NGOs. The Western aid that actually made it into Africa mostly found its way into the bank accounts of top bureaucrats. After funding overpriced infrastructure projects built by well-connected locals, some money trickled down through the economy to buy these Chinese-made goods. What was left after that mostly ended up in the hands of the now-numerous mobile phone companies; people loved to talk. Few saved any money in order to build local capital. The trillion U.S. dollars that had been shipped to the continent since the end of World War II had accomplished almost nothing except impoverishing Western taxpayers while corrupting Africans. Government foreign aid largely served to transfer money from poor people in rich countries to rich people in poor countries.

"Charles!" Kollie called back to him, and waved him over to meet the vessel's captain, just emerging from inside the superstructure at the main deck level.

Charles came forward, and his smile grew. He watched as the captain and Kollie greeted each other warmly. His smile expanded as he approached, and he quickened his pace. His arms started spreading out.

The captain saw him. Charles saw the captain's face transition from uncertainty, to hopeful bemusement, to positive recognition. The captain leapt toward Charles, his arms likewise wide open, and the two men grabbed each other in an embrace. The captain was the larger man. Charles winced under the pressure.

"Charles! Had I known you were here in country, my young friend, I would have contacted you upon my arrival in port."

"No way you could know I was here, Anders, but I knew where *you* were! Kollie here helped us get into the port. Do you remember TJ?"

Captain Anders Freberg stood tall and bearded, a modern-day Viking, but arrayed in a short-sleeved white cotton uniform, four gold bars on each black shoulder board. He turned. "TJ, yes, of course. It has been many years. When I was captain of the 'Africa Grace.' Many years back."

"That's right." TJ shook his hand. "What a time that was."

Captain Freberg said, "Did you know that Charles sailed with me for three months, what, has it been two years ago now?"

Charles nodded. "That's about right. Fully 'round the Cape, across the Indian Ocean, and through the Strait of Malacca and then up and down China for a time. Fond memories."

"I am so pleased that my chess partner is back! If you sail once again, I'll get a piano on board at the first opportunity." He turned to Kollie. "Charles played for the Danish queen and the British queen as well, so he said."

Charles nodded. "More important, back in New York, I've just signed on to play a few concerts for the common folk." Royalty were mostly either the spoiled scions of successful gangsters, or inbred members of the lucky-sperm club. But then, there were the occasional few who broke the mold. One in particular.

"Have you heard from Caroline, Charles?"

"Yes, we stay in touch. But I suspect you see her much more often than I do."

"She tries very hard to be anything other than the princess that she was born to be. The Danish people have adjusted to her … shall we say… less-than-royal ways. They grow more fond of her every year."

Someday, perhaps, Charles would find his way back to Caroline.

"Anders, I'm here to sail with you once again, if it's indeed true that you're heading to North America."

"Then welcome aboard. We head across the Atlantic after we offload. You will have the first guest cabin of course."

"I'll take it." Charles turned to TJ. "The last trip I bunked with the crew. This ship is bigger, though."

"But I only have her for another year; they're already laying the keel for my next command. I will show her to you. She'll be a beauty, and enormous. Thirteen thousand TEU. No half measures for me."

Charles tried to imagine a ship with more than twice the shipping capacity of a Panamax vessel, which itself was enormous and able to carry cargo amounting to almost 5,000 TEU: twenty-foot-container equivalent units. Anders's next command would be massive. "Will you get through Malacca still?"

"She'll be a wide ship, not a deep one. She'll get through the Strait of Malacca."

"Congratulations." Charles reached out to shake his friend's hand. "Now, before you offer me the first class guest accommodations back to the U.S., I need to tell you what I hope to ship in your holds."

*   *   *

Most ships going from North America or Europe to Africa came in full but went out empty. The continent's exports consisted mostly of raw petroleum, unprocessed ore, latex rubber, and timber, all cargoes unsuitable for a container ship. Captain Freberg's ship would not be entirely empty on this return trip. It spent the next day loading containers of bamboo, which did not travel well on bulk-cargo ships. Bamboo flooring had emerged as the new thing in the U.S., and bamboo furniture remained popular in some markets. It was, after all, a renewable resource, and therefore green. The U.S. tax code provided a subsidy for it, serving to confirm that the politicians cared about Mother Earth. One of TJ's brothers owned a major collection site for bamboo exported from central Gondwana.

The ship left directly from the port with its bamboo, Charles, and his special cargo all safely on board. They followed the West African coastline, stopped for bunkers and a day of rest at Cape Verde, and then headed west at twenty-five knots in the open ocean, toward Baltimore.

13

Legal Permits and Permissions

"WHY the hell did you buy twenty containers of bamboo, Charles?"

Charles kept his feet far apart for balance, not yet reaccustomed to the firmament after bobbing around on the Atlantic on Anders's ship. "I like bamboo, Maurice. It's eco-friendly."

"Eco, schmeco. So's dirt. Do you need that walking stick, or is it just for show?"

Maurice did not offer Charles a seat, so Charles slid a stack of folders off a chair and took a seat anyway, after handing Maurice the bamboo walking stick he had taken to carrying with him for the past few days.

"It's a gift for you. Take the base off. But be careful. Cut bamboo is razor sharp."

Maurice carefully removed a rubber foot from its base. He looked down the dark hollow interior of the bamboo shaft. He rubbed his finger along the cut end and instantly said "shit!" as he dropped the stick. Out poured hundreds of blue pills, all over his floor.

"Hey, watch out there, uncle. I told you it was sharp. Now the fibers in your carpet are all going to stand up straight."

Maurice sucked on his bleeding finger. He pulled it out of his mouth to ask, "This is Viagra?"

"Well, actually it's Fiagara. With an F."

"How much do you have of this stuff?"

"One million pills in the hollow center of the bamboo scattered among the containers I acquired. It's why bamboo is so straight and hard, didn't you know?"

"I do now. Fiagara. That sounds Nigerian. You sure it's Viagra?"

"Not Nigeria. Actually, it's made in India. It's the same stuff. Very reputable company. Of course I had it assayed. I got you that supply there, now on the floor, for when you get off your ass and start losing weight so you can get some women again."

"Charles, I get women, make no mistake. Money is very attractive, and I have lots of it. They don't even see my weight."

"Prostitutes, Uncle? Really?" Charles wasn't passing a moral judgment so much as assessing the difference that two hundred pounds and thirty years could make on a man's approach to a problem. Like most young men, certainly those born after a certain time, Charles never needed to engage the services of a professional sexual therapist. While living in Asia, he became well aware that girls from good families didn't idly spend time with foreigners. And the ones who hung around bars would go home with you if they liked you, expecting a tip the next morning simply because it was the right thing to do. Not at all like the culture in North America, where it was a cash and carry transaction.

"No! I mean they are attracted to me, and the only reason I can think of is that I have money. I don't *pay* anybody!"

"Oh, thanks for explaining. But really, Maurice, you need to lose some weight. In the two months since I saw you last, you gained a few pounds."

"Probably. I still don't go out much."

"That's gonna get worse."

"I know. I know. I know." Maurice smiled up at him. "Fantastic, kid. You're really doing it. You're officially now a drug smuggler."

"My father would be proud."

"Don't tell him, kid. Do *not* tell him."

"I won't."

"Shall we order Chinese? Or, better, in celebration of the origins of your Fiagara, Indian?"

* * *

Stephan walked into Tristana's office and closed the door. He glanced over at Rainbow, who sat with a notepad on her lap, recording the day's list of chores as Tristana dictated. He stood silently, his face flat. Tristana stood up from behind her desk as if she were the accused about to hear the final verdict in a murder trial.

"Don't keep me in suspense, Stephan. They approved us, didn't they!"

"Final approval." His face erupted into smile. "It's done. No more BS from, or for, the FDA! Sybillene is approved for market!"

Tristana ran around her desk and threw her arms around her assistant. Tears flowed as they jumped around in a circle. "We did it!"

Stephan pulled Rainbow up from her seat and hugged her. Tristana opened up her office door and shouted out to the handful of people she had maintained on payroll. "We did it!" A cheer went up from all, and moments later, dusty bottles of sparkling wine popped and yellowed plastic flutes appeared. The bottles had sat in the drawers for many years, awaiting this moment.

The phone rang, and Stephan almost fell over his desk as he reached for it, knocking over an open bottle of champagne. He caught it before it hit the floor and then answered the phone. "Visioryme. Can I help you?"

Instantly his hand went up, catching Tristana's attention. She couldn't smile further without her face cracking, but somehow she did as Stephan enunciated loudly, while pointing flamboyantly at the phone with his spare hand. "Why hellooo, Mr. Knight. You heard already? Yes… Yes… I'm sure that would be fine. Please do… Yes… We're celebrating… Yes… Really? Yes… I know… Goodbye."

Tristana asked him without saying anything. Stephan mouthed the word *tomorrow*, and gave her a thumbs-up and raised his eyebrows up and down in Groucho Marx's universal innuendo.

"Tomorrow?" Rainbow asked.

Stephan replied loudly over the chatter, "He says he has the money to build out the manufacturing."

"He's come up with the money?"

"So he says. Ten million dollars."

"What a day!" She threw open the door to the clean-room manufacturing space that, along with storage and processing areas, took up most of the building. It was dark, as it had been for over a year, since the last FDA-required registration batch of Sybillene had been completed. The machinery—boilers, giant separation columns, stirrers, shakers, analyzers, powder fillers, clean-room equipment—all lay silent, faintly reflecting the intruding light. She shouted into the ghostlike facility, "Hey, clean room! Get ready, you're gonna be busy! Filled to the brim with bamboo and excitement!"

She turned to Stephan. "We'll need to get hold of some bamboo. It takes at least a month to get here. If Charles really has the money, we're in business!"

"Actually Tristana. He said he already has the bamboo. Twenty containers full. All expenses paid, free on-board at the Baltimore Port Authority."

"How the hell would he know?"

Stephan shook his head. "I have no idea."

Rainbow whispered to herself, "I do."

They drank sour champagne and cried and laughed and made phone calls. And they watched their stock price rise as the news poured out through the small number of analysts who even knew Visioryme existed.

Tomorrow, many, many new ones would be paying attention to the prospects of Visioryme. It was a great day for the company, a pivotal day.

Tristana was as happy as she had been in years.

But a certain sick feeling in her stomach wouldn't go away.

*   *   *

Stephan greeted Charles the next day with a smile and hug, something Charles didn't mind from people he liked. Charles reserved his affection not for humanity in general, but for certain individuals in particular. He hoped the whole office was in the same sort of mood as Stephan.

Tristana opened her office door a moment later, and Charles received a very warm welcome. Stephan watched, grinned, shook his head, and said, "Get a room."

"How did you hear before we released the news, Charles?"

He felt like playing with her. "Maybe your husband called me to let me know. Maybe he's a friend?"

"Yeah, I don't think so." Tristana's face, so bright a moment before, dulled suddenly and completely. But briefly.

Mentioning her husband was a bad idea. In his mind, he hit himself.

"Think he's a bit jealous?" Charles asked.

"Should he be?"

"That's a question for you, not me."

Perhaps Tristana would not want to risk what the next minute's discourse might evolve into. But he knew she wanted to continue.

"Are you conflicted?" he asked. It could have only one meaning.

She responded immediately. "Entirely. Aren't you?"

"Yes." But not in the ways she hoped. Who she might evolve into remained unclear to him. She was immersed in impending change.

She said quietly, "I'm a married woman."

"I'm aware of that."

"What's that mean to you?"

Charles replied, "It means you have a contract with Donald—a boilerplate contract written by your church and the state decades ago, or hundreds of years ago. It's not likely a contract optimized for you and Donald. Unless you rewrote it with a prenuptial agreement."

She shook her head. "No prenup. I didn't want one. That was years ago. I was foolish and in love."

"Love?"

"I thought so at the time."

"We have a lot to talk about. Dinner tonight?"

"Of course. Charles, Rainbow is staying with us at the house regularly now."

"I heard. I think that's great. Where is she?"

"She's only here some days. She likes to go running many days."

Charles chuckled. "Yes, she's quite the *runner…*"

"She's a smart kid. Inventive, a hard worker. I just couldn't stand her having to do that long commute every day to whatever horrid place she lives."

Charles reflected back to Gondwana. Even Rainbow's mattress on a tile floor beat a grass mat on dirt. "I'm glad it's working out."

"Well, it is for me. It turns out I've needed the company. Donald can't tolerate her. When *she's* there, he tries to *not* be."

Charles repeated, "I'm glad it's working out." He lifted his briefcase to his lap and slid his hand inside to remove a folder. "I have your bamboo."

"I heard. I don't know how you knew to get it."

"Maybe I knew FDA was going to clear Sybillene. Maybe I just guessed." *Maybe*, he thought to himself, *we just got lucky when TJ's brother chose the bamboo in which to mule the Fiagara.*

131

"Yes. Well, it's amazing. But, Charles, it's probably not the right bamboo. Not the right fungus."

Charles handed her the folder. She opened it. It held a set of analyses on Johns Hopkins letterhead, from one of the mass-spectroscopy laboratories. She studied it for over two minutes, then, while still reading through the papers, pressed a button on her phone.

"Tim? It's Tristana. I'm glad you're available." She punched the speakerphone button. "Hey, I have Charles Knight in my office here."

"Hello, Mr. Knight," the voice said.

"Hello, Dr. McBride."

"Are you excited about your investment?"

"Every day. And you?"

McBride replied, "Yesterday was the culmination of many years of work."

Charles felt a flair of exasperation and impatience even before the PhD academic scientist finished the sentence. Though he tried—for a moment— he could not refrain from correcting the man. "I'm not sure about that, Dr. McBride."

"What do you mean?"

"Visioryme hasn't pulled in a dime of revenue from it yet, nor helped more than a handful of research patients."

"Oh. Well, I meant that the hard part is done. We got FDA approval. That's not easy."

"No, it's not easy. And I don't mean to denigrate or minimize all the effort it took. You'd already created a good product, and *that* was worthy of a celebration. But I have trouble celebrating the approval of some faceless bureaucrats who should never have been involved in the first place."

Charles let that sink in for a moment. It was a rather harsh thing to tell a man eager to celebrate his victory.

He couldn't soften it much. "Now we have to start building a company that produces value for customers. With a little bit of luck, and a lot of hard work, we should be able to turn out a quality product at an affordable price. Thanks to you, we may have a better mousetrap, but, contrary to the old saw, in this business the world won't beat a path to our door. My point is, FDA approval just eliminates a roadblock. We're not successful until we get millions of these things in the public's hands."

Only silence came from the other end of the line. Tristana raised her eyebrows.

His words had come as a shock to McBride; only one in a hundred academics would have a clue what he was talking about.

"I stand corrected," Dr. McBride said.

"We're all a bit too giddy here too," Tristana piped in.

Charles added, "Me? I'm celebrating that maybe the bastards will stay out of our way for a while. That *is* worthy of celebration."

Tristana said, "Look, Tim, I've got analyses of a supply of bamboo. It looks good to me."

"When did you order the bamboo? I thought we were out of money?"

"It came from Mr. Knight." She looked at Charles. "Charles was obviously optimistic."

"And the analyses?"

"Mass spec. Johns Hopkins. Also provided by Mr. Knight. I'm faxing them now."

"I'll call you back in a bit. But I'm going to want to repeat them."

Charles said, "Sure. Please be quick. We have to start producing and selling product. We aren't on an academic timeline, here. We're hanging by a thread, just like always, and FDA approval doesn't make that thread any longer or stronger."

Tristana added, "And it's Charles's money we spend each day now."

That reality would weigh on Charles every day that went by.

"Understood," the academic scientist replied.

Tristana disconnected and said to Charles, "You better be careful, or you're going to make more than one man jealous today."

Charles stood up while he said, "McBride. Scientifically jealous?"

"Yes, Charles. I certainly don't mean romantically jealous. Sybillene is his baby."

"Why not romantically?"

"He's a professor."

"Professors were eunuchs in Chinese imperial courts. They aren't eunuchs here. How old is he?"

"I think about fifty-five."

"And how old are you?"

"Thirty-eight."

"You're beautiful, and I rest my case."

Charles held the office door for her as she went out. She placed the lab results on Stephan's desk as she went by and said, "Please get these to Tim right away. We're off to dinner."

Stephan pulled his chin back into his neck. He nodded vigorously at Charles and then turned to Tristana. "You go, girl!"

14

Evils and Expletives
of Competition

"HELLO, Alpha."

"Hello, Paladin. Been a while."

"It takes a while."

Dirty snow clung along the sides of wet streets while slush filled the holes in the sidewalks, waiting to refreeze overnight. The twilight of a gray January sky mimicked the depressed mood of the city. There was a storm coming.

"You good?"

"Always," Charles replied as he sat down on a cold concrete park bench a couple of yards from where Alpha sat.

"You know, Alphabet Men is almost outa stock already."

"Your guys burning through a thousand a day still?"

"Double that."

"I just got us plenty more. Are you bringing in more teams?"

"I got guys set to pound the pavement of D.C. and surrounds."

"Where did you get them?"

"Other factories."

"Are you taking 'em out from under some distributors?"

"It's an open job fair, Paladin. They see the same advantage we did. The boyz may be ignorant, but they ain't stupid."

Charles scrunched his face. "You think it's gonna make their former employers unhappy? Taking their sales force? Are you planning anything to mellow out the tempers of the multi-kilo guys?"

Alpha replied, "Been thinking about it. We got one particular who's making noise."

"Who's that?"

"His name's Tadeus Jones. Tomo's his man. Rainbow says you met Tomo."

"Yeah. I remember him. Last time I saw him he was painted with a red laser dot." Charles sensed the rational fear that arose within himself on hearing Tomo's name.

Alpha snorted. "Yeah, that's Rainbow's original neighborhood. Tomo remember you too. He's unpredictable. Tadeus too."

"What d'you think? Take 'em head on?"

"Yeah. You want to play in that game with me?"

"It's necessary. So I do."

"Tonight then—nine PM. We'll leave from the pool hall."

Charles stood as the first winds of the impending blizzard worked their way through the city.

"I'll be there."

*　　*　　*

Sleet curved upward toward Charles's face, carried by thirty-knot gusts that circulated among the buildings and exploded out of the alley in front of him. Alpha stood next to him, underdressed for the onslaught of the midwinter storm.

"Should we reschedule on account of weather?" Alpha shivered.

Charles had butterflies in his stomach. They appeared any time he faced a new and dangerous situation while feeling unprepared. He should pay heed to these butterflies. But he didn't just then. "We're taking this head-on, right?"

Alpha nodded. "It may not go well."

"I don't expect it to."

"Are you ready?"

"I'll pretend like I was born ready."

He wasn't ready. Charles was far out of his element here. But it needed to become his element. If you are faced with something you fear, learn what you can and deal with it. He'd learned what little Maurice could gather about Tadeus Jones. Maurice used one of his myriad connections—most of whom owed him treasure, introductions, or intelligence. In this case, Maurice had provided someone in the DEA the opportunity to pay a long-owed debt. Via his network, Maurice could get the goods on anyone, and as usual, Maurice found a way to come through with just the right information.

Alpha said, "Then we're in."

Alpha climbed the stone steps to the first-floor entrance of a five-story multifamily dwelling. In keeping with this fairly high-rent district of town, the exterior of the building and entranceway were immaculate.

He pressed a buzzer. "Tadeus. It's us. Open the door, man. It's freezing."

The door buzzed, and Alpha and Charles walked through. Charles wore a long black overcoat and Alpha a wet leather jacket. Neither removed their outerwear. They passed the elevator, and walked up the inside stairs.

The apartment known as 2C wasn't like the others in the building. Apartments 2A and 2B no longer existed. Apartment 2C wrapped all around the structure, looping the inside stairwell like a horseshoe. Tadeus had the whole floor.

Sterile white paint coated the walls. Charles pointed to the two old doors to the former apartments. "Do those still work?"

"I think so. Can't swear to it. Only been here a couple of times. This guy distributes much more than I can deal. He's a level up from where I generally hang."

Alpha knocked on the door, which a moment later opened into a room that had three televisions, all on, all loud, on three different stations. A delicate Asian man opened the door, acting like a houseboy. His long jet-black hair sported a prominent streak of fluorescent green down the middle, like a punk striped skunk. He wore tight tweed pants and a black turtleneck shirt that clung to his scrawny torso. He made a half-hearted attempt to frisk Alpha, which met with a brusque "Fuck off" and a shove. The man then dramatically turned his back on them and sashayed into the next room.

Two men sat on the couch: one massively obese; the other tall and thin. The fat man didn't budge. He didn't even look at Charles and Alpha. He just stared at a television screen.

Alpha said, "Tadeus, how's shit?"

The tall, thin man replied, loudly enough to be heard over the televisions. But he didn't look at Alpha. He looked at Charles. "Shit is real shit.

137

Surrounded by shit. I don't like feeling surrounded by shit." Tadeus's mustache resembled Adolf Hitler's, and lay atop pallid and pockmarked skin. The mustache spoke of active self-absorbed branding and attention seeking.

Alpha had described Tadeus as a reasonably predictable dealer, with a reasonably uncontrolled temper and modestly loyal employees. He seemed modestly unhappy. Charles began his own study of the man from his position slightly behind Alpha, but couldn't gather much from either his visage or his posture. He surmised some traits that would generally apply to a city dealer. But were they applicable to a man who lived in a high-end apartment in a higher-end building? The traits Charles imagined were more likely to relate to characters from movies he had seen in his childhood than to this man in front of him.

A quick assessment of the room revealed more. To either side of the bright-red leather couch stood end tables with unusual lamps. The one on the left appeared to be constructed from an AR-15, muzzle down, with a lampshade sitting on a bulb socket attached to its stock. To the right stood a vertical AK-47 with a naked fluorescent bulb emerging from its muzzle. Other than the illumination from the televisions, these gun-shaped lamp fixtures provided the only lighting in the room. On the walls hung six movie posters, expensively framed, advertising in turn *Wall Street*, *The French Connection*, *The Bourne Identity*, *Bloody Sunday*, *The Last King of Scotland*, and *The Omen*. The films this man chose to honor were about speculators, drug dealers, assassins, terrorists, warlords, and the end of days. Pretty dark stuff overall. A shelf prominently displayed hardcore-porn magazines; some had fallen onto the floor and lay strewn around. Empty beer bottles, empty potato chip bags, McDonald's cheeseburger wrappers, and other garbage littered the place. The occupants' habits didn't match the apartment's high price tag.

At first inspection, this home provided nice digs for a midlevel distributor. Or perhaps a high-level multi-kilo player whose pissed-off wife had recently kicked him out. That seemed more likely, based on nothing other than the mismatched plates, bowls, and glasses that lay around on the few tables, all of them kitchen orphans that a woman might allow her soon-to-be ex-husband to take with him as she slammed the door on his ass, hopefully as he left forever.

Tadeus still didn't look at Alpha as he spoke, but rather at the floor. "So, what's this I hear about you taking Tomo's guys out from under him, huh? I hear that same shit from Lindi. And Kines too. You been … um … recruiting my thoroughbreds. Stealing my jugglers. How am I to trade? I hear you gonna be selling clean drugs too. That true? What I hear?"

Alpha motioned Charles forward into the room. "Tadeus, this is Paladin. I work with him."

"Paladin, huh? What the hell's that? Some kind of freakin' video game name? Where you takin' my men?"

Charles said, "Tadeus, it's my pleasure…"

Tadeus stood up then and shouted, "Yeah? Well it ain't *my* fucking pleasure!"

Charles had anticipated this sort of reaction. He could deflect the man's loud voice, and he could parry a verbal threat. But if the man became violent…

"You like movies?" Charles asked, unfazed and unintimidated.

Tadeus replied, "What?"

"Do you like movies?"

To a man who evidently chose to instill fear with a loud voice, a calm and fearless response might trigger frustration.

"What's that got to do with the price of shit in Mexico?"

"I like movies."

"Yeah? Well, good for fuckin' you."

Charles walked the room slowly, pausing in front of each movie poster on the wall. "Each of these movies holds memories for me. Who can forget Gekko from 'Wall Street'? Michael Douglas. He may have broken a law, but he never cheated or stole from anybody."

Tadeus said nothing.

Charles walked to the next poster. "'The French Connection.' It used to be the way that opiates came into this country from about 1930 to 1980 or so, right? The cops are just as criminal as the bad guys in this movie, only they have badges." He moved on.

"'Bourne Identity.' Great book. OK movie. Assassin, but a good guy, right? Bourne always has the moral high ground.

"And 'Bloody Sunday.' Terrorist massacre. Ever wonder why the idiots pick innocent targets when there are so many guilty targets to choose from?

"'The Last King of Scotland'—Forrest Whitaker played Idi Amin superbly. It's a morality tale about how power corrupts, right? Makes you wonder if a warlord can ever be a good guy."

Tadeus offered no reaction or opinion. But at least he looked at Charles and maybe settled down some.

"And then 'The Omen.' With the way things are going, I gotta wonder if the Antichrist is gonna show up soon." As he walked around from poster to poster, he examined every nook in the mostly bare apartment. He studied the windows and gained the ground knowledge that just might be needed later.

Tadeus waved his arm around. "So you watch the same movies. That supposed to make us friends for life? This is all fucking irrelevant. What's real is that you're fucking stealing my men."

"Do you have contracts with those men?" Charles asked.

"You're fuckin' right I do. They work for me, and I pay them. They stay loyal to me, or they fuckin' suffer pain. That's the contract."

Charles spoke calmly, his voice still gentle. "The first part of that is a contract. The second is a threat. So it's inherently void from inception." He straightened out the poster of *The Last King of Scotland* while he surreptitiously examined the locks on the inside of the door.

Tadeus said, "My men are my men."

The front-door buzzer signaled, and the Asian man retreated through the apartment door.

Charles watched Tadeus closely now, as the man's temper mounted. He shouldn't push too hard. But they would all have to know each other's stances. Might as well get them into the open. "Are you saying they don't have the freedom to take another job?"

"They fuckin' better not."

"They're not free to work for better pay, less risk, better hours, and better prospects for controlling their own destiny, their own fate?"

"Sure, they are. The harder they work for me, the more money they can make and the better their fate."

Charles replied, "But most still live with their parents. They aren't making much money, but they take a lot of risk. You aren't doing these men much good, Tadeus. And if you threaten them if they leave, then you're just enslaving them."

"Fuck that slavery shit. I pay them for their work. If they don't think I pay them enough, fuck 'em. They can get another fucking job cuz they ain't worth shit and I don't need them."

"So, are we agreed?" Charles put his hands in his overcoat pockets and stood directly facing Tadeus.

"What?"

"If they don't think you pay them enough, they can get another job. Your words, minus a couple of fucks and shits."

"Fuck you, *Paladin*. Fuck you."

"Tadeus. You can offer them a better deal, better pay. And your men may then choose to stay working with you. Otherwise, I might hire them. Alpha might hire them. Burger King might hire them. Whatever. They're free to leave. So to keep them you have to pay them more."

"If I pay them more, then I gotta charge more. People buy less, and I sure as fuck don't want that."

"Yes, that would seem to be bad, from your point of view. So, what do we do, Tadeus?"

"You get out of my fucking town. That's what we do."

"I'm not going to do that. So what do we do?"

"I fuckin' kill you right now."

Charles chuckled. "And I'd prefer you didn't do *that*."

The apartment door opened then, and the little Asian stepped in, followed by Tomo. Tomo stopped halfway through the door.

Charles watched Tomo's face turn from confusion to recognition to anger.

"Wha' da fuck?" Tomo looked over at the couch. "Tadeus, what this cracka here for?"

Charles greeted Tomo with a wave and wry smile.

Alpha nodded and simply said, "Tomo."

Tadeus frowned. "Paladin here stealing you too, Tomo?"

"What?"

Tadeus pointed at Charles. "This the guy been backing Alpha. Taking our crew."

"Yes, that's me," Charles interjected. "Like you, Tadeus, Tomo wants me dead. So I hear."

Tomo took two steps toward Charles, but Tadeus waved him back.

Charles took a sheet of paper from his left coat pocket. On it he had listed a few selected tidbits of information about Tadeus, information that he shouldn't have been able to acquire. "Read this." He reached out, and Tadeus took it.

Charles kept his right hand in another pocket where he held his .45-caliber 1911. It was his first choice for a handgun, although too large for easy concealment. His coat had deep pockets.

Tadeus stared at the note as Charles tucked his left hand back into his coat pocket.

"How did you fuckin' get this information? Was this shit from you?" He turned to Alpha.

Alpha leaned against a wall to his right and looked questioningly at Charles before replying. "Not me, Tadeus. I don't know what that is. Paladin knows things. Lots of things. But he don't necessarily tell me."

"Anyone who knows this shit don't live to tell it." Tadeus nodded to Tomo. "Take this trash outahere, Tomo. All the way out."

Tomo moved toward Charles again.

Alpha, gun now in hand, moved to block Tomo. "Back off, Tomo."

Charles saw a shadow move through the door behind and to Alpha's right.

"Down, Alpha!" Charles yelled as his left hand came back out of his coat pocket, armed with something that didn't look like a gun.

The green-haired Asian had emerged from the next room and flew through the air at Alpha, wielding a five-inch blade palm down. Alpha couldn't turn fast enough, and the man's body drove into his side, but the knife didn't move to cut flesh. Instead, it fell from the man's strained hand as a high-pitched continuous scream emerged from his frothing mouth. Alpha's attacker collapsed onto the floor. Two wires were embedded in the man's chest through his thin turtleneck. The wires coursed to the black device in Charles's left hand. Dozens of tiny pieces of paper floated down through the air like a ticker tape parade. His face expressionless, Charles held the trigger down on his Taser while the skunk man twitched and squealed in agony.

Tomo, Tadeus, and the fat man all watched the impromptu show, mesmerized.

Charles didn't focus on the writhing body. Instead, he had to watch both Tomo and Tadeus. Charles's eyes were colder than the sleet outside.

Alpha rose and looked down at the squirming figure. Drool soaked both the carpet and the green stripe in his hair.

"Tadeus," Charles said as if the room was otherwise sane, "if you kill me, the information you see in that letter will be provided automatically to certain friends of yours who won't appreciate what it says. And that will happen while my body is still warm."

Tadeus turned. "Fuck you, Paladin."

Charles released the trigger on the Taser. He pulled out his 1911; the hammer was already fully cocked. Its trigger required very little pressure. He raised the muzzle away from the floor, slowly, getting closer to Tadeus. "Oh, and to be clear, if those who might read this letter choose not to act, I've arranged with a friend for you to be … dealt with. Among other things, he's an expert shot with a rifle and a night scope." He glanced at Tomo knowingly. "Don't worry. You'll have some warning. He'll paint you with a red laser before he blows a hole through your chest."

Alpha had his gun aimed at Tomo again.

Charles said, "Tadeus, this leaves you the following choices. First, leave us be to conduct fair business with men who may choose to work for me. I'll leave you alone. That's easy, since we don't even sell the same products, or have the same customers. Second, you kill us, or even try to, and then you'll die yourself, with no doubt or alternative or equivocation. Killed by your friends, or killed by mine. Dead either way."

"If I leave you be, you take my men." Tadeus spat the words out like a challenge.

"We don't *take* anything from you. They may choose to work with us. They may choose to work with you. They may choose to work with us both. It is not for us to make those choices for them."

"I win nothing here."

"You can win. We can give you something, Tadeus."

"What?"

"We won't take your *customers*. We're not competing with you for dope fiends, crack addicts, or meth heads. We won't supply, distribute, or promote the products you sell. Look at it this way. We're like two stores on the same block. One sells food, the other sells hardware. We may compete for employees, but not for customers. In fact, people who come to my hardware store may get hungry and stop by your place. Who knows?"

"Mind if I sit in my own home?" Tadeus asked.

Charles slowly raised the muzzle of the 1911 the rest of the way, to the center of Tadeus's chest. He held the gun perfectly steady. The two men stood four feet apart. "Make yourself comfortable."

Tadeus sat back down next to the fat man. "Threatening a man in his own castle. Not a way to make friends, Paladin."

"I won't threaten you after today, Tadeus, assuming you don't threaten me or anyone who works for me, or any of my clients. If you start a war, no one will profit from it. You'll spend money and time and effort just watching your back. No one wins from that, Tadeus. But I'll lose a lot less than you."

"Your life is a lot to lose."

"A lot to lose, but with little likelihood."

"Who the hell *are* you?"

"I'm Paladin. And as I said, I won't threaten you if you don't threaten me. We can, in some manner, exist as neighbors."

Tadeus turned his head to look at the fat man, whose attention had returned to the television. Other than to stare at the tased man drooling on the floor, he hadn't budged the whole time.

Now the fat man looked at Tadeus and nodded slowly once.

"OK. Your way." Tadeus affirmed to Charles. "We do it your way."

"It's not my way, Tadeus. It's *the* way."

*   *   *

Charles and Alpha walked three blocks directly into the cold wind, ice assaulting their faces. Climbing into Charles's car provided some relief.

"Holy fuck, Paladin. Holy fuck."

Both men shivered and exhaled in unison as Charles started the car and blasted the defroster to clear the windshield. The wipers swept back-and-forth, making slow work of removing the layer of ice. Finally, he was able to pull into the street, maneuvering through the roads, starting the trip back to Southeast, eager to be away from Tomo, Tadeus, and the little green-haired butler.

"You think we pulled it off?" Charles asked.

"I think maybe we did. Maybe *you* did. But you was gonna get us killed in there."

"There's rarely profit in killing."

"You know that. I know that. Tadeus, he's not normal, though. He's emotional. Unpredictable. More than a little crazy. And he's into weird shit. That green streak of hair is just *one* of his little creatures."

"Yeah, I figured. Tadeus is a danger for sure. But he's not the one I'm most worried about."

"Yeah, Tomo's a loose cannon."

"No, not him."

"You mean the fat man?"

"Who was he?" Charles asked.

"Not seen him before. Tadeus's importer, maybe."

"Why do you think that?"

"The dude was calm, composed, cool," Alpha replied. "We didn't scare him."

Charles replied, "I agree. Fat Man's been in much worse situations. He saw that we were rational, talking sensible business, so he stayed at ease. He's probably more comfortable with us than he is with Tadeus."

"But he's dangerous."

Charles nodded. "I think so. Like Tadeus said, if there are fewer dealers on the street, there will be fewer people getting pushed, fewer users. Fat Man then sells less product to Tadeus."

Alpha agreed. "And Fat Man won't be liking that."

"And Fat Man won't get targeted if we're killed either. Only Tadeus."

Alpha nodded. "That's right." He added, "What was on that paper?"

Charles laughed. "It turns out that Tadeus is an occasional confidential informant to the DEA. He's been knocking out his competition by running to the G."

Just like the regular pharmaceutical companies, Charles thought.

Alpha shook his head. "Then he's a dead man walkin'."

"He is if word gets out. To the Fat Man, Tadeus is replaceable. We offered something to Tadeus. We told him we wouldn't compete with him. But Fat Man doesn't care about that. He just wants more distributors and end users. Right now, he's immune to the consequences of killing us, and will benefit from our deaths."

"I saw Tadeus get approval from him."

"So he's above Tadeus on the tree of life. Was that approval given in order to end the excitement, do you think?"

Alpha replied, "Maybe. After we left, he might have told Tomo to kill us."

"So what do we do about the Fat Man?"

"We need to learn, first, who that guy is. Then we need to figure all the angles."

"I'm with you. Let's learn and figure fast though. I don't like the idea of being dead."

"Me either, Paladin. So, you wanna go meet the next guy, or have you had enough for one evening?"

Charles thought for a moment, analyzing his condition. His heart still beat hard. "I've got good blood flow. I'm good to go that way." Then Charles thought better of it. "But I'm not prepared. We got time. We can do this slowly and carefully. More carefully than tonight, right? What do you say we call it a night."

Alpha shrugged. "Oh, Paladin, next time someone tries to knife me, would you mind shooting him with a real gun instead of that pansy-ass Taser?"

"Sure, pal. But killing Tadeus's weird squeeze would've started a war for sure, one that we're trying to avoid. Just think, that Taser gave you a ticker tape parade."

"What was that stuff?"

"Stupidity. It's the registration number for that Taser typed onto confetti. When the Taser's fired, those pieces of paper release all over the scene. Cops can trace who owns the Taser because the company does a felony background check on all their buyers."

"So with the help of a cop friend, Tadeus could trace you? What you thinking, boy?"

There were certain little joys in life that Charles provided for himself—little bits of pleasure that no one else would understand. Charles looked at Alpha after he made the next turn on the increasingly slick streets. "Nah. Their system isn't foolproof. I registered that Taser using the name of the chairman of the Federal Reserve."

15

A Parolee and an
Enemy of the State

AS a parole officer in the Big Apple, Anthony Scibbera spent his professional life lying. He certainly misled the people who wrote his paychecks. But it wasn't like the people who paid him were worthy of much respect. Or even deserved of the truth. At least not all the truth all the time.

Anthony—everybody except Jeffrey called him Tony—acted as a fifth column, working against the team whose uniform he wore. Why would he do such a thing? Because, as it turns out, his team was wicked.

Tony was quiet and subtle, but a revolutionary: an underground agent only pretending to work for the alien invaders that had taken over his country.

He sported a large mustache, the kind that might have been found on an Ottoman Janissary of the 1800s. It was his one affectation. Likely it turned some women away. But, thank heavens, not all of them.

Living a professional life of lies contributed to his substantial stress, but he had support. He had taken a year off after college to travel the world and write, and some of his writing got published. His writing brought him to the attention of the man who recruited him to the underground.

In his mind, his real boss was Jeffrey. Jeffrey was a man's man, and his scars proved it. Tony did not have a single scar anywhere on his skin, and wanted to keep it that way; he wasn't into action or violence. Although they rarely met, Jeffrey provided Tony's only connection into the underground, to the *Island*, to the place that just might be the future of the world. He had been there, once.

He spent today, like every day, in the mindless bureaucratic machine, trying to pull people out of its gears before they were crushed to pulp. He would have preferred throwing a monkey wrench into its gears, but he had to avoid discovery, or he would, himself, be mangled by the machine. At most he could add some friction by dropping some well-directed sand into the machine: misplace a file, check a few extra boxes, put in a good word for the right person, and by so doing, one at a time, throw a dying starfish off the beach back into the sea to live another day.

Of course many of the people he processed were just garden-variety scumbags; the system almost never made them better, and generally made them worse. They'd stay criminals until they became too burned-out for the game. But, occasionally, he could dig an unopened tin of caviar from the garbage. He knew how to game the machine, and how to make it send him the people with whom he wanted to interact. People who might identify with the underground.

Lawbreakers, not criminals.

Per the system, Tony was not supposed to cut anybody slack.

"You do it by the book. And if you don't, you're breaking the law. And you're an idiot if you stick your neck out for one of these lowlifes." That's what they told him during orientation, many years back. It was the prime directive, dictating the corporate culture of the robots that logged hours in the gray, depressing office.

That instruction still came repeatedly from his supervisor, who'd started out as a screw on Riker's Island, but moved up in the world. Tony suspected why the guy went to work in a prison, a place no normal person even wanted to visit. And where, as a screw, he knew everyone hated him. The guy was more degraded and bent than the people he'd guarded. Maybe he'd jockeyed for his promotion to this office because he could hurt more people, Tony thought, for more money and less risk, than he could at Riker's.

Tony was hired to just be a cog in one of the machine's wheels, and to do as he was told until he retired with a sweet pension. Instead, he chose to fight the underground war against it.

He glanced at his schedule. Albert Peale was next. Good. He liked Peale.

"How are things going with the *Weekly Observer*?" Tony asked Peale as soon as he sat down.

"It's been a long winter, but it's almost over."

Albert Peale was a mostly bald investigative journalist, small in size, but bighearted. Despite having lived in New York City for all of his seventy years, he remained uninterested in most financial stories. He saw himself as a people person, not a money person. Unfortunately, his lack of interest in money matters caught up with him. His poor tax accounting at his small newspaper conspired with his naïve bravery and his willingness to critique some powerful politicians. The politicians railroaded him into the slammer for three months, and now into the probation system for three more years.

Peale's treatment stemmed from his being just a bit too persistent, digging up some dirt that certain people preferred to stay buried beneath other layers of dirt. Peale thought it was unjust. But the people who felt threatened thought he got what he deserved for sticking his nose where it didn't belong. When a system senses a threat, it will try to neutralize that threat. Attack the system, and you can expect a counterattack. All organisms—amoebas, persons, corporations, or governments—have at least one thing in common: a prime directive to *survive!* The system went after Peale and tried to seal him off from the world. When Peale got out on probation, Tony had swooped in to claim him.

Tony enjoyed seeing Peale, one of the tins of caviar. Peale served as a reminder of his true purpose.

"Spring is coming, and things are going to start getting better, Tony."

"Yeah?"

"Yeah. I think I'm onto something that's going to get my paper some real attention going forward. Start making some money finally."

"Fantastic. I want you to tell me more, but let's check off the damn boxes first. You know the drill. Are you well?" It wasn't an idle query. The paper on the clipboard in his lap had a numbered list of questions for which the system demanded answers.

"Yes."

"Employed? I'll check that off. Have you ventured more than fifty miles outside of Manhattan?"

"No."

"Are you using any illegal drugs?"

Peale didn't answer right away, and Tony looked up at him.

"Peale, you're not using drugs, are you?"

"Tony, this stuff is really interesting." Peale addressed him as a human being, not a parole officer.

Tony's shoulders fell perceptibly. "What are you talking about, Peale?" He didn't care about drug use per se, but the system sure did, and he did not like wasting his time trying to cover for some probie's drug use. Junkies were always unreliable, untrustworthy. The first to squeal and roll over. Even if they had other good qualities, you were a fool to rely on them. He was annoyed and surprised that he had, it seemed, misread Peale.

It had been a better-than-average day so far, dealing with some of his favorites—the subversives infiltrating the hive mind of a system that feared them. Peale was a favorite. But he wouldn't be for long. Tony had to conserve his energies for what Jeffrey paid him to do: protect the good probies from the bad system. He avoided trying to redeem lost causes.

Peale responded to Tony's exasperation. "It's not illegal. It's this new *prescription* drug."

"Peale, what are you talking about? You're gonna have to show me your prescription. You know the drill. Anything you put in your body besides food, including what your doctor prescribes, has to be reported. I may not always be here for you. If someone else in this office nails you with a random drug test, you go back to the can. You know I'm on your side. But there are limits…"

"Shit, Tony, you know I'm not into drugs. Never have been."

"So, what are you talking about?"

"The wife of a friend of mine. She's been suicidal for a long time. Since childhood, I think. She keeps trying different ways to sorta kill herself. She never succeeds. Maybe it's a cry for help."

"Sounds like a borderline personality." *Borderline* described adults, mostly women, who never psychologically matured past about age eleven years, even when they were thirty. Tony had seen his share. Impossible to cure, and very difficult to interact with, borderlines often undertook intentionally unsuccessful suicide attempts in a dysfunctional effort to manipulate people. They might superficially slash the skin on their wrists, or threaten to jump off a moving bus.

Avoid borderlines if at all possible, Tony advised his probies. "Hanging around with crazy people tends to make you crazy, Peale. I don't have to lecture you about hanging around with these people."

"Yes, that's her. Borderline. Well, they gave her some brand new antidepressant. Came out less than a month ago. It's inhaled. It's called Sybillene. Supposed to be great, works real fast. Well, she gets home from the pharmacy with it and does her thing—you know, she's supposed to take one puff, but instead she sucks in like ten puffs of the stuff in a half-hearted attempt to OD on it, right? That's just the way she is. But it doesn't kill her. It doesn't even make her sick."

"So what happens?"

"My friend said it made her think clearly."

Interesting, Tony thought, *but probably crap.* He politely prodded, "What, like smarter?"

"Yes, smarter, more rational. I don't know what she'd look like on an IQ test, but she's less flighty. Much more together. She said she could see that she was being an idiot always trying to cut herself, poison herself."

"A cure for borderline personality? You can't cure that."

"Well, maybe you can. She's doing great, my friend says. I went over to their place, and she seemed like a new person. Hasn't tried to knock herself off in weeks."

"A lot of these psychoactive prescription drugs might seem to improve horrible situations, but mostly by turning people into zombies. Or tightening down the lid on a pressure cooker, with nasty side effects. Maybe it's just a coincidence. Maybe she's just not stressed right now. Who knows why she's acting normal?"

"Maybe, Tony. But she's toking the Sybillene three times daily, ten puffs at a time, going through the stuff like water. And she's not the only example. Here, look at this. It's Sybillene." Peale handed his probation officer a green plastic inhalation device that resembled an asthma inhaler.

Tony turned it around in his hand.

"So I tried it, Tony. I took a couple of puffs. That did nothing. So I took a few more. Nothing. But I took ten puffs and then something weird happened."

"Peale, I'm your probation officer. Did you forget that?"

"Oh, screw that." Peale dropped his voice to a near whisper. "I'm almost seventy. I don't really give a damn. That's a big advantage of being over the hill. Plus, I know you aren't any normal probation officer. You aren't here to screw me back into the joint. That's not what you're about. You're more like a guardian angel."

151

Tony chuckled. None of his charges had any idea how close to the truth that was. "Peale, I can't protect you from being stupid."

"But that's what I'm saying. It isn't stupid. Sybillene makes you smart."

"Did you actually get smarter? You gonna win the Nobel Prize for General Brilliance next week?"

"Look, Tony, this is subjective. It's not as if I can prove it with a controlled study. I don't mean academically smart. But clear thinking, perceptive, street smart. Most drugs cloud your perception, distort the way your mind works, make you lie to yourself. Not this stuff. This stuff helps you see reality. For instance, I understood something I had never grasped before."

"Go on."

"Yeah, well, I was thinking about the business, my paper. So I was thinking about money. I was looking at some cash just before I took the Sybillene. I'd just watched the movie 'National Treasure,' and pulled a dollar bill out of the pile to look at it. I had been looking at the details on it, the eye in the pyramid and whatnot, for a while before I inhaled the Sybillene. Right after that, like within like a minute, the dollar bill started to make some sense."

"What do you mean?" Tony's forehead wrinkled as he listened.

"Scattered bits of information I had in the back of my mind came together. Look, when I was a kid the dollar bill used to say *silver certificate*. I remember that. Back then, it wasn't just paper. A store clerk would give you real silver for it. Four quarters or ten dimes, because back then those coins were silver. In fact, before 1933 all the paper money in this country was redeemable in gold or silver coins. In 1933, Roosevelt pulled all the gold coins out of circulation; they made it illegal to use gold as money. During the Vietnam War, they stopped redeeming the silver certificates for silver and took silver out of all the coins. The dollar bill used to be a promise to give you money, but now it's just a promise to give you another piece of paper. Now look at this." He took a dollar bill out of his pocket. "It says *Federal Reserve Note*. Is it any wonder that the dollar doesn't buy what it used to? It isn't the same dollar!"

Peale stayed silent for a minute, as if reflecting, so Tony prodded. "What do you mean?"

"I mean that the dollar is now just a lie. It's counterfeit." He waved the Federal Reserve note in the air in the middle of the parole office and raised his voice. "This thing is just an *IOU nothing*!"

152

"Hey, keep it down, Peale. The system here is light in the humor department."

Peale dropped his voice and looked around sheepishly. "With all I've been writing about, and all I've read, I must have known this in the back of my mind. But I've never been a money guy. Now it's become crystal clear."

It was an unusual insight, and Peale had just raised one of the issues that the underground considered most important. Yet Peale had never before hinted that he cared in the least about such matters.

Peale spoke more quietly. "This piece of paper is designed to help the bankrupt federal government pretend it's rich—they can create trillions of them. They use these things to bribe states and local governments and voters too. It's done through the banking system. The banks buy government debt with fake money. And they credit the government's account with Federal Reserve notes—dollars."

"Money from nothing?"

"Yeah. You ought to do a little research. I did, after I had this insight. Before the Federal Reserve was created in 1913, banks could only lend the money that was deposited with them. They were real banks then. They kept your money secure if you put it in a checking account, but they charged you. If you wanted to earn interest, you opened a savings account, where they would loan it out, once, for interest. They paid you three percent, charged the borrower six percent. Now, the banks get to loan out your money ten times over, because the borrower redeposits it into his own account. You couldn't do that, but *they* can. The government and the banks don't produce goods or services for money like we have to. They essentially counterfeit it. It's the biggest fraud ever committed. The banks and the government win, and the people get hosed."

"Hosed how?" How much did Peale, seemingly quite out of the blue, suddenly understand? Could it really be this ... Sybillene?

"Remember, it is *fake* money that gets loaned to the government, but the taxpayers have to work *real* jobs to service the government's debt. People end up working to pay for the whips and chains that their masters abuse them with."

"I've not heard it said that way before."

Peale's enthusiasm seemed boundless. "If you double the number of dollars, then sooner or later prices for everything will double. That's what inflation is all about. Inflation isn't caused by the greedy butcher, baker, or gasoline maker; it's what happens when the Fed and the banks create dollars out of thin air. They do it to feed the government's addiction to spending, and the bankers take a percentage. The average guy tries to save dollars, but they're constantly losing value as the Fed creates more of them. It's criminally insane. People's life savings are stolen bit by bit, while the government is empowered and the banks are enriched."

Tony was surprised, not by Peale's insight, but by Peale himself. This recognition was common knowledge among libertarian economists and historians who were trying to expose the realities of this evil *to* the people, and among those at the very top of the major banks that parasitized *off* the people. But no more than a tiny fraction of the population at large had a clue how they were being conned every day. Sure, the government took in a huge amount in taxes. But it took in almost as much again, using the banking system, through printing money.

Peale somehow had the wool pulled off his financially ignorant eyes— apparently by means of an inhaled antidepressant. It had taken Tony years of reading before he fully understood the nature of money.

Tony knew too that, as with all frauds, the U.S. dollar was a precariously constructed house of cards. Or rather a *mansion* of cards. What they were doing to the dollar would destroy what America was meant to be. As the scheme fell apart, the government would maintain control by employing increasing amounts of force.

That future had already arrived. "So Peale, you've never given this any thought before?"

Peale replied, "Not really. Almost nobody thinks about these things. But that's the fantastic thing about this drug. Sybillene's not like other drugs—it doesn't give you a high like coke. It doesn't take you to an alternate reality like peyote. It doesn't fog your mind like pot or most psychoactive prescription medications. It *clears* your mind. It doesn't give you visions like acid—it lets you see what's actually in front of you. It doesn't make you *feel* powerful, like meth—it actually gives you the power to think."

"Any side effects?"

"Not that I've noticed, or at least nothing you don't want. And it gets better. It doesn't just help you think clearly, it helps you see through all sorts of lies. It works when you're listening to news shows. Watching commercials. Listening to politicians talk. When I use it, I can see when the emperor isn't wearing any clothes."

Tony pulled on the tip of his mustache. "There are lots of naked emperors wandering around these days. It helps you see through lies, huh?"

Peale nodded. "It's not like it gives you knowledge. But it does help you to understand knowledge. I think you have to know something about what you are looking at for this, uhh, *Naked Emperor* stuff to work."

At that moment, Albert Peale invented the street name for high-dose Sybillene.

Of course, neither man knew the significance of this exchange. Not then.

Tony asked, "What do you mean?"

"Naked Emperor doesn't tell you what you don't know. It tells you what you know but can't recognize, or won't admit."

Tony studied Peale carefully. If what Peale said were true, Naked Emperor would change the nature of the world. *If* it were true. He sighed. It seemed unlikely.

"And you think ten puffs of this Sybillene stuff," Tony raised the green plastic tube, "caused you to see all this?"

"I think it did. The stuff gets into your brain fast. It takes the blinders off. It's a little scary…"

"Maybe it does, Peale. But it *is* illegal for you to be using this stuff, because you don't have a prescription for it."

"Whatever. You ain't gonna ding me for that; I have you figured out." Peale smiled conspiratorially.

"Yes, maybe you have. But you aren't the only one I have to protect. I have others under my charge. I can't risk them all if I let *you* get away with doing something stupid that some other PO catches you on while I'm on vacation. I can't protect you from stupidity."

Peale smiled as he picked at a rough spot on his fingernail. "You know how I figured you out, Tony? I took ten puffs of this stuff, and I figured you out. Or at least I made a damn good guess." He dropped his voice to a whisper. "You don't work for *them*, do you?" He waved his arm around the open floor of the office, filled with shoulder-high cubicles populated by an army of probation officers, civil servants deciding who has to go back in front of the judge and off to prison, and who stays clear. "You work to help me keep doing what I do, running the newspaper. I bet you don't even work for the state of New York. Not really. You work for someone else, some uberwealthy guy who thinks he's fighting for truth, justice, and the American way. And maybe he is. You're working for Batman. Isn't that true, Tony?"

Tony chuckled inwardly. Jeffrey would get a laugh out of being compared to Batman. Nobody had previously suspected what Peale had just stated. The truth itself was actually even more grandiose, some might say paranoid. Maybe there was something to this Sybillene stuff. *Naked Emperor.*

"Peale, you want me to keep doing what I do, don't you?"

"Yes."

"Then never mention what you just said about me to anyone else."

"I would never. Sybillene told me what would happen if I told anyone about you."

"Yeah?" That was a bit ridiculous. "What did Sybillene say would happen?"

"You wouldn't just get fired, Tony. You'd likely get killed."

Maybe Peale was right about that. Tony served as an underground operator, a traitor to the collective political mind. And traitors, when discovered, suffered capital punishment, or died before trial. Sure, it wasn't a civil war with armies and shooting. But a war raged nonetheless, and he was a subversive: an enemy of the state.

The planet was ruled by people whose money and power depended on a constant supply of deceit. Tony was a guerrilla warrior, working in the system, but not for it. This Sybillene, this Naked Emperor, just might be a major weapon—if Peale wasn't deluding himself.

That was a problem with so many who went through this office. Most had an angle; most were running some kind of scam. No matter how much he may have liked them, he couldn't trust them. In this dark world, deception was as natural as sex and as necessary as food. But if Peale wasn't just shucking and jiving for some reason, this Sybillene stuff had some real potential.

He would check it out and talk to Jeffrey.

Tony could not know that another person in New York City, a man with nearly unlimited money and power, had also just become aware of this new psychoactive drug. And that man also thought Naked Emperor might change the world. But he was determined not to let that happen.

And when that particular man became so absolutely determined, even Leviathan would bend to his will.

*   *   *

None of Dr. Paul Samuels's staff related to him—beyond a polite "Good morning, Dr. Samuels," or "May I get you a coffee, Dr. Samuels," or a "I'll have that file for you immediately, Dr. Samuels." He had no friends—no old pals from high school, college, or grad school. No golfing or bridge buddies. None of his many minions knew anything about his personal life—if, indeed, he even had one. Paul Samuels lived the life of a workaholic. The elite respected his knowledge, but didn't like him. His analytical ability and judgment earned him a reputation for exquisite foresight. So people wanted him on their team, whether or not they enjoyed his company. And nobody enjoyed his company.

But his lack of charm hadn't stopped his climb to the peak of power and wealth. He savored providing policies, strategies, and plans to high government officials, and he held to an ideological framework that aligned well with those who had guided his career. He was a reincarnation of Machiavelli or Richelieu or Bismarck.

Somewhere in the dim past, Paul Samuels had been a college student, and may have even had fun, once or twice. After college he'd worked as a sell-side hack at a Wall Street sweatshop, but soon fled to graduate school where he learned all the magical power of modern economic philosophy before returning to Wall Street, where he engaged in some successful gambles with other people's money. This, along with a fortunate comment at a panel discussion, brought him to the attention of the Federal Reserve—where he took up a research position for a year before migrating to the U.S. Treasury with a concurrent professorial position in academia. Augmented by these credentials, he parlayed his Treasury gig into a highly paid position at the most powerful Wall Street investment bank, an entity that covered the financial face of America like a giant vampire squid. He increasingly associated with the people who mattered, providing the academic rigor they valued. And so, through a combination of innate intelligence, hard work, good fortune, and connections, he recently had become the president of the New York Federal Reserve Bank.

The papers he'd written in his first Fed stint had remained influential. The elite within the Fed recognized the importance of his particular field of economic investigation, which, however, remained unknown to outsiders. They declared his work to be, in essence, a continuing top secret project.

Early in life, while but a minion himself, he'd killed his wife one night in a moment of uncontrolled frustration. He'd since blanked from his mind what had triggered the murder. It had long ago ceased to matter. The death of his wife was attributed to an unidentified thief that had invaded their house—a fairly simple fabrication that garnered him sympathy as well as freedom.

He had no children of his own, but his wife's daughter became his. He hired superb nannies for her, and ensured that she received a first-rate, albeit conventional, education. Although he worked constantly, he undertook much of it from home, giving him time with his daughter. He considered her a project, a physical projection of his legacy. He taught her how he thought, how he put useful valuations on objects and people, and how he obtained what he wanted, whatever that might be. Much more interesting, and useful, than playing with dolls…

But over time, for reasons he failed to comprehend, she grew distant. He rarely heard from her anymore.

Samuels leaned forward on his desk, which was the size of a small aircraft carrier, and turned his attention to a report he'd requested.

He was pleased to see that a young woman who'd come to his attention years before had authored the report. He trusted her work far more than most. Over time, in some ways, she had taken the place of his stepdaughter. He started to deem her a project too. And so he taught her how he thought and how he obtained what he wanted. Unlike his stepdaughter, she absorbed his teaching like a sponge.

The report made it clear she hadn't just gleaned low-hanging and fallen fruit. She'd actually gone out and aggressively harvested data. Her report fleshed out the earlier one-page document, but he needed much more information.

Most people would ignore the issue in question, but Samuels stood at the very top of his profession for a reason. He didn't get there without getting a whole lot right.

He read the pages carefully. The document gave him some hope, but did not entirely alleviate his concerns. They had been here before, and by *they* he meant his predecessors. And they had barely gotten through that period of history. It was a drug that had prompted the danger back then, just like now. But this drug might be much more of a threat, and be even more difficult to eliminate.

Maybe the company that made this Sybillene stuff would fail out of the gate. Maybe FDA would take it off the market.

He wouldn't count on maybes.

His mind sent thought tendrils out toward the possible futures, anticipating what would materialize if this drug were allowed to persist in the world.

What he saw was destruction of their whole system.

He rarely sought the input of others in similar positions around the globe—the quiet monarchs of the financial world. Should Einstein have consulted with a group of high school algebra teachers? Of course not. Besides, he had time to act on his own.

He would, however, need eyes on the ground at FDA. Someone he could trust implicitly. He knew just what he would do. And just who he would send.

But he'd need a favor to make it happen.

Samuels picked up the phone and called the president of the United States.

16

Truth and Consequences

DONALD Debocher's new job turned out to be boring. He knew better, but had fantasized accompanying his own SWAT team, wearing flak jackets and gas masks to shut down companies, guns ablazing. But that was DEA territory. Being director of enforcement for FDA provided no such excitement.

As a matter of fact, he really didn't have much to do. The thought crossed his mind: perhaps he'd been kicked upstairs.

A file awaited on his desk: an informational bulletin, written by a junior clinical reviewer at the Center for Drug Evaluation and Research, about some minor adverse event. Scrawled in pen on the filing tab at the top was the subject title "Visioryme—Sybillene." Approved three months ago, the stuff had only been actively on the market for four weeks.

He'd been hoping to avoid what was likely inevitable in this new job. If this file contained a can of worms, would he screw the cover down tight? Would he protect his wife's interests at risk of his own career?

His wife's company had become substantially Charles Knight's company, not really hers anymore, even though she still thought of it that way and owned a ton of shares. Knight had a controlling interest, and although he had declined to take any official position in management, she now essentially worked for him. Knight had bought the results of her hard work with money that, near as Donald could tell, derived from his role in a gigantic mining fraud in Africa. Knight was young, good-looking, rich, very sure of himself, and now worked closely with Tristana at Visioryme. Far too closely.

An image of the two of them together intruded into every corner of his mind. She obviously respected him, even put him on a pedestal, and almost certainly lusted after him. Donald's mouth turned down at the passing thought.

He could see, when they talked during those rare dinners at home, that her eyes brightened involuntarily when she mentioned Knight, glistening like those of an incandescent whore trying to attract new clients. Then her eyes would return to normal, only to become those of a vixen in heat again, just for a flash, at the next mention of his name. He suspected Knight passed through her mind in those moments, that Knight elicited a Pavlovian response in her. And the moments happened far too often. The left side of his upper lip, as he sat at his desk, lifted in vulgar envy as he imagined Knight with her, touching her, taking her.

He knew their marriage was coming to an end, their life together now increasingly an exercise in mutual antagonism. It had been good for a while, when they had first married, both starry-eyed about their futures in the drug business. A public-private partnership. They even made jokes about how she would create drugs just so he could enjoy trying to stop her. But, as the old saw goes, women hope men will change, and men hope women never will. She changed. She wasn't that same trusting person, confident the system would protect her and work for her if she just did her part. She had stopped cooperating and no longer enjoyed the game. She seemed selfish, bitter, and angry.

FDA had been good to her and her company. They had given Visioryme the benefit of the doubt. In the old boy network that controlled FDA, he'd been able to subtly and quietly speed things along. His intercessions and nudges had saved the company years of time and perhaps hundreds of millions of dollars that FDA would otherwise have demanded. In fact, in his mind, he was as much responsible for the company's success as any of its scientists or lawyers. But she didn't see that she was practically getting a free ride. All she did was complain about how slow FDA was, how much money and time it cost them, and how FDA demoralized her staff.

Ungrateful bitch.

He knew that all married couples change over time. Sometimes growing at different rates, sometimes in different directions—and that was the best case. Sometimes one partner might expand while the other contracts into a ball like a slug exposed to light. Especially when they married young, when few really knew who they were, or what they'd eventually want.

Tristana had changed too much, become too selfish. She no longer wanted what was best, just what was best *for her*. He was now pretty sure she thought *Knight* was best for her.

It was as if his own work at FDA, abiding by the rules and now enforcing them, was neither noble enough nor adventurous enough for her. If she wanted the excitement of being manhandled by the bad boy type, the playboy, the criminal, the dark person Knight certainly must be, well, then she wasn't worth holding on to. Be done with her.

But he hated the thought of Knight winning, while he, the good guy, lost.

He grasped the file and began reading. He analyzed every word.

Sybillene's dark secret *had* been found.

There were three reports. Isolated, apparently harmless, but strange. Three reports to the FAERS—the FDA Adverse Effects Reporting System—of strange events occurring in association with Sybillene use. No harm. No danger. No sickness. Just strange.

Of course, these things were like cockroaches; if you saw one, you certainly had an infestation. And if three reports had been sent to the voluntary FAERS system, that meant there were hundreds of unreported events.

In his mind, nothing FDA needed should be voluntary. But for this one case, he was glad it was.

He thought for a long minute, staring at the cover of the folder. He struggled to balance competing interests, and in the end carefully tucked it into the bottom of a drawer in his desk. It would go unnoticed, for a time at least. Maybe it would go away. It was amazing how adverse effects of modern pharmaceuticals could be ignored if the drug had friends in the bureaucracy.

He could rediscover the file anytime, if need be.

Knight might own most of Visioryme, but Tristana, and therefore he himself, was a substantial shareholder. And since FDA had waived his conflict of interest, there was little point in shooting himself in the foot. Although the company's share price had spiked on FDA's approval, it had then fallen back. If Visioryme became financially successful, its share price would rise, and he would win big. If it failed, well, then it failed. He would be almost as happy to crush Knight as to pocket millions of dollars.

His phone buzzed. "Mr. Debocher, I have two gentlemen from Freich-Planck Pharmaceuticals here for your two o'clock. Then Ms. Heidel is waiting here to see you right after."

He couldn't remember what either meeting was about.

"Send in the Freich-Planck gentlemen."

Donald held decidedly mixed feelings about the slick executives from Big Pharma. They typically earned several times more than he could ever hope to at FDA, not counting their stock options. They somehow managed to look down on him even while they played at being obsequious. It was as if they thought they owned FDA. But he knew he could ruin their day, any day, every day. Some days the master kicked the dog, and some days the dog bit the master. Most days, it was hard to tell who was who.

Freich-Planck probably wanted to coax his cooperation in their massive lobbying efforts to ensure that their new $1,000-per-month drug for opiate abuse would find its way into the bloodstream of the nation. The company was encouraging every level of government to mandate it and subsidize it. To that end, they'd been stoking the media with stories about the rapid growth of the *opiate epidemic.* Clearly, the company was anxious to become an addict to the huge profits their mediocre drug would generate.

Donald stood up from behind his well-manicured desk to greet them as they came through the door.

"Good of you to see us, Mr. Debocher. I'm Frank Starwell, chief counsel of Freich-Planck." The man passed over a business card.

"Stone Timmons, vice president of compliance and regulatory affairs." His card found its way likewise into Donald's hand.

Big players, not low-level stooges. Something else was up.

"Well, what can FDA do for Freich-Planck?" Donald asked, activating his best customer-service-oriented political attitude. "Please, sit." He indicated a maroon vinyl sofa and the three chrome-and-black vinyl office chairs nearby.

Starwell—the alpha male in this room—towered over Donald, who couldn't help but feel intimidated. He spoke fluently, never stammering, with clear tones, fine enunciation, and profound confidence. It was as if he were not only in charge of this FDA office, and his company, but the country and the world as well.

"Mr. Debocher, information has been trickling in to Freich-Planck about an imported generic version of Viagra, being sold mostly in the

Washington, D.C., area. We think this has been going on for several months now, and seems to be accelerating. The drug is misbranded, sir; it hasn't gone through FDA channels. We were afraid you might not yet have heard about it."

Donald nodded sagely, but had no previous knowledge of it. Viagra was not a Freich-Planck drug. So why did they care? He asked, "And this interests you because…?"

"Here in D.C., we've seen some unexpected small declines in the sales volumes of our own branded erectile-dysfunction medication, Goplena. Just a couple of percentage points. We checked into the situation and discovered this illegal importation scheme. It's not much volume. But we're concerned for public safety."

Donald understood now. "FDA appreciates your concerns about public safety, and keeping us informed. The nutshell, however, is that Freich-Planck is feeling spillover from illegal competition?"

"Hardly anything. But it's better to nip these things in the bud."

Donald rubbed his chin, mostly bored. These guys would take forever to do their postapproval regulatory paperwork, but would pound on FDA's door to jump all over some illegal competitor as if the world was going to end. "What's Pfizer doing? They got their patent on Viagra extended. Aren't they protecting it?"

"We don't know. I'm sure you'll agree, it would be improper for us to discuss problems with a competitor."

"So you want FDA to intervene."

"This generic Viagra, as I said, is misbranded."

"What is the stuff?" Misbranding was one of those critical issues, something that FDA could not allow.

"It's manufactured by Cintina Pharmaceuticals, an Indian company. The drug goes by the name Fiagara. We have reports of it being sold in D.C. and Baltimore, and we now suspect New York and Boston as well. It's spreading."

"Honestly gentlemen, this is the first FDA has heard of it. A threat to your bottom line, perhaps, but not a crisis. Is Cintina directly marketing it?"

"I spoke with their general counsel, and of course they deny providing any of their drug for sale in the U.S. Nor does the company have any marketing or sales presence here in the U.S."

"What else do you know about it? Is it the real drug at least?"

"We doubt it, Mr. Debocher. We suspect it is loaded with melamine and fillers, with very little actual drug."

The regulatory man, Stone Timmons, added, "Very little API."

Donald nodded, but he knew they hadn't actually looked. He could tell by how confidently they lied. It would be quite unusual for a drug containing little or no API—the active pharmaceutical ingredient—to be sold in the U.S. Companies had far more to lose than to gain by shorting customers. Most drugs cost nearly nothing to manufacture; chemicals are cheap. The big expenses lay in regulatory approvals and marketing, not API.

He said, "Do you have any of it in hand?"

"Just a few."

"*With* you?"

Timmons shuffled through his briefcase and pulled out a Ziploc bag containing a foil-wrapped package of ten blue pills. He gave it to Donald, who examined it front and back.

"Looks high-end. Not street stuff. We can send this to the lab and check its exact composition. But I suspect you're mistaken about it being counterfeit, Mr. Starwell."

"It's misbranded because Cintina's drug isn't FDA approved for sale in the U.S. We're here to inform you, as chief of the enforcement division, of the fact it's being sold in the United States."

"I hear you, gentlemen." This must really be affecting their revenues more than they admitted.

"We have only the safety of the public at heart."

"Of course. Well, if you supply all the information you have, I'll get someone on my team to start looking into it."

Starwell replied, "We sincerely thank you for your time."

The exchange confirmed that, as much as he'd like to change salaries with them, Big Pharma execs were uptight assholes. They came whining for help from him, over just a fraction decline in sales. "I'll see what FDA can do about this situation, gentlemen."

But he didn't mean it.

He showed the men out of his office, and caught sight of his next appointment, who sat primly just beyond his secretary's desk. She had caught sight of him too, and smiled.

"Ms. Heidel is it?"

She nodded.

"Please come in."

He held the door open and inhaled as she stepped past. By so doing, he enlarged his chest, sucked in his gut, and had the opportunity to register her scent, all at once.

"Please call me Sabina." She provided neither business card nor a title, and Donald tilted his head to indicate he expected more information, but he didn't get any. She moved directly to sit on the maroon sofa to the side of his still-new office.

He closed the door, and when he turned back, she had her shoes off and her feet resting on his glass table. It was somewhat irregular to have one's feet up on a table during a business meeting, but as Donald's brain refocused from its neocortex to the limbic areas, her feet didn't bother him.

"Ms. Heidel? Sabina?"

"Mr. Debocher. Since we are going to be working together, perhaps I can call you Donald?"

Donald sat down on the black chair adjacent to the couch. Sabina's brilliant red hair, obviously not her natural tone, clashed with the sofa, but that hardly mattered to Donald. He wasn't looking at her hair.

"Please do." He had no idea who this person was. "Who are you with, Sabina?"

She didn't answer. Instead she said, "I'm here to learn everything I can from you, in your role as the chief of the Enforcement Division. And to provide whatever assistance is needed. Consider me your special assistant. You tell me what you need, and I'll make sure you get it. We should work hand in hand, constantly."

He studied her closely. "Are you sure you're in the right place?"

She replied, "Pardon?"

"I apologize. I don't recall that I ever asked for a special assistant."

"Oh, Donald," she laughed. "You didn't."

"Explain?"

She reached and placed her hand on his knee. His eyes, like those of fifteen-year-old boy, fell victim to nature. He stared down her dress, and his imagination ran free. She noticed. And he didn't care.

Her voice drew Donald in like a siren's song. "The president assigned me as part of the Government Efficiency Enhancement Initiative."

Donald was aware of the ridiculous program, and hoped he'd never have anything to do with the rigmarole it entailed. But it was well known to be the president's pet program to improve government function. Today's lovely surprise visitor constituted his first actual exposure to it. If all the people temporarily moved from one agency to another looked like Sabina Heidel, he'd sign up.

The thought of spending time with this woman enticed him. The problem was that he had few interesting tasks he could assign her.

But he did have something.

Donald stood, walked to his phone, and pressed the intercom for his secretary. "Yes. Cancel my afternoon meeting with Hill and Domm. Reschedule for the AM. I need to orient Ms. Heidel for a while. And check on the availability of Seth Fowler at DEA to meet with me. Sometime tomorrow perhaps. Tell him it's a contraband-drug case."

He went back to Sabina and sat down.

She, with obvious intent, moved closer.

*　　*　　*

The three women sat around a kitchen table.

Suzy felt the excitement that comes from instigating a conspiracy. "So y'all really wanna do this?"

Her friend from the club, Holly, whose natural beauty was enhanced by diligent diet, exercise, and cosmetic surgery, and diminished by chronically poor self-esteem, could not contain her excitement. "I do! What the hell, if it kills us, it kills us."

Kerri, the most intellectually inclined of the three, added, "If it doesn't kill us, it'll make us stronger. It didn't kill me. It helped me clarify my thoughts. Didn't hurt at all."

They each held a green plastic inhaler of Sybillene.

"Let's do it one at a time. Suzy, you go first."

"It looks like a short li'l green dildo," noted Suzy. "Do ah put this in my mouth?"

All three giggled.

"Yup. And suck it real hard. Ten times!"

They giggled more.

"No, I mean it," explained Kerri. "You suck on it really hard and fast. That's how the powdered medicine gets into your lungs. Then it goes to the brain. And then you'll see what happens."

"If you say so."

The other two nodded.

"We'll watch you first." Just to be on the safe side, Holly wanted Suzy to be the test dummy. This stuff might be like most things—from Godiva chocolates to sleeping pills: A little bit could be great. But too much could kill you.

Suzy held the green device to her mouth, and inhaled the powder into her lungs ten times. As she sucked, her eyes questioned, seeking the support and assurance of the others. After the tenth, she smiled, nervously.

"It has an aftertaste—kinda like the way my bamboo lawn furniture smelled when it was new," Suzy said.

Nothing happened for several minutes, and the other two women started whispering about irrelevancies, such as their husbands.

Then Suzy noticed a change. "Oh. Oh. Wow. So *this* is Naked Emperor."

Holly stopped talking. "What's happening?"

Suzy's eyes were fixed, staring straight ahead, not at either of her friends.

"Suzy, are you OK?" Holly's voice evidenced concern, as she contemplated what the papers might say about someone having a catatonic seizure in her house.

But Suzy wasn't concerned. Not in the least. She could feel her body and brain tolerating the medication easily. But not all was fine. Oh god, not all was fine.

"What's going on, Suzy? What's happening? Are you OK?"

She spoke slowly, carefully. "I am OK. I believe I am thinking logically. I am seeing things." Her voice sounded normal enough, but her diction had increased in precision and her syntax had changed. She sounded confident, clear, focused. She seemed to have transformed from a Southern magnolia to a female version of Mr. Spock.

"You're talking a little funny. What are you seeing?" asked Kerri.

"Are you hallucinating?" Holly asked.

Suzy replied slowly, peacefully. "No. I am not hallucinating. Holly, I see something. I understand something. Very clearly. About my husband. I see he is having an affair!"

Kerri looked at Holly. Suzy kept staring ahead. Holly said nothing.

"I see it so clearly now. Jack is definitely having an affair. The meeting in Boston three weeks ago. He was so late picking up the boys last Thursday.

No interest in me for the last few weeks. A tiny fragment of a blue pill I found in his pants pocket in the laundry. The meal charges on our credit card bill from the Boston trip were from a different class of restaurant. The way Holly spoke his name yesterday. A new scent on his coat. The scent Holly uses." She paused and took a breath and then said calmly, "Holly, you are having an affair with my husband. There is no sense in denying it. The facts add up. I *know* it."

Kerri turned to Holly. "Holly?"

Holly's face fell to an ashen gray, and she breathed fast.

At first, Holly said nothing. A moment later she stood up. Suzy kept staring straight ahead. It wasn't a thousand-yard stare, nor the stare of hypnosis, but the way a thinker might focus on the middle distance to obviate distractions.

"I'm so sorry, Suzy. I'm so very sorry." Holly's face had taken on a patchy redness—a combination of humiliation and guilt. Tears flowed, and she gasped.

Suzy slowly turned her head and looked at Holly. She said serenely, "It is all right, Holly. It *is* all right. I have just figured something else out. Something even more important."

Holly asked, humbly, tenderly, "What's that, Suzy?"

Almost in staccato, with emphasis on each syllable, Suzy replied, "I do not love my husband. I just realized that I have not loved my husband in years. I can see that we have been living a lie."

Holly walked around the table and put her hand on Suzy's shoulder.

Suzy turned her head to look at her. There was no malice in her mind, or in her soul. Or in either her expression or words. "Holly, it is truly OK. And it is your turn to suck on the Naked Emperor." Suzy yawned.

Holly sat down, and took her turn. A few minutes later she stared straight ahead, looking at neither of her friends, and said, "It is happening to me too. Suzy, I do not love Jack either. I do not love myself, actually. And I finally know what I need to do. I need a life. I will start by getting a job."

17

Home Is Where the Beast Waits

RAINBOW had made space for herself in the corner of Tristana's office. Tristana liked having her there, even if for only a few days each week. When she was around, Rainbow served as her Girl Friday, complementing Stephan's Man Friday role. She was not only willing, but—particularly for a kid—capable. Like most teenagers, she wasn't all smiles. But she proved a pleasant companion for Tristana. Something of the daughter she wished she'd had.

Tristana absentmindedly turned her swivel chair away from Rainbow.

"Charles, sales have been fair at best. Honestly, we've been struggling." Tristana held tightly to the phone, waiting. She had mixed feelings when talking to Charles. Excitement, fear, anticipation, nervousness. She felt an acute business accountability on calls with him. He rarely let anything slip by. Sometimes his calls were simply unwelcome. She would rather avoid these calls and have a romantic lunch with him instead.

He said, "We're more than a month into sales now. Are we cash flow positive?"

"No. We've just begun the ramp-up process. This takes time. Most doctors are loath to prescribe something new. There's too much risk, too much liability in today's world. If something worked for them in the past, they stick with it until they retire. Large sums of marketing money are usually required to overcome that inertia."

"When will the company book a profit, do you think?"

"We *can* probably book a profit within a few months, if we're willing to slow down depreciation. But it would be artificial."

"No. Stick to the rules for depreciation. If we inflate the price of the stock artificially, we'll draw in the wrong kind of shareholder, and scare away the kind of shareholder we want. Plus, the sooner we show a profit, the sooner we have to pay taxes. Profit will come. In the meantime, are you building inventory?"

"We're trying to keep inventory low. It helps our cash flow."

"Of course it does. But if I were to give you a million more dollars, could you turn that into packaged and ready-to-go inventory?"

"Why?"

"I think we may need it soon."

Tristana squinted. A stupid idea like that put a crack in her respect for Charles Knight. The man, for all his apparent intelligence, had suggested something foolish. But who was she to turn down a cash infusion?

She spun her chair around toward Rainbow, switched to speaker phone, and turned to what she thought was a more valuable subject. "We have some *good* news. We've had more small pharmacies requesting stock. A rather big bump in requests just in the last week or so. If it continues, our sales numbers will look a lot better next month."

"Everybody loves good news."

"It's a start at least. I hope we get more."

Knight said, "Maybe we should sell it door-to-door."

"Door-to-door?" Tristana smiled toward Rainbow and shook her head. Rainbow grinned back.

Twenty seconds of silence passed before Charles said, "Tristana, what do you know about Naked Emperor?"

"Naked what?"

"Naked Emperor. You haven't heard the term?"

"Can't say I have. What is it?"

"It's a new drug people are using. Middle class and wealthy people are using it to clear their thinking. Naked Emperor is Sybillene."

Tristana's face flushed then. Charles probably heard the quick involuntary breath through the line, a response to suppressed guilt.

Rainbow picked up on the sudden change in her boss's appearance.

Tristana turned off the speaker and held the receiver to her ear. "Tell me more" was all she felt comfortable saying.

171

Charles continued. "I was doing an online search, and saw a report in one of the New York City neighborhood papers about it. If it's true, then inhaling ten times the recommended dose causes Sybillene to turn into Naked Emperor."

She asked, "*Ten* times the dose?" *That would probably be about right,* she thought. "That's what I read."

Don't let Sybillene become a street drug.

As was usually the case with her, fear emerged first. "FDA or DEA could hurt us," she said, "or maybe even shut us down entirely. Does it get people high?"

"I haven't read that. The information I've come across so far is entirely complimentary. Ridiculously so, in fact."

"Hmm."

"What do you know about this, Tristana?"

As always, Charles came to the point.

She was not ready to answer. "Charles, I miss our lunch meetings."

"As do I. But don't change the subject."

"I should tell you what I think, in person. Lunch tomorrow?" She closed her eyes, hoping he would make the three-hour train ride down from New York.

"Tomorrow then. Sleep well."

She wouldn't sleep at all.

For the rest of the day, she had scheduled manufacturing meetings, regulatory meetings, a meeting with accountants, and most importantly a meeting with the contract marketing team. It amounted to far too much for one afternoon. The only thing missing was a meeting to schedule more meetings. Her ego must have been bigger than her mind when she let Stephan set up all these appointments. But now, it was impossible to focus on any of this stuff. She pressed a button on her phone.

"Stephan, I need you to postpone the accountants 'til later in the week. And the regulatory staff—push them out to Thursday, will you?"

"So Charles is coming down tomorrow," Rainbow prompted.

"Yes. Something has come up. Rainbow, I need to put a new task on your plate. Please go online and learn anything you can about a street drug called Naked Emperor."

Rainbow nodded. "I heard," she said. "I'll find out all I can."

*   *   *

That evening Tristana headed home even later than usual. Rainbow had gone back into the city for the night, to what sort of horrible place she did not want to imagine. She preferred having Rainbow stay with her. Her presence took the edge off of Donald dominating the house with his darkness.

She stopped at a shopping mall to wander around for an hour, and then the gas station to top off her half-filled tank. The cold evening soaked through her inadequate coat, but she further delayed getting home by heading to a 7-Eleven for a bag of chips, a Coke, and a *People* magazine, a proven recipe—a veritable trifecta—to become fat and stupid.

After finally pulling into her driveway, she sat and listened to a couple of random songs, attempting to gather courage. But the songs on the radio didn't have the effect of "The Ride of the Valkyries" or "La Marseillaise." She finally managed to extract herself from the car, knowing that the morose humors holding the house in thrall would soon consume her. Its doorway felt like the maw of a beast.

Donald had to be lurking inside, like a troll. His car sat in the driveway. The lights were on in the house.

"Hi, Donald." She tested the water with her gentlest voice, intentionally uplifted, when she found him sitting in the kitchen.

"Well, hi there, sweetums!" Donald replied with a smile on his face. Smiles came rarely to him these days. And a term of endearment… Well, he had not employed such a thing in at least a year. "How was your day, Tristana?"

"Just a day," she replied cautiously.

"Feeling good?"

"Yes?" She said it suspiciously, intentionally so, with a rising pitch as if she were questioning whether *yes* was his desired response.

"Any news today?"

"Not really." God, she hoped he wasn't trying to get romantic.

"Did the new sales figures come in?"

"Soon. Not today. Tomorrow maybe." She shuffled around in the refrigerator.

"Oh." He nodded his head. "Do you want to go out to dinner?"

"Oh, Donald, no. I don't. I'm too tired. I'm going to snack, go to bed, and read a book. Sorry."

173

"Oh."

He sat at the table in silence for a time, while she stood and ate a cup of ramen noodles. She shook off foolish echoes of guilt for not preparing a meal for the two of them. She looked at him as he read some junk mail a bit too carefully. He *was* trying to get romantic, in his clumsy way. A few years ago, she would have been thrilled. Not now.

But she could derail him in a flash, and chose to do so.

"Charles Knight is in town tomorrow." She saw him involuntarily flinch, a movement visible only because she watched so closely for just that response. "To go over our financials."

"Hmm," he replied, pretending to pay little heed.

"How was your day? Chasing down all the naughty companies trying to pull pranks? Slaying the evil dragons trying to defy FDA authority?" She wasn't sure if she was taunting him, yanking his chain, or just continuing efforts at conversation. Most likely a little of each.

"It's been slow until today, really. In the last few months, we've only done a couple of raids. If I don't develop some activity, they may cut my division down. You know how it is: if you're not growing, you're shrinking. There's a lot of politics involved, and we've got to show we're doing something. Use it or lose it. But, now something may be up."

"Whatcha got?"

"Usually I couldn't tell you, but this I can. Because it's not an American company. Not even a company that does legal business in the U.S. There's generic Viagra manufactured by a large Indian pharma company, and it's coming into the U.S. and being sold, without prescription."

"A lot of it?"

"Yeah, one of your big-cousin pharma companies here in the U.S. thinks so at least. Joint private-public operation. That should make headlines."

"And the DEA?"

"Yeah, I'm meeting with Seth Fowler tomorrow."

"How's Seth doing?"

Donald turned another shade darker, falling into his usual routine after struggling to be friendly. "Why do you care, Tristana? You don't like Seth."

"No, I don't. You're right. I think he's a power-mad state trooper with a major screw loose. He's a psycho in a suit, complete with beady eyes and a sick leer. He would 'Heil Hitler' if he got the chance. And I don't like the way he controls his wife."

"You don't like his wife either."

"What's to like? Anyhow, it sounds like you're into something fun. Good for you." At least it should keep him occupied.

"And if I play my cards right, it could be the springboard for the next step up the ladder."

"My, aren't we ambitious!" Then she quickly backtracked on the snide comment. "You're climbing faster and faster, Donald!"

"Yeah, contraband generic Viagra, it's a whole new game. Selling door-to-door, on a large scale."

"Door-to-door?" Twice, that phrase, in one day.

"Yeah, actually door-to-door."

"So, you think DEA is going to care? That Fowler is going to be interested? Those guys deal with narcotics, not erections."

"I have to make him care. Those guys and Customs are the two most knowledgeable agencies about illegal imports. FDA doesn't have people that work much in that area. And when it comes to street distribution—well, I'm not sure how to start. A joint agency bust will get a lot more attention, and maybe FDA can broaden its mandate. The numbers are probably pretty high. Millions of pills."

"Wow. That's a lot of erections. Or one *giant* one."

"Funny."

It was not *that* funny. But Donald hadn't taken the opportunity to expand upon her lewd comment, so maybe he'd pulled away from being romantic. One more dig, another reminder about Charles, should do it for sure.

She said, "I won't be home for dinner tomorrow night."

Donald shivered in suppressed anger. The effect was perfect.

18

Devil's Brew

SPECIAL Agent Seth Fowler had a pole on his front lawn with a U.S. flag flying twenty-four hours a day; a small spotlight lit it up all night.

After college and a hitch in the army with the military police, he had begun his career as a South Carolina state trooper. The state police were like the army's MPs, but offered better pay, more authority, and the freedom to do things the way he saw fit when on duty in his cruiser. Ninety-nine percent of the job consisted of ticketing speeders. After all, the public had to know they were being watched. And revenue needed to be generated to pay the costs of pulling people over. It also assured his supervisor he wasn't just sitting at the side of the road reading a magazine.

He'd learned a lot from several years of contact with mundanes on the highways. Almost all of them broke the law, and most of them would lie about it. Some of them treated him as if he were no more than a puffed-up version of the grade school hall-safety monitors every normal kid hated; if they revealed such an attitude, they invited additional charges or a vehicle search. Some had especially aggressive attitudes, which was usually cause for them to "step out of the car, sir," and, if he felt he had to physically discipline them, charge them with assaulting an officer. Some of them acted as though *he* was the one defying the law, as if *he* was the one committing the crime.

But most of them just cowered in their cars, hands on the wheel, smiling like good little citizens or ingratiating children. "Yes, officer." "No, sir." "I'm sorry, officer." "It won't happen again, officer." Anger and frustration stayed mostly concealed by fear. During those years, Fowler learned how to leverage the power of fear.

All mundanes were capable of being criminals, and that was how Seth treated them. Give them an inch and they'll preach about their rights—as if rights had any meaning beyond television cop dramas—and then take a mile. So don't give 'em the inch.

He had given an inch once, and it had proved a mistake. When internal affairs investigated, the perp—who was never prosecuted—became unexpectedly eloquent and convincing. He made Fowler look bad. How twisted was that? It left a black mark on his record. The next time a similar situation arose, he aimed more carefully and shot the lying weasel dead. No way that perp would talk. Fowler took pride in being one of the relatively few cops who had ever killed a man. Not far below the surface, he hoped the opportunity would arise again.

At a certain point, however, he realized there was no future in wearing a paramilitary costume with a silly Smokey the Bear hat and handing out tickets all day. State cops weren't featured on any of the popular police shows that filled his TV in the evening. At best they served as go-fers for the heroic federal agents who assumed control of any important case. He put in applications with all of those federal agencies, was accepted by the DEA, and moved to Virginia.

The Drug Enforcement Administration meshed well with his personality. Nobody was innocent—only the rare Mormon in the wilds of Utah hadn't blown dope, snorted coke, or popped a pill at some point. And everyone figured the government either already knew about their crimes or could find out. Everyone committed crimes, whether they knew it or not. With 190,000 pages of the U.S. Code on top of even more state and local statutes, there were plenty of ways to ensure that any man, woman, or child could be prosecuted as a criminal, if necessary. The average person's guilt, fear, and general insecurities empowered him, and Fowler used the power whenever possible. It made work so much easier, and more fun.

Fowler didn't know why his fellow agents at the DEA didn't particularly like him. But neither did he care.

"You're a jerk, Fowler," one of his fellow agents said, for no reason he could ascertain, as he walked passed him in a corridor.

"Asshole," said another agent to him after hearing about how Fowler threatened jail time to an old woman dying of cancer who used marijuana to alleviate her pain. She incriminated her own grandson, who scored it for her. The power of love? Let's talk about the power of fear!

A couple years back, there had been rumors—leaked by his old partner no doubt, damn him—that Fowler had tainted some heroin and stuck it back on the street.

They didn't know the half of it.

Sure, the other agents didn't approve of him. So what. It's not as if they didn't have plenty of their own dirty laundry. Just as all the entrances to the FDA building served as revolving doors for Big Pharma, the DEA was similarly subject to regulatory capture. The industry they regulated—in this case illegal drugs—eventually wound up having some influence over the bureaucracy, or at least some of its agents. The money, huge, came in the form of cash, or in offshore deposits. When given an offer of *plata o plomo*—silver or lead—the discreet and intelligent agent took the silver, especially after being on the job long enough to realize how ungrateful the political stooges at the top of the administration were. And the people of the country? The so-called lawful citizens? There weren't any.

Fowler got the job done and enforced the laws. Every cop was sworn to enforce the laws—no matter if they were cruel, wicked, or unjust in a particular case. The law had to be upheld, no matter what it said or what means were required to do so.

Why? He never asked that question.

Of course, to enforce the laws, one had to be above them.

His particular combination of strict and successful enforcement actions conspired with some dumb luck to move Fowler upward in the DEA faster than he had imagined possible.

"Hey, Seth." Debocher came through the door and reached over the desk to shake his hand with a practiced appearance of sincere enthusiasm. He needed more practice on the actual shake, however. His soft, limp grip felt like liverwurst. "Thanks for seeing me."

Seth replied, "Since you and Tristana moved out of the neighborhood, we never see you." They had lived alongside each other in Burke, Virginia, a D.C. bedroom community full of people just like themselves.

"We should fix that soon. Tristana said just last night how much she misses you and Kate."

"So, you've got a new tip for me?"

Debocher held his finger to his lips and shook his head.

There was a rap on Fowler's partly opened office door, and a woman looked around it as she pushed it aside. With flame-red hair, green eyes, rounded cheekbones, and a body that was the consummation of female perfection, the woman instantly triggered a set of genetically programmed responses in Fowler.

"Seth, this is Sabina Heidel. Sabina is my new special assistant. She's shadowing me. Learning the ropes."

Fowler's respect for Debocher rose two notches and his distaste for him tripled. "A pleasure indeed, Sabina."

He had difficulty transferring his gaze from her and back to the pale, irritating Debocher.

Sabina pulled a chair up and crossed her legs.

Only then did Fowler realize he hadn't even stood up when she entered.

Debocher then began discussing his suspicions about a new kind of drug ring. As Fowler listened, he realized that Debocher didn't have a clue.

Debocher's special assistant added color to the presentation. "This is quite an outrage," she said. Sabina Heidel sounded like a righteous victim of a horrible crime, assuming a position of moral superiority to demand that justice be served. Looking at her made Fowler want to be the one to serve that justice.

"It's a bit out of our purview here," he said. "Generic Viagra is not covered by the Controlled Substances Act. You'll need to talk to Customs, and I suppose the U.S. Marshals."

"Yes, we know," Debocher replied. "But this is a drug ring. Illegal importers of illegal drugs. And from what I understand, you're our go-to person to help address illegal importation by drug rings. Am I mistaken?"

"Hey, don't get me wrong. I know how these organizations work, sure. But if Viagra is all they're dealing, then I can't officially do anything, not without permission from above."

Sabina said, "Can you get the permission? I would think that once they've set up a network to distribute a garden-variety drug like Viagra to an upmarket clientele, they're in position to move anything and everything."

Fowler considered. Although far outside of the DEA's turf, this might fit perfectly with an idea he had but had not gotten around to executing. "Honestly, I doubt I can. But perhaps I could help arrange a joint operation with Customs. Have you talked to the local and state authorities? That's probably the place you should go first."

Donald shook his head. "Seth, this is a multistate ring. It needs to be handled at the federal level. If I approach your division chief and he agrees, would you take an assignment to a joint operation with FDA, with the involvement of Customs?"

"I would be working with the both of you?"

"Yes, under my authority."

"Let's see what the boss says." If this broke new ground for the DEA, it would be a feather in his cap. Perhaps it would necessitate a new division that would need a new chief. The one thing every high-level bureaucrat wanted was justification for Congress to provide them with a larger budget to oversee.

*   *   *

"Mr. Knight!" Stephan hugged Charles with ever-increasing enthusiasm each time he came into town and visited Visioryme. Charles accepted the intimate greeting, while privately hoping these affectations would taper off.

"Charles!" Tristana greeted him with similar, but less demonstrative, enthusiasm.

His mind wandered to thoughts of kissing her. The keenly anticipated event hadn't yet occurred. And despite the temptation, Charles thought of several reasons it shouldn't.

Tristana and Charles walked into her office. "Can you come in too, Stephan?" She waved him through the door.

A casual observer might describe Stephan as nonthreatening, harmless, and relatively unimportant in the Visioryme corporate structure. His flamboyant nature made some think he was more interested in show than content. In actuality, he was insightful, reliable, and critical to the company. He could speak his mind forcefully when necessary. That was an increasingly rare—and therefore increasingly valuable—trait in a culture dominated by yes-men. Stephan could run the company if need be. He knew the people, the science, and the technology.

"Hi, Mr. Knight!" Rainbow popped out from where she sat surrounded by various papers.

"Hey! Good to see you. How do you like office work?"

She shrugged in response.

Charles asked Stephan. "Have you arranged for the additional inventory I requested?"

"I got the ball rolling," he replied. "But Tristana thinks it's stupid."

Tristana cast Stephan a frown. But then she said, "I *do* think it's foolish, Charles. It makes no business sense. It just starts the clock ticking on the product expiration date."

"I understand all that."

"Hmm. If you have money to burn, I'd rather we spend it on marketing and reimbursement consultants."

Tristana wasn't wired to think like a speculator. If you think demand was going up, buy while something is available and stockpile it. In other words, the time to buy straw hats is in the winter. The time to buy umbrellas is when it's not raining.

They sat down in Tristana's small office while she pulled out some papers containing the most recent sales figures. "This is where we are, Charles."

Charles read through them for the next few minutes, analyzing numbers, seeking information between the lines.

"Not great."

Tristana came back at him on the offensive. "Maybe we shouldn't order that extra inventory now, huh? Welcome to the medical industry, Charles."

Charles hadn't slept and felt testy. Visioryme's financial figures aggravated the condition.

Tristana glanced at Stephan before speaking. "Anyway. As you're aware, the way things work in the pharmaceutical industry, once we get through all the scientific development and actually have a viable product, we earn the privilege of getting to fight FDA. If we win there—which we have—then we fight for insurance coverage, while selling pieces of our flesh to layers of middlemen, like pharmacy benefit managers, plan sponsors, and third-party administrators. We have to make our case to *everyone but the patient* that our drug is worth what we're asking. If these intermediaries all say yes, we might get paid nice high prices and be on easy street. We might make a fortune. If they refuse to pay, then we end up selling only to a small number of patients who don't have insurance, and who want the Sybillene enough to spend their *own* money on it. It's hard to make more than a small profit off pharmaceuticals when people have to pay their own money for them."

Charles smiled internally. "There are ways."

"Can you believe it?" asked Stephan. "Can you believe that people still have to pay their own money for their own medical care?"

Charles struggled, and his face fell. He'd liked Stephan, at least until this moment. Had he misunderstood the man's character?

Tristana must have seen his discomfort. "Charles, Stephan is being sarcastic."

Charles exhaled, relieved. "Oh, good." He looked at Stephan. "It's hard to tell with you sometimes."

"He's kind of a libertarian," Tristana assured Charles, "although he doesn't really know it."

Stephan nodded. "I'm not into politics."

Charles said, "It's not just politics, it's philosophy."

Stephan shrugged. "All I ask is for everyone to stay out of my way."

Tristana shook her head. "I told you, Charles."

"That's good for openers, Stephan. I like you again." He felt much better.

"And I like you, Charles." Stephan said this in the deepest heterosexual voice he could muster.

"As I was saying," continued Tristana, "we might get these multiple layers of third-party payers on board—most importantly Medicare—after a year or two of fighting and negotiating. Start picking up a few of the state Medicaids, then we're finally a contender in the market. At that point the playing field starts to level out some. And that's when we have a chance."

Charles started feeling worse again. He asked, "Level field among FDA-approved insurance-paid medications, you mean?"

"Yes."

"And everybody on the whole playing field is massively subsidized."

"What do you mean, Charles?"

"I mean that once someone else is picking up the tab, the patient has no motivation to pick the cheapest drug available, 'cuz saving someone else's money doesn't matter to him."

"Yes, that's *exactly* my point, Charles. That's what I was saying before. We can't make much profit when people have to pay their own money for Sybillene. But once Medicare, Medicaid, and private insurers start paying, Sybillene will cost very little to the patient. They'll *want* it as if it only cost ten dollars. But we'll get *paid* much more. That makes for high-margin, high-volume sales. This is exactly how we cash in. It's the motherlode."

Charles didn't think of a motherlode the same way that Tristana did. This all sounded to him more like a load of shit.

She said, "If patients had to pay for their own medications, all our profits would be cut by eighty percent or more. We love FDA *after* approval, because they keep our competitors out."

"But we hate them the rest of the time," Stephan added.

Charles shook his head. "All of that screws up any possibility that anyone will make a rational economic calculation or even shop around. So the cost of drugs skyrockets."

Tristana replied, "That's true. But once we've got the system on our side, it's *our* profits that skyrocket."

Charles said what he felt. "I thought pharmaceuticals are supposed to make you better. But this makes me *sick*."

"Yeah, it's sick. But a sickness that will make us financially healthy if we play our cards right. The key is that insurance approval, particularly the Centers for Medicare and Medicaid Services. Without it we're nothing, also-rans, outsiders. You can't compete with the covered drugs. Ever tried competing with government-subsidized products?"

Charles's exposure to government had been entirely unpleasant to date. "I don't much appreciate having my own money used to buy the rope they use to hang me."

"We're still in near-death mode, Charles. And you can rest assured that our competitors at Big Pharma are already lobbying FDA to pull the plug on our life support. I'm sorry. We're in a world of hurt until our reimbursement consultants can finish negotiations and get us where we need to be."

Charles thought a moment. "Reimbursement consultants? What, pray tell, do they do?"

Stephan elucidated. "Every health-insurance industry employee, including at Medicare, starts their company orientation by spending seventy-two hours with no sleep saying the word *no* over and over again. Reimbursement consultants are the only ones who have a clue how to get through those automatic programmed denials. They're the pilots that navigate through the medical-government-industrial complex."

Charles couldn't argue with what these two knew. But it was one reason why he thought insuring for trivial issues, or indeed anything other than major catastrophe, was stupid, and by stupid, he meant *self-destructive*. If he needed major medical care, then Thailand, India, and South America were less than a day away, the costs were only ten to twenty-five percent of those in the U.S., and the quality of service was at least as good. Luxury medical care could be found on the cheap, if you made an effort to look for it. But why bother to look when you're spending other people's money?

Tristana added, "But our consultants haven't succeeded yet. When they do, it's a whole new ballgame."

Charles shook his head, dejected. He said, "A ballgame in which only friends of the stadium owners get to play." Why was he still learning lessons at his age? When would he be wise enough to know better? Dealing with this type of thing made him feel as if he were living in a parallel universe where everyone saw crazy things as normal.

"So we're trying to go from failure to fraud? Is that it?" Charles looked back-and-forth between Tristana and Stephan. "Our path to success is defrauding the public and using the FDA to quash the competition? *That's* our business strategy?"

Charles felt that sensation in his belly again: his body's way of reporting his disgust. It wasn't just that the whole industry was corrupt; it was that everybody seemed to think that's the way it *should* be.

Charles suddenly wanted to get out. Get as far away as he could. Staying in a concrete-bound and highly regulated business would inevitably lead to personal corruption.

He could sell his shares. Since FDA approval, the stock had remained high despite its negative cash flow. He might profit substantially if he acted soon. But the price wouldn't stay up once analysts saw insiders selling. He'd never be able to get out with a position the size of his. No pharma giant was jumping in to buy Visioryme, and the analysts were just beginning to realize that. The market was littered with struggling pharma companies dying a slow death.

Tristana replied sheepishly, "I'm afraid that's our business model. That's the model for this whole industry. But, on the bright side, we *have* created a wonderful new medication that could help millions of people."

Charles pondered the possibility. "If Sybillene helps get patients off the zombie medications, then that's worth doing."

He looked for justification to stay involved in this company. Although the immense waste of time and capital in the pharmaceutical business appalled him, he had ulterior motives for staying in it. Plus, Visioryme seemed to have a superior product. He looked up from the papers and asked

Stephan a question that seemed off the topic. "Can you track how much Sybillene is being used off-label?"

"It's hard to track. Once a drug is approved, doctors can prescribe it for anything." Stephan's knowledge, gained in the trenches, supplemented Tristana's degree in regulatory science.

Charles shook his head. "I'm sorry, I guess I didn't mean to say *off-label*. I mean how can we track how much Sybillene is being used without a prescription?"

"Stephan," Rainbow explained, "Mr. Knight told us yesterday about a new street drug called Naked Emperor. It's probably Sybillene used in high dose."

"Oh *really?*" The glance Stephan cast at Tristana, combined with a fairly blatant inflection in his voice, now assured Charles that the two of them knew something more than they had admitted to.

Charles's trademark smile had vanished. "OK, you two. Let it out. And get your tails out from between your legs." Charles kept his face firm. This sort of thing could raise issues with the FDA that could bankrupt the company. But on the other hand, it could open up a whole new business plan, and one that appealed to Charles much more than the nonsense that Tristana and Stephan had just laid out.

Stephan looked at Tristana with his eyebrows raised and his face twisted in a way that only a gay man can pull off, a wordless expression of chastisement combined with an "I told you so!" Stephan added a verbal accusatory "Well, *girlfriend?*"

She sighed and then said, "A few years back … we did our toxicity and dosing studies in dogs… Some of the dogs may have gotten … smarter. We didn't have the time or money to pursue it. Our mandate was to get the drug approved, not open a new can of worms. So we let the sleeping dogs lie, as it were. After the highest-dose Sybillene was given to the dogs, which was a lot more than ten puffs' equivalent, the next morning the dogs were all out of their cages. They all figured how to open the levers that locked them in. I'm not kidding."

"Maybe a handler screwed up."

"Of course that's what we thought. The study required three separate days of overdosing the Sybillene. We suspected PETA, so we stationed a security guard outside of the lab, and in the morning the technicians walked in to find that the dogs were out of their cages again. We had to repeat the whole study. The contract lab was so embarrassed that they did it for free."

"Yes," Stephan added, not the least bit embarrassed himself. "It was a bad time for us. I worked for that lab then. No one had the nerve to theorize that the dogs knew how to escape from their cages. The lab officially ended up writing it off as a PETA attack and a sleeping guard."

Tristana said, "But both of us have wondered about it. Dr. McBride is aware too." She shook her head. "But between operating on a shoestring budget and pushing paper to the FDA, we haven't gotten around to seeing what's up with that."

"I see. Have you tested humans at high dose at all?"

"Not that high. Two puffs was no more effective than one for treating depression, and there was no toxicity in animals at *any* dose of the drug, so higher-dose regimens weren't tried in humans."

"Interesting. What did Dr. McBride think about this? Surely, he'd want to pursue the possibilities."

"And we promised him the opportunity as soon as we got some traction for the drug's primary use ... and some money to finance further research."

Rainbow said, "I've been reading what's getting posted online about Naked Emperor. People say they see truths that they had previously blocked out of their minds. People say they think more clearly."

Stephan said, "We would need to do IQ tests."

"Somebody already did that," Rainbow responded. "On himself. He said his IQ didn't change."

"So much for making people smarter with a drug."

"One person, one experiment," Tristana noted. "Doesn't count for much. Plus IQ testing may not be the right measure."

Charles said, "I went to the effort of meeting a guy named Peale. He's the editor/publisher of a little city newspaper called the 'Weekly Observer' in Manhattan. His team put together the first story on Naked Emperor, and he claims to have given it the name. What Naked Emperor seems to do is help people see things more clearly."

Rainbow chimed in. "There are postings about bosses realizing which employees are stealing, knowing when a car dealer is lying about a car, seeing through war propaganda, realizing when the media is lying and twisting truths, identifying boyfriends who are cheating."

Charles added, "And recognizing alternative facts and factoids for what they are. Oddly, it started with Peale equating the Federal Reserve with a criminal counterfeiting organization, which impressed me as a most-unusual assertion for a local paper. It was part of the story he wrote about Naked Emperor, where he also mentioned an anecdote about our drug helping a woman with borderline personality. There are a bunch of reports about how it helped people see through the lies they told themselves. They say it cuts through denial and personal defenses. It's pretty compelling stuff. There may be a lot of exaggeration, and it's all anecdotal, but for whatever reason, this thing is going viral."

Stephan reached over and put his hand on Tristana's knee. "Darlin', you need to try some Naked Emperor yourself. Seems like just what the doctor ordered."

Charles chose not to comment, and his lack of comment left the office in silence for a time. No one needed Naked Emperor to understand what Stephan intimated.

But Rainbow stated it plainly. "Really, Tristana. My bet is that if you toked some Naked Emperor, Donald would find himself buried to his neck in your backyard."

Stephan brought the subject back to business. "This might lead to new patent claims. New indications for use if we do the necessary studies."

Charles said, "Lots of human studies. We're talking big money."

Tristana added, "Or veterinary studies. Maybe help dogs learn how to be better drug sniffers. There's undoubtedly consulting money to be had from Customs and the DEA."

"Ooh," Charles said quietly. "Not my first choice. But how about seeing-eye dogs, or dogs that help people with other disabilities?"

"Sure. And there could be a ton more uses," Tristana added. "But we're getting *way* ahead of ourselves here. Right now this is nothing but hype. Let's get the science team on board. Rainbow, can you give us all a summary of the info you pulled up on Naked Emperor?"

"Sure," Rainbow replied. "It's mostly just people posting."

"It'll be a start."

Charles said, "Tristana, you're the one most knowledgeable about … what do you call it? … *regulatory science*. We need to think through the risks of this."

Rainbow revealed her teenage innocence, if she could be called innocent. "What risks? How can anyone complain about people seeing the truth? That can't be a bad thing."

Charles replied directly, "Not bad? It's fantastic! It would be on a par with discovering the cure for old age and cancer. But there *are* major risks."

Naked Emperor presented plenty of dangers and opportunities for Visioryme, and for those who ran it. A crisis loomed. It was no accident that the Chinese ideogram for *crisis* was a combination of the ones for *danger* and *opportunity*.

"You mean, something we didn't find in all our toxicity studies?" Stephan asked.

"More like a nuclear explosion than a slow-acting poison, Stephan," Charles replied. "If this is real, then Naked Emperor helps people see truth buried in complexity or obscured by propaganda or misdirection."

Stephan nodded. "I agree with Rainbow. That sounds like nothing but a good thing. Where's the problem?"

"Who in this country might want to conceal the truth from the people? Stephan, who would you guess?"

"People who lie, obviously."

"Of course. Can you name one group who fits that bill the best?"

"Politicians?" Stephan joked.

"Yes. Politicians," Charles said straight-faced. "And all their cronies. Solar-power manufacturers who want subsidies. Corn farmers demanding ethanol mandates. Pharmaceutical companies wanting to keep competition down. Banks who don't want people to understand central banking. Scientists trying to get grants. The White House, when it wants to start a war someplace. People who make their living by race baiting. Nationalists who say that patriotism means supporting the government."

Tristana said quietly, "And a lot of powerful lobbies."

"Sure. And hundreds more new enemies of Sybillene. The whole establishment. The Deep State, who want everything to stay just the way it is, no matter who's in the White House. And whether or not Sybillene *actually* exposes any of their lies matters little. Just a reputation for exposing lies is enough to trigger the attention and fear of people who don't want to be caught."

"Charles, you're paranoid. This isn't Nazi Germany or Soviet Russia. Nobody's trying to hide the truth from the people—assuming anybody even knows the truth. That's tin-foil hat thinking."

Years earlier, Charles had learned to control his irritation when people stated blatantly false notions. Tristana was probably just regurgitating what some college professor had told her years ago. So he tried to respond calmly.

"Tristana, people lie all the time. I didn't see you rushing to tell the world about the effect of Sybillene on dogs. Nor have you suggested we hurry up and inform the FDA about this issue."

Stephan asked, "Should we head this off with a press release?"

"That depends. Would we have anything to *say* in a press release?" Charles asked. "We have less knowledge than the people who have used Naked Emperor personally."

"Yeah. And that has to change this very night." Stephan jumped up in his trademark energetic manner. He pulled a handful of silver foil packages from a drawer and handed one to each of them with a flourish. "I give you: Naked Emperor!"

Charles nodded, "Shall we all get high and see if any of our emperors are wearing no clothes?"

Tristana said, "I'm game. After dinner tonight?"

Stephan added, "You know me. I like the whole idea of seeing any emperor naked. I'm turned on by naked power. Not so much the power, but definitely the naked part." He spoke with a particularly prominent lisp for this last line, and they laughed.

Rainbow said, "I'm gonna pass."

Tristana said, "I wouldn't allow these crazy men to experiment on you anyway, Rainbow. So you're off the hook."

"Oh, it's not that. I've already used Naked Emperor. Several times. You all gonna have fun!"

19

Maximum ProPG Pathways

AT dinner they decided, with some regret, to avoid alcohol. No point in adding an X-factor that might complicate their impromptu, nonclinical study. After dinner, Charles booked a hotel suite, and the three sat around a table on which Stephan placed a lit candle. "For ambiance," he said. Each of them held a green plastic Sybillene inhaler.

"From what Rainbow said, the effect takes a few minutes to kick in, and lasts about ten minutes." Tristana said. "I volunteer to go second."

"OK, girl, I'll go first." Stephan started sucking from the device, clicking and turning its top each time to get the next dose ready to inhale.

Charles warned him not to make any crude sexual jokes when any of the three of them inhaled. He figured the warning would go unheeded.

Stephan waited about thirty seconds after his tenth inhalation before he smiled. "Oh god. Oh my god. I see the truth! I had no idea." He paused and then said dramatically, "I'm gay!"

"Cut it out, Stephan!" Tristana and Charles both said at the same time.

"Sorry. I had to."

Charles reached out and patted him on the shoulder. "OK, but let's take this seriously now."

"I will." Stephan settled back on the soft chair.

Charles and Tristana watched as his eyes relaxed and focused on nothing, straight ahead of him. He stayed like that for over a minute before Tristana asked, "Stephan, are you all right?"

He spoke slowly. "I am fine, girl. I am fine. Nothing wrong with me."

"What are you feeling?"

"Happy. Calm."

"Any insights into the world?"

Stephan inhaled deeply, and then exhaled. "Getting there. Something is happening. Be patient, girl." His voice was mellow, his speech slow but perfectly enunciated, his use of verbal contractions held in abeyance as some effect of the drug, and perhaps an indicator of its presence.

After another minute, Charles asked, "Stephan. Do you feel high?"

"No, Charles. I feel normal. Except…"

"Except what?"

"Except I knew right away that the dogs were not released by PETA. PETA would not break in on one night to let just some of the dogs out of their cages, then risk coming a second night to do it again, would they? And they would have taken credit for it. It was not PETA. The dogs were improved by Sybillene. I suspected so immediately, and mostly suppressed it."

"Is that all you're thinking?"

"No. There are all sorts of flashes, as things pop into and out of my mind."

Charles handed him a one-dollar bill. "This is what got the whole Naked Emperor story out there, when Peale looked at one of these after ten puffs. What's this to you?"

Stephan examined one side and then the other. After over two minutes had passed he said, "It is just a piece of green paper."

Charles turned to Tristana with his eyebrows raised.

Tristana picked a controversial topic where everyone had an opinion, but few possessed true knowledge. "Stephan, what do you think of global warming?"

Stephan spoke every word in a gentle melodic voice; up and down his tone traveled. It was pleasant and calming to listen to. "I hear you. You put it in my mind. Let me see. I think… I think… OK, it is starting to make sense. In science, it is dangerous to combine certainty, bias, and emotion. There is very little civil discussion of the actual science anymore."

"What do you mean?"

Stephan continued, "I am a reasonable man. I am not in the petroleum business, nor do I care much about the future of coal mines. Yet, after all the publications and movies, why is it that I do not trust the story of

191

anthropogenic global warming? Am I blind? Am I ignorant? Or is it something else?

"It now occurs to me that those who choose to enter the climate field in college are already inclined to a certain view instilled by the politics of their parents and reinforced by their childhood teachers. The most passionate of them successfully climb the academic ladder, garnering the right mentors and the department support. Those who write grant proposals *supporting* the theories of older climate scientists are most successful, while any proposal skeptical of dominant climate theory has less chance of being funded. Then, if any funded climate research accidentally proves unsupportive of the accepted theory, the researcher is unlikely to go to the effort to write a manuscript. Why? Because it opposes his views, is unlikely to be published anyway, and could hurt his career if it *were* published. Those who write supportive papers get promoted. They get to teach others how they think, and decide who wins future grants. And so the next generation is brought into the fold.

"Only supportive data tend to be collected, written about, or published in the scientific journals. And only the most sensational of *those* get picked up by the media. If it bleeds, it leads. And so blood is all the public gets to see and base their conclusions—and their votes—on.

"The net effect is that scientific objectivity is overwhelmed by layer upon layer of bias beginning in childhood and extending to professorships, grants, journals, and on to reporters. I perceive seventeen layers of self-reinforcing bias. Yet most climate scientists deny the existence of even *one* of those layers of bias."

Charles said, "Very logical, Stephan. Believing because of trust in what you are told sounds like a faith more than science. And because of this layered bias you describe, the climate priesthood is not a particularly trustworthy source."

Stephan said, "Exactly. So I have learned that I am *not* a climate change denier, but rather I am a climate-*science* denier, because the very field has no credibility."

Tristana asked him, "Stephan, is this something you've considered before?"

"I read the occasional article. I know about academic reinforcement bias in pharmaceutical research, even at Visioryme. However, I had never put it all together to recognize what is wrong with the global warming data. I can now see how the field has become immersed in its own self-reinforcing multigenerational momentum. At the same time, many of those who *deny* it do so for political and emotional reasons, and do not seem to understand *why* they do not believe it. I think this lack of trust in the scientists is why. It seems like people who work anywhere in the climate field are no longer capable of separating truth from their own fictions. As a result, I have no idea if human-induced global warming actually exists or, if it does, whether it is a problem or a benefit."

"So what do you recommend?" Charles asked.

"The solution is simple. The climate scientists all need to puff Naked Emperor."

Tristana said, "*Everyone* needs to puff Naked Emperor! The so-called climate deniers and climate hysterics may not know why they each believe what they do, but Stephan may have just explained it all."

Charles considered for a moment. "My guess is that it won't just be professional environmentalists who are going to feel threatened by Naked Emperor. All kinds of professional activists will be enemies of Visioryme."

Stephan said, "Not all of them. The environmentalists are mostly well meaning. If they start taking Naked Emperor, it may help them focus their efforts towards the most significant threats to Mother Earth, which may not be carbon dioxide at all. Naked Emperor will help them distinguish scientific truth from religious dogma. They will stop lying to themselves, and that is the first step to health."

Charles chuckled. "Oh, that brings up another group. Some of the big-haired megachurch pastors *really* won't like Naked Emperor."

Stephan said, "I feel like I should sleep now, but I am not particularly tired."

This caught Tristana's attention. "That's interesting. Maybe your brain wants to sleep in order to consolidate the new thinking; sleep helps you process and remember thoughts and ideas. According to Dr. McBride, new neuronal connections in your brain are strengthened during sleep, when the ProPG-induced neuronal connections are modified most effectively."

Stephan asked, "OK, you two, who goes next?"

"I volunteered to go second. Here goes nothing…" Tristana inhaled the drug, ten breaths, holding her breath for six seconds after each inhalation, like a pot toker, smiling self-consciously as the two men watched her.

After a few minutes, Tristana's breathing steadied, and she began looking into some distant place, her eyes gazing straight ahead. She said nothing for a time. And then she chuckled. And then she cried.

"What is it? What are you thinking about?"

She, too, spoke slowly. "I do not want to discuss it. But it is important. To me, personally. I realize that I have been suppressing something."

Stephan urged her. "This is an experiment, Tristana. It is OK to tell us anything."

"What I am thinking is not for public knowledge. It is just for me for now."

"Wow, girl."

"Is that all, Tristana?" Charles was concerned for her. She had a lot to be emotional about. "Let's not push her, Stephan."

"I would appreciate that," she replied. "I can tell you that this drug causes me to think clearly, more rationally. It helps me to reach into parts of my mind where other parts of my mind do not want me to go. I want to see what happens over the next few minutes. If all seems OK, it will be your turn, Charles."

Charles nodded. "You both speak slowly and select your words carefully, enunciating with, I think, no use of contractions. Interesting."

Stephan shoved Charles playfully. "I'm using contractions now, Charles. It isn't as if I'm not using 'em."

"Well, maybe the effect of the drug has passed."

A few minutes later, Tristana started looking at Charles. Her eyes sparkled, her face was bright and flushed.

"I think I'm done," she said. "And I feel happy. As if my mind were the Augean stables, and Hercules diverted a river to clean it out."

Charles laughed. "Maybe Naked Emperor causes us to wax poetic too. Well, if you both feel fine, it's my turn."

Charles followed the procedure. He took one puff of Sybillene, and then added nine more until he was at full Naked Emperor dose.

He then sat and waited. He didn't feel anything in particular. He let his eyes focus on something in the distance. Maybe he should slip into meditation. He let his mind wander. There was no effect that he could ascertain. He slowed his breathing. He focused his mind on a few topics in the news, but no cosmic breakthroughs burst into his consciousness. Minutes passed.

"Charles, what are you experiencing?"

Charles shook his head. "Nothing. I don't think, feel, or sense anything differently. Do I *look* different?"

"You started staring into the distance for a bit, but that didn't last."

"I did that purposefully."

After a bit longer, Charles added, "Still nothing."

"Should we challenge you with something like we did to Stephan?"

"Sure, go ahead."

He heard her ask Stephan, "What do you think we should probe him with? No jokes now!"

"No jokes," Stephan replied. "I don't know... Oh, I got it. Charles, who killed JFK?"

Charles considered the question for a while. He tracked through all the information that popped into his brain, pulled things from his memory that he had not considered in some time. Then he said, slowly, "Well, lots of folks would have wanted him dead more than Lee Harvey Oswald did—the CIA, the Mob, Lyndon Johnson, Castro, the Russians, Dulles. All of them were capable of manipulating Oswald or turning him into a stooge. Jack Ruby's involvement has always made me wonder. He had no identified motive for killing Oswald, and he repeatedly stated that he was part of a big conspiracy. There was clearly something very important with Ruby that we never learned. And at this point probably *will never* learn. But, to answer the question directly, I have no idea who actually killed Kennedy. I just know that the official narrative is obviously incomplete in ways that are suspicious.

"And I know that the last gun an assassin would choose was the junky World War II–surplus Italian carbine they say Oswald had. And if he was going to do it, why not shoot while Kennedy was coming towards him, head on? Not when he was already going away, a difficult-angle shot."

Tristana said, "Well, that's interesting, I guess. But you were supposed to tell us some exciting new insight."

Charles replied, "I don't think I have any new insights about JFK. Nor have I awoken to any lies I had been telling myself. I feel nothing different. No new data, nor any new insights."

Tristana suggested, "Maybe your ProPG pathway is already fully active? Perhaps?"

"Possible. Or, the stuff just doesn't work on me."

Tristana said, "Let's try something more personal. What do you think about me, Charles?"

"Precisely the same thing I thought about you before I took Naked Emperor."

Stephan asked cheerfully, "And how about *me?*"

Charles laughed. "With Naked Emperor in my system, I finally have seen the truth. And the truth is—get ready for it, Stephan—the truth is… you *are* gay!"

20

Two for the Price of One

"PALADIN, we been missin' you." Alpha chastised him. "Where you been?"

Charles replied, "Just acquiring product for you to sell, sir."

Once Charles peeled back most people's social veneer, he was often saddened and disappointed by what he saw. But not with Alpha. Alpha had been forced to wear a Halloween mask to deal in the ghetto all these years. Once he took off this mask, he became more, not less, appealing. Alpha's ghetto bravado faded when around Charles, replaced by a growing acceptance of his role as an honest businessman: a partner Charles could trust.

Charles had been away, in foreign lands and on the ocean again. He lazily grew a short beard, now at its most itchy point. He had gone through this many times over the years and was used to the experience. He would soon have to decide whether to shave it off, or wear it as trimmed stubble, as had recently become fashionable. Fashion may be foolish, but it provided a convenient excuse to avoid shaving every day.

On the other hand, he had a piano performance this week and didn't relish an urge to scratch his face during a part written to be played *prestissimo*.

"Our revenues are ramping up. It's getting busy. We ain't dealing in controlled substances, but we *do* have uncontrolled demand. Your money-washing process holding out?"

Charles grunted. "Eh, it's getting maxed out. We'll need to think of something new."

"There's always the old-fashioned way. You know, takin' risks."

He didn't like taking unnecessary risks. But the choices might be between stopping the growth in the business and being satisfied, or moving larger sums of money than his system allowed for. He looked at Alpha and saw a man who wanted to keep expanding.

"Any trouble with the local police?" Charles asked.

"They don't care. No harm, no foul. They happy that we're peddling innocent shit. Our sales force is working selling stuff to help men get laid, and lower their cholesterol and all the other stuff that they can't afford from the pharmacies. We may be responsible for cleaning up the drug trade some in this city. Some of the cops, they think so."

"Because we changed the jobs of a bunch of street dealers?"

"Myths become real, Paladin. They hear that we taking dealers out of the shit, and they believe it. Coke and H always gonna be there, homeboy, I ain't gonna lie to you. Addict is a addict. And coke can keep a man harder than marble."

Charles raised his eyebrows. "I didn't know that."

"No word of a lie. But you gotta put it on right."

"So inhaling it doesn't do the trick?"

"No, snorting too much makes you limp. But topically, it works. I heard of a guy who had wood for more than a day, and the docs had to cut off half his dick. No lie. After I heard that, I never did it again. Plus, it made my dick numb. That's no fun."

"Yeah. Coke makes everything it touches numb."

"Point."

Alpha shifted uncomfortably.

"What is it, Alpha?"

"Well, our girl, Rainbow, she's one of our best runners. And she bringing distribution too. I feel real guilty about my part in what happened to her mamma, like I told you."

"As would I," Charles commiserated.

"When she came to kill me, I damn well nearly killed her back." Alpha shook his head. "She's real smart. I think she introduced you and me so's maybe I'd get out of that line of business. No kid in the hood would bring a clean, white uptown boy like you into my office selling Viagra. She took a big risk, and I respect that. "

"And you in turn took a big risk on me, and *I* respect *that*. So the team is happy?"

"Ya. There's more safe money dealing yuppies than crackheads. The cops get some free blue pills, and the bald cops get free hair-growth pills. They be cool."

"I like that. That hair-growth med is a testosterone blocker. That's how it works."

"Yeah, I read the documents."

"Can't hurt to block a little testosterone in some of those cops."

"Straight. Anyhow, so far the G don't care 'bout us."

"Yeah, Alpha, that's what I'm here about. The government shouldn't care, but Big Pharma started to notice. And Big Pharma has influence on the government."

"What you hearin', Paladin?"

Charles wondered if Rainbow had ever given his real name to Alpha. If she had, Alpha never acknowledged her reports on him. "I've got intel that there's a joint task force in development. FDA and Customs are working with consulting support from DEA to address our operation. Near as I can tell, they don't know much right now. I doubt they're putting much effort into *little ol' us*. And the guy in charge is no rock star. But it's a reminder to be careful. Are you keeping up firewalls?"

Alpha bobbed his head. It was equivocation. His speech lost much of the practiced street talk. "If the G uses enough threats and offers enough deals, they can get up to the Alphabet Men. Since day two, we have built that wall up high. But we didn't build it on day one, you know what I'm saying? Still, it will be hard for the feds to see through it unless they stumble into us accidentally, or if they start making deals with Tadeus or the Fat Man or one of the other multi-kilo dealers. Cuz *they* know who we are."

"We know Tadeus will sing to the narcs, Alpha. We need to think about how to better secure ourselves from the government. Just in case. In regard to Tadeus, how are things on that seedier side of the tracks?"

Alpha nodded. "We've made a couple a enemies there."

"Fat Man?"

"Maybe. You might have been right about that dude. One of those guys don't like what we up to. Fat Man pulling strings."

"What's he doing?"

"So far he's having his boys *threat* our dealers. Couple of guys got beat up. It's all under the radar so far, but he threatening more. Trying to hurt us. The dude want only narcotics sold on the street, and only by him."

"That sounds like Fat Man. Will he kill anyone?"

"He could. It's his next step. He losing some employees and therefore some street cred."

"So, agenda item number two for today is how we deal with the Fat Man. Item three is supply and inventory and storage. Item four is complaint resolution. Item five is moderation of growth: we can't outgrow our cash management. Six is an update on packaging and distribution. What else do you have on your list, Alpha? Anything else for today's agenda?"

"Yeah, agenda item seven. I want to add a drug."

"What are the clients asking for?"

"Sybillene. It's a new antidepressant. Sybillene has a bunch of street names. Naked Emperor, Covfefe, Fey, Vatic, Augur, Haruspex."

Charles simply said, "I've heard of Naked Emperor."

He sensed nothing in Alpha's speech or manners to suggest that the man knew anything about Charles's connection to Sybillene. Either Rainbow had stuck to her promise to keep Visioryme and Alpha secret from each other, or Alpha could act better than an A-list movie star.

"Yeah," Alpha continued. "That's the most common name. It helps people see lies for what they are, and liars too. I dunno. I never tried it. Lots of people asking though. Society types. Lawyers, businessmen, doctors, even cops. We've been selling erections and hair to the men, but the women are now asking for Naked Emperor. I guess it helps 'em figure out why their men are trying to grow hair and who they growin' wood for. Relationships and shit. Maybe I'm calling it early, Paladin, but I'm telling you this stuff gonna get hot. Might rival coke and Ecstasy. Another reason to watch our backs with Fat Man. Can you get your hands on any?"

"Sybillene's a new drug. I don't think anybody is making it for cheap overseas yet. But you think it's gonna be that big, huh?"

"Paladin, I think Naked Emperor gonna be huge. They say you don't get wasted. It's a society high. There's big money in society highs."

Charles's mind spun through a dozen business scenarios that ranged from fabulous to disastrous. "Put some sales estimates together."

"If you can supply this stuff, Paladin, that would be a freakin' miracle."

"Not as much as you might think, Alpha."

* * *

200

"Hi, Maurice."

"What do you say, m'boy? Good to see you. How's the drug-dealing business going?"

He hadn't seen Charles's face, for once again, after opening the door, he'd immediately retreated to the couch. Maurice reclined fully before making eye contact with Charles.

Charles said, "You mean the stuff we're selling on the street? God, it's a relief after suffering with Visioryme. The illegal drug trade is a much more honest business."

Uncle Maurice scoffed, while simultaneously downing a can of Pepsi. "Sure it is. Tell that to the users hospitalized when their drugs get cut with poisonous fillers. Lives lost to turf wars and back alley stabbings. Pimps and dealers getting children hooked on addictive substances in order to turn them out as underage hookers."

Feeling wrongly admonished, Charles asked, "Are you finished?"

"Yes, I am. But I'm sure there's more." Uncle Maurice concluded.

"Maurice, I know you know that those things are almost entirely consequences of prohibition. So perhaps I should have clarified. *My* illegal drug trade is ethical. My team assesses demand, orders inventory, arranges fulfillment, and generally optimizes systems to maximize profit. It's the way business is supposed to be. We don't have to pay lawyers and regulatory consultants, and we don't have to keep records for tax purposes. The illegal business has less hassle and less risk than the legal one, and supplies people's needs and wants better. I wish we could do it out in the open; we'd be that much more efficient."

"Talked to your dad lately?"

"Yes. But not about my black market activities. He knows all about Visioryme, though. He's proud of me. He thinks *Visioryme* is the honest gig! Hah. I'm sorry, but he doesn't get it. There's not much that's honest in the legal pharma business."

"What's going on at Visioryme?"

"Sluggish revenues at first, but things have been picking up this last month. I suspect mostly because Sybillene gets used as Naked Emperor... So far, people can only get it through their doctors."

"When did you get back?"

"Just a few days ago. Spent the last month and a bit in India on quality-control detail. And West Africa, picking up supplies, and shipping in more bamboo."

"How many containers of stiff wooden poles stuffed with Viagra this time?"

"Fifty. Not just Viagra anymore. We do other meds too."

"Shit, kid, how are you justifying importing that much bamboo to Customs?"

"It's not that much. Hardly even noticed on a big ship. They're going to let it pass right on through—totally legally—because Visioryme needs so much of it for making Naked Emperor. I mean Sybillene."

"What's that you say?"

"Sorry. I start confusing them in my own head too. But it's nice to get two for the price of one, as it were."

"Clean that up, and keep them straight, m'boy. It'll get you in trouble."

"You're right." Charles couldn't let that happen again. "Customs lets it go through because bamboo is used to make Sybillene, an approved medication with the happy imprimatur of the FDA. We've got all kinds of stamped official papers giving us approval. Hell, if we wanted to, we could probably get the government to *subsidize* my Viagra import system. Medical needs and all. But Maurice, it looks like the *real* money is going to be in Naked Emperor."

"Is Visioryme going to take Naked Emperor to the FDA, and get approvals for that use of it?"

"It would take three years of studies and applications. Lots of time and money. Life is too short to fill it with aggravation. And I suspect that Naked Emperor's going to be very unpopular in a lot of powerful circles. Just like LSD was. So it may get the same treatment, long before any FDA application could get approved for a new *indication*, as they say. It's frustrating, So many roadblocks. So many problems."

"Life isn't just full of problems. Life *is* problems."

"It doesn't have to be."

"Stop complaining. Next lesson: don't act like a victim. Now, what do you need from me?"

"This one's hard. I need information on a man named Juan Marcos. I just call him the Fat Man."

"Hey, I resemble that remark. Watch out."

"Yeah, sorry, Uncle. Are you losing weight?"

"Stuff it, kid. I'm a man of substance. What do you already know about this Juan Marcos?"

"Not much. He's a Tijuana-based cartel character. Seems like a modest-sized operation. Angry enough about what we're doing. We hired off some of his dealers. He's starting to get aggressive. He had a couple of our dealers beat up. I need a dossier."

"I'll see what I can do. But that may be a tough order. I've already tapped my DEA contact."

"I'm sure you can do it. Sooner the better, please. I don't want my men getting killed. Are you up for a game of chess?"

"I'm always up for that, m'boy."

Charles set up the board, pushing aside a pile of documents on the coffee table. As he reclined on the couch, Maurice played with his left hand, occasionally directing Charles to move his pieces for him. Mostly they played in silence.

"Why are you back in Manhattan, Charles?"

"I have rehearsals this week. I have a Friday evening concert with the Philharmonic."

"Good for you, Charles!" Maurice expressed true glee.

"It's part of what they call a Young Person's Concert Series. It's going to be fun. It's a blend of 20th-century European composers. They're calling it 'An Evening of Emotion.' My practice time is limited with all my traveling, and I'm barely able to get competent at the one piece. Prokofiev. It's nice they're giving me a chance, but I'm rather nervous that I'll stink. Will you come out?"

"I'm not big into emotion. It gets in the way of thinking."

"Emotion can have its purpose. It can be a good motivator."

"Rarely, Charles. Usually it is a bad motivator."

Charles shrugged. "When was the last time you were outside this apartment?"

"I'm not a recluse. I went out to the blood-sucking doctor's office in December."

"That was months ago! You've not been out since?"

Maurice thought for a moment and smiled half a smile and shrugged half a shrug. "I guess not."

21

A Piano at War

CHARLES, feeling more nervous than he had in years, walked toward Lincoln Center through Central Park. With an hour to go before his performance, he sat down on a bench in an effort to center his mind. Charles kept a phone reserved for communicating with Alpha, powering it up once per day for news from the front. A message came through.

Alpha had said simply, "Five of our people down permanently today. In public. In front of customers. Delta's dead. Need intervention."

Charles closed his eyes. Blood poured to his face. His heart raced. He thought of Delta, and his fury rose, in great part at himself. His distaste for the criminal acts of government had caused him to turn a blind eye to the same criminal behaviors occurring in the underworld. Bad guys infiltrated all of life's strata. He tried to swallow. This was as much an indictment of his failure to act as it was an indictment of humanity in general. Humans' quick resort to violence demonstrated just how closely they were related to chimpanzees.

Early this week, he should have cancelled everything and dealt with the Fat Man.

One shouldn't blame a scorpion for being a scorpion. But a fate now awaited whoever killed Delta: the same fate that a scorpion would meet—being crushed by the heel of Charles Knight's boot.

He could not let this happen again. His men were dead. His emotions were not.

His jaws came together, and his lips thinned out. His face now looked like it never smiled. His breath came out through his teeth. He hyperventilated in righteous fury, and he encouraged it, perhaps because it negated the crushing feeling of anguish from a moment before. He would wait. He would let the emotions fade. But he resolved to deal with this problem decisively.

Some people in the world just needed to be dead.

He didn't keep track of time, sitting there on a park bench. One minute, perhaps ten minutes, passed before he continued his march to Lincoln Center. He did not need to relax before this performance. He felt out of his body, separate from it. He could not anticipate what his hands would accomplish, how his mind would guide them when he sat in front of a grand piano, in front of the thousands of people, while his spirit fumed. He wasn't nervous anymore.

He didn't speak to any of the other artists backstage. Some looked at him, curious, wondering, perhaps concerned. But each individual was lost in his own thoughts, concentrating on his own performance. Professionalism wasn't so much demanded as assumed without question. Nobody double-checked the performer's preparation. No patronizing paternalism here. An expectation of individual excellence permeated the place, an expectation always met.

Here in this setting, in this venue of excellence, the individual and his or her expertise were considered as one, connected to the other artists by an unwritten contract to create extraordinary musical moments. If they were good enough, the audience would remember those moments for the rest of their lives. But only if they achieved perfection, and their mood climaxed in a crescendo.

The Philharmonic had asked him those many months ago what emotion he would convey with his piano tonight. Then, of course, he had no idea of the events that would precede this evening's performance. He had chosen to represent anger because he thought he could. He had planned to call on the anger he'd felt at the very beginning of his years of travel, when he was a younger man in Africa, when so much was taken away from him. But now, with the night at hand, he personified a much more immediate rage.

When his time came, Charles walked into the spotlight of the auditorium known to most as Avery Fisher Hall, or as Philharmonic Hall, to the anticipatory applause of more than twenty-five hundred pairs of hands sounding from the darkness. He made no motion to the audience, not even acknowledging their presence. Every bit of his being focused on the anger he felt. On Tadeus, on Juan Marcos, in the present; on the SEC and the IRS in the past.

He sat on the bench. He didn't care to wait for silence in the hall. As soon as his hands attacked the keys, the mood of the hall would mimic his mood. Filled not just with darkness. But with fury.

Prokofiev had written his Piano Sonata no. 7 soon after Stalin's secret police, the NKVD, arrested his friend and colleague, Vsevolod Meyerhold. A month after Meyerhold's wife was killed—and a few months before they executed Meyerhold himself—Prokofiev was commanded to compose a cheerful concerto to celebrate Stalin's birthday. After completing this commanded cantata, and now in utter hatred of Stalin, he next penned the three piano sonatas that came to be known as the *War* Sonatas, including no. 7.

Stalin proved the worst, at least in terms of body count, of the political criminals that ruled most of the world in the 1930s and '40s. Yet once he became an ally of the United States in the war against Hitler, U.S. government propaganda transformed him into the good-natured *Uncle Joe*. Forgotten was the fact that, even by the time the United States entered World War II, Stalin had killed over twenty million in his own country. He started with independent farmers, then moved on to dissidents, intellectuals, writers, army officers, and even composers of what he considered degenerate music. Hitler had by then killed *only* a million people. Mathematically one-twentieth as evil as Stalin.

Americans, provincial and protected from the Old World by two oceans, think of World War II as a contest between themselves—with perhaps some help from England—and the Axis: Germany and Japan. But in war, truth is the first casualty. In fact, World War II was mostly a battle between the national socialist Hitler and the socialist Stalin, thugs who shared the same basic values, presented with different rhetoric and trappings. The two tyrants were overt allies until June of 1941. From then on, most of the European war took place on the Russian front, where an overwhelming percentage of the war's deaths occurred.

Hitler's machine stood frozen in the Russian winter. By 1944, the six hundred thousand horses used during the invasion had died of starvation or been eaten by soldiers. The nightmare could have ended then and there, bogged down in frozen battle until both regimes collapsed under the weight of their failed shared philosophy. It could have been the end of two giant personality cults that pretended to empower the people they slaughtered. They should have been allowed to beat each other to a pulp.

The U.S. drug war echoed the horror on a smaller scale: gangsters duking it out for domination of their block. Charles's mind found itself in the Moscow of 1943, Mordor East, where he felt Prokofiev's passion. But he was here too, in New York, even as another increasingly tyrannical government pretended to empower the people it dominated.

He brought up his hands suddenly and smashed them down on the keys; the sounds surged from the Steinway. He focused all his emotion from his shoulders into his wrists, his hands, his fingers. He felt his fingers the way Prokofiev imagined, pulling triggers, twisting out grenade pins, squeezing the throat of an enemy. His arms hurled tense bodies to his left and limp death to his right. He ran his fingers over the butts of weapons, the hilts of knives, the tracks of tanks, the torn cement of buildings, over barbed wire imprisoning people left to the mercy of the morally insane. He clawed at carpet as secret police dragged him away, he scratched at their faceless faces, their emotionless hatred of all things productive and free. He killed Stalin with his fingers on black and white. He killed Tadeus and the Fat Man with the palms of his hands.

His elbows and hands then fell against his sides as his psyche left Stalin's hell and returned to his present. He was done. He opened his eyes to silence. And then he heard a clap, a single clap, and then another single clap, isolated in time and space. Then others joined, others who, no longer mesmerized by the strength of it, realized that the sonata had ended. Their hands found each other, beating hard to make as much noise as possible, in acknowledgement of the motive power of the moment, in belief that they had just experienced the anger and anguish of the composer, while unavoidably wondering about that of the performer.

His arms lay limp beside him. Charles stood then, and so did every member of the audience. He stared at, or rather through, the audience and walked off the stage as he had come on, acknowledging them not at all.

Backstage he found an unlit hallway and moved to its far end. In a dark corner there, unseen by anyone, he crumpled against the wall.

When he could stand, both his own and Prokofiev's anger remained, but the anger no longer controlled him. He filed it in a place to remind him of anguish, to be used when he needed it most.

He would now take charge of his mind and emotions to address a crisis.

The Sunday *New York Times* replaced its previously planned Style section lead with a picture of Charles at the piano, his face contorted by its demand for righteous vengeance. A critical review announced, in glowing terms, that Charles was the king of the emotive piano. It was the first time that a performance at Lincoln Center had caused a headline story to be replaced. The paper's editor-in-chief penned the critical acclaim. He had been at Lincoln Center that night and, by chance, decided to try Naked Emperor for the first time, during the break just before Charles and Prokofiev and Anger took complete control of the stage. His hands had been the first to clap.

22

The Lesser of Two Evils

TRISTANA'S words came rushed and anxious. "I heard you might be back in Washington, Charles. Are you coming by the office?"

"I'll try to make it, if I can. It's late. Everything OK?" He had no time for Visioryme tonight. He reinserted the magazine in his 1911 pistol.

"Not really."

"I only have a minute now. But go ahead." He wasn't interested in the most recent effluent that might have emerged from the FDA. Charles's mind focused on a series of actions that likely would lead to several deaths.

Tristana of course did not know this. She said, "Good news and bad news. The good news is that our sales are rising, and I mean rapidly."

"Everybody likes good news."

"Yes. The bad news is that FDA has sent a letter requesting information about high-dose Sybillene use."

"OK. What does that mean?"

"It means they're looking at us."

"So we're on their radar screen. That's unfortunate."

"Usually. Our science advisory board is on it, and we'll need to answer a lot of technical questions. But this is still low-level stuff."

"OK. But let's prepare for a storm. I don't think it's going to pass by." Charles looked around before speaking deliberately into the phone again. "Tristana, I do apologize, but do you mind if I call you back tomorrow?"

She accepted his apology, and he turned off the phone. His mind immediately left Visioryme.

"Girl troubles?" Epsilon prodded.

"Sorry for the interruption, gentlemen." He looked at the Alphabet Men, less one man. They'd worn increasingly conservative attire for going on five months, mirroring their new market. But they weren't going to be dealing with yuppies this evening. Tonight they dressed entirely in black, with bulky black coats covering Kevlar vests and ski masks that they would pull down from their scalps to cover their faces. Each wore dark sunglasses, except Beta.

"Are we agreed? We kill only if attacked?"

"I think they gonna be shootin', Paladin."

"I expect you're right, Epsilon. Anyone wanna back out?"

"You know that's not happening," Alpha said quietly to Charles. "They gonna 'venge Delta, sure. And we gonna defend what we've built."

Beta drove the unmarked panel van. The thin metal walls of the van would provide little protection from bullets. In military parlance, the van offered concealment, but no cover for the men within. Beta drove them to within a block of Tadeus's triple apartment and parked next to a hydrant. In the moonless overcast night, streetlights alone illuminated the block.

"Beta, go." Charles commanded. Beta jumped from the driver's seat, grabbing a large pair of cable cutters and some other gear. Two minutes later, the rest of the men swiftly emerged from the van, faces concealed.

A crackle came through a speaker in Charles's ear. "Pi, this is Beta. Lights out."

The street lights went first, and then the lights on the buildings flickered and died. As a car turned the corner of the block behind, the only source of remaining light disappeared. Then the men removed their dark glasses.

"Zeta, go."

Zeta, his eyes accustomed to darkness by the sunglasses, ran down the block and within fifteen seconds stood at the locked entrance to Tadeus's building. Zeta popped the door with a crowbar and held it open for the men, like a doorman at the Waldorf Astoria.

Epsilon grabbed the crowbar and led the way up the dark stairs. Charles couldn't have held them back if he'd wanted to. He kept a red-hued glow-stick in his teeth, which provided just enough light to make the climb possible.

They ascended the flight of stairs silently. Alpha indicated the doors leading to ex-apartments 2A and 2B; Gamma and Zeta moved to cover those exits. The other men stood on either side of 2C. Epsilon held the crowbar to pry it open. They slid their masks down over their faces.

The glowstick went to his pocket. "Epsilon, go," Charles whispered.

Epsilon shoved the crowbar into the doorjamb just above the lock and heaved. The lock splintered, and the door flew open. The men stormed into the living room.

"What the fuck is this?" Tadeus hollered.

Their targets had not yet found flashlights or candles to illuminate what they assumed was just a failure of the local power grid.

The Alphabet Men remained silent as Alpha, Gamma, and Zeta cleared the apartment, room by room, military style. Charles and Epsilon set up LED flashlights on either side of the room, aimed directly at Tadeus and the Fat Man, who sat on the couch. They kept their AR-15s aimed at the two men while doing so.

"Who da fuck are you?" Tadeus demanded.

Charles said in a monotone, "If you have weapons, lay them on the table. We're going to search you. If we find weapons on you still, we *will* shoot you."

Tadeus turned to the Fat Man, who shrugged. The Fat Man then shook his head slowly back-and-forth as he pulled a small gun from somewhere beneath his vast expanse of flesh and laid it on the table in front of him. Tadeus reached behind his back.

"Slowly, Tadeus." Charles was insistent.

"Fuck you. Here's my gun." Tadeus threw it down at the table. It clattered as it bounced and smashed into a pottery bowl full of chips, breaking the bowl into pieces.

Epsilon moved to take the guns from the table.

The five men gathered back in the room. Alpha brusquely shoved the Asian man with green-striped hair who had not that long ago tried to kill him. The man fell across Tadeus's feet.

"That's all?"

"Otherwise deserted."

"You aren't traveling safe, Juan Marcos."

"You know my name." The Fat Man spoke now for the first time, his Mexican accent thick.

Charles let his gun fall down to his side and replied, "Juan Esteban Marcos. Head of the Northern Mexico cartel, if you can call it a cartel. Two sons.

Both in the family business. Large estancia outside of Tijuana. You have a bad temper. You beat your sons. You like both dog and cock fighting. You smoke pretty good cigars. You bring drugs straight through the border, perhaps hidden in avocados, given that you have a large avocado farm."

"Who are you?"

"As far as you're concerned, Mr. Marcos, I'm just a man who is not subject to intimidation."

"Paladin?"

Charles pulled the ski mask off his face and replied, "You killed five good men."

Juan Marcos looked at Tadeus, questioning.

"Four of them were *my* men!" Tadeus screamed.

"If they were your men, why did you kill them, Tadeus?" Juan Marcos posed his question as an accusation.

"What you fuckin' asking me that for?"

Juan Marcos's tone stayed measured. "Because I want the truth. Did you kill those men?" His large face turned red now in the full beam of a flashlight.

"They workin' for Paladin. That's enough reason."

"Can you not find more men? Or are you lazy?"

"Fuck you, Juan Marcos."

"I do not like you anymore." Marcos reached his massive left arm up and grasped Tadeus's neck from the back and squeezed. His right arm quickly came over and grasped the front of his throat. One of his heavy feet kicked the green-haired head of Tadeus's lover, still laying by Tadeus's feet.

Tadeus's tall and thin build proved no match for Juan Marcos, whose muscles were accustomed to moving his heavy bulk. Marcos matched each of Tadeus's efforts to pull free with a shove backward into the couch. After a few moments, Marcos rolled his mass off the sofa and onto his feet. He then pressed the full weight of his torso onto his straight arms with thick hands wrapped around Tadeus's neck. One foot now also pressed into the shoulder of the green streak of hair.

Tadeus kicked, or tried to, but one of Marcos's knees was sufficient to immobilize the man's lower half. After a few long seconds, Tadeus lay unconscious. Marcos did not let up until the suffocating compression had stopped the man's heart.

The Alphabet Men watched in silence. The green-haired Asian watched from the floor, where he lay immobile under Marcos's bulk.

Nobody tried to intervene.

When it was over, Marcos slid back down into the sofa, deep breaths heaving his chest up and down. Sweat dripped down his face.

Marcos nodded, and spoke in a monotone similar to the tone that Charles had used a few minutes—and one man's life—ago. "Mr. Paladin."

The green streak of hair screamed from the floor. Squirming out from the now-lesser restraint of Marcos's heavy leg, the man leapt to his feet while hurling a knifelike fragment of the broken bowl. It struck Charles's face, slicing through skin, and then the man was on him, digging long fingernails into Charles's wrist, prying at his gun. The flashlights all turned toward the new motion. Tadeus's surviving lover found the pressure points on Charles's wrist, and wrenched his gun away. Then, three shots echoed through the room. And green hair tumbled to the floor, writhing.

Charles rolled the little man onto his back with his foot. Blood streamed from the man's neck, soaking through his turtleneck collar and onto the floor. Blood filled his mouth. He coughed, his body convulsed, but it took him a minute more to die. His agony ended in a final and permanent silence.

While the man lay dying, Marcos held a small pistol, previously concealed in the couch, illuminated by the LED flashlights that had turned back toward him. Cast on the wall to the left, underneath the movie poster from *The Omen*, a perfectly delineated silhouette appeared: a fat arm holding a diminutive pistol with a faint puff of smoke drifting lazily from the muzzle.

"My gift to you, Mr. Paladin," Marcos said, calmly, as he wiped down the pistol and placed it on the table. "Tadeus will bother you no more."

Charles did not respond. He let the blood drip from his cheek as he looked closely at Juan Marcos. His mind raced through a series of impending moves as a chess player might, but this was a game of life. Kill or not kill.

Alpha pointed his muzzle at the Fat Man. The other men all did the same.

Charles's earpiece cracked.

"Pi, what's going on in there?"

"Beta, Pi here," Charles responded. "We're all fine. Stay in position."

Epsilon said quietly, "It sounds like a sorority. Beta Pi."

Charles looked at Alpha. Only his eyes and mouth were visible. But the eyes conveyed the answer to Charles's unspoken question.

"Mr. Marcos, thank you."

*　　*　　*

Later, as the van moved through the quiet city streets, Epsilon asked, "Why let him live?"

Charles sat still in his seat, watching through the van's front window the buildings of the city, the storefronts, the restaurants, the homes. "I don't know if it was wise, Epsilon," Charles replied a bit later. "But the Fat Man didn't attack us. So, for better or worse, I think we had no choice."

"Let's hope it works out for the best, Paladin."

Charles frowned.

In the dictionary, *hope* falls between *hell* and *hysteria*.

23

Awakening

"WHAT happened, Charles?" Tristana asked him as soon as he approached close enough to hear her in the noisy bar.

Charles reached up and touched his cheek. A bandage covered his sutures, but purple and red swelling bulged out from all sides of the wound. Completely covering it would have made him look like the phantom of the opera.

"No real damage. It'll heal, Tristana."

"What do you get into? Bar fights? Do I need to warn the bouncers here?"

"Oh, a minor tangle last night. No problem. They look worse than I do."

"You got mugged?"

"Some people aren't very nice."

"Charles, you amaze me. Who the hell are you?"

"Just another guy trying to figure out the meaning of life. May I sit down, please?"

"Oh, I'm sorry. Please join me. I don't usually expect people to ask."

"Emily Post used to beat me with a wooden spoon."

Charles settled in across the table from Tristana, who wore a red dress, with more makeup than usual, tastefully done with a deliberate and light hand. "It's good to be here with you. Do you know how long it takes to get sewn up in an emergency room?"

"One hundred forty-seven minutes?"

"Close. Thirty minutes of meaningless paperwork, four hours of point-less waiting, and six minutes of sewing. I was in line behind people who use the ER as a neighborhood pharmacy. The law says they can't be turned away, but it seems most of them don't pay."

"So what happened to you?"

"Oh, they finally checked me in, wanted an insurance card, didn't know what to do when I offered them cash. I don't think that ERs know what cash is."

"Charles, I meant what happened that you needed stitches?"

He leaned his elbows on the table. "Just life in the big city. Let's talk about you."

She glared at him.

But then she softened and shook her head. "You're impossible."

"I consider that an invitation."

"An invitation to what?"

"To get out of this place and do something fun."

"Sounds super. We're all working nonstop, barely sleeping. The whole company's working long hours, doubling up in the manufacturing facility too. Demand is suddenly popping. Your excess inventory is coming in handy."

"That's great, Tristana!" Charles smiled for the first time since the day of the concert. But it hurt his injured face to do so. He had followed the sales volume closely, and his expanding Alphabet Teams had added a bit to the illicit demand for the green canisters. "But please don't let the inventory decline. Push production."

"On the money front, we're not just generating revenues. We're going to show some profit this quarter," she added.

"Greater yet." The smile grew, but his enthusiasm was muted.

"We're getting hit with all sorts of requests for Sybillene, mostly from independent pharmacies, not the chains. Lots of doctors requesting it. Our drug is going viral, Charles, and outside of usual pharma paths. It makes me more than a little bit nervous."

"Again, it sounds like time to do something fun," Charles reiterated.

"What do you have in mind?" she asked.

"Let's go to the Mall."

"You want to go shopping?"

"No, no… The *Mall*. The one with the monuments and the reflecting pool. Let's see what's going on down there tonight."

Tristana looked at him intently, skeptically, but he just smiled back.

Tonight could be special. The Mall would not be empty. Internet banter had caught Charles's attention, but not that of the mainstream media. The fact Naked Emperor had gone viral might become evident to everyone after tonight.

The Mall provided the traditional venue for Americans who wanted to make a point. War veterans, poor people, civil rights demonstrators, tax protestors, and women all had their days in the national spotlight. Nobody received more media coverage per capita than the two hundred people who had gathered to protest a change in transgender bathroom edicts. TV and newspapers increasingly amounted to press-release distribution services for political movements, interspersed with what amounted to corporate info-mercials and some heartwarming psychological soma to make everyone feel either good, or good and angry. Of course, the broadcasts came spackled with commercials, including a surprising number for prescription drugs. People who wanted actual news, as opposed to scripted infotainment delivered by blow-dried personalities, increasingly found it on the Internet.

Most likely the media would overlook tonight's rumored activity. But a different energy had built up to this evening. He wanted to be there and see for himself. This was too important to rely on *reporters*.

"What's going on tonight?" Tristana asked as Charles parked on the west side of the river near Arlington Cemetery. In the dying light of the early evening, thousands of people walked across Memorial Bridge toward the Lincoln Memorial. They held no signs, no banners, and bore no pins to announce their purpose. "It looks more like a polite celebration than a protest."

Charles looked at her. She had to suspect. But she would suppress it for as long as she could.

"Let's go find out," he said.

He popped out of the car and came around to the passenger side, opening the door before she had unbuckled her seatbelt. He offered his hand. She took it, not seeming to mind when he didn't let go.

He was now certain that this evening could proceed to intimacy. He was also certain that he did not love her. There might be some welcome sex tonight. Or perhaps he'd avoid the still-unwelcome complication. Either outcome had its value. Charles's abilities didn't include fortune telling, so he chose not to worry.

Be happy, and go with the flow. Whenever possible.

They walked holding hands toward the bridge, joining the growing crowd moving toward the broad edifice of marble that shone pink and orange in the last throes of the passing day. They hadn't, however, come to worship at the altar of Lincoln. Although the memorial itself was magnificent, most of these people blithely ignored it. It honored, indeed apotheosized, the man as the best of presidents even though he was perhaps the worst. Lincoln closed down hundreds of newspapers that opposed his actions, and jailed thousands of men after suspending habeas corpus. He had forced the South to remain part of a union they had every right to leave. He was directly responsible for the unnecessary deaths of 750,000 people.

All of this was camouflaged with rhetoric about freeing the slaves, something Lincoln cared little about. In fact, Lincoln freed no slaves, for his famous Emancipation Proclamation applied only to the Confederate states, where he held no power. He wrote it as a matter of expediency. His whole purpose was to keep Europeans—who had all successfully abolished slavery without civil war and now hoped for the dissolution of the United States—from supporting the South.

But discussing Lincoln's flaws with an American was almost as dangerous as discussing Mohammed's flaws with a Muslim. Why paint a target on one's chest when nothing could be gained? The fact that all the people passing by the monument tonight paid no heed to it served as a reminder of one way to combat the memorialization of tyrants: ignore the bastards.

Charles observed the throng around him as best he could, while fighting the distraction of her hand in his, the occasional querying, almost imperceptible stroke of a sliding of finger against finger. The assembly was comprised of all colors, all classes of men and women. This was no typical protest used as an excuse for either a party or a riot. Something altogether different was in the air.

"Where are you coming in from?" a woman in a lightweight blue fleece asked Tristana. They had been walking next to each other since the middle of the bridge and had turned to the right together, heading down the paths toward the Tidal Basin, the Japanese cherry trees, and their final destination.

"I'm a local," Tristana replied. "How about you?"

"Iowa."

"Wow. Why are you here?"

"What do you mean?"

"Well, what's going on here?" Tristana asked.

"Oh, you aren't here for the…" The woman stopped for a moment, causing Tristana to stop as well for just an instant before they both started walking again, now slightly behind Charles. He immediately missed the feel of her hand.

The woman said, "It's amazing how disconnected people who work in Washington can be from the goings-on in the real world, huh? I don't mean to be rude."

Tristana shrugged. "It's not rude. It's true. I'm in the private sector myself, but I guess it still applies to me, because I don't know what this gathering is about."

There was that famous *New Yorker* cover cartoon that showed Manhattan Island in great detail, and the rest of the continent as an empty space, with Los Angeles in the far distance. The same kind of cartoon could be drawn for D.C., with the Beltway acting as kind of a cultural moat separating it from the rest of the country.

"It's not a protest," the woman said. "It's an awakening."

"I don't quite follow…"

"You've heard of Naked Emperor, haven't you?"

Tristana stopped in her tracks as her denial disappeared. The woman stopped with her. Charles slowly turned and listened from a slight distance, as the crowds walked politely past.

"Naked Emperor? Yes. I have." Tristana looked around at the people. Charles watched her eyes as they evidenced the growing recognition that this gathering multitude was a result of her work.

"Yes," the woman said, "Naked Emperor. It's got a bunch of names. Sybillene, Viewer, Insight, Covfefe, Truth Serum. If we asked around, I bet we could hear *a hundred* different names. But the universal name is Naked Emperor. It's the best stuff ever."

"What about Naked Emperor?" Tristana stayed still and let the people walk past. Charles saw her struggling, an internal battle between anxiety and pride.

"It's amazing," she replied. "I'm an aeronautical engineer. Naked Emperor helped me discover a design flaw in a project, one that I had entirely failed to see. It took some kind of blinder off me." The woman pulled a familiar green cartridge from her purse. "This is it, here. We are all going to take ten puffs of this, at eight PM."

"All these people are going to be puffing Sybillene tonight?" Tristana nodded to herself, now realizing both the significance of the event and why Visioryme's revenues had shot up. She looked over to Charles, her face filled with a mixture of concern and ebullience. Charles, amused by Tristana's confusion, didn't respond. She turned back to her new acquaintance. "Who organized this?"

"Nobody. It was suggested first by a student newspaper at some college outside of Detroit. It took off on the Internet. It's a huge experiment."

"So, no one is in charge? No one is giving speeches?"

"I haven't heard anything about speeches. We're all just gathering, enjoying the view, and at eight PM we start inhaling." She held up the canister of Sybillene. "It's a perfect evening for it." Her arms waved around, pointing at the ubiquitous cherry trees that lined this part of the city.

Tristana looked up again at Charles, her eyes now showing only the fear, not the confidence, nor the pride. She nodded faintly to the woman, who waved goodbye before catching up to her group. Charles reached out, took Tristana's hand again, and guided her along with the calm flowing river of humanity toward their nexus: the memorial to the president that this type of person would most honor.

Surrounding the Jefferson Memorial stood a throng of peaceful, even contemplative people. They settled into comfortable spots all around the Tidal Basin, leaving little space for more to arrive. Yet more arrived, risking the cars streaming by in order to cross the complex of roadways.

No one around could know Charles's and Tristana's role in all of this. They were just another couple holding hands, two more faces in the crowd.

"This … could be a disaster for us, Charles." Tristana swallowed. "A real nightmare."

"Yes. And there's absolutely nothing we can do about it," Charles replied, not looking at her, focused instead on the edifice that reflected in the unstirred water that lay just in front of them. Charles often joked that his favorite president was William Henry Harrison, because he died after only a month in office, before he could do any serious damage. But he would have liked to have known the president represented by the tall statue in this memorial.

He added, "I don't think this is a gathering of political radicals. These people cover the spectrum."

"This is going to kill Visioryme, Charles. This is going to have FDA all over us."

"You think?"

"Massive off-label use will cause FDA to stop us in our tracks. You don't know these people. I do. Far too well."

"Tristana, I'm not saying that the FDA won't come down hard on Visioryme. I expect they will, actually. But it won't be because of off-label use, although they might use that as an excuse. And they won't be the only ones coming down on us. If what I think could happen here tonight indeed happens, then the entire machinery of the government, and all the industries that rely on them for their revenue, are going to come down on Visioryme. And they won't play fair.

"It'll be a repeat of what happened with LSD. LSD was legal and a big part of the free speech movement, the peace movement against the Vietnam War, and antigovernment protests in general. So they made it a Schedule I controlled substance, just like heroin. Even though LSD is not addictive, doesn't cause violence, and is a beneficial therapeutic. Same with cannabis. Ayahuasca. Peyote. Psilocybin. And several hundred artificial compounds. Anything that can alter a conventional view of reality. They don't want to see anybody taking the Red Pill."

Charles kept looking out at the Jefferson Memorial. He didn't appear particularly concerned, and he wasn't. So he spoke as if he were reciting history, which he was. History repeats itself. He knew his words might fall harshly on Tristana's ears. So he softened them with a reassuring squeeze of her hand. He was loath to let go of that hand.

It was almost eight o'clock.

His mind searched a path through the obstacle course—the gauntlet— that the FDA-pharmaceutical-medical complex would set up against Visioryme. Plus the SEC, because Visioryme was a publicly traded company. The IRS because they had income. Homeland Security would suggest that Naked Emperor encouraged terrorists. When they illegalized Sybillene, the DEA and the FBI would get involved. Multiple arms of the government would start flexing their muscles. But as yet, Charles had no notion of the organization that would be Sybillene's greatest nemesis.

He was sure, however, that Visioryme had no chance. Not if they tried to stay legal.

The crowds of humanity surrounding him now were allies, albeit unarmed and unorganized.

He didn't yet know how to handle it. Visioryme had started out as a means to an end, and provided superb cover for importing bamboo poles stuffed with Fiagara and other pills. But now, the tail wagged the dog. And there could soon be hundreds of millions, billions of dollars to be made from Naked Emperor.

Everyone around them held a green cartridge of Sybillene. Every one of them was made in a production facility that Charles controlled.

They all looked to the Jefferson Memorial. Many people had their mobile phones out, occasionally glancing at those perfectly synchronized clocks as the hour approached. Then hands came up to mouths. And together, fifty thousand people inhaled, hard and fast. It was perhaps the first time in history that the breathing of so many people was so audible, so spontaneously coordinated. It was as if they were practicing pranayama in an immense yoga class. It was a "be-in," the likes of which hadn't happened in the U.S. since the '60s. Tristana was the new Ownsby Stanley, the chemist known as *Bear*, who spread out his White Lightning in the Summer of Love. She had unknowingly become his latter-day avatar, spreading Naked Emperor.

Charles said, "Breathtaking!"

Neither Charles nor Tristana participated. They wanted to observe, unaffected and unimproved by the influence of the drug. After the ten inhalations, people around them offered to share with those who didn't have a canister. Many others then took their ten puffs. Tristana waved off an offer, a bit rudely, immersed as she was in her internal battle between fear and awe. Charles watched.

In a few minutes, complete silence enveloped the Tidal Basin. Some people stood, others sat, some found room to lie down. But what they all did was stare into a distance, toward the Jefferson Memorial, through the stone and to the inscriptions on its walls. Many of the people there had the words inscribed in their mind's eye. Others had it on paper in front of them. Everyone now focused on those words. The words still read at least once by all schoolchildren, before their meaning was negated by everything else they would be taught.

Charles whispered to Tristana. "Watch what's going to happen next."

"You know?"

"Yes."

222

And then those closest started speaking the words carved on the memorial. No one coordinated it, and no conductor kept tempo for the thousands of voices. The sound came like thunder, yet because of their familiarity, the words were entirely clear.

Charles and Tristana listened as the multitude calmly spoke in a concert that could be heard across the Potomac in Virginia:

"WE HOLD THESE TRUTHS TO BE SELF-EVIDENT..."

"Truths, Tristana." Charles spoke into her ear. "When have you ever heard a group this size show an interest in the concept?"

They listened to the excerpt from the Declaration of Independence, recited not so much as a document of rebellion, but as a treatise on the maturation of humanity.

"Have we created a zombie drug, Charles? Look at these people, all staring, all reciting the Declaration of Independence. What have we done?"

"They're not reciting trite brainwashing rubbish, Tristana. It was no accident that they came to this place in particular. Sybillene is no zombie drug. You've created an *anti-zombie* drug. Naked Emperor is the opposite of Aldous Huxley's soma. This is an awakening. Awakening from *being* zombies for so long. Look around you. These people, *enhanced* by your drug—by *our* drug—are right now thinking about what Thomas Jefferson meant when he said that Nature wants us to pursue happiness. Once aware of that, people will come to some radical conclusions. And Tristana, these people are now *all* aware. Some perhaps for only as long as the Sybillene lasts. But for others it may be permanent..."

The thunder of the recitation concluded and the people around them began communicating their new discoveries, their Naked Emperor–evoked realizations. Everyone was ... happy.

Eyes and minds had been opened in these past minutes.

Many of these people would not be slaves again. Jefferson's words, undistorted, regained their original power.

Charles and Tristana listened to the conversations around them. They listened as Americans began, many for the first time in their lives, to think and speak like Jefferson. Charles could not hold back his delight. His smile became broad, infectious. He ignored the pain in his face, for he was the proud father of a newborn baby.

"I think, Tristana, I think our little drug may have just started a revolution."

24

Kabuki Theater

SABINA Heidel sat on the edge of her seat, idly looking from one man to another, paying no attention to any of them. She knew they all paid attention to *her* though, sneaking furtive glances at her blouse, her face, her legs. And when she turned to walk out they'd all stare. Were they fools to think she didn't notice their reaction to her? She could tell even if her eyes were closed.

Her stint at FDA would soon be over. Working alongside Donald Debocher had been like pushing on one end of a boiled spaghetti noodle and expecting the other end to move. A prototypical bureaucrat, Donald was disinclined to *do* anything. Of course, doing nothing avoided all risks. He was worse than the dregs that populated the IRS, whom she despised when she worked there. To this day, her father still ran the IRS, and even *he* couldn't fix the endemic malaise that infected its culture.

Sabina encountered this in every government organization she'd worked in. She loved the power, but despised the people.

When she'd first arrived at FDA, she'd snuck around to get information about Sybillene. Her assignment was clear. The publicly available material proved unhelpful. And when she had asked Donald for access to the rest, he'd agreed, but with suspicion; he dragged his feet providing the files that she needed. In fact, for a slug, he was masterful at delay and misdirection. Better than Einstein at physics, better than Babe Ruth at baseball. Nagging proved pointless. Donald's blatant and profound conflicts of interest stood as additional roadblocks to Sabina's mission. But those same conflicts were potential leverage. Sabina, therefore, recommended that Paul Samuels be patient, and not use his influence to replace Debocher.

When Debocher wasn't idle, or obstructing some form of progress, he focused languid attention on finding the source of counterfeit Viagra. Sabina pretended to care about this scourge of the planet, prompting Donald to make some headway on his initiative. There was little real progress, but that didn't matter.

She was here because Paul Samuels knew Sybillene presented a threat not just to central bankers, but to the entire establishment. The establishment—the *Deep State*, as some called it—consisted of an informal association of top politicians, bureaucrats, generals, academics, media types, and corporate leaders who had an interest in the status quo. They'd managed to cement themselves into positions of power, using the government for leverage. The average citizen thought of government as *We the People*, idealized in a high school civics book. That useful fiction had to be maintained.

Sabina could see how the game was played, and wanted to join the varsity team. She'd set her goal—to rise to the top of the banking system—some years ago. Money and power were fungible. But power rested on a bedrock of money, at least in a developed country. She considered this current deployment to be a worthwhile, if tedious, step in her ascent.

Paul Samuels sent her here because Donald Debocher was married to the CEO of Visioryme. Debocher could not, therefore, be expected to be on the right side when it came time to eliminate Sybillene from the world. Debocher, a successfully entrenched bureaucrat, had to be neutralized. Of course, he could always meet with an unfortunate accident. But finding a proper replacement for him would take time, and brought its own set of risks.

Her job was to act as a Mata Hari, to manipulate Debocher.

She would try to avoid sleeping with Debocher. It was more effective to keep him on edge. He was an easy toy to chew on—an almost perfectly predictable male. She'd sleep with him only if necessary for a critical victory. Years ago, she would have done so purely for the pleasure of controlling him. But now, with some years behind her, she found his type simply disgusted her. She'd slept with billionaires and vice presidents. To allow Debocher to have her would be like allowing a slug to crawl on a princess. Yet she wanted him to believe it was possible.

She dug into Visioryme the best she could, investigating its financing, marketing, and distribution. She strove to understand the science, and the manufacturing processes. She put together background files on its execs, its key employees, and the scientists who created the drug. There was no point, after all, in turning off one spigot if nine other spigots could flood the nation. If college kids could figure out how to make Naked Emperor, or foreign cartels figured out how to import it, they would. The inventors needed to be stopped, not just the invention.

She looked at the board of directors, but had not prioritized the shareholders of Visioryme. Three weeks into her investigation, she decided that had been an oversight. Paladin LLC was not only a major shareholder, but an aggressive buyer of shares. She reached out for help from the IRS and SEC, and learned that a man named Charles Knight was behind Paladin, and therefore behind Visioryme.

She knew that name well. Minutes later, she'd ascertained that *this* Charles Knight was the same Charles Knight she had known seven years ago, the only man to have ever spurned her. The Charles Knight whose financial ruin she'd engineered, which in turn had propelled her up the ladder at the IRS, the SEC, the White House, and now the real bastion of power: the Federal Reserve. The same Charles Knight that could have destroyed her back then, and maybe still could now.

She hated him then, but he'd disappeared. Now that he was back in her world, she hated him even more.

But she discovered nothing about where he had been over the last seven years. She discovered nothing about where he lived or what he did now. She could find no address. She could find no credit card information, and no personal tax returns. Paladin LLC was a dusty company, and Charles Knight was too murky to see through. He wasn't the type to post his trivia to Facebook, or reach out to strangers on LinkedIn.

She reported selectively to Paul Samuels, of course. He could arrange to have FDA pull Sybillene off the market. But he felt a simple administrative ban was worse than a half measure. It would waste a huge opportunity: a chance to do something of historic importance. He'd decided to get Congress involved. The FDA was necessary for the moment, but really just a bit player in a much, much bigger plan.

Even after years of working with Samuels, she was astounded by the man's insight, his genius.

She didn't tell him about her history with Charles Knight. Samuels would pull her out if he knew.

She looked around at the men in the room, meeting about FDA trivia. She'd stay on the job here until Congress acted.

And then she would do all she could to annihilate Charles Knight.

* * *

After the Awakening, no word emerged from the FDA the next day, nor the next few weeks. There were no comments from the police, the FBI, or the DEA. No agency would stick its nose into this morass until after the big guys had chosen the path they would have to follow. But there were plenty of private conclaves between the denizens of Capitol Hill and the regulatory community. And with Paul Samuels.

Meanwhile, sales of Sybillene shot to the moon and beyond.

A Senate subcommittee called hearings to investigate Sybillene. The subcommittee chairman rescheduled the hearing for a day when the one senator with any sense could not be present.

Charles Knight would be the first witness called to testify.

They'd have to wait, because Charles had something more important on his agenda.

Charles had supplied Alpha with some Sybillene, but he hadn't opened the spigot wide. The Alphabet Men wanted as much as they could get. Naked Emperor had rapidly become the #1 request of their clientele, and now beat, by a factor of two, all of the bootlegged imported drugs combined. Charles's civilized money laundering process could not keep up with that. At least not safely. Charles expected two things: first, that the Alphabet Men and people like them might soon become the primary, or even only, distributor of Naked Emperor and, second, that safe money movement would become a major challenge.

By the time the summons to appear before the Senate had been delivered to Visioryme for him, Charles had already agreed to another obligation. He wasn't about to break his promise because some jerks thought they had the power to tell him where to be. He'd try to do both, but the jerks would have to wait their turn.

Today would be the first actual delivery of money using a new experimental system. This was nothing like his carefully plotted transactions at the banks, which would still be used for most of the small dealers. His new system allowed the movement of substantial cash, with a good level of protection from prying eyes. He needed this protection because someday very soon, the authorities would start tracking the cash movement, trying to climb their way up the distribution ladder. The cash, and therefore the ladder, reached up to Charles. So Charles went to great effort to prevent authorities from climbing up.

He had the easy job. The hard part involved the dealers, climbing into darkened subway tunnels, avoiding detection by cameras while not getting run over by trains.

And so he sat by the railroad tracks, away from the nearest station and the nearest camera. He dressed as a bum, with the hood from a windbreaker covering his head and the bill of a baseball cap obscuring his face. The tracks lay above ground here at the far reaches of the metro's tendrils, southeast of Anacostia, before the Green Line came to an end a ways down at Branch Avenue.

Charles sat waiting on a pile of discarded railroad ties. They'd been pressure-treated in massive chambers with a wood preservative distilled from petroleum. It was reminiscent of the method Dan Smolderhof had used to fabricate drill-core results back in Gondwana to fake a multibillion-dollar gold discovery. Here the effects smelled like diesel fuel, and didn't look like gold.

The next train would be the one. It wouldn't be stopping.

It appeared four minutes later. The sound was deafening as the train tore by, screeching as it curved to the right on its way to cross Suitland Parkway. Charles pressed a button on a remote control just as the last car passed.

He didn't see it fall, but he did see something bouncing along the tracks, chasing the train for a few yards. The mechanism worked, for there in the middle of the tracks lay a zippered brown leather satchel. Ten seconds later it was in his hands. He left the scene at a brisk, unobtrusive walk.

The satchel had a claw that could grab onto a hose or pipe or thick wire. The simple device would release its grip upon receipt of a radio signal. He only needed the train number to release the satchel anywhere, on any line they chose, and no one would know where that would be. It was an effective way to move cash.

The satchel contained three short stacks of hundred-dollar bills. About $30,000. No point in risking big money on a test run.

The system worked, for the moment. Maybe, if things went sideways, he would have to set up a system to ensure that GPS trackers and other such high-tech gadgets could be countered.

Charles climbed into Xander's Mustang, drove to Branch Avenue, and parked. Still looking like a bum, he climbed aboard an inbound train.

Just maybe, he would make it to the Senate hearing on time.

*   *   *

"Never before," began the chairman of the Senate Committee on Health, "never before has one drug been used, improperly, by so many people so rapidly with such disregard for the labeling and marketing restrictions provided by the scientific experts from FDA. Users call this drug Naked Emperor, Insight, Covfefe, Freshview, Open, and many other names. Its official name is Sybillene, and it presents a grave new threat to the integrity of the system that keeps our nation's pharmaceuticals safe and effective. We're facing a health crisis for America. I call on Mr. Charles Knight, the controlling shareholder of Visioryme Pharmaceuticals, the manufacturer of Sybillene, to stand before this committee and testify under oath."

Tristana and Stephan sat two rows behind the committee chamber's witness table. Congressional staffers had screened them as potential witnesses, but Tristana didn't make the cut because of her husband's position with FDA. To make the nepotism public was hardly in anyone's interest. Stephan had proven too obnoxious during his interview, and his gayness made it entirely too politically incorrect to attack him. But Charles, with his history of illegal stock speculation, tax evasion, insider trading, and many years outside the U.S. engaged in who-knows-what other illegal acts, seemed like the perfect witness for Congress to pillory in order to vilify Sybillene. So he would be the man of the hour.

But he was late.

Tristana turned her head to look for him.

"Charles Knight!" the chairman called again, exasperation evident in his voice and visible on his face.

A hum rose in the packed committee room as people started looking around. One doesn't defy the U.S. Senate lightly. A contempt citation usually came accompanied by jail time.

The rear doors opened, and Charles came through. He'd been running. He stopped as soon as he came in, taking in the situation.

"Oops," he said quietly.

Charles wore baggy green pants with pockets on the thighs, and a cheap windbreaker. His clothes weren't particularly respectable in the first place, and had picked up some extra grime alongside the train tracks. His hair lay disheveled. He perspired from his run to the chambers, and he hadn't shaved in more than a week.

He carried the small leather satchel, which had been searched with great amusement by a security guard at the entrance to the Capital Building. "Who you planning on bribing?" the guard had asked—only partially in jest—as he flipped through the wads of cash.

Tristana winced at Charles's appearance.

He saw her sitting with Stephan and Rainbow, smiled, and waved.

"Charles Knight!" the chairman called.

Charles walked up the center aisle. An officer directed him to a seat at the witness table. His mind had a flashback to an adolescent dream about sitting in a classroom in underwear. It's not often, he thought, that someone actually gets to live the dream. He wasn't even wearing a tie. Was a necktie required in this place?

There was no doubt in anyone's mind that Charles Knight didn't fit in.

Forty-eight hours earlier, three young congressional staffers—who believed they were messengers of the gods—had provided him with a pre-pared statement. They *assured* him that *assuring* the committee of his desire to cooperate fully and accede to their wishes would help things go smoothly, and *ensure* the best possible outcome. He, in turn, *assured* them he under-stood. With mutual assurances firmly in place, the choreographed meeting should proceed as desired.

He looked behind at the audience. Rainbow's now-multicolored hair stuck out from the crowd as much as Charles's rough attire.

He then looked upward toward the committee members, seated in their positions of authority over the plebeians below them. One leaned to whisper to another, grimacing at Charles as he did.

He didn't apologize for his tardiness; that would set the wrong tone. After all, they were the ones interrupting his business day. The scuffed, oily satchel resting on the table proved it.

After some preliminaries, and a request to explain his position with Visioryme, Charles spoke.

"Ladies and gentlemen of the committee, I sit before you as a man who
has declined the opportunity to be the chairman of the board of Visioryme
Pharmaceuticals. I serve in no official capacity for the company. I declined
the honor and opportunity for one reason—so I could avoid a small percentage of your SEC's rules and prohibitions on trading. A company I own
has been a large shareholder of Visioryme for many years, although, until
recently, I was quite unaware of that fact. Oversights like that happen when
one has to 'get out of Dodge,' as they say. The IRS and SEC stole the vast
majority of my assets some years back, and I felt it prudent to stay out of
harm's way for a while.

"It's irrelevant that my only crime was uncovering a giant fraud and
stopping a war in Africa. These agencies, your agencies, took my money
under the pretense that I broke a law. The reality is that *they* broke the
law—at least if falsifying documents and suborning witnesses is against the
law anymore. It's common practice in your world, where right is determined
by might, and you hold the biggest guns."

Murmuring arose behind him. The congressmen shuffled through their
copies of Charles's prepared comments, confused. A few staffers pulled close
to their bosses, shaking their heads. Charles would give them no time to
interrupt. What he had to say was brief enough.

He went on. "There are essentially only four ways to deal with evil. You
can bow to it, and let it rule you. You can pretend it doesn't exist. You can
try to run, and hope it won't find you. Or you can confront it, and attack it.
Only the last alternative has a chance of success for more than a moment.

"I am here today at your request, as a free American who now controls
a small pharmaceutical company. Visioryme is, like every other organization
in this business, required to waste an obscene amount of time and money
hiring legions of lawyers, lobbyists, and regulatory consultants, simply to
stay in business. Despite the costs imposed and barriers erected by this body
and the unconstitutional agencies you people have established, we've succeeded in bringing a new and exciting product to market that treats depression faster than any other pharmaceutical intervention *ever* has. We still go
through hell each day, fighting for the Centers for Medicare and Medicaid
Services to give us their approval, without which we cannot even enter much
of our market. But with CMS approval comes a nefarious regime of price

controls. Indeed in the end, because of the systems you have created, neither Visioryme nor our customers will have much say in what we are paid for the product of our labors.

"Nowhere does the U.S. Constitution grant authority to the U.S. government to set or control prices. Yet you do. Or be involved in medical care. Yet you are. Nowhere does the U.S. government have the authority to create an FDA, or to in any way regulate medication or medical devices. And yet you do. The health and longevity of Americans has been compromised for decades as you people have slowed and stopped all manner of innovation in drugs, devices, and technologies. And your misguided efforts have exponentially raised the costs of those drugs and devices that make it through your artificial gauntlet. Medicine is a high-tech field, like computers and telecommunications. Medical costs could have, should have, and would have fallen radically were it not for you. Because of you they've done the opposite.

"You people self-righteously claim to be protecting Americans, when in fact your laws only protect yourselves and entrenched special interests while killing more people every year than the army does in a typical decade.

"Now, you in Congress are upset because the People have found new ways to benefit from our antidepressant, Sybillene. The new benefits have not been approved by your bureaucratic minions at the FDA, but neither have they found anything dangerous in this new use of Sybillene. There are no reports that this use, what has become known as Naked Emperor, has harmed *anyone*.

"However, there is danger. You are *absolutely right* about there being a danger. But the danger of Sybillene is to *you*, senators, not to the public. If you used Naked Emperor yourselves, you just might see the fraud that you perpetrate every day. You might realize that your very existence is counterproductive to everything that is good in society, and that you create poverty at every turn. You're hypocrites, and so it might be dangerous for you to take Naked Emperor. Because you might feel a need to jump off a high bridge and end your sad, destructive lives. So yes, you have reason to fear.

"Furthermore you need to fear because Naked Emperor enables Americans to see *you* for what you are. It allows them to see through the lies and propaganda you, your colleagues, and your useful idiots in the media spew forth. And that's why we're here today, isn't it? Naked Emperor can take away your power. It will expose the destructive nature of the state, and the three dark forces that support it: taxation, currency inflation, and fear. It can expose the fact that your government is morally and financially bankrupt, and that you are parasites leeching the blood from America. It can expose the fact that your two major political parties are just two sides of the same false coin.

"And ladies and gentlemen, I predict that Naked Emperor is going to trigger the rise of a new movement, an apolitical movement, that will disempower your parties and dismember the national government. People will recognize that you politicians aren't the solution; you're the problem.

"So, yes, this is a crisis for you. Mr. Chairman, your committee fears that Sybillene is a health crisis for America. You have it entirely wrong. You've succeeded in conflating the country and its government, which are two different things with very different interests. Sybillene is a crisis for the health of the United States *government*, because it is the best treatment conceivable to bring *America* back to health.

"You have no health justification to take Sybillene off the market. There have been no reported health dangers of any kind, and it is proven effective as an antidepressant. So, senators who sit before me, above me on your high seats of authority, what lies are you going to employ to justify what you are no doubt going to do?"

Charles sat back in his chair and stared at the chairman. He had made eye contact with each of the politicians during his testimony. It had been many, many years since anyone had dared speak in front of the august body in this way. Perhaps a few of his words would make it out of this chamber and be read by someone, somewhere in the world, and change that person's course through life. But that was not his purpose.

Charles knew that trying to make an impression on the government officials here was pointless. They were mostly sociopaths, with a few psychotics successfully hiding behind a mask of sanity. All of them were narcissists, feeding on the power they'd acquired. Charles wondered whether even Naked Emperor could pull the thick wool from their eyes. Some people were nonhumans in human form. Some people, the genuine sociopaths, were beyond redemption on any level. If Sybillene had toxicities, they might appear only in such people.

"Mr. Knight, what you have said here today bears no resemblance to your submitted written comments approved by this committee. I hereby order the verbal comments that you have provided be stricken from the Congressional Record, as being inconsistent with the agreed-to comments."

Charles leaned in to the microphone before the chairman had finished speaking. "Mr. Chairman, I made no such agreement. Had I made such an agreement, I would have abided by it, as I always do what I agree to do. I have no doubt you will succeed for a while longer at suppressing the truth. But you cannot do so forever."

The chairman stood, red-faced. "Mr. Knight! Your services are no longer needed by this committee. You are excused, and you will be escorted out of this chamber immediately."

"Well, Mr. Chairman, your lack of questions would suggest that you understand what I have testified about. And that is happy news for me. Oh, and I appreciate the escort."

Charles stood and turned his back on the committee as hundreds of voices filled the chambers. He winked at Stephan. Cameras flashed picture after picture of him, photographers calling his name for a good face shot, reporters asking him a litany of questions. He left the hearing room ahead of two men in police uniform, and worked his way out of the building, down the Capitol's white marble steps, around a corner, and into a six-passenger black limousine that Charles had waiting. Tristana and Rainbow caught up and climbed in behind him. Charles, now sitting knee to knee with Tristana, saw the rage on her face.

He turned his head to speak to the chauffeur through the open barrier that separated him from the passengers. "Would you mind stepping out for a moment?"

Charles turned back and said, "Tristana, you should stay for the rest of the hearing." He did not want this conversation now. She needed to cool down.

Tristana said, "You pushed them too far. Now there's no chance that they'll even give us the benefit of a doubt. They're pissed off." Tristana's tone combined fury with fear and sadness. Her voice came out as a croak. "Too much, Charles. You lost everything for us."

"Hardly. We still have our integrity. And that's what they really wanted to take from us."

"Integrity? Charles, you don't know these people! They can't, and won't, tolerate ... opposition."

He replied calmly. "I know that."

"Then why?" She pointed at Rainbow. "And you wanted Rainbow to hear this? What attitudes are you trying to teach?"

"Well, a few things. Including to seek the truth, speak the truth, and stand up for what's right."

Rainbow took in the altercation, but said nothing.

"Tristana, I thought out my testimony carefully. When you're under attack, what are the options? You can run away. Or you can pretend you're not being attacked, and hide your head in the sand like an ostrich. Or you can supplicate, beg for mercy, roll over on your back like a whipped dog and wet yourself. Those responses just feed the enemy power, while destroying your own soul.

"Or you can try to argue the matter with them, work within their system, hire more lawyers, parse the law, and play their game. That's what most people do. But it's a mistake to play the other guy's game on his home field and with their referees making the calls. Tristana, if we try to hide from it, or bow to it, or play their game, we *lose*. We have to confront them head on, call them out, show no fear, and where we can, deny their right to exist. When dealing with these types, the best defense is a strong offense. That's the only way to keep our integrity. And it opens the door for a chance at success."

"Damn you!" Tristana's voice grated. "In your battle for integrity, you've destroyed Visioryme! They'll close us down. All of it gone, just so that you could grandstand. They're going to ban Sybillene, you know. Visioryme is dead. Maybe you can afford to be financially wiped out for your integrity. But I can't!"

Charles reached out to take Tristana's hand. She rejected him fiercely.

He shook his head. "Banning Sybillene is the best thing that could happen to us. We're about to be freed from shackles. You'll like walking without dragging a ball and chain, Tristana."

The limo's muted TV was tuned in to a financial news show. A picture of Charles appeared, taken moments earlier; a talking head opined on what Charles had just done. Charles didn't much care what the news reader said.

Tristana, lost in fear, saw the stock chart for Visioryme on the bottom of the screen. "The share price is already down twenty percent. That's on top of the thirty percent decline over the last few days since this hearing was announced."

"What are we trading at now?" Charles alternated his gaze between the street and Tristana.

"Four dollars. And still falling."

"All the weak holders, trend followers, and amateurs who bought it on hype without studying the fundamentals are getting washed out of the market. It's got a lot further to go. I expect it will bottom at around ten cents."

"Why do you think that?"

Charles was silent.

"You're actually trying to destroy Visioryme, aren't you?" Tristana asked.

"On the contrary. I'm making sure it survives. My holding company, Paladin LLC, started selling Visioryme into the spike that followed the media attention of the Awakening. In some accounts I took a substantial short position. I've been reporting it all, don't worry. Just no one has noticed yet."

"What if they had asked you, Charles? At the hearing?"

"They would have asked, had they been willing to let me speak more. So my little monologue had the fringe benefit of ensuring that they wouldn't."

Her face darkened further, something Charles had considered a moment earlier to be an impossibility.

Charles continued. "Visioryme stock had gotten ahead of itself."

"So you sold? You went short?"

"Why not? Our stock was overbought and bubbling up on hype. And it wasn't *our* hype. It wasn't anything we said or did that prompted it. Selling shares made sense to moderate the mania. It was the responsible thing to do."

"But *shorting* us? Really?"

"Of course! There's always someone willing to write put options. I was speculating that something like this congressional hearing would happen. If the government now does what you fear, those options will serve us well."

"Us? How does it serve *us* well, Charles?"

"Tristana, we're dealing with snakes in suits; it made sense that the government would land on us. The hearing we've just left is going to be a financial gift. At some point, I'm going to cover my shorts and put the profits back into Sybillene. Remember, Tristana, the stock market is a voting machine, not a weighing machine. And I really don't care what the opinions of the voters might be, since they're usually wrong. So, when it gets back to being a penny stock again, I *will* be buying."

"You'll be buying a dead company with no product. FDA will pull our approval."

"We will still manufacture and sell our product."

Tristana had not caught up with where he was going. Her face revealed dread, pain, and anger as she processed the massive loss in value her stake in the company would suffer. And her loyal employees. All their options, now worth nothing. She said almost in a whisper, "We haven't even started getting regulatory clearance in overseas markets. And now we won't for sure. Our revenues are going to stop cold."

"To hell with regulatory! I'm sick of hearing about regulatory."

"And the shareholders?"

"The shareholders that bought for the wrong reasons are now all bailing for the wrong reasons. I'll be doing them a service by providing a bid for their shares when nobody else wants them. Yes, they are going to panic about the hearing. I can't control what people do, or what goes on in their heads. But I can profit from it. It's pretty much like Will Rogers said. 'It ain't what people don't know that's the problem. It's what they think they know that just ain't so.'"

Tristana's tears flowed now. "I don't get you. I don't understand. The government is going to put us out of business. Then what happens to the company? To our employees? And why are you going to be buying when we'll have no sales? And why the hell are you *smiling?*"

"Because Visioryme is going to make us, and the employees, lots of money. I intend to take this company private. I suggest you tender your shares like everyone else. Someday, after you are divorced from your cretin husband, you can buy back your shares from me at a very favorable price. That I promise. The same offer will be available for all of our loyal employees and early investors. The next step is to move Visioryme out of the country. And we will never report anything to this government again. Or pay them any more tax. Or, I can assure you, ever again waste time at a sideshow like the one we just left."

Rainbow, who had been listening and attempting to understand the world of stock markets, coughed to stop the conversation, straightened her shoulders, and announced, "This is going to be the best thing ever for Sybillene."

Tristana, who had become Rainbow's mentor and clearly grown fond of the girl, let her anger win out. She barked back, "What the hell? You have no idea what Charles just did to us, do you?"

Rainbow reached over to take Tristana's hand, and Tristana let her. "Tristana, we don't need the government to allow us to market Sybillene."

"Of course we do! Don't you understand? When FDA takes away our marketing approval, we *can't market*. We can't sell any drug! We'll have no revenue. We'll have no money. We'll go bankrupt!"

Charles smiled and nodded to Rainbow. She reached out and took the leather satchel from Charles. She unzipped it and turned it over. Onto Tristana's lap it emptied. A mountain of $100 bills.

Rainbow rubbed Tristana's hand. "We come from very different worlds, Tristana. You've been very kind to introduce me to yours. But now it's time I teach you about mine."

* * *

Back in the Senate hearing room, the chatter had started to die down. Discussions of Charles's dismissal by the chairman—and Charles's dismissal *of* the chairman—were replaced by the repeated hammering of that chairman's gavel.

"We will now move on to the next witness. Dr. Manuel Disite of Harvard University. Please begin your comments with a presentation of your credentials."

Stephan was an astute interpreter of body language, from any angle. But it didn't take an expert to tell from the man's posture, haircut, clothing, word choices, and intonation that Dr. Disite was an academic through and through.

The man sat up straight. He turned to look back over his shoulder. Stephan followed his gaze toward a stylish woman with red hair entering at the back of the room. She stood tall on heels, beautiful and shocking in a green dress, a shade expertly matched to not just avoid clashing, but to accent her dyed hair.

Dr. Disite was under the spell of the hot lady in green.

"My name is Dr. Manuel Disite. I am a tenured professor of biochemistry at Harvard University. I'm in the medical school faculty, and vice chair of the Department of Toxicology. I have extensive experience in analysis of a variety of psychotropic substances and narcotics."

The chair interrupted him to ask a question, to which they already knew the answer. "How many papers have you published?"

"Over one hundred and sixty just in the field of controlled substances."

"Very good. I will assume that the committee will stipulate to your expertise. Please, Dr. Disite, inform us about Sybillene."

Disite, well funded with NIH grants, knew on which side his bread was buttered. He could be relied on to approach any real or imagined drug question from the correct angle.

Dr. Disite shuffled his prepared comments and then read them directly off his paper. Stephan could see them. There were no red marks, no changes. The professor would read what the congressmen already had in their hands. He rattled off some chemistry to confuse the listeners and confirm his credibility. He made great leaps of logic based on assumptions that he presented as fact. In the end, he summarized his comments in a sing-song rote voice: "High-dose inhalation of Sybillene is highly likely to interact in further unforeseen ways with the neurochemistry of the brain. It appears to be a classic drug of abuse. It provides no substantial societal benefit over other available, proven, and less expensive antidepressants. I do not believe that the risk Sybillene presents is balanced by any real benefits."

"Do you consider Sybillene to be addictive?"

"I expect so."

"Do you consider Sybillene to be harmful to the body?"

"Very likely."

"What is your recommendation to this committee, doctor?"

"I recommend that Sybillene be placed on the Schedule I tier of controlled substances. This schedule is reserved for drugs for which there are no medical justifications for use that outweigh the risks."

"Thank you, Dr. Disite. Are there other questions for this witness? Hearing none, I call Mr. Donald Debocher."

Stephan sucked in his breath. Tristana had said nothing about her husband coming to this meeting, let alone being a witness in front of this committee. It had to be a surprise appearance. Stephan twisted back, looking toward the hearing room's main entrance.

The door opened, and Donald marched in. His suit was uncharacteristically well pressed, and he stood more erect than usual. The man acted like he had entered his native element, about to serve as an expert witness in a process programmed to get what the senators thought was best for themselves, the government, and maybe even the country.

After the standard preliminaries, the chairman said, "Mr. Debocher, please state your credentials for the record."

239

Then Donald, too, looked over his shoulder at the striking red-haired woman, the same one that had caught the attention of the academic witness a few minutes earlier. Stephan saw an exchange, a glance.

Donald said, "I am the director of the FDA's Office of Regulatory Enforcement."

"How long have you served in that position?"

"Almost eight months."

"And before that?"

"I've been with FDA for my career since graduating from Brown."

"Are you familiar with Sybillene?"

"Quite familiar."

"What is your view on it?"

"There are definite safety issues with its use in high dose. They present a clear and present danger. It is my view that Sybillene cannot be effectively restricted to the low-dosage, FDA-approved usage. At least not by any currently known technology.

"So there is no way that Visioryme might package it differently to prevent this problem?"

Debocher replied, "No effective way that we at FDA can conceive of. To eliminate Naked Emperor, Sybillene would have to be removed from the market entirely."

"And has FDA yet taken away marketing approval?

"Not yet. We have been examining the issue for several months. We are collecting information still."

"Will removing Sybillene cause any damage to the U.S. health care system as a whole?"

"No. There are numerous alternative medications."

"So you see no harm to the population if FDA were to revoke the approvals for marketing of Sybillene."

"I do not."

"Are there other questions for Mr. Debocher?" the chairman asked the committee, looking to his sides and behind.

Stephan could not let this go unanswered. He stood up, totally out of order, as if accepting the invitation to query, and said loudly and with conviction, "My name is Stephan Liggett, Visioryme's VP of public relations. I have a question, Donald. Will removing Sybillene harm any individual with otherwise-untreatable depression, when Sybillene is the only drug that works for that person?"

The chairman did not want to offend an openly gay man. But the man was out of turn, and the question interfered with the purposes of the committee. "Please sit down, Mr. Liggett. You are out of order."

Stephan ignored the chairman. "Also, Donald, did you mention to the committee that you are the husband of the CEO of Visioryme, the manufacturer of Sybillene, and that you are jealous of Charles Knight's relationship with her, and that you are a sniveling little government bureaucrat?" His voice gained a more lilting tone with each word, and he looked right at the red-haired woman in the green dress.

"Mr. Liggett! Please remove yourself from this room immediately, or I will have you removed." The chairman pounded his gavel.

"No problem, Mr. Chairman. Don't forget to strike my comments from the record." Stephan bowed to the committee and walked slowly out the back door, allowing plenty of time for pictures to be taken.

"No pictures of Mr. Liggett in this hearing room!" the chairman shouted, but to no avail. Photographers, recognizing the value and the rarity of a genuine money shot, disregarded his wishes. Stephan was the perfect follow-on to Charles Knight.

Hearing something from two people, especially if they appeared to be very different, wasn't just twice as effective as hearing it from one person, but ten times more. The reporters knew that people found it much easier to believe things, good and bad, because others also believe it.

Stephan turned at the back of the room and pulled from his cloth briefcase a bag of green Sybillene canisters. He started handing them out to whoever reached him the fastest. "Free Sybillene for anyone who wants it! Free Naked Emperor for anyone who wants it!"

Lots of people wanted it.

"Mr. Liggett, depart this room! Security, escort Mr. Liggett from the premises immediately." The chairman screamed now, just to be heard over the clamor for free Sybillene.

Two security guards politely helped Stephan leave the building. Each asked for and received their very own canister of Naked Emperor.

"Thanks for accompanying me out of the building, Jack, Fred."

"A pleasure, Mr. Liggett," the one named Fred replied in a conspiratorial tone. "I hope someday we can assist the chairman of that committee out of this building."

Stephan threw them both an informal salute and a grin that would endear him even to the most skeptical homophobe, and marched out into a balmy spring afternoon, high on life and wondering if he might soon be arrested for illegal distribution of prescription drugs.

*   *   *

"I think we should take a break." Tristana told Donald as he entered their house. She handed him a small suitcase.

Donald took one more step inside the front door. After gauging his wife's resolve, and his role in the impending destruction of her company, he silently took the suitcase. Without further acknowledgement, he turned and shut the door.

She sat on the stairs and caught her breath, her marriage failing, her company in ruins. Years of frustrating work on both fronts destroyed in the space of a day.

Tears were inevitable, and she allowed them to flow. But she would not allow herself to lose control. Tonight she would sleep, mourn, and turn off her mind in front of the television. Tomorrow, she needed to prepare the company for what lay ahead.

Rainbow looked down from the top of the staircase. Tristana heard her footsteps, and she slid to the wall to make room for her to pass. But Rainbow settled in next to her. And then Rainbow reached both her arms around her and whispered in her ear.

"Thank you," Rainbow said. "Thank you for all you do for me."

25

After-Action Report

"WAY to go, Charles!" Stephan jumped up to greet him as he came through the office door at Visioryme.

"You aren't furious with me, Stephan?"

"Why would I be? You were awesome. Your antics are all over the news! I don't know what got into me, but I decided to be your Mini-Me."

Charles raised his eyebrows and pursed his lips. "Most of the media are going to paint me as Dr. Evil, so I'm proud to have you as my Mini-Me. I heard about what you did in there. I loved it."

"A drug dealer in the Senate chambers!"

"How is your boss now? I haven't talked to her since she got out of the limo yesterday. She wasn't happy with me."

"Oh, Tristana *still* isn't happy with you. You all should talk. She kicked Donald out of the house." Stephan waved his hand, directing Charles to walk straight in.

Before Charles went to face Tristana, he turned to Stephan. "Are you up for an adventure in Africa? An overseas assignment?"

Stephan said, "Will there be elephants? I love elephants!"

"Well, you won't see any of those. But there will be plenty of snakes."

"Probably fewer than there are in Washington. I'm in. I want to go somewhere I can juke, joke, jive, socialize, and generally be left in peace."

Charles nodded. "We may have to build that together, because right now such a place doesn't exist."

He shut his eyes for a couple of seconds, in anticipation of what he had to face next, and then walked into Tristana's office. She sat behind her computer screen, head down on her desk. He glanced around. No Rainbow.

She looked up at him, and he saw the dark shadows under her eyes.

She went straight to business.

"They're going to ban Sybillene, Charles. Two House subcommittees are sending a bill to the floor for immediate action. They're bypassing FDA on this. The speaker and the minority leader are both sponsoring the bill and waiving the procedural rules right and left. National security, national emergency, whatever. It's expected to pass, essentially unanimously. The Senate committee you testified before has a similar bill heading to the Senate floor."

"I'm sorry, Tristana. It was the only path forward. And it took me a long time to find it." It was OK that she let her anger out at him. But he would keep his disappointment in her to himself. She was a decent person, and he was fond of her.

"What path is that, Charles? What path have you taken us down? From what I understand, it looks like the road to perdition."

Charles protested. "Look, if our reimbursement consultants—even saying the word is horrifying—even if our reimbursement consultants were successful…"

Tristana interrupted, shaking her head in bitter despondency. "We won't be needing *them* anymore, so *that* should make you happy."

Charles kept his cool. She had not suggested that he sit down, but he slid into a chair, and leaned toward her. He said quietly, "It actually *does* make me happy."

"You've ruined me both professionally and personally, you know. Is this what you do, is this what drives you? Ruining people?"

"I heard you kicked Donald out."

"I'm not just talking about me. And I'm certainly not talking about Donald! I'm talking about *Rainbow!* Teaching your devil-may-care thwarting of law and order, your suicidal flirtations with disaster … as if this is all *normal!* If she follows in your footsteps, she'll wind up in a group home, jail, or worse."

"Very possible. I'm glad you've given her a chance to follow your footsteps as well. She may be able to learn more from you than from me."

Tristana's face softened. "She stayed with me last night. After Donald left. She's a good kid. She told me a lot more about her life than I had any inkling of."

"You know her better than I do, then."

"Well, I am grateful for that. She said she saved your life. Maybe more than once."

Charles chuckled. "That may be true. She helped me through one pickle, and got me out of a jam."

"You've never explained your relationship to her. Is she the child of one of your old girlfriends'?" Tristana looked at him bitterly.

The accusation, intended as an insult, triggered his anger. But he suppressed it. He, and others, had just turned Tristana's world upside-down. He exhaled slowly, opened his eyes, and spoke evenly.

"No, Tristana. I met her not long before you did. She's a kid from the streets, and you and I have given her a boost up."

"I don't know how I can keep myself financially afloat going forward. But she's welcome to stay with me as long as I can keep the house."

"Maybe it's not as bad as you think, Tristana. Let me have a chance to make this right."

"What choice do I have?"

Charles nodded. "You have plenty of choices. But only one or two *good* choices. Can I tell you how and why I struggled so much recently? Struggled with Visioryme?"

"I didn't know you were struggling. And I don't know how it could matter anymore. But go ahead."

"Thanks. As I was saying, if our reimbursement consultants had been successful, the result of their success would be that insurance companies would effectively work with CMS to stick a price control on Sybillene. The price of Sybillene would be determined not by us and our customers, but by third-party payers. The price they chose might, or might not, be sufficient for us to make a lot of money. That, you'll recall, was your business plan for our success. Remember? So if we accomplished our aim, and our reimbursement consultants won, our success would come from leeching blood from a moribund medical system. *We'd* be the parasites."

Tristana sat still, staring at him.

He continued. "But maybe the CMS and insurance regimes would set a price so low that it would prohibit Visioryme from making any money. After all, it's all at the whim of some faceless cubicle dweller." He stopped himself from adding, *like your husband Donald.* "That would be a death sentence for Visioryme, but it would look more like leprosy than a guillotine.

Imagine Visioryme, left to the whim of government employees like the ones you wait in line for at the DMV. First FDA, then CMS, then who knows what other agency would climb up our butts. And all the while Big Pharma would be lobbying against us, to protect the products they've already got on the market. Even if we were somehow successful, it would be because some bureaucrat felt magnanimous. A sick victory. I couldn't be a part of it.

"Look, Tristana, if we were co-opted into the machine, I was going to *have* to sell all my shares of this company, no matter what, just to maintain my self-respect. My selling would have badly injured the company, yet I'm unwilling to be a leech, sucking the blood from society. So I found a way out."

"What way is that? You have yet to enlighten me. Please hurry."

"Tristana, they were going to ban Sybillene no matter what I said. That became obvious to me on the night of the Awakening. I didn't need Naked Emperor in my system to see that. Naked Emperor is simply far too dangerous to them. That committee wasn't going to let anything positive about Sybillene get on the record. So I had to get attention, to become a Naked Emperor celebrity. Basically the same strategy Howard Hughes used when they were investigating him, or Oliver North, when he was facing prison because of the Iran-Contra scandal. I had to stand up against them. Treating these political creatures with the disrespect they deserve earns the attention of those who will become our customers.

"With a little luck, the bloggers and small-press types will see me as a friend of the common man, as opposed to a suit working for Big Pharma. Politics is all a matter of perception. You have to turn the tables on these people."

Tristana shook her head. "So you'll become a celebrity. You made the news. What's that get the rest of us?"

"Tristana, don't you see what we've got here? We have the best drug made in the last fifty years! Maybe ever! *Naked Emperor does for the soul what antibiotics do for the body.* It cleans out dangerous infections. And we're the only ones who know the tricks necessary to make it. Nobody will be able to make it but us, at least for a few years. We're going to sell in vast quantities both here and in overseas markets, so much that it will blow your mind."

"You mean illegally?"

Charles stated with more vigor than he intended, "I *really* don't care what's legal!"

"They're going to list Sybillene alongside heroin as a Schedule I controlled substance. They put people in prison for *life* for selling those drugs."

Charles sat down. "Look, I'm concerned with what's ethical and moral, not with what's illegal. If you want to be sure you're on the legal high ground, you need to understand that what *they're* about to do—banning Sybillene—is what's illegal, Tristana. The Constitution doesn't give Congress any power to ban our drug."

Tristana shook her head. "Nobody cares about that anymore. The Constitution won't stand up and defend me in front of a jury."

"That's true. But the Constitution is one of the few places that morality and legality are even on the same page. If we don't stand up for what's right, nobody's going to do it for us."

Tristana sighed. "I understand, Charles. You're acting like Don Quixote, tilting at windmills. And I almost empathize, I do. But it's academic, because FDA … and now the DEA … they aren't going to let us manufacture and sell Sybillene!"

"Of course not." Charles chided her. "But think what fun we'll have going underground. There'll be *serious* demand now. And with Sybillene illegal, the price of Naked Emperor is going to skyrocket. These people have given us billions of dollars by criminalizing its use. Do you think there'd be any serious money in heroin, cocaine, meth—any of them—if they weren't illegal?"

"But if we go underground, our manufacturing costs will go way up too."

"Don't count on that. How much of our manufacturing costs go to oiling the FDA's machine, but add nothing to the safety or efficacy of Sybillene?"

"I don't know. Maybe fifty percent."

"That's a lot. Underground, we can focus just on safety, efficacy, and efficiency. Not arbitrary rules and useless inspections. Even after the cost of security measures we'll have to take, the final costs might wash. And we won't be paying any tax. That itself will increase our net another fifty percent."

"Do you know how long it will take to rebuild our manufacturing process?"

"I don't, Tristana. But I do know that I asked for a very large inventory. And that I asked Stephan to ship it all out of the warehouse. I hope that's OK."

She shook her head. "I don't think I care."

"I think you *will* care. Soon."

He found a bit of hope when she next said, "If we go underground, how on earth are we going to market it? You think anybody is going to touch a Schedule I drug?"

"Rainbow and I have that covered," he said. "It's time to introduce you to a friend of ours. But I have to warn you, he's not a society gentleman."

26

Burning Down the House

"OK, gentlemen, time to shut them down. This is why we get paid the big bucks." Donald Debocher's attempt at humor failed to establish rapport with the three U.S. marshals standing as close as each could get to Sabina Heidel. He didn't have much in common with them, other than an obvious appreciation of Sabina. "President Cooligan has just signed the Sybillene ban. It's law now. So let's go into action."

The loss of his wife's value—his value—in Visioryme didn't bother him anymore. It had collapsed; it was gone. Now he would make Visioryme valuable to himself in other ways. He stood up and patted down his well-pressed suit. He could no longer tolerate wrinkles. He made a mental note to stop by the new tailor Sabina had recommended, to pick up his newest purchase. Italian. She'd suggested that a man with his public sector experience would be aggressively sought by the private sector. At a much higher salary. But only if he could add value. And, perhaps even more important, *looked* like he could add value. Why not start looking the part now?

Sabina had insisted on participating in this raid. He didn't know why she cared, but he wouldn't turn her down. Not when he was so close to having success with her. He had bided his time, put forward his best charms, and she'd begun to respond. He'd lost some confidence in his own charms over the last week, but today, she really seemed interested in him.

Obviously, he had to go on this raid too. After all, Sabina worked under his mentorship. Plus, he wanted to. He imagined it the way the DEA might raid a crack house, breaking down doors, guns blazing, handcuffing everyone in sight.

But this was not the DEA. It was an FDA operation carried out by U.S. marshals who had long provided calm and civilized interventions on facilities that FDA wished to close. They never arrested anyone on such raids.

Sabina, Donald, and the marshals climbed into a black SUV. Kevlar vests, automatic rifles, gas grenades, and assorted paramilitary gear crammed the cargo space. Everything one might need to confidently enter the unsecured headquarters of a small, unguarded one-story pharmaceutical company in the back of a strip mall in suburban Virginia. But it still wouldn't be like the DEA.

"Only one vehicle?" Donald asked the driver.

"We have state-police backup. Don't worry. We'll have plenty of support."

"Then we're good to go." Donald liked using the military-sounding phrase. He felt the power of command.

One of the marshals looked at another and rolled his eyes.

Donald's adrenaline had surged in pulses since he'd made the decision to accompany the marshals. From the third-row seat, he looked forward at Sabina, who sat next to one of the marshals in front of him. Why was she sitting next to *that* guy? He looked at the marshal. With a hard jaw and a large crew-cut head, the solid, muscular man stood about six feet four and looked like a professional football player. Sure, the guy was handsome, but he was just a marshal, a pawn in the game. He felt his lips curl and his stomach twist. His knee began bouncing slightly. He felt now much as he had felt throughout junior high school.

He told her, "Sabina, don't worry. Stay back behind us and you'll be fine."

Despite the fact it was Donald's first raid too, he postured at being in charge. How he hoped Charles Knight would be there so he could see his face when he shut the company down. That his soon-to-be ex-wife had dedicated her youthful energies to that enterprise, instead of to her husband, made Visioryme's impending death that much sweeter.

"What about your wife, Donald?" Sabina turned and asked.

"Ex-wife," he said. She wasn't his ex-wife yet, but it seemed wise to get Sabina thinking of her that way.

She could have taken the opportunity to express sympathy with an *Oh,*

I'm sorry to hear that... Donald was glad she didn't. A grateful smile would be preferred, and indeed, she smiled. Donald took it as a warm invitation.

He said, "Tristana is going to have to deal with it. She's made her choices. And *I* don't have a choice. Our job is to be impartial in the enforcement of the law."

Others in the vehicle recognized the contradiction. This operation had become decidedly nonobjective and entirely partial.

The marshal sitting too close to Sabina asked Donald, "You could have issued Visioryme a warning letter, don't you think? Or maybe had an administrative court send them a cease-and-desist order?"

Donald spat back, "Would you have us issue a warning letter to a company that was manufacturing heroin? Would Al Capone have respected a court order? I don't think so. Visioryme is manufacturing dangerous illegal drugs. We gotta shut them down hard and fast. So *that's* what we do."

The marshal shrugged, silenced for a moment. But then he came back by saying, "But then isn't this the purview of Seth Fowler and the DEA now?"

"We already have enough cooperative work with Fowler on the Viagra Initiative." The term *Viagra Initiative* for the joint task force among DEA, FDA, and Customs had an aggressive, determined ring to it. Donald thought that it would make a good title for a book. Maybe he would try to write one, featuring a dashing, hands-on *Chief of Enforcement*. But first they needed a measure of success, and so far they hadn't even received official approval for the task force to go into action. It took months to get anything done. The nebbishes in legal slowed down the government to magnify their own importance, even as the government worked so hard to solve all the problems the citizens kept causing. He hated the paper pushers in legal, and the thought occurred that they probably hated him.

"I hope we get approved for the task force soon." Sabina prodded.

He felt so close to finally getting her. She had let him know, in only slightly uncertain terms, that he was going to have her soon. He wanted her now. Perhaps tonight would be the night, and the prospect of what might come after this daring raid made him doubly excited. Donald took his eyes off her just long enough to glance at the side of the face of the big-jawed marshal, who was looking down at her perfectly honed legs as they angled off the bucket seat and crossed. Donald could track his gaze along her thigh to the edge of her short skirt, for she was turned and sitting sideways on the seat, one of her knees almost touching the thigh of the adjacent marshal. He wanted to push that knee aside. Or push the marshal out of the car.

"Wilkins, how long have you been a marshal?" Donald asked the man who offended him.

The man's bass voice came back quickly. "Ten years. Ten long years."

"Why long years?"

Lantern Jaw replied in what sounded like a rehearsed response. "Babysitting witnesses is boring. We aren't Tommy Lee Jones in 'The Fugitive.' And shutting down pharmaceutical and medical-device companies at the beck and call of FDA—it's hardly the thrill I had hoped for in life. So, yeah, ten years is a long time."

"If you don't want to participate in this, you can get out of the car right now." Donald asserted himself.

It didn't work. Wilkins turned around in his seat, pressing his right leg completely against Sabina's knees as he did so, and stared at Donald. Donald had no ability to maintain eye contact against that intense glare. He saw that Sabina looked at him as he turned his eyes out over the passing terrain of the suburbs, as if there was something important out there. "Or you can stay," he said quietly, trying to sound patronizing.

Wilkins just shook his head slowly as he turned forward, breaking the connection between his leg and Sabina's.

"All right, gentlemen," Donald said in a loud voice, striving to regain the authority he felt he had lost, "let's talk about how we're going to do this."

The driver said, simply, "How about we knock on the door and ask to come in?"

"I don't think that's the way I want to play this," Donald replied. "This is a high-profile operation. The government has determined Sybillene is a very dangerous drug. This isn't a garden-variety FDA search and seizure. It's entirely possible there will be people on the premises who'll violently resist our action today. You're aware of Knight's conduct before the Senate committee."

Wilkins responded. "You know these folks. We don't. This is your baby; you're calling the shots. If you want us to go in hot and fully equipped, we will."

"Yes, we will."

"And then we will confiscate their—what is it, bamboo and mold—that they use to make the Sybillene?"

252

"We will destroy it, confiscate all the Sybillene, and every piece of equipment they use to make it."

"Destroy the bamboo?"

"The way you would ingredients in a meth lab. It's what the new legislation demands. The wording commands us to destroy all supplies and equipment used in the manufacture or processing of Sybillene."

"OK. I hope there isn't a warehouse full of the stuff."

The driver of the SUV interrupted, "We're half a mile out from the target. Time to suit up." He pulled into a parking lot toward the back of a convenience store and the four men and Sabina pulled their vests and tactical gear from the back of the vehicle. Sabina put on her vest and tactical belt as slickly as the three marshals, and was fully suited up before Donald had even figured out how to lash his Kevlar vest closed on the side.

Each marshal sported an M4 carbine with two extra magazines for a total of ninety rounds of ammunition. Wilkins took the gun Debocher had picked up and exchanged it for a seemingly identical weapon, nodding his head as he did so to convey some unknowable message. Wilkins watched Sabina pick up one of the weapons, and while barely looking, rapidly cycle the action, loading a round from the magazine into the chamber. Wilkins held out his hand and shook his head. Sabina gave him a face, flicked her index finger to release the magazine, and cycled the action once again to expel the unfired cartridge, deftly catching it as it flew out the side ejection port. She left the action back as she handed the weapon to the marshal with a shrug, and tossed him the cartridge as if she were flipping a coin. She climbed back into the vehicle without another word.

Twenty state-police cars were scheduled to roll and surround the building. The driver confirmed the radio frequency for communication with the staties. "Ten minutes," he said.

Donald commanded, "Let's start moving in." He did not want any state-cop types showing up and distracting any reporters he hoped would appear. He'd invited a few.

Wilkins pressed the mike attached to his collar. "Ingress team is inbound."

After a short drive, the marshals, Sabina, and Donald climbed out of their car and moved to the front door of the Visioryme building. They lined up two-by-two to the left of the door, Donald alone at the rear. Wilkins pulled the door open a few inches, barely exposing himself to anyone who might be within. He opened the door the rest of the way, and then led with his gun, following the muzzle into a brightly lit carpeted corridor. Loud music and laughter emanated from around the corner.

"What the hell are they celebrating?" Wilkins asked no one in particular.

They moved up the hallway and through a double doorway into an open office space, with scattered desks but no cubicles. Windowed conference rooms lined the far wall, and between the conference rooms was a broad set of glass doors leading out the back of the building. The doors lay open, letting the spring air inside. Fifteen people, presumably employees of the company, laughed and talked out back. A few danced.

The revelers seemed unaware of the arrival of five new people in their building, dressed in black and carrying automatic rifles, silently padding along the carpeted floor, checking around corners and into closets as they went, clearing the spaces as if they were entering an al-Qaeda training facility. Wilkins opened a metal door and peered into a cavernous empty space that was once a clean-room manufacturing facility. Donald approached the back doors with an abundance of caution, despite the fact that the place was devoid of danger. Wilkins shrugged, grabbed a donut from near a coffee machine, and started nibbling. Sabina smiled at him and nodded toward the obvious collection of people out in the daylight.

Donald didn't see Sabina's smile because he was moving stealthily toward the open door, slithering along with sidesteps, creeping closer to the crowd. Then he was at the door. A young man wearing a lilac shirt and a pink tie turned toward him. When he saw Donald emerge from the relatively dark interior dressed in tactical gear, he started and squealed, but only for a moment. Then he laughed.

"Donald! Oh, Donald," Stephan howled. "You are *so* funny. Rainbow, come look at Donald! I've never seen him look so delicious! Hey, everyone, Donald is here, and he brought friends!"

The partiers looked toward the doors and through the glass, and saw the incursion team. The Visioryme employees should have stepped back in fear, a logical response when confronted with armed paramilitary. But they didn't. Instead, they laughed and pointed at the group. Donald's face grew darker, and his frown coalesced into his trademark sneer as he lifted his upper lip, exposing a canine tooth like an angry dog. He saw Tristana, and next to her that whelp, Rainbow, dressed entirely in black, like the street urchin she had unsuccessfully pretended not to be.

The marshals came up to him now and stood by, waiting for Donald to take the lead and speak. He remained silent, however.

"U.S. Marshals, ma'am," Wilkins spoke loudly to the attractive woman who had come forward.

"I'm Tristana Debocher, CEO of Visioryme. What can I do for you gentlemen?" She looked at all of them in turn, except Donald. "We have cake, champagne, and cheese and crackers. And there are burgers and hot dogs on the grill." She pointed toward an area near the back wall of the building where smoke rose from a charcoal grill. A brisk breeze carried the pleasant smell through the now-expanded gathering of people. It also carried with it the gentle scent of bamboo, great bundles of which lay stacked behind the back wall of the building, rising to the roofline. Wilkins said, "Ma'am, we need you all to prepare to be searched. We have orders to seize all materials related to Sybillene."

"Yes, we know. We're celebrating, see?"

Sabina came outside through the doors then. "Just what are you celebrating?"

"Oh, it's *you!*" Stephan screeched, hands held high. "From the hearing! The lady in the green dress! May I say that *you are fabulous*. If only I were so inclined, I would be all over you, girl!"

Charles Knight emerged from behind the crowd, walking directly toward Sabina. He stood tall in front of her, very close, wearing an amused smile, and looked down into her eyes as he analyzed her. After a long moment, he said for all to hear, but directed to Sabina and only Sabina, "We're celebrating our freedom from exactly the kind of insanity that sent *you* here."

Donald wasn't a very astute observer of people, but even he could tell there was something going on. Knight and Sabina stared at each other. Donald, out of reflex, pushed his way between them, unintentionally shoving Sabina backward. Donald looked up into Knight's face then and said, his sneer profoundly enhanced, "Knight, if you in any way hinder the activities of the marshals, we *will* arrest you. Do you understand me?"

Knight looked down at Donald now, with an expression almost of pity, but more of disgust. "Donald, I don't believe I'll ever understand you." His gaze fell on Sabina. "But I think I now see one more reason why you act like such a jerk."

Donald raised his carbine in both hands and, like a hockey player cross-checking an opponent, rapidly extended his arms to shove the whole side of the weapon into Knight's chest, trying to force him backward. Every action tends to cause an equal and opposite reaction, and this time proved no exception. Knight barely moved. His left foot fell back six inches, and his head came forward two. Donald, however, bounced right off Knight's chest, lost his balance and stumbled backward, tripping his left foot over his right, falling. He smashed into the charcoal grill, spilling its burgers, hot dogs, and red-hot coals in a broad swath. Donald rolled as best as he could to ease his impact on the tarmac and avoid getting burned. But as he did so, his finger squeezed the trigger of his weapon.

A disaster could have occurred just then but for some foresight on the part of Marshal Wilkins. When Wilkins had switched Donald's gun, he had given him a civilian model M4, which lacked full automatic mode, its lower receiver offering a choice between only safety and semi-auto. Had Wilkins left him with the automatic selectable M4A1, the weapon would likely have emptied its thirty-round magazine over the next several seconds, and people could have died. As it was, one round belched through the muzzle toward the steel charcoal grill, ricocheting through a window into the rear of the building.

The partygoers fell back reflexively, and a few screamed in shock. All laughter stopped, and some dove to the ground. The marshals crouched down, except for Wilkins, who tackled Sabina to cover her from any potential spread of bullets. Knight did precisely the same for Tristana, and the two men found themselves lying next to each other on the ground, each on top of a beautiful woman. They faced each other, noses all of twelve inches apart.

Knight raised his eyebrows knowingly, and Wilkins shook his head slightly. As the echoes and screams died down, each man gently raised himself. As soon as Wilkins had done so, Sabina jumped to her feet and was down by Donald's side, removing the weapon from his hand as he lay on the ground.

Wilkins moved over toward Donald and helped him up. Donald straightened his tactical gear after he stood, wiping off dirt, adjusting his belt and vest. His beady eyes assessed the damage, the Visioryme employees, then the marshals. He didn't look at Knight, Tristana, or Sabina.

"Stay there." Wilkins ordered Donald. "We'll take it from here."

"The hell you say," Donald replied, pulling himself together, trying to reassert command. He reached over to Sabina and took back his carbine.

"I'm fine. Everyone move back." Donald pointed the muzzle at Knight. "Strap him to something."

Knight raised his hands up in front of himself, close together, as if he were holding an invisible basketball. He said gently, "Now Donald, I am not here to intervene in any way with your law enforcement activities. I won't bother you. Besides, you're the one armed to the teeth and firing your weapon wildly. Perhaps you're the one who should be cuffed." He looked at Wilkins before saying, "No?"

"Shut your fucking hole, Knight!" Donald snarled. He turned to one of the other marshals, pushed his shoulder, and shouted, "Restrain him now!"

The face of that marshal showed controlled fury. But he looked at Wilkins, who hesitated for a moment before nodding slightly.

Wilkins said in a calm tone, "Accompany Mr. Knight over there. Make sure he's unarmed, and see that he stays still while we're on the premises."

Knight replied, "I will stay still. No need to waste one of your men on me. You all have plenty of work to do. The new law says you have to take all our supplies. There're still about ten containers' worth of bamboo lined up here." He pointed at the wall of bamboo. "It's going to use up all the trunk space in your state-trooper cruisers. Plus a few semi-trailers."

As if on cue, a contingent of body-armored state-police officers stormed through the door and lined up with their weapons trained on the unarmed employees.

Wilkins held up his hand to the state troopers. "We're good here. Accidental discharge of a weapon. No injuries. Please return to your positions."

Knight added, speaking loudly to the troopers, "Yes, we appreciate you keeping us all safe from anyone who might barge in here and shoot the place up."

Donald moved over to Knight and shouted at him through clenched teeth. "Knight, you will say nothing more. I will have you arrested!"

"For what?"

"Interfering with a federal agent."

"You tripped over your own foot. Arrest your foot." Knight's sardonic smile was entirely devoid of sympathy.

Donald could not contain himself further. He jammed the butt of the rifle into Knight's ribs. Knight pulled back sufficiently to prevent the blow from being forceful enough to break them, but it came hard enough to leave a painful bruise.

Wilkins moved alongside him immediately, restraining Donald from striking another blow.

"Debocher, that's enough! Who the hell do you think we are?"

Tristana cast Donald a withering look and went to Knight's aid, but he waved her off.

Wilkins moved to talk quietly with Tristana, and Donald couldn't hear the exchange. Twice Tristana looked at Donald and shook her head. She did it a third time, but vigorously, and with a frown. While they continued to talk, Knight spoke up.

"Donald, why this fit of aggression? Your superiors will be displeased when they hear about your coming in here armed to the teeth and assaulting us."

"Knight, you might have had this place locked down and ready to start a war. The lives of my men are paramount. I wasn't taking chances."

"Donald, we are a *pharmaceutical* company. Do you really think we have anything to gain by shooting at government agents? I'm all in favor of putting the FDA in its place, let there be no doubt about that, but I'm not going to do that by shooting up some unsuspecting U.S. marshals. What sort of crazy thoughts are going through what passes for your mind?"

Donald glared at him.

Knight came at him with a verbal assault. "Maybe you're a rule junkie who gets passionate about whatever new regulation comes off the president's desk. Maybe you're mentally unbalanced. You should consider that as a real possibility. Maybe you're trying to impress the ladies." He indicated Sabina. "I don't know. Or maybe you're just a power-hungry jackass. Again, I don't know."

Donald dripped sarcasm through gritted teeth. "Maybe I'm gonna kill you, Knight. I don't know."

"Nice, Donald. Nice, Donald Debocher." Knight pointed at him and turned to look over his head at the back entranceway.

Only then did Donald notice. He followed Knight's gaze to a security camera. There were others. A quick scan revealed that this entrance had two cameras. And there were three more on poles that overlooked the back of the building and the stacks of bamboo. Those cameras would have captured Donald's accidental firing of his weapon, and the rifle butt to Knight's ribs.

"Where is the security room?" Donald asked Stephan.

Knight interjected, "You mean, where do we keep the recordings from the security cameras?"

"Where?"

"They're everywhere, Donald. Streamed live. This whole thing has been streamed live. And the fire will be too."

Donald's fear focused his mind on his own appearance, and his self-concern became apparent in every line of his face. So much so that Charles's mention of *fire* did not enter his consciousness. "Streamed to where?"

"To *everywhere*. We estimate that there are fifty thousand people watching this party live. They'll then post it on social media, at least the juicy bits. And Donald, there have been some nice juicy bits. Don't you think?"

"You're a fucking asshole, Knight."

"I'll let the viewers decide who's the asshole. These cameras—they do audio too. A gunshot at a party makes for great audio. I bet there are ten million views on YouTube by this evening. You'll be famous. Isn't that what you always wanted?"

"Fuck you. Fuck you!" Donald looked up at the cameras again, raised his middle finger, and waved it from camera to camera. Then he raised his voice and he stared bitterly at the camera. "Fuck you all. From this time forward there will be no more Naked Emperor. It's done. Fuck you and all your druggie friends."

"Nice, Donald. Nice." Tristana shook her head in disgust.

Visioryme hadn't left FDA with much to take or destroy. The shelves lay empty, and the machinery of the manufacturing clean room had been removed, leaving only scattered pieces of trash and some old shelves and tables. All that remained for the FDA to confiscate was bamboo and fungus. And maybe not even that.

Knight pointed to the stacks of bamboo that lay against the back of the building nearby, from which billowing smoke had just started to rise. It had taken a while for the charcoal from the grill Donald had knocked over to ignite the bamboo.

Perhaps Rainbow had surreptitiously kicked some burning coals under a particularly dry bundle, and some of the charcoal starter fluid too, although the streaming video noted no such thing.

Once the fire began, the hollow bamboo stems quickly became an inferno. Flames leapt up, shooting through the stacked rows of highly combustible bamboo tubes. Superheated air raced through them, feeding the flames. The bamboo internodes, filled with hot air and steam, exploded as they heated. It sounded like dozens of automatic weapons firing thousands of rounds. Within thirty seconds, the plume of fire rose more than fifty feet high, and the breeze spread the blaze horizontally, racing along the bamboo stacks. The heat pushed everybody back.

The place looked and sounded like an active war zone. As fires tend to do, it mesmerized all who watched, burning higher and hotter. The repetitive cracks sounded for all the world like gunfire and attracted everybody in the neighborhood. The bamboo tubes shot flames like torches toward the adjacent steel wall of the Visioryme building. The steel warmed, bent, and fell inward long before the firetrucks appeared. The roof collapsed upon melted computers and burning file cabinets. The employees of Visioryme, the U.S. marshals, the FDA man, the state troopers, and an expanding throng of neighbors watched from a safe distance as Visioryme Pharmaceuticals went up in smoke.

Donald felt animalistic elation as he watched Tristana and Knight's enterprise disappear.

Tristana, Knight, and Rainbow stood watching the blaze. Donald moved up to Knight and shouted at him. "We will track your distributors and confiscate any Sybillene in transit. We'll arrest everyone you are connected with who bought Sybillene in the last week. *Everyone* knew Sybillene was going to be outlawed. I am going to burn them all for daring to buy it. And most importantly, I'm going to burn you, Knight." He pointed his finger right into Knight's face. "I am going to *burn* you."

"I don't know, Donald," Knight replied calmly. "I think you just burned yourself. How do you think you're going to find the distributors and the recent shipments? Where do you think we kept all our records? The names of all our distributors? All our sales information? All our shipping paperwork? Where would we keep the data about who bought the last supplies of Sybillene?" Knight waved toward the conflagration. "*We* couldn't destroy our records without breaking the law. But you just did. All the information Visioryme had is burning up in front of your eyes."

With the increasing heat of the flames, Knight's icy stare melted into a smile, a reflection on Donald's dissipating career.

Rainbow gave Donald a grim reminder. "Just remember, you fired first."

27

Building the Dark Side

"YOU get busted up again, Paladin?" Alpha asked.

"Yeah," Charles replied, wincing from his bruised ribs as he leaned against the bar, hoping a beer would arrive soon. "By a *true* thug this time, not some little punk loser with green hair like last time."

"Who did it?"

"A government boy."

"We need to be worried?"

"It had to do with another matter. But a related matter."

Alpha pursed his lips and nodded.

Charles said, "Can I introduce you to a friend of mine?" They had cemented a mutual trust over the months they'd built a business together. He waved Tristana over from the far side of the bar. "This is my friend Tristana. She works with me in my day job."

"Right. I know that name."

Tristana smiled and shook Alpha's proffered hand. "I had no idea that Charles had so many interesting colleagues."

"Yes, ma'am. We *are* interesting." He turned to Charles with a grin. "So, your name is Charles, huh?"

Tristana glanced at Charles, with a look of horrified guilt. "Oh no. I'm so sorry. Was I supposed to use some alias for you?"

"I go by *Paladin* in my other life, Tristana, but that's OK. If Alpha doesn't already know my real name, he will in about a minute."

261

Alpha said, "OK, homeboy. I keep telling you. Rainbow don't tell me shit. She's loyal to you, and she's loyal to me."

Charles nodded. "As it should be. If you didn't see my command performance last week with Congress, you'll see me on YouTube. We need to talk about Naked Emperor."

Alpha said, "Yeah, I don't follow the news, but I heard they made Sybillene illegal and burned down the company that makes it. That's gonna put a crimp in supplies. You still gonna be able to get it for us? I got us a healthy number of street orders. Rainbow going hard at the computer shit and social media. She's got her homegirls kicking the stuff throughout town too. They selling shit like wildfire. Women like that Naked Emperor, and turns out they like to buy it from females."

"I got you the very last batch of legally manufactured Sybillene, Alpha. To bring you up to speed, I'm the major shareholder, and soon-to-be principal owner, of Visioryme Pharmaceuticals. Tristana is its CEO."

Tristana clarified. "He's the major shareholder of a twisted mass of rubble, and I'm CEO of a pile of ashes."

Charles couldn't help but taunt her. "It's liberating, Tristana! You're getting in the mood already!"

"Not much else I could do, Charles."

Alpha said, "Wait a second, Paladin. *You're* Charles Knight? The guy that the Naked Emperor crowd keeps talking about as some kind of folk hero?"

"Yes. Although I don't quite see myself that way…"

"The pieces be coming together! You know they want you to run for president."

Charles scoffed. "Some people have a real sense of humor."

"But what you gonna do now? Can you still manufacture the stuff someplace?"

Tristana said, "We're sure gonna try."

She was getting into it. That pleased Charles no end.

"Good. That stuff beats everything else we sell."

"The price of it has got to go up, Alpha. I've got you a large supply. But it'll take months to get more manufactured. We saved barrels' worth of raw powder, but can't load it into canisters yet."

"Hey, Paladin. It's powder. What's wrong with a hundred-dollar bill and a nose, yo?"

"Not happening, Alpha. We're going to keep this on the straight and narrow. If we sell the stuff outside its sealed inhalers, some people will start cutting it with powdered sugar, or God knows what else. And then we lose trust."

"True dat." Alpha mused.

"You'd probably cut it yourself, wouldn't you?"

"Old habits die hard, Paladin."

"Let 'em die, Alpha. One key to building a brand is reliability and quality control. You'll have the largest supply in the country. This is going to be our brand. We've gotta jack the prices up—I suggest you look at five to one, for openers—and make our profits now, because it may need to carry us for a while."

Alpha said, "Competitors gonna come, if the prices are high."

It was a logical observation that everybody in the illegal drug business was aware of, but that legislators and regulators remained oblivious to. If the DEA made a big bust, and took a ton of cocaine off the streets, that simply raised the price of what remained. If the price doubled as a result, say from $5,000 to $10,000 a kilo, then the profit for the importer might go from $2,500 to $7,500. That provided more capital to the importer, and more incentive for others to bring in more coke. So the more they confiscated, the more was imported. If they arrested the head of a cartel, it simply created a job opening for a new guy. And perhaps a temporary vacuum in the market, allowing the organization of three new cartels. The illegalization of drugs was exactly what made dealing them profitable. Just as the illegalization of Sybillene would ensure massive profitability for Charles and Alpha and everybody around them.

Charles couldn't help but smile at the thought.

"Competitors may try," Charles said, thinking a bit. "And I don't know that I mind if they do, as long as they don't try to pass the stuff they make as *our* product. Here's the problem: Sybillene is hard to make. What I worry about is that there will be lots of counterfeit stuff without any Sybillene in it, and it might make people sick, or they won't get the effect. Our brand has to be a guarantee of quality. That's one of the many unintended consequences of the DEA's controls: not being able to advertise our brand publicly actually makes the public less safe."

Alpha prompted, looking at Tristana, although he didn't know who her husband worked for. "Hey, maybe the FDA could regulate those damn counterfeiters and the DEA take them down!"

Tristana smiled wistfully. "Wouldn't that be a trick. But for some reason, the FDA doesn't like us."

"So what can we do to prevent counterfeiting?" Alpha looked at Charles.

Charles redirected his question to Tristana.

Tristana offered, "We need to visibly brand Sybillene…" She coughed. "I mean Naked Emperor … in some way that's impossible to copy. Holograms? Or how about a code number on each canister, like software identification numbers?"

"That's an idea."

Tristana continued. "The purchaser can type the numbers into a website, and the website will confirm whether that serial number is real and spit back how many times someone has typed that specific number in. If more than zero, the purchaser would become suspicious that the canister was fake."

Charles looked at Tristana with rising appreciation. She had embarked on a journey of transition. Her business brain now focused on solving real problems instead of artificial problems created by government hacks.

He said, "We can do that. Overseas, in some country where it's hard to track the owners of the site. It's not an immediate priority, but it'll be needed soon enough. We should do everything we can to make sure our clients know what they're buying."

Tristana said, "I can ask Rainbow to look into it. She's got all sorts of friends."

Alpha looked at Tristana. "Right. You the woman that Rainbow stayin' with."

Tristana looked up at Alpha. "You didn't know?"

"Rainbow keeps secrets real well."

"Should we plan to, um, stop the competition?" Alpha prompted, hesitancy in his voice, so close to Tristana.

Charles frowned. "We don't have that right. If others come in with counterfeit or even the real drug, the buyers can choose their stuff if they want to. As long as they don't try to pretend it's ours."

Alpha said, "Makes sense to me. Hard for us, of all people, to argue against competition, huh?"

Tristana said, "And if theirs *does* look like ours?"

Alpha looked at Charles, who nodded and said slowly, "Then, girl, there gonna be another fire."

Charles chuckled. "Alpha, they've shut down Visioryme, but I don't know that this will be the end of the government's involvement. There's a real chance that this is going to get hot. When it does, how will you keep your dealers from getting arrested?"

"Paladin, you're just some rich pharmaceutical-company owner. Down here on the street, getting arrested, going to prison, it's part of life. But you looking at a guy who been avoiding arrest for years. Trust me."

Charles tried to do almost everything by delegating to people who knew what they were doing. But sometimes he forgot.

When they left, Tristana couldn't help but ask, "How in the world did you ever meet a guy like that?"

"Rainbow introduced us."

"Why?"

"I'm in the drug business. So is he. We were each just expanding our networks."

* * *

Seth Fowler shook his head. Sabina Heidel sat adjacent to Donald, but not as close as she used to. Seth said, "Look, I've known you for a long time, Donald. But you screwed the pooch on this one."

"I did nothing wrong," Donald replied. "The guy knocked me over and my gun went off. Not my fault."

"Well, if that's how you remember it… But the way it's spinning all over the Internet is that you're a psycho government agent and Charles Knight is a normal, reasonable guy. You shot up the place during a *barbecue*, and then set fire to the whole damn building! The video and audio are all over the net."

"Fuck that. I was enforcing the law. I'm entirely in the right. It's not on the video, but I saw that pyro brat that lives with my wife kick charcoals under a stack of bamboo. She could have killed me and a whole lot of others. I've got the law behind me, and the truth will come out."

Fowler scowled and replied, "From now on, we can't wait for the truth. We have to *make* the truth. And that's tough when we have competition.

The problem with this Naked Emperor is that it seems to point out when people are lying.

"Truth serum."

"Nothing like that. Sodium pentothal destroys your will and clouds your mind. Naked Emperor *strengthens* will and *clears* the mind. But they're equally dangerous. And the stuff is going to be out there for a while."

"We're trying to track the wholesalers and distributors who bought the last of the drug from Visioryme," Sabina offered. "But the records were destroyed and the memories of the Visioryme staff seem to be failing them."

Fowler looked at her quizzically, further revealing his foul mood. Donald's antics reflected badly on everyone even tangentially involved with him. He directed his ire, albeit gently, at Sabina. "I'm sorry, Ms. Heidel. Why are you involved in Sybillene?" Perhaps he could get some control over the woman. But her face was stone.

Donald cut in quickly, "Ms. Heidel is an ad hoc member of my staff for the duration of our joint projects."

"I see."

Sabina asked, "Sybillene is now in your purview at DEA, isn't it, Seth? Since it's a Schedule I controlled substance…"

Seth replied, "It's definitely in the DEA's sphere of operations, yes. And since I'm already involved with FDA, the director has asked me to be the point man on everything related to Naked Emperor. It's one reason why I called Donald here today. I'm taking over anything to do with Sybillene."

Donald said nothing.

Seth went on. "And here's the other news. It looks like you and I will be working together. Your Viagra Initiative, as you call it, has been approved by DEA, finally. I think that was the last hurdle to our taking on your counterfeit-drug problem. Your counterfeit Viagra task force is a go. We're going to start shutting down the erection factory."

Sabina smiled faintly. She didn't care one bit about this.

Donald nodded. "Good. About time."

Fowler continued, "On one condition."

"What condition?"

"Given your recent activities at Visioryme, my boss insists that DEA run the show. We won't be equal partners. You'll report to me."

"Fuck that, Fowler. This whole counterfeit-drug operation is my world, my idea. It is not even DEA's purview. You said so yourself."

"That was then, and this is now. It's non-negotiable."

"Fuck that. Fuck you."

"Do you kiss your mother with that mouth, Donald?"

The left corner of Donald's mouth lifted, expressing the darkness that constantly ran through his mind. "Fowler, for DEA to run this, we'll have to go through the whole approval process again, with FDA and with Customs."

"No, I don't think we will."

Donald waited for Fowler to explain.

Fowler smiled. "My boss is at the White House right now. He's meeting with the president."

28

The President Learns a Lesson

PRESIDENT Cooligan sat on the couch in the Oval Office. This wasn't his real office, which was immediately adjacent. But the famous room was useful for more than just ceremonial activities and impressing some select members of the public invited to look through the door. The room was at once intimate, yet intimidating, and a convenient venue for meeting with small groups. Its prestige helped the president to get what he wanted with private discussions.

The president looked at his chief of staff. "Dick, what do you think of this stuff?"

Dick Stafford replied, without any change of facial expression. "As you know, I have concerns. Let's hear from the vice chairman. He asked for the meeting. And then let's hear what DEA has to say. Their director is also here."

The president asked his secretary to send the vice chairman of the Federal Reserve into his office. Tradition held that the president of the New York Federal Reserve Bank also be the vice chairman of the Federal Reserve Board of Governors. Cooligan referred to him as Mr. Samuels, Professor Samuels, Vice Chairman Samuels, or *that patronizing weasel*, depending on his mood.

Most people at the higher end of the economic ladder knew the *chairman* of the Federal Reserve by name and often by face. After the president himself, the chairman was probably the most powerful man in the world. But few outside of financial circles knew the *vice* chair. He had been selected twelve months earlier, and outsiders might presume he would still be finding his way through the intricacies of the job. That would be a false assumption. The man had known for years that he would be the next head of the New York Fed. He knew the intricacies of the international financial systems far better than any elected official. And now he controlled the operations of the largest bank in the world—the bank that the U.S. government primarily went to for financing its activities.

"Vice Chairman Samuels, how are you?"

"Well, Mr. President. Thank you."

"And your family?"

"My daughter has grown up, Mr. President. I'm an empty nester."

"Mine too, professor. Let's hope they do well. Now, what's on your mind about this Naked Emperor? We've shut it down, but I hear you think that's not enough."

"Allow me to cut to the chase. This new drug, Naked Emperor, is a clear and present danger to this government and the entire economy of the United States."

Samuels's use of the phrase *clear and present danger* caused Cooligan to salivate. The Supreme Court had long ago decided that freedom of speech, and all other freedoms, weren't absolutes; the nine justices regularly set aside the Bill of Rights with a stroke of a pen, allowing presidents to do whatever they thought might be a good idea at the time.

"Banning Naked Emperor, as Congress and your administration have just done, is not sufficient. It's already gone underground."

"You know this how?" the president asked.

"The information is all over the Internet. It seems unequivocal."

The president turned to Stafford. "I thought no one but Visioryme could make the stuff. I thought it was nearly impossible to recreate. Bamboo, fungus, complex chemical modifications, all that rigmarole."

"That's what we were told, sir," Stafford replied.

"FDA burned all that bamboo and fungus, yes?"

"Accidentally, but yes."

"Has that idiot from FDA been fired?" the president asked.

Stafford replied, "Debocher? No. I don't think we should."

"Why not? He opened fire with a machine gun in a Virginia suburb!"

"We need him, Mr. President." Stafford nodded his head slowly, sending a message.

The president nodded back. He knew Stafford was telling him that Debocher possessed a useful personality type, traits that should be kept in reserve and deployed when needed.

At first blush someone looking at Debocher might think him entirely undesirable. But a skilled puppeteer sought out characters like Debocher. A man with so many flaws is readily manipulated to do whatever might be needed. And those same flaws could make him an excellent fall guy when *that* was needed.

He looked back to Samuels. "Tell me, Vice Chairman, why you're so concerned now. We just passed a strong law. Why don't we wait to see what its effects will be?"

"Mr. President. I cannot stress enough that I believe, as does the rest of the Fed's board, that Naked Emperor presents one of the gravest threats to our national security in the last hundred years."

The phrase *national security* caused Cooligan to salivate more. The ambiguous, flexible term had come into fashion after World War II, could justify almost anything, and seemed to demand bold and immediate presidential action.

"You've been listening to the congressional committees' propaganda. Don't be dramatic."

"I am *not* being dramatic, Mr. President." His tone was firm, and cold.

"The biggest threat to national security in the last hundred years? Really? How about Hitler? How about the Cold War? How about terrorists?"

Samuels replied, "We mustn't drink our own Kool-Aid. Shall I remind you that once Hitler invaded Russia, he was never a threat to the United States? The Cold War? The Soviets would have collapsed a decade before they did if we hadn't propped them up. Terrorists? They're distractions, largely primitives living in caves; more Americans die from lightning strikes each year. Most importantly, these were all *external* threats, Mr. President, and therefore far less important than what Naked Emperor could visit upon us."

Neither the president nor Stafford felt a need to comment.

"Power relies on two factors: economics and psychology. These things, respectively, control the world outside of us, and inside of us. The most important is psychology, however. That's why a giant elephant can be ordered about by a skinny little boy—because the elephant's mind has been trained to believe he must obey.

"The fact is that our present monetary system—and therefore government finances and much of the economy—is based on a similar training. Training to have confidence in the dollar. If confidence in the dollar disappears, then the economy collapses. Chaos results. A serious lack of trust in our money, our financial system, and our leaders—and I'm not just talking about the usual grousing from perennial malcontents, but broad-based skepticism—could result in the delegitimization of our government in the eyes of the ... proletariat."

The president saw Samuels twinge, using such a politically charged word. His dossier indicated that the man had been a Trotskyite in college, and he was still sympathetic to that worldview. Like many in the higher echelons, he was a neoconservative for international policy and a progressive in domestic matters—dedicated to ensuring that the state maintained control in all areas. He was one of many converts from socialism to the merits of a directed market economy, because it was practical.

Cooligan agreed with Samuels in many matters. They agreed that an economy with private property, markets, and entrepreneurial activity maximized tax revenues—something the Soviets didn't realize until they were far beyond bankrupt. And they agreed that a strong state was required to properly direct the masses, so that wealth flowed where it should. The model was illustrated by the prominence of a specific Roman symbol on the reverse side of the old Mercury dime, and on the official seal of the U.S. Tax Court, and directly at the front of the House of Representatives. This symbol consisted of an ax, representing the punitive power of the state, surrounded by rods—*fasces* in Latin—representing corporations. The public-private partnership made them both more powerful.

Samuels said, "I don't know how or why Naked Emperor works, and I don't really care. For all I know it could drop people into some type of narcoleptic trance. Maybe it does for people's rationality what Ecstasy does for their emotions, or LSD does for their imagination. But it causes them to see the world in different ways, and what they are beginning to see poses an extreme threat."

Stafford said, "We can see the problem. We've already acted."

Samuels shook his head. "Congress isn't stupid, at least when it comes to things like this. They know they can't withstand the scrutiny of people influenced by this drug. The masses might see some ... inconvenient untruths. You, Mr. President, supported the new law because *you* can see the risks.

And I applaud your foresight. I didn't want to take your time during the creation of the law, because everything was proceeding properly. Had there been some legal snafu or constitutional concern, I of course would have felt an obligation to step in." The vice chairman spoke as if he were the regent counseling a slightly dim boy king in some medieval palace.

"Well, Professor Samuels, it wasn't such a hard decision. I've long believed the Constitution should be a living document that needs to evolve and change with the times. And in times like these the Constitution often poses unnecessary constraints that hinder our getting on with the business of governing."

The vice chairman responded, "Again, your opinions are one reason why you are in this office." And, perhaps quickly sensing that he may have over-reached, he added, "That's why the people voted for you; they feel the same way."

The president wasn't noted for either his IQ or his general knowledge, at least outside the political arena. Those characteristics were not just over-rated, but actually problematic for men who rose to the office. His strong points included flexibility; an affable manner; good looks; a great memory for names, faces, and anecdotes; charisma; and driving ambition. He glanced at Samuels, who didn't alter his deadpan expression.

Cooligan didn't particularly like this man from the Fed. Nor the fact that he had far too much power.

Samuels—the man with too much power—said, "The chairman has met with you once or twice, I know. I assume he has provided information you need."

"It's always instructive to sit down with him, thank you." He really didn't care for the man's smarmy impertinence. But there wasn't much he could do about it.

Samuels said, "Yes. I am glad for that. But do you *really* understand? Most politicians do not—it's a matter of specialization and division of labor, of course. Most people, including legislators and executives here in D.C., have a very limited understanding of the monetary system. That hasn't mattered up until now. But the situation has changed."

"What are you saying?" The president took in the direct and insulting challenge to his intellect, knowledge, and power, coming from this small nerdy man sitting on the couch across from him. Someone who he himself could appoint—or not—to be the next chairman. He held the man's future in his hands. Almost as much as Samuels held *his*.

"Do you know what it takes to keep this economic system working?" Samuels asked.

Expecting a lecture from the man, neither Stafford nor the president responded. The people from the Fed always lectured, and always patronizingly.

Samuels bowed his head. "Very few people are aware of this. But I think you should be. As you know, the Federal Reserve has a substantial research arm. I'm referring to more than just collecting statistics and analyzing economic indicators.

"My research specialty is a hybrid of sociology, psychology, and economics, and the way they interact. It's a fairly new field, not something we promote to the world at large. It can best be described as the study of how fiat money affects the mass psychology of societies. Most people think of money—if they think of it at all—just as something in their pockets or in their bank account. They think of it as a given, like the seasons, or the earth revolving around the sun. But it's much more. Money is to a country what blood is to a human body."

The president said, "Go on." Like most people, Cooligan had never paid much attention to the nature of money itself. He knew fiat money came from nothing, as opposed to a commodity money, like gold or silver, that had to be dug from the ground or obtained from others who had worked to dig it up. All national-level politicians took advantage of fiat money: it's so much easier to pork-barrel-spend and buy votes if you can just print money up whenever needed, as simple as pressing a button. But the distinction between commodity money and fiat money seemed meaningless, interesting mainly to academic types like the man before him. From a practical point of view the dollar was, well, still "sound as a dollar." Although, oddly, that phrase was rarely used any more. Academics such as Samuels would have much more to say on the subject, and no doubt say it confusingly.

The president had yet to come out of a meeting with the Fed without agreeing with whatever they wanted him to change his mind about. They were convincing nerds.

Samuels said, "There are hundreds of sociologists, economists, and psychologists who have researched this over the last century, at various central banks, universities, and think tanks, laying the groundwork for what I'm telling you. The world economy is integrated, and it makes sense for the state and the private sector to act in concert whenever possible."

President Cooligan said, "Goldman Sachs?" It was a safe guess. The firm had risen from being one among many, to dominating the markets. It was now known in the business as *Government Sachs ...* or the *Vampire Squid.*

"Of course. Among several others."

"And you are a leader of this academic field?" the president asked.

"I'm influential. It's why I'm here today. As you well know, the world's economy has been on shaky ground for quite a while."

"And just what does your socioeconomic-hybrid psychology-research mumbo jumbo tell you that we don't already know?" The president was known to put his foot in his mouth when talking extemporaneously. That was one reason his handlers insisted he give speeches from teleprompters. He had little knowledge of economics, but few of his economic counselors' predictions ever seemed to come true either.

"Mr. President. This is a science that helps us to understand how people interact with various forms of money. What happens to the value of money, its quantity, and its price—interest rates—determines whether people are carefree or angry. Whether they want war or peace. Whether they want to vote for a leftist or a rightist. Many, many things. Everything, really."

The president waited. He was used to thinking the world turned around politics, and what he did from this very office. Not sure how to prompt for more information, he stifled a yawn.

Samuels continued. "Currencies are like the public stock of the governments that issue them. A strong currency shows people have confidence in the government that issued it, much like a high stock price indicates that a company is doing well. There are differences, of course. A company gets its revenues from selling things that people need and want; a government gets its revenues through taking what it wants from its citizens. A share certificate is backed by a company's earnings and assets; a dollar bill is backed only by the labor of the citizens forced or convinced to pay taxes. And people don't like to pay taxes, especially if their standard of living is stagnant or falling. So managing the U.S. money hasn't been an easy task since the late '60s. Most relevant to us is how fiat currencies alter decision making at the individual and societal level."

"Right, right."

"Mr. President, I believe in our system. The Fed was founded in 1913, and over the years it's become more and more important. It's questionable whether the U.S. would have, or even could have, joined in World War I if the Fed hadn't been there to help finance it with paper money. We now realize the Fed created the stock market bubble of the Roaring Twenties by facilitating easy credit, until the animal spirits got out of control, and things ended badly in 1929. In 1933, you'll recall, Roosevelt made it illegal for Americans to own gold, because there had been too many dollars created. Up until then, every twenty-dollar bill was just a receipt for an ounce of gold held in the Treasury, and gold coins circulated in daily commerce. We had to default on that promise for Americans, and raise the price of gold to thirty-five dollars an ounce for foreign governments, devaluing the dollar. But the dollar was still the best currency in the world, and the U.S. was still the best place to be, with World War II looming.

"The next big event occurred in 1965 when Lyndon Johnson took silver out of coins. He claimed it was because the rise of vending machines made it impossible for the government to keep enough silver coins in circulation. But that was a bald-faced lie. The fact was that the supply of dollars was exploding because of his 'guns and butter' policies—meaning his spending on both the Vietnam War and his immense expansion of domestic welfare programs.

"We had printed so many dollars that, naturally, the dollar became worth far less than the ounce of silver that had for centuries defined the very term 'dollar.' Our predecessors—yours and mine—had a choice: print less money and fund less warfare and welfare, or keep printing money but take the silver out of the coins to avoid the coins' becoming worth more than the dollar bill.

"So beginning in 1965, we replaced the silver coins with cheap cupro-nickel tokens that look almost exactly like silver coins."

Samuels reached into his pocket and handed the president a quarter.

"In 1971, Nixon entirely reneged on the government's promise to redeem its dollars to foreign governments for gold. So now, for decades, there's been no legal limit on how many dollars can be created. Since 1913, when the Fed was established, the dollar has lost about ninety-six percent of its purchasing power, by our own statistics. And those are, I have to tell you, somewhat-flexible yardsticks. At this point people don't save the way they used to. Even if they know nothing about economics or history, they know holding dollars is a losing proposition against inflation.

"People have an inclination to try to produce more than they consume, and save the difference. They instinctively know that's what you have to do to last through the winter. And perhaps become wealthy. But it doesn't make much sense to save paper money, and so they tend to save less. Especially when we're forced to keep interest rates low. So there's less real capital for the government, or anyone else, to borrow. At the same time, we now have many trillions of dollars outside the U.S. For a long time now, the main U.S. export hasn't been wheat, or computers, or even weapons, but dollars.

"Foreigners accept dollars still, partly because Nixon cut a deal with the Saudis. The U.S. would guarantee their theocracy, if they'd price their oil only in dollars. Of course, that helped create a lot of foreign demand for dollars, and, as you know, explains many of your predecessors' Middle East policies.

"But foreigners are less and less interested in buying, or owning, the U.S. government's paper. The Chinese accepted dollars because we were their major market. Imports from China keep down prices here in the U.S., so the average Joe doesn't notice the inflation as much as they did in the 1970s. It's been a good trade for many years; we give the foreigners our dollars, and they give us real goods.

"But now they're choking on dollars, and increasingly see them as an unsecured liability of a bankrupt government. The paper dollar is looking like a hot potato, an Old Maid card. They used to trade their paper dollars for U.S.-government Treasury bonds, but now they know that's just more paper. So we at the Fed—the 'lender of last resort'—must buy massive amounts of not just government debt, but even mortgage debt. If we don't do this, interest rates will have to rise to attract lenders to buy Treasuries, and that would be a disaster for the largest debtor in the history of the world."

The president scrunched his eyebrows down. "By that you mean?"

"The U.S. government, certainly."

"Right. Of course."

Samuels went on. "Now, the Fed tries to inflate the currency slowly enough that nobody loses confidence in it. The Republican politicians like it because inflation makes the GDP numbers look good, and government debt is paid off just by the loss of value in the dollar. The Democratic politicians like it because we inflate the currency mostly by giving them new money to spend. And everybody likes a booming stock market, and low interest rates. Of course it's true that the rich get richer because they're the ones who own stocks that rise from the new money printing, own real estate, and have the credit to borrow. We keep the perception of inflation down by redefining of terms. Believe me. *Don't believe your lying eyes.*"

Cooligan was unsure if that last line was an attempt at humor, or just a statement.

Samuels added, "People tend to have confidence in the numbers we report. And when inflation appears in the stock market and housing, people believe it makes them wealthier, so we can keep the process going. But we know that the dollar is based mainly on confidence. Unfortunately, confidence can blow away like a pile of feathers in a hurricane.

"We have to be proactive. It's not as if we're about to become Germany in the 1920s, or Zimbabwe or Venezuela today; the U.S. has accumulated an immense amount of wealth. But not once in the history of the world has there *ever* been a society that operated on fiat currency that did not in the end suffer complete economic collapse."

Samuels seemed to be predicting an economic catastrophe. The president looked over to his chief of staff, who did not look back.

The vice chairman continued. "We believe we can manage the situation. It may become necessary to impose foreign exchange controls, so Americans can't take their capital out of the country without approval. We certainly want to control and reduce the use of cash. It would be better if all transactions were digital, through a bank account; that way we can much better monitor what people earn, and do, and have. It may become necessary to use the military to keep things under control. It may be necessary to impose some order on the Internet, which is a hotbed for the kinds of rumors that cause instability. It's important to have the draft legislation on hand, so that we can maintain control."

"*We* maintain control?" The president prompted. "*We?*"

"Yes, Mr. President. We. This is why we're so concerned about the effects of Naked Emperor. Let me re-emphasize this: the system rests on confidence, belief, and mass psychology. We can't have the equivalent of someone yelling 'fire' in a crowded theater. The system is too fragile for that. We can't have people crying out that the emperor has no clothes."

Only then did the president understand the symbolism of the name of this new drug. He felt the fool for not getting it earlier. His own psychology moved to defend his delicate ego from the man's impertinence. He lashed out. "And *this* is what you people have saddled us with? I thought the situation was under better control!"

Samuels shook his head. "Saddled you with, maybe. Empowered you with, certainly. Frankly, the U.S. government could never have become as powerful as it has without a flexible fiat currency. The U.S. dollar and government debt are our two largest exports, because our dollar is accepted everywhere. That provides us with immense power. Both of our major exports are created with the stroke of a pen! We can give dollars to foreign governments to ensure they stay on side. We can finance the world's largest military and security complex. We can provide medical, retirement, and welfare benefits for over half of the population. And, very important, we can export those dollars, at essentially zero cost, in exchange for German cars, Japanese electronics, Colombian coffee, and the Chinese bric-a-brac that fills the Walmarts. The fiat dollar has allowed us to maintain a much higher standard of living than would otherwise be the case.

"We're quite aware that by any normal accounting standards the U.S. government is bankrupt. Even its so-called assets, like the Post Office, Amtrak, or Fannie Mae, are actually huge liabilities. But, as a practical matter, the U.S. government won't be *considered* bankrupt as long as people are willing to accept the dollars that the Fed creates. Can you name one other bankrupt entity that wields any power at all, and even *expands* its power every day? Only the United States' federal government has that luxury.

"It's enabled by the universal acceptance of our fiat currency. Fiat currency—the modern U.S. dollar—is why the United States government, and why you, sir, have power. You owe your job, your authority, your power, to the Federal Reserve. In effect, you stand on our shoulders."

"Really? How about the fact that I have been elected by the people. How about the fact I'm commander-in-chief?"

Samuels shrugged off the questions as naïve and irrelevant. It didn't much matter whether the population voted for Tweedle Dee or Tweedle Dum.

"Mr. President, you have listed your goals for your presidency. They all require large sums of money. We can create that new money when it's needed. If we don't, the U.S. government will be *in fact* bankrupt, and it will then lose all its power. France in 1789, and czarist Russia in 1917, collapsed because their governments were bankrupt. The chaos would be much greater if it happened here. Thus, I repeat, loss of confidence in the dollar, and our ability to manage it, is the single greatest risk to national security."

It had been a most-disturbing presentation, provided by someone in a position to know. The magic words *national security* of course caught his attention. But he also thought of personal security. If this happened on his watch, he'd be blamed.

"Well, I thank you for that, Professor Samuels," the president said. "I'm not interested in this collapse happening on my watch—that's one fact you can rely on. It sounds a bit like what Hemingway once said: you go bankrupt slowly at first, then all at once. I'll trust you to keep us on the slow part of that slippery slope."

Samuels tilted his head. "That's where my work comes into play. My research seeks, for the first time in history, to prevent fiat currency from collapsing the economy and destroying the government that prints it. It is a very important field."

"I hope you're making progress!"

"Absolutely, and indeed we have had success. We've had fiat currency for over one hundred years, Mr. President. That in itself is almost unprecedented in world history. And the economy thrives, on average. That would have been impossible without the results of the work my predecessors and I have undertaken."

"I would hardly say we're thriving. Maybe *on average* progress is being made, but the average is elevated mainly by the superwealthy."

"The rich getting richer is an inevitable and not a necessarily undesirable consequence of fiat currency and the inflation it causes, Mr. President."

The president pretended to understand. "I don't know much about monetary theory. But I know the system nearly collapsed a few years ago. The sucker nearly went down."

"And it will again," replied Samuels. "Perhaps very soon. Nothing goes on forever. Even Keynes, whose theories inform almost all economists today, was aware of flaws in his own system. When someone asked him about the long-run consequences of a fiat currency and government deficits, Keynes replied, 'In the long run, we're all dead.'"

Stafford chimed in to say, "That's hardly a reassuring notion to anyone who cares about our future."

Samuels shrugged. "It all depends on whose future, and which possible future, one is concerned about. Over the last thirty years, we've learned many tricks to help overcome these collapses, defer them, divert them, so that the currency, and our system, survives. We intervene when needed."

"Well, that makes sense," Stafford said. "Of course you should do anything necessary to keep things together."

"We intervene in ways other than just printing more currency and keeping interest rates low."

"What do you mean?" The president sensed something new forthcoming.

"We teach. Call it indoctrination, if you wish. It's a question of properly educating the public. We have special teachers."

"Teachers? Who?"

"Very public figures. On television, in the newspapers. They're celebrities in a way, and the public has confidence in their opinions. You know them all by name. I think it's fairly obvious."

"And what do these talking heads teach?"

"I said it was teaching in a special way. We call them *pushes*."

"Pushes?"

"We've learned that we need to *push* here and there, targeting both particular individuals and society at large, often in subtle ways, to keep the balance in favor of currency stability."

"How do you do this?"

Samuels shook his head. "Suffice to say our pushes involve a variety of different methods to redirect the people and their fears. Of all the emotions, fear is the most potent motivator. More than love, greed, or hate. Fear is why it's easy to sell everything from regulations to financial bailouts to war. I suspect we'll need a few meetings for you to put it into context."

It was another dig at the president's intellect, and he didn't miss it. If Samuels had been that supercilious with a president like Lyndon Johnson, that good ol' boy would have verbally outdone a Marine drill sergeant before physically evicting him from the office, and then making it his life's work to destroy him. Ronald Reagan might have interpreted the insult as a compliment. Bill Clinton, well known both for his knowledge and his high IQ, would have smiled and nodded, while paying no attention and contemplating mayhem. Bush and Obama would each have nodded and done as they were told.

But this president had only modest grit, modest affability, and modest intellect. So he spat out, "Try me."

Samuels said, "The purpose of our pushes is to protect the Federal Reserve System. For instance, we encourage people to fear deflation, even if they don't know what it is. At most they know it's what happened in the 1930s' depression. We get key people to publicly beg us to fight against the impending disaster of deflation."

"So that when you inflate the currency, you're heroes."

"It certainly provides us a mandate for inflation, doesn't it?"

"Give me another example."

Samuels frowned, considering. "Mr. President, we use big words."

The president could barely restrain his anger now. He clamped his teeth, and his cheeks visibly tightened. Even his nose flared.

His chief of staff interceded.

"Mr. Samuels, we don't appreciate being talked down to. Nor does it aid the cause of cooperation."

Samuels again tilted his head to the side as if apologizing and replied, "I didn't mean to suggest you wouldn't understand. Not at all. I meant that in our public statements we use *big words*, confusing terms, that often make no sense to the general population, or to Congress for that matter. They're hard for the average person to comprehend, but that's all for the best. TARP, Quantitative Easing, ZIRP. People only need to know that we're not about to let *their* bank fail."

The president breathed and said, a bit boisterously, "But the financial gurus, the academics, *they* know."

"It's hard for those types to admit that they don't really know what we're talking about, even though, to be quite candid, a lot of it is intentionally contradictory gibberish. 'Fedspeak.' Greenspan and Bernanke were masters of it. It's nothing new. The Oracle at Delphi, or a clever carnival mentalist, is hard to prove wrong if they say something cryptic. People play along. We have the advantage in that everybody's wealth depends on our success. *Everyone* hopes we're right. Everyone is rooting for us. Nobody wants the bubble to break, to see banks fail, the markets crash, and businesses go under. They *want* to have confidence in us. What other choice do they have? The whole system is based on confidence. So we engender confidence. In us."

"It's a confidence game. So you're saying you're a con artist." The president said it as a joke. But jokes are funniest when they're true. "What's the legality of all this?"

"Sir, there is no U.S. law that prohibits what we do, I assure you. But, it is still something that needs to stay in the shadows. The tools that we employ work best when the subjects aren't aware of them."

"You mean, like a placebo."

"Yes, in many ways very much like a placebo."

"I'm interested in hearing more about this, Mr. Samuels. And soon."

"Yes, we must have further discussions. Once you understand, you will find our methods helpful to the programs you are undertaking during your term in office."

"It sounds like propaganda. Re-education."

"As I said before, we prefer to use the phrase 'pushing.' *Re*-education suggests that they were once *educated*. Almost no school in the country teaches its students about the Federal Reserve or fiat currency. That's quite intentional, and took a great deal of *pushing* on the part of my predecessors to accomplish."

"You're still doing that?"

"No need to anymore. How can the teachers teach when they don't understand it themselves? How can the professors educate when they themselves are oblivious? So it naturally comes off the curricula."

"Well, that's good, I suppose."

"Yes, that is good," Samuels replied. "But still, I don't even want to contemplate what would happen if kids start using the drug en masse in the schools. It's better for everyone if they just memorize and repeat the right things. We don't want to see cars with *Question Authority* bumper stickers in school parking lots, of all places. If young people don't think they should obey their leaders, there's no telling where things could head."

"How does your *pushing* relate to Naked Emperor?" the president probed.

"I'll reiterate, Mr. President. The methods we employ, these pushes, work best if the subjects aren't aware of them. If people had a sound education in economics and history, our work would be harder or impossible. Fortunately, most people are concerned mainly with sports scores and celebrity divorces. They devote their energies to getting a bigger house or a newer car. But Naked Emperor changes a lot of dynamics. We've studied Naked Emperor in several subject groups, and the results are profound. In the presence of Naked Emperor, our pushes not only fail to work, but seem counterproductive."

"What does that mean?"

"It means that if enough people get hold of Naked Emperor, the measures we'll need to try to balance the ship when the next collapse occurs won't be enough. If Naked Emperor stays available to the population, the U.S. dollar will collapse, and this government with it."

"How soon?"

"We don't know. Naked Emperor has tossed all our models on their ears."

"We've already outlawed the drug. What else do you want me to do?"

"What did outlawing marijuana do for marijuana, Mr. President? In the end it just amounted to free advertising for a plant that was previously only used by Beatniks and Mexicans. That's what this man Knight has done with his presence on Capitol Hill. You have to do more. The public needs to take this seriously. It's critical that Sybillene be obliterated off the face of the planet."

The name *Knight* rang a distant bell in the president's memory.

The president shrugged. He turned to Stafford. "What else *can* we do?"

Stafford replied, "Well, we can turn the heat up, Mr. President."

The president nodded.

Samuels pushed a bit harder. "Half measures have never worked for drug prohibition. I advise you to move very quickly and fiercely, Mr. President. We may have little time."

The president nodded slowly. "The director of the DEA is outside this door. I'll start with some private discussions."

Samuels nodded. "Thank you, Mr. President. Please keep me informed. We should talk frequently."

"That's a two-way street, Mr. Samuels."

"Clearly, Mr. President. So, please do keep me informed."

"I meant that I expect much more information from you in the coming days."

"Of course, of course… Oh, I have a favor to ask of you, Mr. President. I have a colleague who needs a change in her position. She's the woman I asked you to place in FDA."

Stafford whispered "Sabina Heidel" to the president.

Images flashed through the president's memories, back when he had much more time and energy for escapades with women like Sabina.

Samuels continued. "She's done at FDA. She needs to go to DEA now.

Right next to whoever is going to be charged with the elimination of Naked Emperor."

Now *this* was in the president's comfort zone. Favors begot favors. And he had some particular favors in mind for Sabina. "I'm happy to help with anything that's in my power."

Samuels replied, "We're on your side, Mr. President. *Everything* is in your power."

"How comforting."

Samuels added as he went out the door, "Thank you for your attention to this Naked Emperor issue. We have much to do in very little time."

29

Small-Small Time

"TJ, we have very little time. At the rate the stuff is selling, even with all the stockpiling we did, we'll be out of product in two months, maybe less."

"Charles, you want to have a pharmaceutical manufacturing site up and running in *two months*?"

"Nope, we need it sooner. We have to be *shipping* product in less than six weeks. But we have a shortcut for the first batch. We already have the drug made, and it's on its way over in barrels. It just needs to be loaded into its canisters. So, do you think you can do it?"

TJ thought for about ten seconds and answered, "With some training, yes." It was a simple, short answer, but not one given lightly. TJ had competence, integrity, and connections. So it was as close to a guarantee as you were likely to get in a difficult environment like Gondwana.

Volumes of new laws and presidential decrees, and the need to visit scores of turf-conscious and easily offended bureaucracies, each with its own protocols and fees, made *legitimate* business frustrating and, without tenacity, impossible. But, at the same time, if one possessed the right connections and knew whom to pay, navigating the corruptocracy could be much easier than undertaking legal business in the United States. As Tacitus pointed out, "The more numerous the laws, the more corrupt the state." Corruption was not only inevitable, but necessary and salubrious in a place like Gondwana. Without corruption nothing would happen.

Bureaucracies didn't matter to Charles. He didn't care about their rules. With the government of Gondwana both incompetent and broke, the rules proved very flexible. Charles loved this place. In Gondwana, as in most Third World countries, a briefcase full of cash would get the job done.

The U.S. also had undecipherable and contradictory laws, but there it was dangerous to bribe government officials, at least by giving them money directly. So, the promise of a fat job after the official left office served as a standard ploy. Directorships and consulting fees were hinted at. If the person held a high-enough profile, a few months on the speaking circuit collecting six-figure honorariums could be arranged. Maybe a seven-figure subsidized book contract. And of course invitations into all manner of sweetheart deals.

In the U.S., bureaucrats and politicians waited until they were out of office to collect the profits from their time in public service. The shrewdest circled back-and-forth through the revolving doors of cronyism, switching between private and public every few years.

For instance, early in her career one insufferable first lady and presidential wannabe became one of the world's most successful cattle traders, despite zero knowledge of commodity futures. Starting with a $1,000 account, a friendly broker stuffed it with winning trades when things were settled at the day's end. The ploy was called *sleeving* because the broker swept the day's winners into one sleeve for one set of clients and the losers into the other sleeve for different clients. The first lady made $99,465 over a couple of months—one of the best records in history. Few people thought to ask what happened to the other $535 of the obvious bribe.

T.J. Wandeah navigated the government-bribery complex professionally. He cared about their rules, sort of. Whereas Charles had the instincts of a scofflaw, TJ simply liked to avoid hassles. He kept Charles out of trouble, as he had years ago, in this same rough country on this same rough road.

They bounced along the highway to Djenne County, bottoming the Toyota Land Cruiser's suspension every hundred yards or so, TJ alternately accelerating to make some progress, then decelerating to a near stop to avoid blowing a tire or breaking an axle in the road's next crater. It had once been paved, during colonial days. But what pavement had survived the erosion of the rainy seasons had been torn apart during the wars.

"Let's find a location. The equipment's on its way."

"How's it getting here?" TJ asked.

Charles replied, "Captain Anders is bringing it in."

"Is he a drug smuggler now?"

"No laws here or on the high seas, or even in the U.S., about shipping pharmaceutical equipment offshore. He's clean for the moment."

"And the scientific and technical staff?"

"We're sort of smuggling them in. Also via Anders. We don't want to make it easy for the U.S. to figure out that several of the Visioryme staff have moved to Gondwana!"

"Oh, good. The port in Djenne is reopening soon. Did you know?"

"Yes, Anders is on it. Anything to save driving on these roads. He's sure it'll handle his ship."

"No doubt. The Chinese have rebuilt the facilities. For ore from the mines. It used to be the largest port in Gondwana. Then the wars…"

"Yes. The wars."

The wars had essentially destroyed Djenne County, not so much by violence as economic dissipation. The iron mines up north shut down, and then the port closed. With the port closed, the rubber plantations in the county couldn't ship latex. So it had been hard times in Djenne. The area was reduced to subsistence, people scratching out a living planting tubers in jungle clearings.

Charles said, "I expect we'll stimulate the local economy a bit. Nothing like a pharmaceutical factory to get the ball rolling."

TJ dodged a huge chasm in the road with a river pouring through it. Charles bounced up in the passenger seat and winced.

"You know what they say, Charles?"

"This, too, is Gondwana?" The country's informal PR slogan was supposed to draw attention to a pristine beach, or a quaint market. In fact it could refer to anything from an assault on the president's palace to a dead dog lying on the side of the road.

"Right, my friend. We have a beautiful country, but *this too is Gondwana*." The car smashed through another hole. "You are relearning this country well."

"An education can be painful and expensive."

"There are things that you don't know, though, Charles. So, especially in Djenne, you should stick with me."

"What things?"

TJ looked straight ahead and reminded Charles about things that few people imagine are still part of the world. "The secret societies are very active in Djenne. You do not want to be out wandering in the bush. Ever."

"I thought the secret societies were recently banned by the government."
TJ laughed. "So was Sybillene!"
"Good point."

The secret societies remained important throughout West Africa, but especially out in the deep bush. Their role was much like that of the union in an industrial town in the Northeast of the U.S., or a church in the American Bible Belt. They had one for the men, called Poro, and one for the women, called Sande. As cultural institutions, their roots spread deep, and influenced nearly everyone. Males were initiated into Poro, mostly at puberty, through ritual and mentoring in the bush. There were stories of foreigners being consumed by the bush never to re-emerge. Ritual cannibalism wasn't an old wives' tale, but a reality. All the bizarre rites of voodoo in Haiti and Santeria in Brazil originated here.

The Freemasons, the Mafia, the CIA, and hundreds of other organizations in the developed world were enshrouded in layers of secrecy; the Poro and Sande were West Africa's equivalent. How much of what was said about them was true? It didn't matter. Fear of what *might* be true was sufficient. The immense psychological power of taboos maintained an impenetrable oath of secrecy among their members. Peer pressure and social opprobrium enforced ancient customs. Traditions were the supreme law in almost any culture, certainly superseding civil laws made by some far-away central government. More often than not that was a good thing, in the same way that the cultural reticence of Italians or Argentines to pay taxes exerted at least a modicum of control on their own regimes.

A Poro devil, in fetish dress, was no more likely to be defied as he oversaw the decisions of Poro men under the natural canopy of the bush discussing the issues of the day than would the pope, arrayed in robes and mitre, speaking to devout Catholics. The secret societies influenced life here the way the church in the thirteenth century did Europeans, albeit with varying degrees of fervor and sincerity. The secret-society members weren't raging crazies, but rather businessmen, pastors, farmers, laborers, and politicians. The omnipresent Poro and Sande were the true establishment.

TJ said, "Most of what they do is cultural, mutual support in times of need, rituals to become an adult. The teenagers may go into the bush for long periods during their transition, to learn the ways of the ancestors. Most of that is very good. But, they will kill, as individuals or as a mob, if they think evil is among them."

Charles had encountered some very nasty people in Gondwana. But they were foreigners. Sabina Heidel came immediately to mind. However beautiful, she was the embodiment of human evil. And that evil had slithered back into his life.

"Do they still target foreigners?" he asked.

"If the foreigners are evil, Charles. If they are evil. But people everywhere think that people they don't know, with different looks, different customs, might be evil. So it's risky for an outsider—even if he's a good person."

This was why there were almost no living albinos in Gondwana. Or, for that matter, any country in sub-Saharan Africa, even though about one in forty thousand babies was born with the condition. Being born white in a black society was tantamount to losing the cosmic lottery. Ritual killings still happened. In East Africa, witch doctors used the bones, skin, and teeth of recently killed albinos to make potions.

The bouncing of the vehicle and constant acceleration and deceleration took a toll on Charles's back. After an hour more, he switched the driving with TJ. At least now he would know when the car was about to swerve or when the brakes would be slammed on, because he would be doing it himself. His back began to feel better almost right away. He thought back to his old friend Xander Winn, who insisted on driving the roads of Africa, for the same reasons, so many years ago.

"It's the muscle tension from not knowing," he told TJ.

TJ nodded. "So, tell me what we have to do to build a production plant."

"Anders delivers in one week. He comes into Freeport and then can get here within a day after that. If the Chinese will offload the cargo."

"They will, Charles. Just pay them."

The Chinese had replaced the Europeans as a colonial power throughout Africa. They were efficient, well capitalized, and in it strictly for the money—like the Europeans of a hundred years before. They were very *unlike* the Europeans of today, who sent kids around in Land Cruisers to write reports on how much good the money their governments sent was doing to fight poverty, completely unaware that most of the money went right back to European banks, or to the Chinese. The European people, and their governments, squandered hundreds of billions out of guilt and altruism. The European *banks* were smarter.

The banks loaned newly created fiat money to governments on the verge of bankruptcy. The government officials in the impoverished country pocketed the money, after a generous kickback to the guys who signed off on the loan, and stuck it back in the European banks. When the inevitable financial collapse occurred, the banks might forgive part of the loans. The international communities considered the banks heroes when they first loaned the money, with much fanfare, to the suffering Africans. And heroes again when they forgave the debt of the poor suffering peoples. In reality, the loans of fake currency cost the banks nothing, and they ended up forgiving the loans in exchange for mineral rights and real estate. It was a neat game. The government officials got rich, individual bankers got rich, the banks acquired some assets. And the people got poorer, with nobody the wiser.

The Chinese, strangely, acted the most honorably. They bought mineral rights from the corrupt governments, paying both in cash and by building needed infrastructure, accomplished via the usual kickbacks to officials on both sides. But at least something useful got built.

Charles said, "Thanks be to the Chinese. At least until a couple hundred million migrate to Africa and it precipitates a race war."

TJ looked over at him. "Ha. It's likely to be a three-way affair. I promise you're going to see my countrymen, and millions more from Nigeria, and Senegal, and the whole continent, on rafts to Europe. Why stay here when they'll give you money just for *being* there?"

Each man recognized the other was correct, and then went back to the matter at hand.

"When did you ship the manufacturing equipment out of the U.S.?"

"About thirty minutes before the FDA and the U.S. marshals came in guns blazing."

"Really? They fired weapons?"

"It was more incompetence than intention. Anyhow, we'd worked the previous forty-eight hours straight to get the functional equipment out of the building. We closed the container doors on the last of the trucks, and sent it on its way. We were celebrating when the FDA barged in."

"So the FDA didn't confiscate any of your equipment?"

"Just one donut."

"Well done, Charles."

"Well, the FDA did get some empty plastic canisters—the inhaler devices—that came in from Brazil later that afternoon. Nothing we could do about that. And the bamboo got burned of course. But that came from right here. All things considered, I've no complaints."

"How bad was that fire?"

"The building was a mass of twisted metal and tar. But since the mortgage was paid off, the insurance money netted some cash. The FDA actually did us a favor."

"You were lucky."

"It wasn't all luck, TJ. We knew they were coming. And more *will* be coming. At this point the U.S. is going to make a major push against Sybillene. They view it as a matter of national security. You hear those magic words, anything goes."

TJ folded his eyebrows in concern. "So, what do we need to make Sybillene?"

"The Brazilians make tons of plastic inhaler devices—same things that FDA intercepted. They aren't a problem; anybody with a plastic mold can crank them out. The Brazilians are going to ship them to Djenne, via a roundabout route. Later we can also buy some molding equipment and do it ourselves. But there's enough for us to do right now. We need a big building, and a big generator. We need to get locals trained. We need housing for the Visioryme people. So we have a real construction project in the offing."

"This area is rougher than the capital city, you know. There is only one hotel."

"Is it ... *nice?*" That wasn't quite the word Charles wanted to use. Maybe *acceptable*, *livable*, *usable*, or perhaps *tolerable* would be more realistic. But he didn't want to insult his friend, in case one of TJ's brothers owned the place.

"It used to be. Now it's not so nice. Only occasional electricity, but it has running water and showers, sometimes. And there are free condoms in all the rooms!"

"It's not what they're used to, but the folks I'm bringing will be OK after they adjust. They can pretend they're kids again, at summer camp. We're tripling their salaries, and they won't have anywhere to spend it. They'll be happy campers. Any ideas for a building we can get hold of?"

"Yes. There is an old mineworks on the top of a hill above Djennetown. The place fell apart during the wars, rains fill it up in rainy season; no one has reopened it. No power, and the rail spur from the base of the hill to the port got all torn up. But it has several substantial buildings that I think we can fix up, and we will work fast."

"Who owns it?"

TJ shook his head in the way that Charles had learned meant that he would rather not say. But he also made that expression when he felt embarrassed, or humiliated. He needed prodding, so Charles prodded. "Tell me, TJ."

TJ shrugged and said, "*I* own it."

"Of course you do."

"Well, I misinform you. My father does. But he is dead, and I am his firstborn. So effectively, I do."

"Will you sell it to me?"

"We can work something out, I'm sure."

"Is this why you said you could do it? You knew you had the buildings?"

"And the people."

"What people?"

"I know most of the people who use to work in Djenne. Good people. They need work, Charles. They need work."

"Do you trust them?"

"They are good people who used to work for my father. Good people."

"Do you trust them?"

"Yes, Charles. I trust them. Many are relatives. They love me."

Charles drove with less skill than TJ, and the vehicle suffered because of it. The car made a series of new noises every time it bounced into a hole or over a rock. Up ahead, two massive trees stood on either side of the road. The trunks measured at least fifteen feet in diameter, and reached toward the heavens. They did so out of the blue too, for nothing on the flat terrain around them stood anywhere near as high. The two trees could have been seen from miles away, had Charles been able to see through the mud-splashed windshield that was impossible to keep clear, or had he been able to look up from the potholed road.

Charles felt compelled to stop at the base of the massive trees, the size of California redwoods. He walked to one of the trunks, and climbed a few meters up the exposed roots, as if they were a mountain.

"You've been through here before," TJ said, "many years ago, but it was too dark to see these trees."

Charles remembered.

"Welcome to Djenne, mister," a boy said from below him, making Charles start. The boy stood next to a uniformed officer. The uniform appeared nothing like the pristine attire of police in the capital. This one had seen its share of mud and time. This man was either a county officer, or not an officer at all.

"Thank you." Charles smiled down at the boy, ignoring the officer.

The officer said, "Mister, I need to see your identification."

"No, you don't," Charles said firmly. He then looked back at the tree, moved in to put his arms up against its wet, thick bark, tilted his head back and stared straight up. It felt like it was falling back on him. This brief feeling of exhilaration helped Charles feel alive. The rush was more real than that any drug could offer. After a minute, he turned and climbed back down the roots, back to the road level, where the officer patiently waited for him. The man looked humble.

"I need to see your papers, sir?" It was a question, essentially a hopeful plea.

"No, you don't. I'm on the way to the hotel, and you have no need to see my papers."

The man's effort at a shakedown remained wimpy. It probably worked on inexperienced passersby.

TJ got out of the car then and walked over. He would not be as polite. TJ spoke in the semi-English patois of the common people. Charles mostly couldn't grasp it, but he heard the name Wandeah, and each time TJ yelled the name, the police officer physically shriveled. As quickly as he had appeared from nowhere, he disappeared. The boy remained.

As near as Charles could tell, the boy said to TJ, "You are Mr. T.J. Wandeah? Oh!"

TJ reached down and offered the boy his hand, which the boy took and shook with that unique complex ritual handshake men used in informal greeting. The boy smiled in delight. TJ handed him a can of Pringles and patted him on the head.

TJ climbed in on the driver's side, and Charles asked him, "So?"

"My name is known here, Charles. I told you my father was a very big man in this town. I have his name. Since he died, I am the big man now."

The town had once had some charm. A substantial church, painted blue, served as the center of the main square. Boarded-up stores lined well laid-out streets, now in poor repair. Chickens were the predominant pedestrians. Two restaurants served the convenient but scrawny chickens to the regulars and the occasional traveler. What used to be a pleasant seaside hotel provided semifunctional accommodations. Most of the town lay in shambles.

"The war years were tough on Djennetown." TJ shook his head. They stopped at the hotel and checked in, delighted to learn that the manager would turn on the generator in a few hours and that there might be four hours of air conditioning. Hot water wasn't in the cards, but some cold running water might be available if the well pump had filled the small water tower sufficiently. That would be a treat.

It took them over an hour to navigate the steep, rough roads leading up to TJ's father's dream—a hill from which he had worked to extract gold for years, according to TJ. After a few days of effort to repair the washed-out paths, it would be tough, but not impossible, for the massive overland container trucks that worked this part of the country to make it up the hill, working around the sharp switchbacks.

At the top of what seemed a never-ending rocky slope, just when Charles was sure they'd lose traction and plunge over the edge, they saw a vista that belonged on a postcard from Paradise. So this too was Gondwana.

They looked over the ocean below. Colossal Atlantic swells crashed into beaches interspersed with rock outcroppings that had kept the sands in place for millennia. Bursting plumes of shimmering white foam shot toward the sky with each wave. The surf's thunderous roar circulated around in the wind; the sounds climbed the hillside like the rumble of a thousand Harley-Davidsons in the distance.

On top of the hill he found another glorious site: two pools of water, each many acres, perfectly clear, algae-free, and entirely undisturbed for who knows how long. If there was sediment in the collected rainwater, it had long since settled to the bottom. The pools lay separated by a rocky divide.

"My father dug these pits many years ago, Charles. They are not particularly deep. Maybe only one hundred feet. He mined gold, Charles. There is gold down there."

"If you say so, TJ." Charles had had his fill of looking for gold in Gondwana. "But they're beautiful pools."

"You want to buy all of this?"

The locals in Africa put little value on the aesthetics of beachfront, only its economic value, which was minimal in a country too poor to allow people to lie on the beach all day. Fifty years before, it had been possible to buy beachfront in Latin America for a song. And fifty years before that, beachfront in California. Someday this beachfront hilltop land could be very valuable. Charles's pharmaceutical enterprise also might increase demand for the rest of TJ's extensive beachfront land. He filed the thought away for future reference.

"We'll talk. But we won't be pricing any purchase based on the historic output of any gold. If I buy it, it's going to be for the buildings and the land. I'm not going to have much time for the beach."

"There is more gold here, Charles. My father was sure of it."

"When was the last time this was operating, pulling out ore?"

"When I was a child."

"He stopped then? Why?"

TJ shrugged.

"It wasn't economic to mine anymore, was it?" Charles asked.

TJ shrugged again.

"TJ, it's not like we have time for core sampling. And for now, there's far more money in Naked Emperor than in gold mining. Frankly, gold mining isn't like … having a gold mine."

TJ said, "Well, for you, I will sell it without counting all the gold that is in the mountain."

Charles let it go for the moment. The buildings had been solidly constructed of concrete, and, although gutted, the walls and floors had survived the years. With effort, they could be resuscitated. Their presence, even as solid skeletons, was worth a fair amount to him right now.

"Is there another road up here? Something that's easier?"

"There was a steep narrow-gauge cog rail line, but I told you it got torn up during the wars."

"Yes, you did tell me. How long to repair the buildings?"

"I can have the buildings all repaired in two weeks, if you have the money. And we'll need a generator and a well pump. We can drop the well pump down into the mine. That water is perfect. Pure rainwater. No arsenic. No cyanide." TJ said it as a fact.

"Are you sure?"

"No," TJ replied in the same tone.

"We'll have to test it. Let's make sure that water is as good as it looks."

Charles gazed out over the view from what just might soon be the most beautifully located pharmaceutical company on the planet. "TJ, I have the money. Let's get cranking on setting up the first international manufacturing facility of Visioryme."

"I will work as fast as the rains will let us, Charles, because we have small-small time my friend. Small-small time."

30

Enemies of America

FOWLER studied the room. Thirty people weren't enough, but their numbers would soon double. And then double again.

"There will be two task forces. Obviously, priority will be given to Sybillene eradication. I will be personally heading the Sybillene Eradication Task Force, which we can call the 'SETF.' Donald Debocher from FDA still will be heading the Viagra Initiative, but will report to me. Customs, U.S. marshals, FBI, the NSA, various state police, and industry are all cooperating on this effort. I will be reporting directly to the president on matters relating to Sybillene."

The crowd murmured, in recognition of what a high-profile operation this would be. Sabina Heidel raised her hand. The overwhelmingly male audience turned in her direction.

Introducing her, Fowler said, "The president has given Ms. Heidel a special appointment to SETF and will serve directly under me." He intended the innuendo. It would strengthen his position as the alpha male in the minds of the officers in the room. "Yes, Ms. Heidel?"

"Thank you, Mr. Fowler. How many agents are available, and how fast will we get them?"

"Obviously this is a major priority of the administration. The president wants this to be a joint federal-state effort as well. The number of available DEA agents is limited. So we will recruit the majority of our team from the various state police agencies. I have the authority to hire as many as we need."

"Why state police?"

"The mentality of the state troopers is well suited for this work."

"How do you mean?"

"I started as a state trooper. They have to have thick skins. Naked Emperor abusers will resist having their drug confiscated. Junkies will use any tactics they can—lies, insults, threats, righteous anger, whatever. Quite possibly violence."

Heads nodded sagely in agreement.

"We know state cops are used to it, and can take that sort of thing. Further, many of them are ex-military, and know the importance of following orders. I don't know how large this operation will grow—it depends on how much of a battle we have to fight—but I can tell you that I have been given a very broad mandate."

The murmurs increased substantially. A new government program being flooded with money almost guaranteed rapid promotions for those involved, with corresponding increases in pay and power. The people in the room had just received an enormous career boost, and they knew it. With that one phrase—*a very broad mandate*—they became enthusiastic converts to the task of eradicating Naked Emperor and making examples of its users.

Fowler held his hands up to quiet the chatter. He spoke with a deep voice. "Sybillene is not your typical illegal drug. To be candid, we know it's been impossible to remove illicit drugs from the market. Those who use them are like an infestation of cockroaches, probably impossible to eradicate but still worth the effort to keep them down to a certain level."

This crowd wouldn't want to hear that there hadn't been a "drug problem" back when everything was legal and anyone could buy cocaine or heroin at the corner store. When such drugs were legal, there was no economic incentive for salesmen to convince people to take them. In fact, those who indulged didn't have the cachet of being hip outlaws. Rather they were looked down on as suffering from a moral failure. Back then, there were few junkies, and no drug cartels. Fowler wished he'd been around when alcohol, the most popular drug, was illegalized in 1920 with the Eighteenth Amendment. Maybe Sybillene prohibition would be *his* chance.

Fowler continued. "With Sybillene, however, it's not just a matter of control. This is total war, and our mandate is to *eliminate* it, entirely and without a trace. This isn't just a matter of public health, but national security. And we're going to break new ground.

"You've each been given a set of documents covering what we know about the drug's manufacture. However, we know almost nothing as yet about its distribution. It seems that what's on the street is all residual from the final manufacturing runs by Visioryme before FDA raided the company. But as that supply winds down, street prices are rising. That will draw in new suppliers."

"I thought the stuff was really hard to make," said a blue-uniformed trooper. "Yes. It isn't like meth. Small labs aren't going to pop up here and there. Although," he lied, "it shares other qualities with meth." Which it did not. But lies would support the greater good. Or at least motivate some of the schlubs who would believe whatever they were told.

"How dangerous is it?"

"The administration has estimated that Naked Emperor could cause more morbidity and economic destruction than all the other controlled substances combined."

A state police officer in brown asked the next question. "What dangers do Naked Emperor perps present to us? Do they get violent on the drug, or coming off the drug?"

"Violence seems to be on the rise." There was actually some truth to that statement, although any violence resulted from armed local police teams violently accosting peaceful Sybillene users, violently throwing them to the ground, and violently interrogating them. No violence had ever been reported in association with the simple use of Naked Emperor, but that was irrelevant.

Perhaps it started with the movie *Reefer Madness*. It took generations to debunk the meme that marijuana caused violence. But the falsehood supercharged the state's war on the plant.

"Use extreme caution when dealing with potential Naked Emperor users. In my experience, they're devious and manipulative. They can seem rational, and be very convincing. We can expect violence at the street level as prices continue to rise and the profit potential to the dealers increases, as is the case for all drugs. We have been given broad-reaching powers in this battle. Make no mistake. This is going to be a war, and we're going to win it. At any cost."

*   *   *

"Make no mistake," the president of the United States stated with authority as he read the material flowing across his teleprompters. "Let me be clear, this drug, Sybillene, which is called by many names including Naked Emperor, but now perhaps best known as Evil Eye, is no garden-variety street drug."

Cooligan liked the name *Evil Eye*. He had come up with the name himself, just yesterday. He smiled, but only to himself, and continued reading, knowing millions of people watched and listened. "The danger of this drug to the user is marked. Profound brain damage is increasingly common. We receive daily, and often hourly, reports of overdoses and deaths resulting directly from the use of this evil drug.

"Thankfully, due to the foresight of the Founding Fathers," the president added, "nothing prevents us from stepping in to protect our people by banning Sybillene and its evil cousin, Naked Emperor, or Evil Eye. Know that we are taking action to protect you. The danger is real, more needs to be done, and I promise you that we can and we will do more. My administration is determined to perform our constitutional duties. We will prosecute these criminals to the fullest extent of the law in removing this scourge from the streets of America.

"When faced with a threat, America will not be idle! To this end, I have created a joint task force, consisting of top federal and state law enforcement officers, including the Drug Enforcement Agency, the FDA, the NSA, Homeland Security, our military, Customs, and various state agencies, all focused on protecting you, the American citizen, from this sudden and treacherous attack on our health, security, and liberty. Do not underestimate our resolve. We *will* achieve a rapid and swift victory in the war on Evil Eye.

"Previously in the War on Drugs, our law enforcement officers have been hampered in their abilities to defend Americans, and in particular the children, against criminals. Change doesn't happen overnight. But we will not repeat the errors of the past. We will move forward by ensuring that our most trusted agencies possess powers they need to protect our citizens from Evil Eye. Already, evidence has emerged associating this drug with known terrorist organizations. Even with our new commitment, there will be setbacks, and mistakes will be made. But let me be clear. We will win this war."

He felt pleased with his words so far. They were words that had been proven over decades to push all the right emotional buttons. Because they were the *president's* words, they would become truth for all intents and purposes. In fact, as he said them, the words became truth to him.

He continued, "But you, the American people, need to fight this war with us. This is not a partisan issue. We are all united with a single purpose, to eliminate this threat before it spreads. We cannot do it without your help. I hereby ask all Americans to do all in their power to fight this war against Naked Emperor, against Evil Eye. You will be asked to do things outside your comfort zone, but for the good of all the people of this great nation.

"This program will use one of America's greatest strengths, which is caring for our neighbors. I ask you to use our hotline, 1-800-EVIL-EYE, to report anything suspicious in your neighborhood. The agents of the Sybillene Eradication Task Force will respond rapidly and conscientiously to intervene on behalf of your community."

The president looked around the room now, for the first time pulling his eyes away from his teleprompter. Expressions of awe and appreciation failed to appear on the faces of the assembled media. There was something wrong, something unexpected.

His acute political instincts took over. Best to leave the questions to the experts. The teleprompter had no further words for him. "Um. Uh. Well, now I will leave you in the capable hands of, um, Special Agent Seth Fowler, of the, um, SETF. The Sybillene Elimination, um, Eradication Task Force."

The president made his most-serious committed face, nodded his head, left the podium, and retreated off the stage before Fowler could make his way up to try to shake his hand. His words had been right, but the response of the press came wide of the mark. He would avoid having any photographs of Fowler and him together, just in case things didn't play out with the new man.

Before he stepped around the corner and out of earshot, he heard Fowler saying, "As the president stated just now, our purpose is noble. We will always walk the path of honor and truth, knowing that we hold the moral high ground in this war against Sybillene."

* * *

"Asshole, wake up!" Fowler shouted as he walked into the interrogation room not forty-five minutes after leaving the podium in the White House press room.

The young man slumped in the cold metal chair heard the angry voice. Pretending to be asleep, he daydreamed of home, of his mother holding his hand, reassuring him, wiping the blood away, giving him Tylenol for the pain. He tried to dream of good things. But his anger and a desire for vengeance—or was it justice?—blocked his reveries.

He had been sitting in that chair for six hours now. His shoulders burned, but his arms had gone numb long before, strapped as they were behind the chair, his wrists bound with a plastic tie that cut through his skin. His head sagged down on his chest. But this new, angry voice would not let him rest. He moved his tongue out of the side of his mouth, probing a new gash in his lip caused by a heavy paperbound book smashing against his face.

Someone, probably the owner of the new angry voice, grabbed his hair and jerked his head back. Too far back. He felt like his neck would snap. Blood dripped down the back of his nose. He coughed out some of the blood.

"Shit!" the voice cried as the hand let go of his hair. "Somebody got a fuckin' towel? Never mind, I gotta go clean this bastard's blood off me before he gives me AIDS."

The voice departed. He strained to pull his head forward, and allowed it to fall back onto his chest. Was it seconds or minutes, or maybe an hour? It didn't matter. The angry voice came back again far too soon.

"You do that to me again, Hazlitt, and I will stuff a towel so far down your throat that you'll never cough anything up again."

Hazlitt stifled a cough as he tried to lift his head. He used all the muscles of his face to pry open his battered eyelids. The left eye opened enough to see a blurry and fogged image in front of him, a face sitting above a partly loosened fog-red tie, over a fog-white shirt, and a fog-gray suit. The hard face sat on a thick neck. The eyes were too close together, the forehead too short, swept back like a Neanderthal's. He saw nothing kind in the man.

"Hazlitt. I hear you're not cooperating. I know you're dealing contraband Viagra. We can nail you on that. But we got you with Sybillene too. Naked Emperor. Covfefe. Whatever you choose to call it, it doesn't matter. You can't hide. Do you understand how long you'll be in prison? Possession of Sybillene is major league stuff. You're headed to a federal pen, and it's not going to be one of the country clubs. I'm talking maximum security."

It was a credible threat. Since Nixon's alcoholic wife, Pat, had stumped for the War on Drugs, the number of Americans in prison had skyrocketed. The "Land of the Free," with four percent of the world's population, incarcerated twenty-four percent of the world's prisoners, half of them for drug offenses. Most of the new pens were variations on the supermax theme. No fresh air. No sunlight. No natural materials. No contact with other prisoners. Russians who had been in both said they preferred the gulags in Siberia, as brutal as they were. The lack of human contact proved worse than the cold.

"For the one inhaler of Sybillene you had on you, I have the authority to hold you for four weeks without you even seeing a lawyer or a judge. Without your family even knowing where you are. Do you understand?"

Hazlitt nodded slightly.

"I own you, Hazlitt."

That was simply not true, and Hazlitt didn't need Naked Emperor to help him realize it. In fact, as he stared at this man through his swollen and bloodied eyes, he realized he probably wouldn't need Naked Emperor to teach him anymore. Naked Emperor had opened his eyes all the way. Now the men who'd been beating him, these members of the Sybillene Eradication Task Force, with their seemingly unlimited police powers, would try their hardest to close his eyes again by beating him to pulp. They'd undoubtedly succeed in a literal sense. But from an intellectual and psychological point of view their efforts would bear no fruit.

"What's your name?" Hazlitt croaked.

"Fowler. I am *head* of the SETF. And I don't take shit from the likes of you."

Hazlitt knew the type. "Fowler." His words came out slurred, his lips and tongue swollen. "I got nothin' for you." Hazlitt coughed. "Send me to prison. But you, Fowler, you have to worry that someday some judge takes a dose of Naked Emperor and lands your sorry ass in the same prison. With me and all my Naked Emperor–using druggie friends. You won't fare well there."

Fowler picked a bloody book off the table in front of him and smashed it down on the top of Hazlitt's skull. It was not nearly as painful there as it was when it crashed into his cheek, or when that other goon had, probably accidentally, almost crushed his windpipe with a blow of the binding against the front of his neck.

Fowler hollered at him through the daze. "Hazlitt. You're not going to prison. You won't live that long."

Whack, another blow, this time on his ear. The pressure of the air in his ear canal peaked in a fraction of a second. Pain coursed through his skull, his cheek, and his teeth as his eardrum ruptured. He swallowed blood, and as he swallowed his ear protested as if it had been pierced with a knife.

"Tell us your supplier, you get to go home in a week. Free and clear." The voice came blurry now, like the image, heard only through his good ear.

But he could still speak. "You get nothing from me, Fowler. You're the enemy."

"Just like what the other guys say," said another voice in the bloody fog of the room.

The angry voice said, "Put this asshole downstairs. Incommunicado. Water only. No food. Nobody talks to him. Nobody. Got it?"

31

Fieldwork

CHARLES pulled a wheeled suitcase—the largest allowed as baggage on U.S. airlines—along the sidewalks of Northwest D.C. But he wasn't on his way to the airport.

He felt rather ridiculous dragging the suitcase around town, looking like an unsophisticated tourist who'd brought the kitchen sink along on his first trip out of town. The good news? Business was booming. The bad news was the difficulty in moving and hiding all the money.

He would let these few smaller dealers finalize the process of washing their deal money through the little capacity left in the bank loans and accounts Charles had set up, but after that, all the local deal money would flow through remote-controlled satchels concealed under metro trains.

The network of Alpha's family and friends had already moved much of their Sybillene supply to feed the multilayered distribution system they'd built up along the Northeast corridor, to Baltimore, Philly, New York, and Boston. Independent distributors spread it from there across the country.

Charles strained to keep the machine supplied. First they had lots of product, but no way to sell it. Now they had a great sales force, but a shortage of product.

It was comforting to have Alpha walking next to him. Two men were not likely to get robbed, especially when one of them looked like Alpha. The suitcase contained thousands of generic Viagra pills, and a few dozen canisters of Naked Emperor. The canisters now retailed for $1,000 each, giving the suitcase substantial value. Each man carried an illegal gun to protect himself. The penalties for the suitcase contents were far greater than those for the concealed weapons. To Charles it was a testimony to how degraded the world had become, that simple tools, substances, and cash were a cause for imprisonment. Or death.

"The best way to carry large amounts of drug is to act like you ain't." Alpha paused a moment. "Paladin, two of our men got busted in the last two days by this Sybillene Eradication Task Force."

"Probably unavoidable." Charles didn't mean to be callous, but it came out that way.

"Can't be completely secure. You don' know, can't *always* know, who's a narc, or a rat."

"I'm amazed there aren't more getting busted, with all the resources and power the government's given that damn task force. Especially here in D.C."

"Oh, they spreading like an epidemic of the crabs in other cities too, Paladin. We'd be in a world of hurt, except that there's this new culture now."

Charles waited for Alpha to continue.

"We sell to the first user, and then he sells to others, who sell to others. It's a big pyramid. That's what we expected. People are getting profits up and down the chain."

"OK. What's new about it?"

"The difference is that people ain't turning on their suppliers if they get snared in a trap. They not helping the police, not helping the DEA, not helping that task force no matter *what* sort of threats they hit with. I never seen this before. Not without major threats to life, limb, and family from the higher lieutenants. And we're not threatening no one, swear to god."

Charles responded, "Strange. Is it loyalty?"

"Loyalty, yeah."

They kept walking.

A block later, Alpha said, "Maybe more than that. It's bigger than that. Kind of … patriotism … to everybody in this game."

Charles nodded. It was before his time, but he'd heard it was like that in the early days of LSD, with Ken Kesey and the Merry Pranksters. Then with people who got into ayahuasca, peyote, and magic mushrooms. People who'd been on trips had a kind of kinship with others who'd also been there.

They approached their destination.

"I'll stay here," Charles said, tucking himself and the suitcase into a lightly used entranceway on a side street only a few blocks from the Executive Office Building, not far from the White House. Alpha reached into the case, pulled out a cardboard box containing five hundred blue pills, and disappeared around the corner.

In ten minutes he returned and said, in a low tone, "Done."

"I assume our man will pick it up?"

"Oh, I suspect he's had his eyes glued to that spot all day... Who else has deposited?"

Charles had gone through the bank statements that morning and knew the answer: "Robert Number Seven."

"Three blocks. Let's walk."

Robert Number Seven was the only name he knew for the dealer whose job it was to pay back a certain specific credit line by depositing cash at a bank teller or an ATM. The faster he paid the credit line down, the more supply he was provided. Charles would let this money-flow system die out. It just couldn't handle the cash volume anymore without garnering attention. This city indeed was Mordor, and the Eye of Sauron was watching.

Constant innovation is the key to any new business. Especially when it's illegal. Following the cash provided the feds the most effective means to climb up the ladder from the street to the supplier. With the bank system Charles set up, there was no way the feds could follow the cash up to the level of the Alpha Team. All the cash from the credit line was extracted before a single deal had been made, before anyone was looking, and then the drug money simply paid the bank back. If the banks could profit off fractional-reserve banking, so could Charles, by leveraging the easy credit it spawned to help him move his profits. Of course the credit lines weren't in Charles's name. Most of the lines he had opened had been paid back now.

"Are we going to do these rounds every week, Charles? This is Rainbow's job. Risky. Below our paygrade."

"I just want a grip on what it's like on the front lines."

"Front lines go to prison, homeboy."

They had two more blocks to walk.

"Hey, Alpha. If your men get too fat from Sybillene, they won't survive the famine if we run out of supply. Keep them caring about the Fiagara and what not, even though the profits aren't as big."

"Don't want to be one-trick ponies."

"Much heat from the police on the Fiagara front?"

"Hardly anything. Local cops don't care. The feds started picking up some of the low-level dealers here and there. But they let 'em go quick. Don't have the prison space to lock up people selling Fiagara and cholesterol pills."

"That's good."

"By the way, Paladin. Do you know what building we just dropped off at? Do you know who's in that building?"

"Not really. Who?"

"It's the SEA's offices. That's the new name they've picked. 'The Sybillene Eradication Administration.' I dropped off five hundred erections to the dealer who sells to their staff."

*   *   *

"I'm telling you, being illegal is great for our business, Tristana. The price of Naked Emperor is through the roof, and their task force is terrorizing any potential competition trying to move fake product. We have to play the hand we're dealt. They dealt us aces when they made it illegal."

Tristana sipped her wine and looked over the glass at Charles's grinning face. He looked younger now than when they first met. It seemed ages ago. A boyish enthusiasm for troublemaking, combined with the satisfaction of beating back the forces of evil on multiple fronts, was good for the psyche. Perhaps life had no meaning other than what you gave it by doing things. Perhaps that's why he took these risks.

"You seem happy, Charles." Certainly a great deal happier than she was herself. She didn't like taking on the establishment. It terrified her.

"This is what I was made to do," he said. "And I don't just mean running a drug operation or two."

She said, "You know they've upgraded the task force. The Sybillene Eradication *Administration*. I'm not kidding. They're putting it on par with the DEA."

"I know. You should be proud. They're certainly ... running for the finish." He smiled, and affected a racetrack-announcer voice. "And they're off.

ATF is out of the gate first, but Defense takes an early lead, followed on the rail by the Bureau of Indian Affairs, OSHA, the EPA, with DEA close on their heels. Mud is flying on the track as they race to see who's the most corrupt and incompetent." Charles closed his eyes.

"And SEA is the come-from-behind horse?"

"And both the horse and the jockey are doping and on steroids. I think I see where they're going with this. Is Donald part of the new agency?"

Just the mention of Donald, as always, made her feel anxious. "From what I hear, only peripherally. He's running his Viagra Initiative."

"How is that going for him?"

Why did Charles have to bring up Donald? "Not well, I hear. They can pick up low-level dealers whenever they feel like it. But since they can't keep them longer than overnight, they don't bother. Judges don't care about these Viagra and blood pressure pill cases. The perps get fined a few dollars. No jail time."

Tristana didn't understand the reasons Charles's grin expanded.

"Donald must be pissed off."

"He's always pissed off."

"Do you know what he plans?"

"No. But I think he's having an affair."

"Oh? I'm sorry. For you, but for his new girlfriend too."

"It's that woman who was working with him at FDA, Sabina Heidel." She told herself she shouldn't care what Donald did. But she did care, and she couldn't help it.

Charles's eyes opened wide, in surprise. "Interesting." Then he seemed lost in thought. After a bit, he said, "I'm sorry, Tristana. Really."

"Why interesting, Charles? Do you think that opens the door for you and me?"

"Actually, I was thinking about Sabina Heidel."

Tristana looked at him in shock. *Sabina Heidel?* "What do you mean?"

"Oh... Not that." He shook his head. "She's superficially attractive, sure. But I've long outgrown any desire for someone like Sabina Heidel. I'm just interested that they're having an affair. You see, Sabina Heidel is sleeping with Seth Fowler too."

She scoffed. "How do you know that?"

"We keep an eye on the alliances our enemies make."

"She gets around, doesn't she? Tramp…" She was glad, though, that the woman was already off with someone else.

"No more a tramp than many of the men out there," Charles replied.

"Are you in town for a while?"

"No. I've got to head back to Africa."

"I wish you could stay." She meant it.

Charles smiled back at her, with eyes that she knew were sincere.

"I'm glad you like me again," he said. "I'm getting used to being hated. But being hated by a decent person—being hated by you? I didn't like that at all."

32

A Most-Flexible Wood

ANDERS sported a black Scandinavian sailor's hat as he puffed on his pipe. Had he been wearing a Norwegian wool sweater, he could have passed for a ship's captain from a magazine ad for aftershave or tobacco. But West Africa wasn't the place for sweaters. He took a puff and exhaled slowly. "Charles, you might need to come up with a different way."

"What's the problem, Anders?"

"This new agency, this SEA, that your government has created…"

"It's not my government, Anders. You know better."

"Yes, yes, I know. Rumor is that this SEA may soon be empowered to seize a whole ship if there is even *one* canister of Sybillene on board. I don't know if it's true."

Charles exhaled. He had only so many tricks up his sleeve. It was one thing when they'd confiscate cash, a car, or even a house. But now even a Panamax ship?

"Any one of our crew might have a canister on them at any time. Ship owners and captains, we're in a bit of a panic."

Charles said, hopefully, "I suspect that's mostly fear, not reality."

"They may have dogs trained to sniff the drug out. We need to be prepared, Charles. Fear is real, even if reality isn't."

Charles frowned, "I'm not sure what that means, but it sounds very philosophical."

Anders laughed.

"It's going to start getting dangerous, Charles."

"I guess the world has always been dangerous, Anders. But I believe Naked Emperor can help make it less dangerous."

They sat on deck chairs on the port bridge wing as the sun approached the horizon during a break in the rains. Almost everything Gondwana imported came through the facility known as *the Freeport*; Anders had to stop here. But soon the recently reopened Djennetown port could become the main export hub, particularly for rubber and iron. And drugs.

Charles squinted. "If there is a real risk of dogs sniffing it out, bamboo might confuse them. Sybillene smells like bamboo."

Anders considered. "Might work, even though a dog's nose is hundreds of times more sensitive than ours. I'm really not too worried. They aren't really searching yet. But if we keep shipping Naked Emperor, we should be more careful than we think is necessary."

"Are you still willing to even take the risk, Anders?"

"My holds leaving this place are nearly empty. You pay well. The purpose is noble. If I didn't want to take risks, I'd get a job in the Copenhagen Department of Motor Vehicles."

"But they could take your ship."

"They can take my ship for *one* canister, which is probably already on board somewhere. One canister or a million canisters. Makes no difference. They'll take the ship for either. We're at the same risk of loss either way. If we have a million canisters, at least we make some money. Anyway, I have plausible deniability, as the lawyers say; nobody goes through their clients' containers."

"Thanks, Anders. But we'll have more than a million to ship. We want to move boatloads."

"But you won't be importing bamboo for Visioryme anymore. So the trick we used for Viagra is dead. How will you conceal the Sybillene?"

"How about bamboo *furniture?*"

Anders considered for a time. "I like that. It's low tech. They can build good furniture here in Gondwana, and some people like bamboo."

"Yes, and one of TJ's many brothers owns a furniture company. He's got lots of inventory. We don't have a lot of time until we need to make a shipment. Will you have space?"

Anders frowned. "Like I said, we have only a few hundred containers for the westbound trip; we'll be mostly empty. It's almost as bad as heading back to China from the U.S. Empty, empty, empty. But this bamboo furniture will take up a lot more TEUs than that tightly stacked bamboo you shipped before. So I make more money on your shipment."

Charles didn't mind that. Right now the shipment's timing mattered more. "We just got the plastic parts from Brazil. We could have them loaded with Sybillene within a week. Soon we'll make everything here."

"I can swing back through Djennetown in about twelve days, if all goes smoothly in Angola and if you're ready to ship."

Charles felt a flood of relief. "I hope to see you then. Hold me that space, OK?"

"Sadly for my company, that will not be difficult, Charles."

*   *   *

Charles disembarked and walked through the port. The brief break in the rain allowed the workers to make some progress offloading. He waved at one of the crane operators, who smiled and vigorously waved back. "Hello, my friend," the crane operator called down, though they had never met. Charles moved on to the expansive port compound's secondary wall, where he'd parked his car. By the time he got there, the rain had started again.

Charles maneuvered the car through the complex stream of trucks, containers, and workers onto the main road leading to the capital, with its even more complex and unpredictable traffic patterns. As usual, a car was stopped in the middle of the road, jacked up to receive a new tire. Traffic swerved around it, barely missing the soaking wet man crouched by the vehicle who seemed oblivious to the danger he was in. One driver distracted at the wrong moment could end his life. Or, perhaps even worse in this country, turn him into a paraplegic.

Charles took his turn weaving around the inadvertently suicidal man and sped on toward the bridge into the capital.

The U.S. embassy complex was uncared for, representing the backwater status of Gondwana. Of course that could change if substantial oil or strategic mineral reserves were discovered. At that point one of the new model embassies would be installed, with a high protective wall, several levels of sub-basements, and embrasures with bomb-proof glass that passed for windows.

For now, however, the U.S. embassy contrasted sharply with the Chinese embassy a few miles away. That magnificent compound had dozens of buildings into which few non-Chinese ever ventured. It wasn't as if the locals were clamoring for visas to travel to the Middle Kingdom.

Charles had little affection for his U.S. travel document. But in a world where government ID was necessary to cross borders, the U.S. passport was better than most, although not as good as those of Germany, Singapore, or even Ireland, as far as visa-free travel was concerned. And if an airliner was ever hijacked, the perpetrators would likely single out Americans for early execution. He had little sympathy for the politics of his countrymen, who regularly voted for the only government in the world that imposed its income tax on them for life, even if they never returned to its soil. A U.S. passport came with serious liabilities.

Still, almost anything, except one issued by an African country, was better than a Chinese passport. The things were actually quite useless until very recent times since their citizens needed a visa to go almost anywhere with it. And consulates were usually loath to issue visas to Chinese. Charles kept a second, and a third, passport to supplement his U.S. booklet.

By the time he reached the embassy, the clouds could no longer hold their heavy load of water. The marines at the gate examined his U.S. passport closely before calling for the embassy's trade and commerce attaché.

"Mr. Knight, I'm Tip Harding. Let's go to my office, where it's cooler. How can I help you?" He carried his umbrella high, trying to cover Charles from the pelting rain.

"I'd like to start an export business in this country, and I wanted to check with you about it." Charles shouted to be heard over the onslaught of water.

"Good move to get us involved early. There are many permissions and approvals to obtain." He shook out the umbrella and placed it to dry in the entranceway.

"Yes. Of course."

Harding steered Charles to a chair, and settled behind his desk.

"What sort of export business are you looking at, Mr. Knight? As you must be aware, little is exported from this country, other than rubber, iron ore, and stories about poverty. And the occasional bush war does cross borders…"

"My thought is to export furniture, plastics, and other consumer goods. To the United States."

"May I ask, have you worked in Gondwana before?"

"Oh, I spent some time here years ago. I know it doesn't make sense, but I've always thought the place had potential."

314

Harding looked at him skeptically. "So you know what you are getting into."

"What do you mean?"

"I mean, you know business in Gondwana isn't easy. There's pervasive fraud and graft. There's no work ethic."

"That's true in most countries, outside of Northern Europe and the Orient."

"But here it's worse. There's no compulsory schooling, so most go uneducated. There are no protections for workers, no health insurance, no fair trade culture, no occupational health and safety protections. Police forces are unfunded, unarmed. You are entering a dismal situation."

With great difficulty, Charles suppressed his grin. What the embassy functionary saw as insurmountable challenges, Charles considered advantages. Beyond the need for regular bribes, the Gondwanan government would stay out of his way here.

Charles's response aligned with his relative youth and optimism. "There are plenty of differences between how things are done in the U.S. and Gondwana, but with the right ideas, decent management, and some capital, this place could be transformed into the most prosperous country in the world."

"Mr. Knight, you're a dreamer. But there's no point in trying to dissuade you. Just don't underestimate the difficulties."

"There will be many, and I appreciate your concern. Bamboo furniture has got my attention right now. It's cheap and ecological. Are there any difficulties, any barriers, you can see in regards to my exporting bamboo furniture to the U.S.?"

The next hour underlined why he generally avoided asking permission from the U.S. government. It would take an enormous effort to set up legal importation of bamboo patio furniture, all so he could import the illegal Viagra and Sybillene hidden within them. There was no way he would have approvals in the ten days before Anders returned with his ship. Approvals would take three months at least. Charles left the embassy frustrated. The functionary was right; he was a dreamer. Another lesson relearned.

He would have to find a way to bypass the bureaucracy. He'd have to cheat.

He swore to himself that from now on he would treat nation-states and their laws with the respect they deserved. Which was very, very little.

33

Import-Export

"SURE, I know a plastics-fabrication guy, Charles. My brother runs the only one in Gondwana."

"Of course he does, TJ. How many brothers do you have?"

"As many as I need."

"How many biologically related brothers do you have?"

"Seven through my father, two through my mother. One through both. Same ma, same pa."

"And the rest?"

"*Masonic* brothers, Charles. It's the way things get done here."

"TJ, that explains much that I never understood."

"You should become a Mason, Charles. It would do you good as a businessman here in Gondwana."

"I'm sure it would. Although I'm typically not much of a joiner."

"It would be good to call you a brother too. Then I could have a brother who owns a pharmaceutical company."

"And a gold mine."

"There's no gold there, Charles." TJ said this with a straight face, but Charles knew him well enough to know that he was laughing inside.

"Yes, there is." Charles pointed back with an exaggerated stare. "Because you said so."

"OK, yes, there is."

Charles sat back. "What's the status of our new facility on the hill?"

TJ said formally, as if giving a presentation to shareholders, "Visioryme's successor, GoldMine Pharmaceuticals Incorporated of Djenne County, Gondwana, is progressing. All the machinery arrived safely. The vats, the boilers, the centrifuges, the stirrers, the columns, the oven, the air filtration. The old buildings are refurbished. We're ready to make new batches. And the two barrels of Sybillene powder that you shipped from the U.S. are here safely too."

"Power?"

"Plenty."

"Fuel?"

"No shortage."

"Water?"

"Look up, my friend. Water is very abundant."

"Is it clean?"

"Clean and pure."

"Bamboo?"

"Unlimited supply right at the base of the mountain. With all the fungus your chemists could want."

"How about the mass spec. Is it working?"

"Dr. McBride and his new man keep it running, but it's not easy, and he will need parts and more supplies at some point."

"Thank you, *Director* Wandeah. You're a miracle worker. Can you start loading canisters of Sybillene soon?"

"We've already started, Charles. Once we got the process going, it's fast."

"We need to get it to the Djennetown port on Friday when Anders stops there."

"Charles, we will have it done. Will you get the next shipment of Fiagara and the rest of the Indian pharmaceuticals on board Anders's ship too?"

"With your help I can. Do you have some extra time?"

"What do you need?"

"I need export documents for containers of your brother's bamboo furniture to go to the U.S."

TJ shook his head. "Don't worry about the export permissions. But you will need import paperwork to the U.S. That's not easy to get, Charles. You have to go to the embassy."

Charles nodded. "I've been there, TJ. They can't move as fast I would like. But I know someone who says he can help with that problem. Won't be legal, though." He thought a minute, and snorted a laugh. "From this point on, I'm not sure anything in my life is going to be legal."

*　　*　　*

Uncle Maurice supplied the counterfeit import documents and called in one of his many chips to arrange for the hacking of the Customs and Border Protection computer to make sure all the documents jibed with the electronic dashes and dots. And by so doing he bought himself ten percent of the calculated profits.

TJ's brother supplied nineteen hundred bamboo desks, dressers, and tables that he hadn't been able to sell because some softheaded NGO had dumped a containership full of donated furniture on Gondwana's economy many months earlier. For added impact, TJ's brother had his factory build special shipping containers partly out of bamboo. If there *were* any dogs yet trained to sniff Sybillene, they would be thrown off at every turn.

When Anders and his crew, directed by the harbor pilot, pulled their ship into Djennetown, the port authority official, the town's residents, and even the Chinese engineers who'd rebuilt the facilities greeted them with cheers. Perhaps it portended good things to come, after many years of bad things.

The containers were loaded in the pounding rain.

The Gondwana port official signed off on the U.S. import documents where Charles needed him to. An intelligent man, he realized precision in the paperwork served no useful purpose. Overlooking numerous laws and ignoring whatever the *real* cargo might be provided him with a fat chunk of extra income.

The partially laden ship prepared to sail with the very first international shipment of Naked Emperor, along with Fiagara and many other medications, tucked into the numerous cavities in the bamboo that formed the structure of nineteen hundred pieces of furniture.

Some of the Visioryme team headed back home on the transatlantic voyage, their teaching job done at the new, clandestine Djenne Visioryme facility. To staff GoldMine Pharmaceuticals, TJ had selected employees from the Djennetown surrounds who at least weren't innumerate or illiterate. He then screened their English since the American team had difficulty understanding the local patois. Although uneducated and unskilled, the trainees

318

were capable and intelligent. They learned the factory work, supervised by three remaining Visioryme staff and a mass spectroscopist from Johns Hopkins brought in by Dr. McBride.

The employees didn't need to know what they produced, what the powder was, or who would be inhaling from the green containers. They had families to feed and their own lives to live.

Stephan, a rootless cosmopolitan at heart, planned to stay indefinitely. He had proven quite adept at working with the Gondwanans, even though they preferred to only work about four hours per day. He masked his sexual preferences. The punishment for homosexuality was severe throughout most of sub-Saharan Africa, such as the death penalty in some countries. In some ways it was a pleasure for him to step back fifty or a hundred years in time on the continent, in other ways not so much.

"That four-hour workday is going to have to change, Stephan," Charles said as they stood on the pier in the shadow of Anders's towering ship.

"Yes. They understand that. But don't see the point of working for more than they need."

"Well, we're not here to change the culture. You might tell them there's a four-hour minimum, but no maximum number of hours. But offer them bonuses for a full day's work. After the first guy buys a motorbike they'll get the idea.

"Now's a good time to focus on the employees; let them sort themselves out, show us who's smart and who's stupid, who's slack and who's sharp. Find a place that fits for anyone with a good work ethic. Fire anyone who needs to be fired. Hire anyone willing to work if they can show you why you should. The idea is to have an *open front door, open back door* policy. Provide loyalty where loyalty is earned. Friendship where friendship is earned. And if anyone crosses us, we stop them with whatever means are needed—legal, illegal, I don't care. Let everyone know that no one messes with us. Tough, but fair. Remember we're running a multibillion-dollar business, we're trying to change the world, and there are a lot of powerful people that want us dead."

Stephan was brought up short. He dispensed with one of his characteristic smarty-pants comebacks. "Agreed."

"The idea is to make sure they understand this is the chance of a lifetime. At the same time, we can't let counterproductive cultural traditions interfere with what we're doing. This place is tribal and rife with superstition. Kind of like the U.S., but much, much more so."

The Italians, the Irish, the Jews, and the WASPs all still had strong fraternal ties in the U.S. Their superstitions centered around rosaries and menorahs rather than voodoo dolls; holy water and matzoh rather than chicken blood.

TJ interjected, "It will take time, but I'll help Stephan. If you take the best people and treat them like adults, they act responsibly."

Charles said, "We're in this for the long haul. The very long haul. Everything we do here can be an investment in the future. And I envision a very bright future for Djennetown."

TJ said, "By the way, Charles, I think you should know. I am running for senator in the next cycle."

"Yeah? Are you getting idealistic, or just craving money and power?"

"Idealistic. I've done some reading."

"My friend, why would you want to jump into that snake pit? Your colleagues will be sociopaths, just like in the U.S. You can do better for yourself, TJ."

TJ shrugged. "My pa was a senator. It's my turn now. Can you bring me something when you come back next from the U.S.?"

"What do you need?"

"A radio station."

Charles shook his head, amused at the degree of outright chutzpah TJ possessed. "Of course. A radio station. Why not?"

"I'll email you the specifics. I need it to run for office. I'm going to start out as TJ the DJ!"

"With that plan, you just might win," Stephan said.

Politics was all about good feelings and name recognition. Political slogans and promises were background noise to the average person, especially in places like this. Only the naïve and the dim truly liked or trusted a politician. On the other hand, you could easily like and trust an entertainer or a soccer hero. A disc jockey would be even better, since he spoke directly to people every day, like a personal friend.

"It will be the only radio station in Djenne. There is no television. I will essentially control the media for the whole county. And I have my pa's name."

The government-owned radio station in the capital served largely as a propaganda organ. Its listeners were interested only in the music that was occasionally interspersed with political blather. The predominantly Nigerian music was rhythmic and melodic. The propaganda? Dry and transparent.

Of course TJ's station would be illegal, but that would only increase its popularity.

A loud blast from the ship's horn filled the port. Charles shook hands with TJ and Stephan. "Goodbye, my friends!"

"The next shipment will be ready in a month," Stephan said.

"Another ship will be here." Charles turned and ran up the gangway. "Start thinking about how we can smuggle this stuff throughout the world. The bamboo trick may not work for long."

34

Everybody Likes Bamboo Desks, Don't They?

"YOU opened a what?" Maurice asked, incredulous.

Charles replied, "A wholesale furniture outlet."

"Called what?"

"Renewable Green Furniture."

"Why?"

"Because, as you know, I'm importing a shipload of bamboo furniture. It arrives in Baltimore in a week or so. I'm calling you from the ship. We're leaving Gondwana right now."

"Why not just burn it?"

"Why do that? Gratuitous destruction runs counter to my middle class values. Do you still have contacts at Columbia Business School?"

"I suppose. I know a prof there who was actually even *in* business."

"Can you find a bright-eyed graduating MBA and get him to cook up a business plan?"

"Here's some free business advice. You're better off with a woman, Charles. They don't party as much as men, and tend to be more detail oriented. Just don't say that in public, or you'll have a litigant, not an employee."

"Yeah, the men would sue me. I'd have an AI robot do it, if I could. Anyway, I can send the inventory and the costs, and she can put together a plan that shouldn't lose money, might even make some."

"If there's a market for bamboo furniture…"

"There might be. If there isn't, I have a backup plan."

"What's that?"

"Burn it. But we've got to be able to sell it in the States at *some* price. Remember, to me it's just packaging material, so any income from it is just icing on the cake."

"I'll see what I can do. By the way, before you hang up, you should know something. Naked Emperor is making even more waves."

"Just what we need. What's new?"

"Weird stuff. Reporters quitting their jobs. Doctors walking out of their practices. There are stories every day in the papers now. Lots of it in D.C."

"Sounds good. If everybody in D.C. quits, the U.S. GDP will probably double."

Maurice said, "Yeah, but it's getting spun pretty darkly by the media. They're labeling them 'quitters,' and they're automatically suspect as Naked Emperor users. Not good. But there is one small positive. There's a new award named after you."

"What's that, Maurice? I couldn't hear you."

Maurice raised his voice. "An *award* named after you. The Charles Knight Prize for Naked Honesty. Maybe it's just a joke. But it goes to the person who posts the most-honest commentary on their YouTube channel. It's getting millions of views and prompting a lot of honest discourse. They're competing to be the most honest. That's due to you, kid. You're the hero of this Naked Emperor movement, you know."

"Thanks, but no thanks."

"At least it's a favorable moniker. It makes you very visible, Charles."

"I don't like that part either."

The government had long made it easy for journalists, writers, and TV and movie producers to apotheosize heroic cops fighting evil drug lords. And they harassed writers presenting the other side, making them out as opportunists, miscreants, or at best hippie freaks. When it came to TV series and movies, the scriptwriters might throw in the occasional bent cop to maintain some connection with reality. But there was hardly ever a good-hearted, honorable, or decent dealer in illegal plants and chemicals. Charles figured he'd be demonized too.

"Charles, these people are getting aggressive. The mainstream-media spin doctors yap about it, constantly. The Republicans hate Naked Emperor because it's an illegal drug, and it causes people to buck conventional thinking. And they won't have their organized religions questioned. And the Democrats are up in arms because Naked Emperor users see how their policies are destroying the middle class, and cementing the poor to the bottom of society. And they just can't have their *secular* religion questioned. None of them like what's being said about their overseas military ventures. There are soldiers who are using Naked Emperor, trying to get early discharges because they feel like underpaid mercenaries. It's a firestorm."

"We're giving people what they want and need, Maurice. Sales are up. Profits are way up."

"Yes, indeed. You need to know that there is something else that is way up, too, Charles."

"What's that?"

"Imprisonments for Sybillene possession. With or without due process. So you and your friends might soon start to have much more trouble selling your junk, if it hasn't started happening already."

*　　*　　*

The president cranked a wicked hook into the trees on the right side of the fairway, bruising his palm and twisting his elbow as the club head took a hard bounce off the ground. He hoped the swing wasn't preserved by some paparazzi.

"Sorry, Mr. President. I didn't mean to give you bad news."

"Stafford, I only get one round of golf a week. You'd think I could have some peace." He reached into his pocket for a ball, only to find it empty. "I'm gonna take a President."

"Well, you're allowed," his chief of staff replied.

His caddie handed him a new ball and tee. The president bent over and pushed the tee into some fresh turf, away from the divot he'd created, took a step back, and waggled in preparation for his repeat shot. He waggled for far too long, well aware it irritated his fellow golfers.

But it made the president feel good to make people wait and watch him. When he finally had waggled sufficiently, he drew back the head of the club and struck a clean drive up the left side of the fairway. The ball rolled out to 220 yards and settled in for a good shot into the green.

"Nice ball, sir."

"Thank you, Dick. You're up."

Stafford got under his ball, lofting it far too high. It ended up in a fairway bunker.

"Do I get a Chief of Staff?"

A gray sky threatened rain but not lightning. The fresh-cut grass, soft underfoot, helped Cooligan relax as the two powerful men and three of their Secret Service detachment walked toward the green. The president asked, "What percentage did you say?"

Stafford walked a few more paces before saying, "Six."

"Six? What was it last year?"

"Less than one percent voted libertarian in your last election, although five percent said they would do so in the run-up *to* the election. One percent was enough to tip the scales."

"OK, so maybe it's still only one percent or so?"

"Actually, it's different now. Twenty percent *say* they will. Our pollsters translate that to six percent that *actually* will do so, when push comes to shove."

"Damn, that's insane. Libertarians are just pot-smoking, free-loving, tax-dodging peaceniks. And you say it's coming mostly out of our side?"

"Yes, sir. But there's also a significant decline in the number of people even interested in voting. That's happening in both major parties."

"It could affect the midterms too then, Stafford."

"Of course. With everything closely divided, it'll make the election more unpredictable than usual."

"And you say that this whole change is being attributed to Naked Emperor? I mean Evil Eye?"

"No one is calling it Evil Eye, Mr. President. We made a good effort with that name, but it didn't stick. Some people are calling it Covfefe, or a handful of other names. But it's Naked Emperor to most everyone. Anyhow, yes, the reports indicate that many of these people have used Naked Emperor at least once."

"What's Fowler doing? Sitting on his damn can?"

"I've got him coming in this afternoon so we can give him a motivational talk."

"Good, Dick. Good. What does Vice Chairman Samuels say about this?"

Stafford replied, "Last time we talked he said he was planning lots of those *pushes* he preached to us about, to try to combat what is becoming an anti-Keynesian storm. I get the impression that he's a bit panicked."

"Fuck him. He's dug this damn hole for us all." Unemployment and inflation were rising. The government deficit loomed larger than ever. And the standard of living of the average voter continued to fall.

"True enough. Can't blame him personally. His sort have done damage, even though they helped get you and me where we are in the world. But you're right. It's a deep hole, and we need him to claw our way out of it. We have to keep him on our side."

The president had a fleeting awareness that, perhaps, things were getting out of control. But this momentary perception soon vanished, as did most other useful thoughts that he'd stumbled across during his tenure.

"Dick, I'm afraid we can't get out of the hole *with* him either."

The men stopped by Stafford's ball. "That may well be true. The ship of state may be taking on some water, Mr. President, but we've got some plans to fire up an extra bilge pump."

35

Who's in Charge Here?

FOWLER waited in the anteroom outside the Oval Office. Sabina sat next to him, as she had so frequently of late, perfectly coiffed and perfumed. His wife's suspicions were heightened by the expensive fragrance on his suit jacket. He would have to be more careful, but only because he did not have the energy to deal with her. It would be more tolerable if Kate skipped the whining and crying and got straight to the inevitable silent treatment.

Fowler was smart enough and ambitious enough that he spent much of his spare time learning what might prove useful. Like many upward-mobile D.C. bureaucrats, he zeroed in on how J. Edgar Hoover had single-handedly—with the clever use of media coverage and secret files on potential opponents—built the FBI from nothing to the most powerful government agency by the time of his death in 1972. Starting with Roosevelt, no president dared not reappoint him for fear that all of their misdeeds and indiscretions, uncovered and catalogued by agents who had carte blanche to look into everything, would be revealed. Starting a new agency, especially one with the powers of the SEA, invigorated Fowler. This was his life's turning point, his potential now much greater than he had ever previously imagined.

The president made them wait two hours after their appointed time. Maybe that was normal. The president's secretary never apologized. It was the *president* after all, and one must consider his time as more valuable than everyone else's put together.

He recalled the story about Clinton's Air Force One holding the traffic at LAX for a half hour, with the lame excuse that he was getting a $200 haircut. The press launched into an uproar about *Hairgate*. Seth had it on good authority that the haircut only provided cover. Word had it that the prez was being serviced by a famous actress. Whether for presidential hair-cuts or presidential blowjobs, there was always an important reason for the delays.

"I suppose we should consider ourselves lucky to meet with him at all," Sabina offered.

Fowler felt superior in that he had met the president several times already. "He's just a dirtball like the rest of them, Sabina. Don't be too impressed."

"Seth, I don't impress easily."

"You seemed impressed last night," he whispered.

"I said I don't impress *easily*."

The president's secretary caught enough of the tone of the conversation to be annoyed. At least she looked annoyed as she stood up and waved them to the door, on which she rapped twice before pushing it inward.

She spoke formally, as if presenting to the queen at court. "Mr. Fowler and Ms. Heidel, sir."

The president and his chief of staff sat on the couches. Dick Stafford beckoned them over. Neither man rose from his seat.

"It's good to see you again, Sabina. Seth."

It caught Fowler off guard. *Again?* Had Sabina met the president before? She'd said nothing about that. Fowler would get to the root of that, later.

Sabina and Fowler stood for an awkward moment until the president indicated two armchairs that closed a loop with the couches. As they sat, Stafford said, "So, Seth, how are things proceeding at the new agency?"

Seth shuffled a bit. He was pleased with his new Senior Executive Ser-vice rating. He was above even GS-15 now, and the salary and perks that went with it were substantial. However, he couldn't *honestly* say he was pleased with how things were going at his new agency. But this wasn't the best time for honesty. "The Sybillene Eradication Administration has started off well, sir. We're organized, and making progress."

"Progress... How do you measure progress?"

"Sir, we've identified and detained dozens of dealers in six cities. The street price of Sybillene has gone up twentyfold. *Twenty*fold. That's prog-ress. *We* are responsible for that."

Stafford said, "Or the law that banned Sybillene production is responsible. Who can say? But you're saying the supply is down, and that's why the price is up?"

"Yes, sir. We have been effective at keeping supplies at very low levels."

"What about Visioryme. Could they still be manufacturing it?"

Fowler replied, "They don't have any other facilities and wouldn't dare if they did. There's nothing out there but residual drug, from before the law went into effect."

The president said, "Good. That's something. It should burn out naturally, then. Problem's going to go away."

Stafford said, "I don't think so, sir. The price is up, true. But so is the volume."

The president asked, "Have you found who is dealing it?"

"Not yet," Fowler replied. "It's very hard to move up the ladder. They've got the parts pretty isolated. We haven't made it up to any central nexus yet. There may not be any central kingpin at this point. The drug was shipped all over the country in the months that Visioryme was legally selling it."

"So you aren't looking?"

"Sir, we have dozens of men undercover trying to obtain positions in the sales networks in various cities. The only way they can get up the ladder is by climbing it organically. We had one agent placed successfully in the network trying to track the supply. He was told where to pick up the drugs. He went, and the drugs were there, waiting for him. But they never supplied him with more. Naked Emperor junkies seem to catch on fast. We never see the suppliers; we haven't made the higher connections. And how they move the money remains a mystery, although we're closing in on it. But, negatives aside, what we're doing has had an impact, judging by street price."

Sabina coughed. It was a good reason for everyone to look at her.

The president said, "You have something to add, Miss Heidel?"

Fowler didn't like the tone the president used. He was flirting.

"Yes, sir. There is, of course, another explanation why the price is so high."

Fowler didn't like the tone Sabina used either. She was flirting back.

"And what might that be?"

Sabina said, "Demand, sir. Demand is way up. Everybody and their Sunday school teacher wants to get hold of Naked Emperor, despite the high price."

Stafford nodded. "I suspected as much. And that high price is going to pull in drug to fill that need."

"Yes, it will." The president agreed, letting them know that he too had a grasp of economic principles. "So … what are you going to do about that, Seth? It seems like your success is partial, at best. Suppliers will come."

Seth did not reply fast enough.

"We can get radical, sir," Sabina suggested, as she grabbed the ladder in anticipation of a giant step up.

"What do you mean by *radical?*"

"How badly do you want this off the streets?"

The president replied instantly. "Very badly."

Sabina eyed President Cooligan. "Just what are you willing to do?" she asked.

Stafford cut that conversation short. "Seth. Sabina. I am sorry that we don't have time for more discussion right now. The president has a commitment. Let me walk you out."

Their three minutes were up, and Sabina and Fowler nodded politely to the secretary as they walked past.

As he stepped out of the Oval Office, Stafford said, "I'll be back in five minutes, Mr. President." Then quietly to his secretary, "Ms. Hampton. Can you please get the president his afternoon snack. He was getting hungry."

Stafford channeled Fowler and Sabina down the hall to his office in the other corner of the West Wing. Once inside, he closed the door.

"Sabina, I'm familiar with you, your credentials, your connections, and your resources. I've got no doubt that you're capable of anything we may ask."

Fowler felt himself being ambushed. Who the hell was this woman, that the president and Stafford knew her at all? Apparently she wasn't just another hack from the president's Efficiency Enhancement Initiative.

"Seth, you're the best person for this job. With Sabina's help, I think you can pull off precisely what needs to be done."

"And what's that, sir?" Fowler prompted.

"We need to change the rules of play. We need to use their tools against them."

"Just what do you mean, Mr. Stafford?" It was Sabina's turn to prompt.

"As I suspected you were about to explain to the president, we need to seriously ramp up the operation. Sabina, you may need to do some things that we can't."

"And what's that, sir?"

"Take executive action. That's for you two to figure out. And from what I think you were about to say to the president, you've already figured it out."

Sabina nodded. "I understand, Mr. Stafford."

"Do whatever it takes to get Naked Emperor off the streets. When the normal methods don't work, you need to think outside the box. So think outside the box."

"Sir, are you giving SEA new authorities?" Fowler asked.

"This is a matter of national security. We're asking Congress to expand SEA's authority to hold the accused longer without trial, tap phone lines without warrant, presume guilt, and use deadly force when contending with people under the influence of Naked Emperor. Starting today, we're positioning Naked Emperor users in the media as domestic terrorists. This office can't—formally—give you more authority. But, Seth, you'll have it from Congress shortly. So I don't think anyone will fault you for leveraging that power in the meantime. As well as making your new powers obvious to the man on the street."

Fowler replied, "Sir, I think we're on the same page."

"And look, Seth. As Sabina said, there's a demand side to this equation. We have the media on a rampage against Naked Emperor. Fox, MSNBC. Left and right: Rush, Maddow, everybody. Only the late-night comedy shows aren't on side. Maybe they're high on the stuff. Those bastards are *promoting* it."

"You could ... correct them, sir."

"That's still beyond the authority of the executive. And if the White House did try to muzzle them, they might have the balls to throw it right back in our teeth. They talk for a living, so they tend to take the First Amendment seriously. But I think that you two might just find a way to bring them around. The key is to decrease the demand side, right? Take the shine off Naked Emperor. So see what you can come up with. Get out there and be heroes. Now, I need to get back to the president. Thank you both. This conversation, of course, never happened."

"Yes, sir."

* * *

"How far do we go?" Fowler asked Sabina as they climbed into the staff car that would convey them from the White House back to SEA's new offices, only seven blocks away. In his eyes, her stock had shot upward today. How could it not, after the president and his chief of staff had endorsed her so?

She slid up the partition to exclude the driver from the conversation. "I think Stafford wants us to go as far as we need to."

"What did he mean about your resources, Sabina?"

"It's not important that you know."

The answer angered him. He didn't want to feel small.

Sabina asked, "How many unfilled Sybillene canisters were delivered after the Visioryme fire?"

"About five hundred thousand."

"Have you destroyed them yet?"

"Not yet. I know we have to. But they've got to go to some kind of environmental facility. We can't just set them on fire in the street. I'll get somebody on it…"

"Don't. I think there are some inventive things we can do with those empty canisters."

"Such as?"

"Think back to your time as a state trooper, Seth. Are the people most likely to use Naked Emperor good people or bad people?"

"That's obvious. They're whining, unpatriotic malcontents."

"Should those people even be allowed to vote?"

"God no."

"Would the world be better off without them?"

"God yes."

His anger faded. She was beautiful. And crazily dangerous. It excited him.

"And what about your connections, Sabina? Stafford mentioned connections."

"Yes, we haven't tapped those either."

"Who are you talking about?"

"In this town, Seth, we like to operate on a 'need to know' basis. It's better for everybody. I'll tell you when I need to tell you, or when you need to know."

His anger flooded back. "Sabina, I need to know now, and you need to fucking tell me anything I ask for!" Fowler's eyes went dark, and his jaw clenched.

Sabina waved a hand through the air. "Oh, stuff it, Fowler. Try to control me and I'll bloody your face all over this car."

Fowler leaned toward her, reflexively raising his hand to punish her for the impertinence. But he thought twice, and held himself back. She seemed to not have noticed.

After a few minutes of waiting in the D.C. traffic, Fowler said, "Who do you think you are? I'll have the authority to sink ships, shoot down airplanes, and imprison people without trial. What tools do *you* have? What do you bring to the party, Sabina—apart from a good piece of ass?"

She looked at him with a flat expression. "I bring a two-pronged plan and the resources to carry it out. First, we have to kill a lot of people. Second, a lot of those people have to be innocent. But don't worry; they'll die in a good cause."

To help Fowler make this ethical transition, which for him didn't require a long psychological journey, she asked the driver to change their destination to the Willard Intercontinental. There, in a room on the sixth floor, Sabina let him have her, unrestricted and uninhibited, for the entire afternoon.

From then on, there was no longer any question who was in control.

36

Executive Action

"PALADIN. We got trouble." Alpha's voice came through the satellite telephone intermittently. Charles was in the middle of the Atlantic, heading northwest.

"What's up, Alpha? Remember, these phones have ears."

"Right. Two men down in public."

"Damn. Who?" Charles would need to be very cautious on this call. "Never mind. Don't use names."

"No one you know."

"Fat Man?"

"Maybe his men. I don't know."

Still five days out from the Port of Baltimore, they were making good time, but there was no way to speed up the voyage. The news made Charles feel sick with the same anger he had felt at the Philharmonic Hall. He spoke slowly through clamped teeth. "What do you want to do?"

"I'll find out what I can."

Charles said slowly, "I'll see what I can dig up from my end. Call as soon as you know something."

Charles retreated to his cabin and composed an email to Maurice and sent it through the satellite upload. He encrypted it with an elegant program based on the premise that the best encryption didn't even look like encryption. Or even look like a message. Given enough time, the government's supercomputers in Tennessee and Nevada could crack the most strongly encrypted emails. But only if they knew which of the billions sent every day they should look at. They had no way to figure out which of the millions of photographs sent daily might have a message hidden in its megapixels.

Maurice responded only a few hours later. His odd sleep and living habits offered few advantages. But one of them was that he never slept for long. Maurice's message came through as a picture of a polo pony. The decryption program turned the pony into a photograph of words that Maurice had handwritten on paper. It said, "No idea if Juan Marcos involved, but he has been traveling extensively and is flying into D.C. tonight. Possibly three more of your men killed. One witness claims a female killer. Wore mask. Disappeared into building. Local police investigating. No federal agency looking into it. That's all I've got."

Charles smashed his fist down on the small desk in his cabin.

*   *   *

Fowler and Sabina walked into the room together. The young man sat in the chair, wrists bound behind him, ankles strapped to the chair legs.

He said, "You assholes have had me for a month. I'm sick of being in this room. Your four weeks are up. You've got to let me see a judge."

Sabina glanced at Fowler for a moment. He shrugged almost imperceptibly.

"That's not going to happen, Hazlitt."

Hazlitt shrank a little in his chair. "I ain't saying nothing to you guys. I'm not saying anything except to a judge."

Sabina came up to him, directly in his face, and said, almost in a whisper, "You won't be seeing any judge. We're not going to beat you up. We're just going to kill you."

She held up, one at a time, pictures of dead men, each shot in the head, blood pooled and visible in close-up color pictures. "Do you recognize these people?"

It was clear he did. They were all from his area, working most likely for the same lieutenant.

She whispered again, "I killed these men. I'll take a picture of you too."

Hazlitt looked at Sabina. His eyes transitioned from a cocky certainty to fear. Sabina nodded. "That's right, Hazlitt. That's right. You understand now."

"You can't do that. I don't believe you."

"I don't care if you believe me. There are hundreds of you scum on the street now. And a bunch right here, locked up in this building. If you don't tell me what I need to know, I'll be taking a picture of you just before I start talking to another one of your colleagues. I've got plenty of battery in my camera and no conflicting plans. I can do this all week."

"Fuck you."

Sabina nodded. Fowler cut Hazlitt's ankles free, pulled him up out of the chair and shoved him toward the door. Fowler reached around him and pulled the door open, smashing it into the younger man.

"Sorry, my friend. Won't happen again." Fowler closed the door and then swung it open rapidly, again smashing it into Hazlitt, harder this time. "Oops." Fowler missed his hands-on days with the state police. It was good to get out in the field. And there were some things that couldn't be trusted to subordinates.

The SEA shared the basement of this building in downtown D.C. with Debocher's barely perceptible Viagra Initiative task force. Locked rooms lined the corridor, small square windows in their metal doors. Though recently refurbished, it felt dank and already smelled musty.

Debocher had initially set up all the rooms with videotaping capability. But Fowler disabled the cameras in several. This was nothing new; it was SOP in most police stations to have an out-of-order camera in at least one interrogation room, just in case a suspect needed to be tuned up. These were usually reserved for the ones who wouldn't be seeing the inside of a courtroom—typically snitches. Now, with the SEA's expanding power, he hardly needed videotaped confessions; he didn't need to be prepared for court anymore. A strong suspicion sufficed to lock people up for a good long time. At least until the powers that be decided that the clear and present danger of Naked Emperor was under control.

Martial law hadn't been declared, but it might as well have been.

The basement had a locked exit through which the SEA agents could go directly to an underground garage filled with black Cadillac SUVs, the vehicles that Fowler himself had chosen for the new agency. Cadillacs conveyed the proper image. The excess expense would get lost in megatons of congressional pork.

Fowler shoved the man out the door. Hazlitt stumbled and fell on the painted cement floor. With mechanical brutality, Fowler threw him into the backseat of a Cadillac.

They drove with Hazlitt through Georgetown, the oldest and most fashionable part of D.C., which was his primary sales area. They drove across Key Bridge and up the GW Parkway to Fort Marcy Park, little known except as the site where the body of Vince Foster—an intimate of the Clintons and important player in much of their scandal-filled years—had been found one day, supposedly a suicide.

"Here's where they'll find your body in the morning." Fowler climbed out of the car, opened the back door and pulled Hazlitt out. "You have ten seconds to hook me up with your source, after which you'll find a bullet in your head."

"You can't do this! I have rights."

"Not anymore. Don't you read the news? You have the right to do what you're told. Who's your contact?" Fowler pulled the hammer back on his weapon as he pulled it out of his holster. He aimed it at Hazlitt's left eye. "Five seconds ... three, two, one. No comment? Well, then goodbye."

Fowler pulled the trigger.

Sabina took a picture with her camera phone before getting back in the car. "Shall we go to the Willard Intercontinental again, Seth?"

"Definitely. But we have to step up the pace. I want to make the connection in the next couple of days. Those bastards at the White House won't be patient much longer."

"We also have to figure out how to follow the money, Seth."

"I know."

As he pulled the car out, he cast a quick look at Hazlitt's body and chuckled. "The park police will probably call it another suicide."

37

Chinks in the Armor

"ALPHA, do you want to close operations for a while?" Charles had come as soon as Customs had cleared the ship, taking the train from Baltimore to D.C. He wanted to see Alpha in person.

"Paladin, look, this is normal fare here in D.C. Dealers get killed. Always have, always will." Alpha lifted his twenty-two-ounce mug of beer and drank, but his spirits, like Charles's, were low.

Charles's mug sat untouched. "Yeah, but they aren't supposed to get killed when they're just selling Fiagara and garden-variety prescription medicines." He shook his head. "Three more days, three more men dead. We cannot allow this! Let's deal with this once and for all. If this *is* Juan Marcos, or somebody else who sees us as competition, then we need to stop him cold."

"You're really hoping to deal with this once and for all? Well, that just ain't happening, Paladin. Not in this business. This is trench warfare. You gotta fight for ground every day, and you lose men every time you make a charge."

"Perhaps we should go for the enemy headquarters, and take out the general, not just captains and colonels."

Alpha bobbed his head. "Now you're talking. This isn't for the weak of heart, homey, and I think you know that. It's not a safe profession. That's why I wanted Rainbow in the suburbs."

Charles nodded. "I hear Juan Marcos came into town the other day. We think he's still here."

"Who's we?"

"A friend of mine. He keeps me informed when he can."

"Part of Marcos's operation?"

"Not at all. My friend is wired with government and corporate databases."

"A hacker?"

"Not really. He's more of a data miner and an information broker."

"Whatever, bro, all the same to me. Told you I ain't into computer shit. Man's got to know his limitations." He thought for a few moments. "Do you want to pay a visit to Marcos?"

"You know where he would be?"

"I expect he'll be at home."

"Where's that?"

"You've been there twice."

"I thought that was Tadeus's place."

Alpha slowly shook his head. "Nope. It turns out Tadeus got kicked out by his wife and was bunking at Marcos's place. He always did business out of there. I didn't know that before. Fat Man played his position sly."

"What do you say we go tonight? We'll have a visit with the Fat Man. Let's bring the whole team again. Do you think they're up for it?"

"He's going to have it more defended, Paladin. A *lot* more defended. That guy isn't going to make the same mistakes."

* * *

Fowler found the prospect of killing scumbags even more enticing than doing Sabina. Beyond a rush. Perhaps it was his calling. The scumbag lying on the ground in front of him would cave, or he wouldn't. A win either way, he supposed. You win a war by killing the enemy.

"Don't shoot me. Please don't fuckin' shoot me!" the girl pleaded, sniveling. Sixteen years old and already a whining little bitch.

Fowler lifted the muzzle of his gun, only slightly. "Tell me then. Who supplies you with Naked Emperor?"

The girl fought with herself, deeply conflicted. He shoved the gun into her mouth then and said, "You've got five seconds … three … two…"

She jerked her head back and cried, "I pick it up where they tell me to pick it up. It changes all the time." Tears flowed down her cheeks.

339

"Shit, kid, is that all you got? You think we don't know that? You think we haven't been following you for weeks? What, you think we're stupid? Who tells you where to pick up the stuff?"

Sabina came over and pulled on his arm. "Give the kid a break. Let me talk to her."

Fowler scowled and answered almost into the kid's ear. "Yeah, you talk to her." He took a few steps back and tried to appear to pay no attention.

But he watched as Sabina sat on the ground next to the crying young girl. She put an arm out around her and spoke quietly. "Look … Roberta, is it? Roberta, that man is unpleasant. But he has a job to do, and one thing I know about him is that he'll do his job. Why don't you tell him what he needs to know? Then you can go home. I promise."

The girl looked at Sabina through wet eyes. Sabina took a tissue and wiped her nose.

"But it's wrong. It's wrong to tell."

"Who says it's wrong?"

"Nobody says. It just is. It's just wrong."

"Don't protect criminals, Roberta. They're using you."

"No, they aren't." She was firm on that point, no doubt about it.

"But they *are* criminals," Sabina tried again.

"No."

"Roberta, he's going to kill you if you don't tell him what he needs to hear. He's *going to kill you*. And if he kills you, that's it. You're done."

"I can't. I can't tell him. I can't."

Sabina sat back and sighed. Fowler wanted to move back in. He'd kill this one, and pick up another later.

But Sabina gave him a withering look, so he stopped.

She said to the girl, "OK. We'll come back later to the issue of where you get the drugs. How about telling him where the money goes? The money you take in. Where does it go? You can do that, can't you?"

The girl was so flustered and so young, all that was needed was just a little chink in her armor and they'd be able to march on through. Fowler watched as Sabina deepened that chink.

"I know you've heard that money is the root of all evil, Roberta. It's true. You aren't breaking your bargain if you tell us where the money goes."

"Stash and cash. Different people. Always are." The girl said it like it was cliché where she came from. A comforting mantra.

"Tell me about the cash, Roberta. Tell me something to stay alive."

Fowler watched more conspicuously now. *Good, Sabina. Follow the money*, he thought. Roberta saw him looking. The kid stared at him, right into his eyes, for almost a full minute. Then her eyes wavered, and she turned them back down to the gravel on which she and Sabina sat.

"Money gets dropped off only if we feel good."

"Explain."

"If we feel scared or anxious, we don't drop it off."

Sabina said, "We've been watching you. We haven't seen you hand off or drop any money."

"You missed it."

"Yeah? How?"

"Maybe you guys suck at what you do. But you missed it. I dropped money yesterday."

"To whom?"

The girl laughed, but it was partly a sob. "Not 'to who.' 'To what.'"

"Roberta, don't mess with me now. Where does the money go?"

She laughed then, a confident laugh. "Money goes to a bank, of course."

"What do you mean by 'bank'?"

"Same thing you mean. A bank. Vaults, you know. A bank."

Sabina looked up at Fowler. He reached into the front seat of the Cadillac to pull out a file, Roberta's file, and flipped through some pages. He said, "First American Bank? You stopped there yesterday."

The girl nodded.

"Did you give someone the money there?"

"I gave it to the teller."

"A particular teller?"

"No."

"What did she do with it?"

"She put it in the account, I guess."

"Whose fucking account, Roberta!" Fowler was tired of this game and cut in, despite another withering look from Sabina.

"I don't know. I just have a number and drop the money off."

Sabina stood up, brushing the gravel off her black satin pants. "Stay there, Roberta. Don't move."

Fowler said to her, "A bank account? Really? A drug dealer stashing his

341

money in a bank account? That makes no sense at all. All we have to do is see who takes the money out, who wires it out, who does anything with it."

"Something's not right about it, Seth."

"Well, let's follow the money and see where it leads. We'll check out the bank."

"Should we let the kid live?"

"Keep her in the basement for now. She's the first one who's turned. She'll keep turning our way."

"Willard Intercontinental, later?" Sabina asked, slyly.

Fowler wouldn't turn down that offer. He still obsessed about her, and kept things that had her scent on them, just so he could breathe her when they were apart. She was all-consuming. Only one thing beat his alone time with her now. And he wasn't going to get to do that. There would be no killing today.

38

El Gordo Spills the *Frijoles*

"IT'S a loan account," one of the former state troopers announced at the conference table at the next morning meeting. "The kid, Roberta? She's been paying off a line of credit."

"A loan? Whose loan?"

"One Dr. James Sandridge. According to the bank, he's a young doctor at Johns Hopkins. He's got a big chunk of research money from NIH, so he has a secure position. The loan was originally a three-hundred-thousand-dollar signature line. Apparently banks give loans to docs just with their signature. Makes me wish I were a doctor. He extended it all initially in a long series of cash withdrawals over a couple of months, about seven or eight months ago. Paying it down ever since. It's mostly all paid back."

"What do we know about this guy?"

"Not much yet."

"Keep this close. Don't let him know we're onto him. But I want a full report on Dr. Sandridge tomorrow morning."

Sabina grabbed Fowler after the meeting. "Seth, Dr. Sandridge won't have a clue."

"I don't know, Sabina. You're thinking identity theft, right?"

"Of course it is."

"Sabina, have you ever heard of an identity thief who paid back what he stole? The loan is mostly paid off."

"Seth, nobody with half a brain would pay back his loan with his own deal income. The guy's a doctor. He's got half a brain."

"Maybe. Maybe not. Lots of doctors are stupid, once you get them out of a medical office. Maybe he had gambling debt, and now has to work part time as a money launderer. We'll know in a couple of days. It's the first solid lead we've got, at least. And hell, it makes sense that doctors would be part of the supply chain, doesn't it?"

Sabina shook her head. "This is something very different, Fowler. I think we're up against something more sinister."

"What do you mean?"

"None of this makes sense, unless…"

"Unless what, Sabina?"

"Unless whoever is running this thing is a boy scout."

Fowler waited, but Sabina did not elaborate.

She shook her head and changed the subject. "We need the culture on our side, Seth. There's a man I want you to meet. He's a critical part of my plan to cut down on demand for Sybillene. You'll need to work with him."

"Who?"

"His name is not important. He's a relative of mine, rather remotely. He has a special personality and special skill set. And he lives here in D.C."

"What's special about his personality?"

Sabina tipped her head, looking into the distance, her eyes cold. "He's a man who has no soul."

Other people hearing of such a person might shiver, fearing evil incarnate. Fowler, however, looked forward to the opportunity. He might be able to learn a few things.

"And what is this man's special skill set?"

"Seth, he will kill anyone, no limitation, no hesitations, no regrets. He requires no justification and has no restrictions. The innocent. Children. Makes no difference. He'll carry out any assignment with no fear. He has only one rule, which is that you have to pay him."

"And this man is a relative of yours?"

"His type isn't easy to find." She looked into the distance and said lazily, "I'm always on the lookout. They aren't who you might think, and appear quite average in most regards. Ordinary criminals tend to commit ordinary crimes. The greatest artists are usually those you'd least suspect."

"What do you do if you find someone like him?"

"Take him under my wing. Mentor him. Train him. Guide him."

"How often have you done that?"

Sabina's laughter was sinister. "I'm mentoring one right now. My current mentee will serve his purpose, but he's not yet able to do what we need."

"And what's that? What do we need?"

The way she answered him, the tone of her voice, her body language, combined to make even a man like Seth Fowler shiver involuntarily. She said, "We need to shoot large groups of children in their schools and have it blamed on Naked Emperor."

"Shit, Sabina," he said. "You don't have a soul yourself, do you?"

"Neither do you, Seth. That's why I've spent so much time mentoring you. Tonight, you'll meet our soulmate—in a manner of speaking. And tomorrow, it's going to start raining hell."

*　　*　　*

They initially planned to go in hot. But before they even climbed into the van to head to Marcos's apartment, Charles changed that plan.

"Remember, gentlemen, we don't know that Marcos is responsible for killing our men. Tadeus killed them before, but we don't know if Marcos is doing it now."

The new plan wasn't perfect, but had they gone in firing, the three bodyguards Juan Marcos now kept with him might have tagged some Alphabet Men. Charles liked his Alphabet Men.

Instead, they smoked them out. They knew the layout of the apartment. Six canister-grenades of FOX F.O.G. pepper spray hurled through the second-floor windows were more than adequate.

The men inside were experienced enough to know that they *should* have trained for this, but hadn't. They had to choose between grabbing a weapon to fire, or being able to see their target. Understandably, they wanted their guns, but they underestimated the effect of the chemical and stayed inside too long. They came out blind.

This time, the Alphabet Men didn't turn off the power in the neighborhood. But they *had* unscrewed the light bulbs in the stairwells and hallways. It was dark outside the apartment door, and the retinas of the guards that came out of Juan Marcos's suite certainly hadn't adjusted to the dim light. Their pupils rapidly dilated to let more light in, but that just caused the mucus coating their eyes to blur everything further.

They tumbled out the apartment door, pushed aggressively by the bulk of the coughing and gasping Juan Marcos. The three guards tried to set up in a defensive perimeter by crouching outside the door, but Marcos fell over them and crashed to the floor.

"Don't fire! No dispare!" Charles yelled so that all could hear. "Nobody fire!"

Yelling that phrase with authority was enough to blunt the excited reflexes of everyone in the hallway. Juan Marcos lay on the floor, his girth crushing one of the guards. In five seconds, Beta and Gamma held their weapons directly in the faces of the guards and Zeta had extracted a gun from the crushed third guard. Within a minute, Juan Marcos and his men were disarmed, sitting on the floor, panting, inhaling fire with each breath.

"Let's everyone get some fresh air..." Charles suggested.

The Alphabet Men guided their captives down the stairs. "Careful. One more step."

Outside, in the dark corner of the small yard in the back of the building, Charles handed each a wet washcloth he extracted from a plastic grocery bag. "Here, put this on your eyes." But it did little to help the flow of mucus from their noses.

Marcos suffered the most, violently coughing and sneezing. The fat gangster lived a sedentary life, and his respiratory system labored even when he sat still, without the added burden of pepper aerosol. Other than the sniffling and the nose blowing, they sat quietly, knowing armed men were out there in the blurriness. If anyone else was in the building, they didn't notice any noises in the backyard.

Still, the Alphabet Men stayed tucked out of sight of nosy neighbors. Charles stayed close to Marcos and his men, keeping them supplied with paper towels to help them mop themselves up. It took ten minutes before they could start talking.

"Juan Marcos. At some point I hope you accept our apologies for our aggressive stance. I thought it the safest for all concerned. And so far, although you're miserable, nobody's been hurt. Let's keep it that way."

Marcos coughed and wiped his nose. He said, "I do not feel safe right now, with your men aiming their weapons at me."

"Yet *I* know you're safe, as long as you stay here quietly," Charles responded.

346

Marcos squeezed his eyes closed and then opened them, slightly more able to see. He nodded then. "What do you want, Mr. Paladin?"

"Eight of my men are dead. Eight. We need to talk."

Through Marcos's discomfort, his surprise was evident. "Is that why you're here?"

"Isn't that obvious?" Charles replied.

"I've seen the reports of dealers getting killed. Bullets in the head, all of them, I hear," Marcos replied. "I didn't know they were your people. I heard they were in the Naked Emperor network. Not selling your Viagra."

"They were our men."

"It was not us, Mr. Paladin. We had nothing to do with their deaths."

Alpha approached Charles as he stood above Marcos, who sat amid a growing mass of paper towels on the grass and dirt of the backyard. Just enough light came through the shaded windows nearby to see facial expressions. Marcos's expression was pained and nervous.

"If not you, Mr. Marcos," Alpha probed, "who?"

Marcos sneezed six times and tried to clear his throat, coughing and spitting. Before he could catch his breath to answer, Zeta came out of the building, wiping his eyes and nose, and pulled Alpha aside. Charles watched as Zeta whispered, and then walked over to hear.

Alpha said, "How much?"

Zeta replied. "Hundreds of boxes. There's a whole room filled with them."

"What did you find?" Charles asked.

"Sybillene. A huge stock of Sybillene."

Charles cocked his head to the side. Zeta handed him a canister. In the darkness, it looked like an authentic Visioryme Sybillene canister. Charles deftly separated the plastic parts and tapped some white powder out of the device and onto the palm of his hand. He touched some of the powder to his tongue and in a moment spit it out on the ground.

"Not Sybillene. This is something very different."

Zeta and Alpha each then tasted the powder. Both shook their heads.

"Bitter. Doesn't have any bamboo smell. Any idea what that is?" Charles asked.

They shook their heads again.

Charles put the canister back together with a quick motion of his hands. He came back over to Marcos. "What is this?"

347

"Naked Emperor. Surely you have seen this before."

"What is the powder? It's not Sybillene."

Marcos shrugged. "Who cares? If people will think it's Naked Emperor, it then *becomes* Naked Emperor to them."

"You sell that junk and pretend it's Naked Emperor?"

"I haven't sold any yet. But I plan to." Marcos shrugged.

"That's just wrong, Juan Marcos."

"What are you, a boy scout? What do you care? You sell Viagra and steal all my dealers off the streets." Marcos coughed again and wiped his eyes. "Unless … unless you're trying to get into the Naked Emperor business now too, Mr. Paladin. Ah, you must be. Am I right?" He coughed once more. "I wouldn't think you would have the cojones for real illicit drug smuggling. I figured all you would sell was hard-ons and wellness. In fact," he coughed again, "you agreed with me; you promised to me that you would stay out of the illicit drug trade. For someone who seems so concerned about integrity, Mr. Paladin, you seem unable to keep your word."

"It would be a fair point, but at the time, Sybillene was legal. And, to be clear, we were fully in this business before it was made illegal."

Marcos leaned back some to better see Charles through his squinted eyes. "There was no Naked Emperor business when it was legal."

"You're mistaken, Mr. Marcos. There was a business. But until they made it illegal it was only marginally profitable."

That was a point Marcos understood perfectly. Drug laws were a drug lord's best friend.

"In any event," Charles continued, "we're going to have to attend to these counterfeit Sybillene canisters."

"I tell you what," Marcos offered. "Why don't you take some of them. Free product to sell. My gift to you."

"We don't sell fake drug."

"You *are* a boy scout."

Charles and Alpha retreated so that they could whisper out of earshot of Marcos and his men. "We'd have to burn the building to get rid of all that stuff," Alpha offered.

"Other people live here. We need another solution."

"Let's get them back upstairs. It's aired out now. We'll figure a way to dispose of the garbage."

Charles paused a minute. "You know, very often the simplest solution is the best one. I've got an idea."

There are numerous waste-management companies in every city, and some of them keep long hours. They found one that sent a giant trash truck around at eight o'clock in the morning. The Alphabet Men quietly walked box after box of counterfeit Naked Emperor down the stairs and threw it all in the maw of the truck's dumpster. The hydraulics activated, and each time the heavy steel compacter closed they heard thousands of canisters fracturing like popcorn popping. A $500 tip satisfied the crew's curiosity.

Alpha pointed his weapon toward Marcos, now sitting on the couch. "What do we do with him and his men? Kill them and leave them here, I suppose."

Charles walked over to Marcos. "You present us with something of a conundrum, Marcos. You haven't broken our previous agreement. But, for all I know, whatever is in those Sybillene inhalers could have hurt people. And it certainly would have hurt the market for our product…"

"Mr. Paladin, I have a solution. I will give you information, and you will let me be. I understand the way you work. I have no desire to step on your toes."

"What information?"

"My source for the Naked Emperor. The counterfeit Naked Emperor of course. I think it will be a very surprising revelation to you."

"Go on."

"Will you let me go?"

Charles considered. "Do I *need* to know your source for fake Naked Emperor? Shouldn't I assume you manufactured it yourself?"

"I did not do so. And, I give you my word, Mr. Paladin, that you *do* need to know where it came from."

Charles had no intention of killing Marcos anyway, so he said, "OK. But you accept exile to Mexico if, after you tell me your information, that's what I decide. And you don't bother my men."

"I have not and will not bother your men. The supplier of this product has me under far more pressure than your men with the guns do now. There may be ways that we can work together to our mutual advantage. You're a competent man, Mr. Paladin, and also a man of your word. I am not a stupid man, and I understand the value of these things."

"What is your source?"

"Mr. Paladin, do we have a deal?"

"Yes, we do."

"Then I will tell you." Marcos squirmed on the couch, uncomfortable and underslept. "All these boxes that your men are disposing of. All of this counterfeit drug? It all came from the same man that I suspect is killing your men. It came from Seth Fowler at the Sybillene Eradication Administration."

39

Quality Control

"IT'S a complex combination of compounds, Charles. MDMA—also known as ecstasy—LSD, and psilocybin are included. It looks like they were trying to mimic some of the effects of Naked Emperor with whatever miscellaneous drugs they had stashed away from drug busts over the years. But those drugs aren't usually inhaled, so I don't know how well it would work, or how fast it would kick in. People who have used the real stuff would know this isn't it. But there are a ton of first-time users, and first-time users would be thrown off, not knowing what to expect."

Tim McBride, as its inventor, probably knew more about Naked Emperor than anybody on the planet. McBride refused to trash-talk his baby, and was therefore treated in the press like a scientist who worked for an oil company. Scientific research had become as politically correct as that of Lysenko in the Soviet Union. Lysenko tried to show that principles of Marxism even extended to biology, and essentially said, among other things, that a giraffe that repeatedly stretched for high leaves would give birth to a baby with a longer neck. This notion appealed to Stalin and his belief that the New Soviet Man could be cultivated and bred. Biology in the USSR became politically correct, as opposed to scientifically correct, and fell decades behind the rest of the world. Stalin was not alone in trying to impose his ideological views on research.

The U.S. government did everything they could to make McBride's life miserable. They'd already barred him from grant funding, a powerful disincentive for anyone doing research, since an overwhelming majority of the money for pure science came as distributions from the state. They spread word to professional journals that publishing his research might be problematic. They pressured his university to withdraw his tenure, on the grounds of involvement with an illicit drug. They maligned him publicly, had him audited by the IRS and sanctioned by the FDA. McBride quickly learned who were the good guys and who were the bad guys, and found he was now one of the latter. He now regretted his decision to come back from Gondwana after setting up the lab for GoldMine Pharmaceuticals on TJ's father's hill.

Although he already knew the answer, Charles asked him, "Why do you think the SEA would be trying to stick this fake stuff in the market?"

"It's diabolical, Charles. You see, there's something else in these things, too. It took a while to figure it out. These canisters are loaded with vanadium chloride. It's a powerful reductant, and creates hydrochloric acid in the airways. Ten inhalations could kill some people, and certainly make people sick, depending on the amounts. But there aren't even any controls on how much is in a given canister; it's like this stuff was thrown together in a kitchen. And one of the canisters had a fatal amount of cyanide. The SEA is trying to make people sick. Or kill them."

Charles nodded. "They even set these canisters up with fake serial numbers similar to those we use for quality control. They faked a serial-number processing website. It's actually quite clever on their part. They're far more serious about eliminating Naked Emperor than they've ever been about any other drug."

"They're truly scared."

"Yeah. Scared enough to kill."

"What are you going to do?"

"I don't know yet. But I have an idea what *they're* going to do."

"What's that?"

"They'll do what every government does when they see they have a revolution on their hands."

* * *

The new supplies of Naked Emperor imported from Gondwana hit the streets initially in ten cities, and spread out from there. The price dropped only a small amount, and that did not last long. People had become accustomed to paying whatever was demanded for what Naked Emperor would be able to teach them. Demand kept growing, despite the propaganda about how dangerous the chemical was. No Naked Emperor user believed the news anymore.

Naked Emperor had no chemically addictive properties. It brought no high, and resulted in no dismal withdrawal to compel the user to access more drug. Yet it seemed Naked Emperor was psychologically addictive, in the way reading a book that changes your life could be. Users became addicted to the truth. They believed that truth would set them free.

Meanwhile, the media painted a bleak picture. "Naked Emperor ruined my marriage and my life" became such a common theme that church pastors used it as an excuse to preach against the evil substance, instead of helping parishioners deal with bad marriages. "Naked Emperor cost me my job" headlined another series of stories, the journalists strategically leaving out the fact that these fired employees had been caught stealing. As time passed, the reports became more emotional. But, like all good propaganda, they contained an element of truth. "Naked Emperor tore me away from my family and friends." "It ruined my life, but I couldn't break the habit!" "Naked Emperor caused me to lose my religion, and now I'm lost." Churches, temples, and mosques united in condemnation of a drug that threatened to destroy the country's spiritual foundation, and cost them untold donations and tithes.

A twelve-step program emerged, called SA, for Sybillene Anonymous, and received a massive infusion of emergency funding from HHS, the Department of Health and Human Services. We can help people "only if they live long enough to get to us," the SA founder said. She spoke with great credibility, because she was the sister-in-law of the president of the United States.

And all that was before the phony Naked Emperor started killing people.

*   *   *

"It's all bullshit, Tony," Peale told his probation officer. "All the bad stuff you hear about Naked Emperor. It's all bullshit. The government is making up these stories. The whole thing is a fabrication!"

Anthony Sciberra sat across from the newspaperman who had started the whole Naked Emperor buzz. "There's *hysteria* out there."

Peale nodded vigorously. "You know, I never understood that line from that movie, where Jack Nicholson says, 'You want the truth? Well, you can't handle the truth!' But now I understand. Some people can't handle the truth when this stuff puts it in front of them. All of a sudden their denials and ego protections fall away and they get hit with a boatload of guilt. It makes them confront their own stupidity. So, yeah, Sybillene is dangerous to some people. But it's not *poison*!"

"Peale, Sybillene *is* poison. Just not to *people*. It's poison to ideas that conflict with reality. It's the opposite of PCP, which makes people irrational and violent. Sybillene makes them rational and thoughtful. Imagine how dangerous Sybillene would have been to the Nazis. It might have stopped them altogether."

"Yeah, it would have helped most Germans, but not the Nazi leadership. They were sociopaths. Negative moral compass. They intentionally caused harm. Just like the political leadership in this country is doing now."

"Peale, avoid sounding paranoid."

"I think just like you, Tony, and you know it. Look, I'm an editor of a newspaper. I make a living being objective, not schizophrenic. You know I take my job seriously. You know I'm a truth seeker."

Tony replied, "Peale, I know you're an honest guy on the right side of things. If you weren't, I wouldn't be your PO. And you appreciate that?"

"Yeah, I got it."

"I told you that I'm not supposed to hear about your drug use. Do you want another PO?"

"God no!"

"And I don't want you with another PO, so let's keep these conversations confidential. You're saying Sybillene isn't like the government or media are making it out to be. Why don't you prove it? Expand on what you're telling me. Do your own study. Interview users. Find out how many of them had any adverse effects. Get data that don't come from the government agencies or their lapdogs or the mainstream media. Get some data that even *you* can trust."

"My paper doesn't have the resources for that kind of project. I'd need to pay people for their work."

Tony said, "How much do you need to get the story put together in a week?"

"I don't know. I can get interns and volunteers to do some of the work. Maybe ten thousand dollars."

"I can help with the money."

"How?"

"I have some funds that I get from … well, you know, *not* from my job here."

"Oh, right. You work for the City of New York. But you work for someone else too. I know."

"Yeah … a lot of people moonlight. But the point is, I'll get you that ten thousand dollars to do that study and get it printed. Get it on the wire. Get it everywhere."

"If you get me the money, I'll do the interviews. I hate lies."

Tony contacted Jeffrey later that day with an ordinary cell phone. Jeffrey didn't need secret codes or secure lines. He didn't seem to care about that sort of thing. Maybe he should. Maybe that's why he had so many scars. Jeffrey didn't hesitate to supply the $10,000.

"This is very important, Tony," Jeffrey said over the phone. "Peale is important. Charles Knight is essential."

* * *

"Seth, I've got something. I think we've got a break." Donald Debocher had walked into Fowler's office without even a nod to his secretary.

The pressure from the White House weighed on Seth Fowler. He suspected that the sudden upsurge in the supply of Sybillene would get him fired. He pretended to yawn, for the sole purpose of diminishing Debocher. "What've you got, Donald?"

"Sabina has been helping me some on the Viagra Initiative. We've just gotten mandatory access to all the pharmacy sales data. Anyhow, we've been looking at sales for the last few months, sales of real Viagra and the other erectile-dysfunction drugs. The legit ones. They were on the rise for a while, but now sales are declining again. Sabina thinks a new supply of generic Viagra has hit the streets."

Fowler didn't hide his lack of interest in this bit of trivia. Now that he ran SEA, tracking down illegally imported Viagra fell far below his pay grade. But one thing Donald said did catch his attention: *Sabina.* "What the hell is Sabina doing working on that? We have real crap to deal with."

355

"It was her first project with me. She's interested!"

"She has more important obligations now."

"Are you jealous, Seth?"

"Of you, Donald? Get real."

"Right. I'm outa here." Debocher turned and marched toward the door like an injured teenager.

Fowler rolled his eyes. "Get back in here."

Debocher stopped.

"So what's the break you say you found, Donald? Not just analysis of pharmacy data, I hope."

Donald stopped partway out the door, but kept his back to Seth. "You want to hear this, or do you just want to compare the size of our dicks?"

Fowler leaned back in his chair. Donald slowly turned around, to see Fowler in a position that suggested less aggression and more interest.

"Seth, Sabina has been tracking Sybillene's street price. Its price had a small but definite drop about a week before legit Viagra prescriptions slowed way down. She's said all along that Viagra would only serve as a gateway to something bigger."

"You think they're related…"

"Why not? Mostly high-end customers. Makes sense for the dealers to be the same people."

"One of the Naked Emperor dealers we picked up last week admitted to dealing Viagra too."

"It's hard to get these guys to admit much of anything. But I bet there are a lot more like him."

"You think this is just street-level dealers? Or is this all one organization?"

"Track the Viagra, and maybe you'll find the Sybillene source, Seth."

"Maybe, Donald. Maybe you're right. How are you coming in regard to that tracking? I haven't had a report from you in weeks."

Donald exhaled. "Yeah, Seth, now it's my turn to say *fuck you*."

"Donald, just tell me. You always gotta play these damn games…"

"We had to lay out a lot of cash for the lead. We've tracked several large shipments of generic Viagra—you know, Fiagara—coming out of India. Going to an interesting place."

"Yeah. To *here*."

"No. To a wholesale pharmacy in Gondwana."

"Gondwana? Where the hell is that? Africa, right?"

"Western side, yes. Millions of pills at a time."

"Sounds like a lot of big black erections. What's interesting about that?"

"Black erections don't interest you? I assumed they would…"

Fowler groaned. "What have you learned about this Gondwana wholesale pharmacy?"

"Not much yet. But I've heard that the Gondwanans take Fiagara along with a gin-based eggnog, and claim it makes their penises bigger. I shit you not. Eggnog. Apparently it's a huge hit in the country."

"Do you believe it?"

"I don't know. The place is small, and dirt poor. It's suspicious. I'm going there myself to ask the locals. I leave tonight."

"The South American cartels are starting to use those shithole countries in West Africa as trans-shipment points. Anything's possible. Check it out if you want. Eggnog, hah! Don't kill too much time over there. Get in and get out."

Donald turned to leave. He stopped, once again, as he walked out the door. "Oh, Seth. I forgot. Charles Knight… Border Protection says he flew to Gondwana about a year ago."

Seth sat up now. He said slowly, "Knight has a history in Gondwana… Viagra in Gondwana… Knight owned Visioryme. Visioryme created Sybillene. Has he been back there since?"

"If he has been, it hasn't been tracked."

"I *am* more interested now. Go to Gondwana, Donald. See what you can learn."

"As I said, I'm on the way." One last time, he started out the door. This time he walked through and out. He left the door open. He was almost by Fowler's secretary's desk when he turned again and said, quite loudly, "Oh, Seth. Sabina is coming with me."

He stayed close enough to enjoy Fowler's expletives.

40

Field Trip

"WELCOME to Gondwana, Mr. Debocher!" Tip Harding, the U.S. Embassy's commercial attaché, smiled as he reached out to shake Donald's hand. Harding's eyes quickly deviated to the woman standing next to Donald. Sabina glowed through the light sheen of perspiration that covered everyone who'd been outside. Heat and humidity affected everybody here; it was worse than Houston during a summer heat wave. But at least it wasn't raining, for the moment.

"Thanks for meeting us, Mr. Harding. This is Sabina Heidel, special assistant to the president, on assignment to FDA and SEA."

"Impressive. Nice to meet you. I've been following news of this SEA. Powerful organization. No limits to that authority. They've got more oomph than Homeland Security, what with all the dangers of Naked Emperor."

Sabina replied, "That's one reason why we're here."

"The government of Gondwana will appreciate your help."

"Why's that?" she asked.

"There's a lot of Naked Emperor use here in Gondwana. It's taken off recently. The government is getting concerned, given all the news out of the U.S. about how dangerous it is."

Sabina and Donald shared glances before Sabina spoke. "I'm surprised to hear that, Mr. Harding."

"Yes. I can get it on the street pretty easily." He paused. "Of course I never would!"

"Where's the drug coming from?"

358

"We presume it's coming in from the U.S. The canisters are the same ones that are sold there. But my information is mostly through the local press, and honestly, the media here aren't big on accuracy. The papers here mostly just push their own political agendas. But we get the 'New York Times' online, and I read the 'Huffington Post,' so I have a good idea what the real facts are. And they're pretty bleak."

Harding led them through the compound to his small office. He offered them chairs and water. "It's cold. And safe. Cold and safe is a rare combination for water in Gondwana."

Sabina looked at the chipped and smudged glass suspiciously. "Thanks."

"So what can I do for FDA, Mr. Debocher?"

"We're trying to track down sources of generic Viagra and other drugs that are being illegally imported into the United States. Millions of pills. We wanted to check on a few things."

"I'll help if I can."

"We've heard that the men of Gondwana think Viagra and an eggnog make them more masculine."

"I wouldn't be surprised. That sounds like something that you would get around here."

"Enough that one of the wholesale pharmacies would order millions of pills from a manufacturer in India?"

"Millions of pills? I wouldn't think so. Maybe whoever is making that eggnog is mixing Viagra in it? That would make sense. But folks here don't have much cash. There are less than a million adult males in the entire country, and a third of them are off in remote areas."

Debocher handed Harding a paper. "Can you help us check out this pharmacy? Somebody named Jayaraman purchased the pills from India. We're not sure if he owns this pharmacy here, or is just an intermediary."

"I can work through our liaison at the Ministry of Commerce or the Ministry of Health. One of them will have some authority to find out."

Sabina asked, "Have you ever heard of a man named Charles Knight?"

Harding pulled his head back for a minute in thought. "Charles Knight? I think so. A while back. Young guy? Long hair? He thought this was a great place to start a business, and he was looking into U.S. import certifications."

"What sort of business?"

"If I remember, it was furniture. Bamboo furniture. Plastics too, I think."

"Bamboo, huh? Did he end up starting this business?"

"I don't think so. I gave him the paperwork, and he left. Never heard back from him. That kind of thing happens a lot. Missionaries come over and want to start businesses to help the economy. Until they figure out how hard it is to export from here. Red tape. Bribes. I figure he gave up and left. Why?"

Sabina smiled tightly. "Mr. Knight is no missionary. Knight owns Visioryme. That's the company that developed Sybillene."

"You're kidding! Well, I wouldn't think there's a lot of money in bamboo furniture…"

"Did he say where he was hoping to set up his company?"

"I didn't think I needed to pursue it. Geesh, you think he's built a facility here?"

"We don't know. Anything else you can tell us?"

"Oh, he did mention Djenne County. That's two counties southeast, on the ocean. About sixty miles. A five-hour drive."

"Five hours?"

"That's if you get there at all. The roads are pretty crappy here, Ms. Heidel, and they sometimes flood out entirely in the rainy season."

She said, "I hate this place. After we check out the wholesaler, perhaps you can help us get there?"

After a year in Gondwana, almost entirely stuck in the embassy compound, Harding would do just about anything to spend time with an American as attractive as Sabina. He changed his schedule and requisitioned an embassy vehicle.

*   *   *

Harding's SUV had more room than the tiny wholesale pharmacy. Prescription drugs from India, China, Ghana, and Nigeria lined the pharmacy's shelves, alongside those of an occasional European or U.S. manufacturer. Sabina saw no warehouse in the back. With the help of a uniformed official from the Ministry of Commerce, who required a twenty-dollar tip, Sabina examined the books: an old-fashioned ledger, its notations in pen. She found no entries for any multimillion-pill deliveries.

"We talked to a Mr. Chandra Jayaraman a couple of days ago." Donald lied. "He told us about his purchases of millions of Fiagara pills."

The diminutive Indian pharmacist shrugged and said in a sing-song voice, "Mr. Jayaraman has been maybe making deals on the side. We can all be doing it. It is quite possibly very, very legal, oh yes." He smiled and shook his head side-to-side.

"We would like to see Mr. Jayaraman. Is he nearby?"

"He is being out of the country."

"For how long?"

"Until he will be returning. It is most hard to be saying." He spoke with an ingratiating smile.

"Can you give us his mobile number, please?"

"He leaves his phone here in Gondwana."

"Do you know a man named Charles Knight?"

No flicker crossed the pharmacist's eyes to suggest recognition. "No, I am not knowing that name."

* * *

In the car a few minutes later, Sabina said, "That was fruitless."

"We'll have to come back to this. Just a bump in the road." Donald scratched at an armpit that was beginning to itch. "Clearly we need to talk to Jayaraman."

Sabina asked Harding, "Will the Ministry of Commerce man be able to keep an eye on that pharmacy and let us know when Jayaraman is back in country?"

"I don't think so. You just need to call his mobile from time to time."

"I have a feeling he won't answer."

The embassy driver, a Gondwanan from Djenne County, swerved around a huge pothole. Sabina buckled her seatbelt after extracting herself from Donald, who also quickly buckled his belt.

The driver said, "In Gondwana, if Africans or Indians or Arabs do no wan' to be foun', they will no be foun'. But you white Americans have no chance to hide. If be white men within fifty mile, you will *know* it."

"Do you know Djenne well?"

"Very well, Miss. Djenne is mah county. Mah village is near Djennetown."

"Can you tell us about Djenne? I think we need to go there."

"It is the best place in Gondwana. It used to be our huge port city. The

361

biggest in the country befo' the war. And it will be again. The ocean is big in Djenne. Huge beaches."

"Do you swim?"

"Nobody swim. Too dangerous." He laughed at her ignorance. "The beaches, people use them for toileting. The ocean wash away the bad stuff. After a time."

Harding chimed in. "Gondwanans don't like the ocean much. They prefer the lagoons."

"Who runs the county?"

"Ooh," the driver replied. "The county supervisor is Anita Mason. We need to stop by her home. Maybe tomorrow. Bring her fish. She will ask you to stay for a meal."

"Are there any businesses in Djenne?"

"Businesses. Yes. Lots. Everyone has business in Djenne. Big companies? No. T.J. Wandeah will soon run for senator, so he hires people now."

"Who is T.J. Wandeah?"

"His father was de bossman of many people before he passed. Now TJ is."

"What does TJ do?"

"Ooh. Many things."

*　　*　　*

The next day brought an exhausting trip, constant acceleration and deceleration, coursing through muddy pools of unknown depth, sometimes diving into them fast in hopes of momentum carrying the car through. Every muscle ached, trying to keep vertebrae from collapsing over five long hours of incessant bouncing. Finally, they passed between two enormous trees, the hallmarks of Djenne County. Fifteen minutes later they stood in front of the Sparkles Hotel's wooden registration desk. The hotel had seen much better days and certainly didn't sparkle.

Harding caught the room number as the young hotel girl handed Sabina her key.

He said, "I'm going to take a shower. But be very careful about the water here. Especially now. The wells get most contaminated during the rainy season. If it gets in your mouth, you'll get typhoid, almost guaranteed. Use bottled water even for brushing your teeth. Don't use ice in your drinks. Let's meet over there in the restaurant at six PM or so? That gives us an hour."

They were the only white people at the restaurant at 6:15 as they sipped very welcome—albeit not particularly cold—beer and nibbled at sliced bread. The loaf had been imported from Lebanon; it was stale, dry, and dense.

They heard a cackling of voices and a high-pitched laugh from the lobby. Donald looked up to see a group of three white men walk into the restaurant. As they took a table not far away, Donald looked closer. There was one man who … who…

Donald stood up suddenly, knocking the table upward with his knees, overturning all three beers. He pushed his chair back, walked over to the table, and stood there. The man he had seen looked up, and his big smile died. But it reappeared just as rapidly.

"Donald! Is that you, Donald?" The man spoke with an exaggerated lisp and bounced up to give Donald a dramatic hug.

Donald broke the embrace and pushed him away roughly.

He said, with an icy smirk, "Stephan, how nice to see you here."

41

Black PR

"GODDAMMIT!" Fowler shouted to no one in particular. He held a photocopy of a front-page article from a small New York City news rag that had managed to get on the wire. "Dammit, send Friar in here, now!" he yelled through his open door to his secretary. He read through the rest of the extensive article that countered, in great detail, everything that SEA had been releasing to the media. He swore intermittently.

Friar—a young bureaucrat who'd been slowly working his way through the DEA ranks before being pressed into the SEA—wasn't excited to walk into that office.

"How did this get by you, Friar? How did this get on the wire? All AP stories that have anything to do with Sybillene are supposed to be approved by us. It's going to be the damn law soon!"

"Sir, it isn't the law *yet*. Look, I've tried, but some of these writers aren't going to buckle. They're stubborn. Ethics, stupidity ... who knows?"

"This is a matter of national security. To hell with their ethics. And they'd better get smart."

"Most of them are just working to collect a paycheck; *they'll* cooperate. But there're still a few old-school guys out there. Think they're Clark Kent."

"Bullshit again! This is a war for hearts and minds." Fowler liked to feel he was on the moral high ground. "This guy's column raises all kinds of ridiculous questions ... causes doubt. We can't win the War on Sybillene if we're fighting fifth columnists and traitors. I want whoever's responsible for this. I want them in my office. They're gonna regret their decision."

Whoever had crafted this story probably knew more than he had published so far, and had to be marginalized.

"Friar, you have to counter this story. Reverse it. Make sure everyone knows that this guy is an inveterate liar. He writes that Naked Emperor is completely safe. Make sure that people know the truth. Ostracize him. Get the IRS on him. Find child porn on his computer. Plant Sybillene in his apartment. Lock him up. Now get out of here."

A few minutes later, Fowler called Juan Marcos on his burner phone, and the news he received from the Fat Man just added to his fury.

Marcos informed him that his boxes had been stolen by thieves. "I am sorry."

Fowler spat back, "What? Stolen? When?"

"Some weeks ago."

"Why did you not tell me?"

"Do you really want a known head of a cartel calling you? No, it is always better for you to contact me, as you and I originally agreed."

"How many boxes were stolen?"

"All of them."

"Who stole them?"

"Several armed men in black outfits. I don't know who they were."

"Your competition, I assume."

"It's a very popular product. Word spreads. These people were well armed and well organized."

Fowler thought for a moment. This would work out fine, then. "So it'll still get on the street."

"One would think so. Why else would they risk their lives to break in here?" Juan Marcos replied.

"This failure on your part voids our agreement, Juan Marcos. You're back on our radar screen. I may be in touch with you again soon. If I find out that you're lying about those boxes being stolen, I'll have you locked up in my personal prison, where I'm the only warden. And you'll only get fed once per week. Make damn sure you don't disappear."

This threat had a ring of truth.

SEA had provided Marcos with only a tenth of the fake Naked Emperor canisters they'd made over the past months. Soon, it would all be sent out far and wide, sold as if it were real Naked Emperor. Field agents loved having something to trade with dealers. Free dope was much more popular than the thousands of tons of free cheese the government had given out years before. But this product was much more dangerous than cheese.

*   *   *

Fowler took the battery out of his burner phone, then returned it to his pocket. One could never be too careful. The FBI, DEA, and NSA were full of snoops that might be monitoring him. Constant surveillance was now a general principle, although particularly applicable in the interagency turf war that always went on under the surface. They might already be keeping an eye on Juan Marcos. It was risky talking to him anytime, so why take additional risk? The only way to ensure they couldn't track a phone was to remove the battery.

Thirty seconds later Fowler's secretary patched a call through to his regular cell phone. He answered after a brief, intentional delay. "Debocher, how's your wild goose chase in Gondwana?"

"We are running into barriers, Seth. Hard to track the Viagra here. Nobody is cooperative."

Fowler had grown accustomed to being treated as one of the emperor's proconsuls in the U.S. He didn't understand that, in Gondwana, few had even heard of the SEA and no one knew his name. And Debocher? He was just a chubby white man wandering around asking questions. But Fowler blamed Debocher, of course, because that was how his brain was hardwired.

"Get your act together, Donald."

He heard no response.

Fowler prodded, with bitterness evident. "How's Sabina holding up?"

"Fine. I'm watching her closely to make sure she's all right. There's a lot of down time in this place."

They exchanged the silence of two males fighting for a woman. Had they been in the same room, they might have come to blows, a battle that Fowler would have won by an embarrassing margin. But at a distance of five thousand miles, silence provided a sufficient means of saying what they wanted to say, and allowed each to flex muscles.

Donald softened first. "Seth. We've got something else."

"What's that?"

"We found where Knight set up Visioryme's new home."

Now came silence again. This time it was expectant. It lasted too long, and Fowler finally prompted with a "Well…?" intended to show dominance over a subordinate. And to show contempt for the soft little man. Inside he scrambled to devise a means of ensuring that credit for any such find would be correctly attributed. To him.

"They're manufacturing Sybillene on a property in Djennetown, Gondwana. They call it GoldMine Pharmaceuticals. It's an isolated place. We got up there. He's got an expansive operation. Several Visioryme employees, including one I've met before. There's no doubt about what we've found."

"Do they know you found it?"

"Yes. We bumped into their team in a bar," Donald added, "where Sabina and I were having drinks before bed."

Fowler chose not to react to the sexual suggestion, but Donald would be punished for it someday. Fowler and Sabina had advanced their relationship far beyond what Donald could imagine. They had killed together. These were the ties that bind. He convinced himself that she was toying with Donald. After all, she liked to mess with the guy's mind.

"Fantastic, Donald. Fantastic. We'll need to get the Gondwanans to shut the place down and arrest everyone."

"I've got the American Visioryme people locked down incommunicado in a local police station, thanks to the U.S. Embassy. But that won't last. Naked Emperor is still legal here. Pretty much everything is legal here. This GoldMine Pharmaceuticals is supplying work for a lot of locals—in the manufacturing facility, building a rail spur, construction, you name it. There's no basis for the Gondwana government to jump on this, and I don't think they will. We need the power of government, but it won't be the Gondwana government, at least not without an inducement."

Fowler figured he would need to get in to see the president. Let him get the national-security advisor and the military in on this. This thing was a cancer, and unless it was completely eradicated, it would metastasize and crop up in other places.

He commanded Donald, "Send me everything you got and call me back in six hours."

"Will do," Donald replied.

* * *

"Donald, I don't know that they're going to do it." Sabina shook her head. "A U.S. military strike on Gondwana won't go down smoothly with a lot of people. Fighter attacks and drone strikes in the Middle East are one thing. But Gondwana isn't a Muslim country with ragheads running around setting off bombs. The president won't go this far. Cooligan's backbone's made out of wet pasta. We need to take them out before the Visioryme team relocates."

Donald smiled for a minute, thinking about Stephan in a Gondwanan jail. "What else can we do?"

"As soon as Stephan and the others are released from jail, you know that they'll clear all the equipment out of the facility just like they did in Virginia. They'll set up shop in a jungle a few counties or countries over, hide it better, and we'll be back where we were."

"I repeat, what else can we do?"

"This isn't a drug problem, this is a people problem. It's really quite simple. If we want the drug problem to disappear, we need to disappear the people who are making the stuff, Donald." She looked at him for a long moment. "Do you understand?"

Donald didn't respond.

Sabina prompted, "Do you want to take out Knight's operation? Do you want to shut him down? You know he's the guy supplying all of the Naked Emperor in the U.S. And he's probably supplying the Fiagara too. He's the guy who broke up your marriage, Donald. Don't forget that. Charles Knight is the guy you and I have been after all this time, and he's right in front of us."

Again, Donald didn't respond.

"There is more I can do to stop him."

This prompted Donald's interest, if only because he had no idea what she was talking about. "What can you do?"

"I'm connected with someone with every bit as much power as the president, Donald. Some would say far more."

42

Evil among Us

"SETH, what's so urgent, my friend?" Stafford smiled as he welcomed Fowler once again into the Oval Office. The president sat in one of the armchairs, his right leg on the table in front of him.

Fowler wanted to cement his image as a get-it-done man. "Mr. President. We've located the manufacturing facility where we believe all the new Sybillene is being made."

"Good. Good. Shut it down."

"It's not in the United States, sir. It's in Gondwana."

"Gondwana?"

"Yes, sir. West Africa."

"I know where Gondwana is, Mr. Fowler."

"Yes, Mr. President. Sorry." It hadn't been an unreasonable comment. Most Americans were challenged to find much beyond Canada or Mexico on a map.

"So, what's the play? Who's our ambassador there?" the president asked Stafford.

Stafford shrugged and walked out the door for a moment to check with the president's secretary.

Fowler tried to keep the momentum up. "Excuse me, sir, but I don't think we'll have time for diplomacy. We have some of their men on ice, but they'll get their equipment out soon. They did that at Visioryme. Cleared everything out before Debocher got to the facility."

"Well, don't let them know in advance this time."

"They'll know. White people in Djennetown, Gondwana apparently stick out, especially when they're in jail without having committed a crime. Our embassy had enough influence to get them arrested, but not enough to keep them locked up."

"What do you want us to do, Fowler, blow the place up?"

"Yes, sir, that's exactly what we need to do."

"A military strike?"

"Yes, sir."

"Stafford, call the joint chiefs. I want their input. Let them know what's up so they can research it. Fowler, you'll need to provide the coordinates of this Djenne, or whatever. Exact coordinates. There must be Muslims in Gondwana, right? Maybe we can say it was a chemical-weapons factory. Say terrorists were making Naked Emperor as part of their plan to undermine liberty. What do you think?"

"No, Mr. President." Stafford came back into the conversation with absolute certainty.

"No?"

Stafford straightened up. "Sir, are we really entertaining the notion of dropping bombs on a pharmaceutical company in a village in Africa without approval of their government? The U.S. went down that exact road not all that long ago…"

The president sat back. "Dick, you've got a point. It didn't go over well when Clinton took out that Al-Shifa pharmaceutical plant in Sudan with a cruise missile. Stayed in the news cycle nearly a month. At least he had a rumor of VX gas being made there. So let's slow this thing down. Check it out, and see which way the winds are blowing today. Let's line up the ducks. Contact our ambassador there. Check with NSA. Something always goes wrong when a president just wants to protect the country. I don't want to be remembered as a president who blew up an orphanage or a church, so let's take this slow and thoughtful. Fowler, keep a lid on this until we see if we can solve your problem for you. If we can't, you'll need to find another way."

Fowler walked out of the office wondering how long it would take for those ducks to be lined up. In the meantime, he would find Charles Knight, if the man was anywhere to be found. He had the resources of the U.S. government behind him. It shouldn't take long.

*   *   *

The next morning, the Djennetown chief of police called Donald and asked him to come to the station.

"Mr. Debocher. We cannot keep three people in jail for more den twenty-four hours widout charging dem for a crime. I know it is different in the United States now, but locking people up widout a reason is still against de law here in Gondwana. And dey are white too. It has been years since a white person has been in jail in Djenne. We have to let dem free, now!"

More important than the chief's ethical and judicial reasoning, the three white men flew under the wing of T.J. Wandeah, a very big man in the county.

Harding wasn't comfortable with locking them up either, but for entirely different reasons. If things went wrong, it would mean a red card, a reprimand, in his personnel file.

"It's not your job to protect some random American criminals, Harding." Donald had told him. "Your job is to protect the United States government and its interests. I can assure you that your cooperation will be rewarded. On the other hand, if you don't pull this off, I might see you charged with conspiracy and complicity. At a minimum it's not going to look good in your file."

But in the end, it fit Donald's plans to have the Visioryme people free to go back to their new factory. Sabina had been very convincing last night in the hotel bedroom that she'd shared with him. And, overnight, Sabina's connections arranged something that seemed beyond the power of a U.S. president.

Stephan emerged from the jail first. Pale, dirty, and unkempt, he failed to crack a single joke as he walked past Donald, ignoring him. He picked up his phone and his wallet from the policeman at the desk. The wallet was intact, but the phone's battery had died. The other two men, a chemist and an engineer, followed Stephan out of the building and began walking down the road toward the hotel.

"How long until they come?" Donald asked Sabina.

She looked at her watch. "A little over three hours."

"That should give Stephan and his friends time to get back up to their facility."

Sabina said, "That would be ideal. I hate this country."

* * *

"Stephan, how are you?"

"I've been better, Charles. A shitstorm is coming. The fan is spinning. Stuff flying everywhere!"

His voice crackled over a doubly weak connection between Stephan's cell phone in Gondwana and Charles's cell. Charles sat next to Tristana on chairs on the deck of Anders's ship in Baltimore Harbor.

They were enjoying a picnic lunch with wine, served on a white-linen covered table, when the call had come through from Gondwana.

"What's happened, Stephan?"

"Donald is here."

"Confirm. Did you say that Donald Debocher is in Gondwana?" Charles looked at Tristana, his face questioning.

"Not just in Gondwana. He's in Djenne, Charles. He had us locked up in the jail here. In the jail! You know how much gay men don't like jails."

"Are you in jail now?"

"No, the chief of police let us out thirty minutes ago."

"What's Donald doing?"

"I don't know. But it can't be good. Donald was with that hot chick in the green dress. Sabina something. And an embassy man."

Charles's mind shifted into overdrive. What might SEA be planning? Send in a detachment of Gondwana police from the capital? Perhaps some kind of U.S. spec-ops team? Something worse?

"Stephan. Get everyone off the mountain. Empty the place. And do it fast. Don't worry about any equipment or supplies. Just get everyone out of there until we sort out what's happening."

"What *is* happening, Charles?"

"I don't know. But we need to keep our staff safe. There's nothing logical or rational about these people."

"Donald said the jig was up, and we were all going down. He didn't appreciate the joke I made about us all going down, Charles."

"I bet he didn't."

"Is Tristana with you, Charles?"

"Yes."

"Tell her I love her and that her husband is a prick and that she should take you to bed while she still has the chance."

"I'll tell her all of those things, Stephan. I promise. Now, get a move on. You may have very little time. And call me in a few hours. Let me know your progress."

"I will."

Stephan never called back.

*　*　*

The United Nations Office for West Africa has a broad mandate. As a U.N. subsidiary, UNOWA supersedes the laws of small bankrupt African nations. The U.N. has its own courts capable of trying anybody, and they protect their own people from sovereign laws that might hinder their missions.

The Security Council informed their minions at UNOWA that a Sybillene manufacturing center had been discovered in Djenne County, Gondwana. It was a matter of world security to eliminate it. The United States encouraged the action, although its U.N. ambassador abstained from the emergency vote. The Security Council arranged for the French Navy to address the situation. They would inform the corrupt and unreliable government of Gondwana only after the Sybillene threat had been eliminated. A decade after the wars had ended, the U.N. still controlled the airspace over the nation, so there were neither practical nor diplomatic concerns.

Just as dusk came to Djennetown, the skies filled with the shrieks of two Dassault Rafale M F3 omnirole fighters, launched an hour earlier from the deck of the French aircraft carrier *Charles de Gaulle* as it passed through the waters near Abidjan. They sped side-by-side over the town and continued on northwest. Two minutes later they had circled back and again flew over the town. With this second pass, two consecutive massive explosions followed the roar of the jets as the planes each released two 227 kg standard ordnance bombs on the mountaintop. A minute later, while concrete and metal still rained on the surrounding hill, each plane launched two AASM Hammer missiles from six miles out. The GPS-guided air-to-surface weapons sped across the sky, turned downward onto the hilltop, and exploded, flattening and burning anything that remained. On their last pass the jets blew whatever scraps that had endured into fine rubble by emptying their GIAT 30M cannons into the ruins as they streaked by. The planes burned through the sky once again for a final photo reconnaissance, then headed back to their carrier, mission accomplished.

*   *   *

GoldMine Pharmaceuticals ceased to exist after the bombs landed. Parts of it were scattered for hundreds of yards down the hillside: shattered blocks of concrete, twisted bits of metal, smoking slivers of wood, and melted pieces of plastic. Various parts of eighteen bodies lay interspersed among the devastation.

Stephan Liggett hadn't suffered. One of the bombs had detonated thirty feet from him. The massive concussion tore the flesh off his bones, but he was aware of nothing beyond a burst of light that lasted for a millisecond, at which point his own light expired forever.

Smoke drifted from the mountain. The people of Djennetown gazed, horrified, at the hill. Some screamed in terror, and ran into the streets looking for answers, looking for their friends and family members who worked up on that hill. Their friends and their family would not be coming home to dinner that evening. They had no idea what they might have done to deserve this.

A thousand eyes watched the visiting U.S. government man and his female companion walk back into the hotel. They looked unaffected, or even self-satisfied, with the disaster. The two entered the restaurant and celebrated with the hotel's last bottle of wine and some stale bread. It would be a long wait for the baked chicken and rice, because the cooks had run from the kitchen to go help on the hill.

It was, as connoisseurs might say, an unprepossessing little wine, having been stored at a rather high room temperature for a couple of years. But its alcohol hadn't been fully replaced by vinegar. Not much of a start for so important a celebration. But Donald's attention wasn't so much on the substandard meal as the banquet of delights Sabina would serve up later that night.

He had beaten Fowler on two fronts today. And he had beaten Knight too. This was the best day of his entire life.

It was the last best day he would ever have.

The cooks returned after a long delay. The chicken was free range out of necessity as opposed to fashion, and rather scrawny. As they prepared their meal the staff talked among themselves in the back of the kitchen. A man met them, and they whispered. One of them made a call on his cell phone. The cooks' hearts raced, the adrenaline pumping.

Evil sat in their restaurant, drank their wine, and dined on their food. Tonight the secret society would undertake its most important duty.

43

Rogue Scientist

FOWLER'S Cadillac SUV raced through the port in Baltimore, tearing around corners designed for slow-moving fork lifts. The three men with him didn't enjoy the horizontal roller coaster ride he provided. The small fleet of black Cadillacs behind him struggled to keep up. They headed toward the pier where a certain container ship had recently offloaded its cargo.

But the pier was empty, and the ship that had been docked there had left hours earlier, clearing the port in record time, headed for international waters. But it had left hundreds of containers, stacked fifteen high on the pier, awaiting their various receivers to deal with the rigmarole. Customs officials had to review the bills of lading to ensure all the arriving goods would be properly taxed.

Fowler called over an ICE official standing near the recently offloaded containers.

"Which ones of these are being received by Charles Knight?" He flashed his shiny silver-and-gold SEA badge, emblazoned with a fanged cobra, the symbol he had chosen for his agency.

The officer's old black vest displayed the outdated term *U.S. CUSTOMS* in large yellow letters. He started shuffling through a thick stack of papers. "It will take a while to figure out. That ship left especially fast. Of course they all do, since those things cost ten grand a day. Maybe they have a captain looking to maximize his bonus, or maybe they knew you were coming. Some of the stuff was cleared through Customs on the web. Some is here on paper. It takes a while…"

"Sort it out as fast as you can," Fowler ordered.

"Some of it's already cleared and gone."

"Already? How was that done?"

"A number of forty-foot containers were picked up by truck. First ones off the ship. They had all the documents perfectly lined up. The port likes to move the containers out of here."

"What was in those containers?"

"Furniture."

"By any chance, was it bamboo furniture?"

"Yes."

"Goddammit! My men are going to want to see all the documents you have for those containers. Who was the receiver?"

"Paladin International Imports."

"Where are they based?"

"Here." The officer extracted a document from the bottom of the pile. "This should have their contact information on it."

Fowler hardly needed to look. It would be a dead end. He slapped the document into one of his men's hands and said, "Follow this up." He could send the Coast Guard after the ship, although that would almost certainly be pointless, and would strain relations with that agency. He spun himself around in a circle and smashed his hands down on the hood of his car.

He'd just let who knows how many more canisters of Naked Emperor into the country. At $1,000 a dispenser, that would likely put hundreds of millions of dollars into Charles Knight's network.

"Goddammit!" Cursing his bad luck hardly reinforced his role as fearless leader. But his agents would continue doing as they were told, as long as their paychecks were issued on time.

Through his anger he saw in front of him on the empty pier, right by the water, what looked like a table with a white linen cloth. He walked over and stood next to it. The table was carefully arranged and set, as if awaiting a couple for a romantic evening. On it sat an empty bottle and two wine glasses. And a note addressed only with the name "Fowler."

The note, written in pen, said, "Remember, you fired first."

* * *

Fowler didn't take long to figure out how he would blow off the intense anger engendered by Knight's note.

The fresh supply of Naked Emperor would be on the street within a day. Well, that was just fine. Fowler knew exactly how to neutralize that. Sabina Heidel had taught him.

He sent a long-awaited text message to a group of ten phone numbers. It said only, "Start distributing our product now."

His planned countermove made him feel like an expert chess player.

But he also needed more immediate gratification. So he took a team and headed for Johns Hopkins Hospital to pay a visit to Dr. James Sandridge, the man whose bank loan was being paid off with drug money.

All told, Dr. Sandridge had completed twenty-eight years of education, including two years of preschool, eight years of grade school, four in high school, four in college, and four in medical school. Then three years of residency and three more of subspecialty fellowship. Now he held a position in the junior faculty of one the most prestigious medical schools in the world, a professional student, grooving into becoming a professional teacher. He'd been in a bubble his whole life, insulated from what most might consider the real world. For the last several years his research pursuits had been funded by the National Institutes of Health. But also by Altria, the politically correct, and meaningless, new name for the tobacco corporation formally known as Philip Morris. Altria's PR mavens felt it prudent to buy a few friends.

He was extensively funded because his laboratory focused on determining why profoundly brain-injured mice reach puberty an average of three days earlier than normal mice, and how that was confounded by exposure to cigarette smoke. There was absolutely no chance his work would ever improve the *human* condition. All he ever did was make mice sick. Such research projects persisted not because of value created, but because so many academic scientists were trained to solve perplexing but unimportant problems by spending large amounts of other people's money. Any suggestion that this might be wasteful was called *an attack on medical research*.

Dr. Sandridge justified his work with the thought it pushed forward the frontiers of cutting edge science—much the way a medieval monk thought determining how many angels could stand on the head of a pin pushed forward the frontiers of theology.

A Fed economist would add that Sandridge's work stimulated the economy. A practical economist would observe that it was a misallocation of capital and a dissipation of wealth, only a standard deviation removed from paying someone to dig ditches during the day and paying someone else to fill them at night. A businessman, interested in creating new wealth, would simply call it a boondoggle.

But no matter. Sandridge performed his science extremely well, with extensively detailed documentation. He turned in his grant paperwork on time. He had every reason to expect that, if his work was thorough and whether or not anybody actually understood or used it, the NIH would fund him throughout his career. He devised unnatural and irrelevant biological puzzles with NIH funding. He then solved the puzzles he created, also using NIH funding. The puzzles advanced science the way crossword puzzles advanced the English language; they were amusing, but essentially a waste of time. His was a first-class ticket in a finely appointed compartment on an academic train headed to nowhere.

His gravy train derailed on an unexpected curve when Fowler, accompanied by six SWAT-uniformed SEA men, burst unannounced into the small auditorium where he sat attending the dean's weekly meeting of lab researchers. It seemed he spent as much time in administrative meetings as he did fiddling in his lab.

"Dr. James Sandridge?" Fowler called out, interrupting the dean's introduction of the school's new regulatory-compliance officer, who would directly oversee the research faculty. The man would undoubtedly require his own weekly meeting.

The dean looked first at Fowler, and then at Sandridge, his face filled with questioning concern.

Two SEA agents zeroed in on Sandridge, guided by the scientists and doctors who had turned to look at their bewildered colleague. The agents positioned themselves behind him, roughly roused him to his feet, threw him against a wall, and handcuffed him.

"Dr. Sandridge, you are under arrest for distribution and financing of Sybillene. You have limited rights as delineated by recent law. These limited rights will be explained to you as needed." Some of the scientists looked at each other. They'd all seen felons being read their rights, perhaps hundreds of times, on scores of cop shows. This significant variation on the Miranda-rights theme would soon become the new norm, to be portrayed each week on the impending season of the new primetime series *SEA: Washington!*

379

The two agents marched Sandridge toward the door.

"I didn't *do* anything!" Sandridge called out to his colleagues. "They have the wrong man! What's going on here? I didn't do *anything!*"

Neither did his friends in the auditorium do anything, other than watch, as the black-suited men dragged him away. They were like a herd of zebras, watching lions pull down one of their number on the Serengeti. The herd stared distraughtly for a few moments during the excitement, but realized there was nothing they could do about it. The animals who attended the dean's meeting would soon go back to grazing. In the meantime, the dean shuffled his feet.

As the last agent walked out, Fowler turned and said, "No one is immune to prosecution if they're involved at any level with the scourge of Sybillene." Fowler made no apology for interrupting the meeting as he further cemented himself in a position where there were very few people in the world to whom he would ever need to apologize.

He certainly wasn't going to apologize to Dr. Sandridge two hours later as he hit him over the left ear with a rolled-up magazine. Sandridge's nose was caked with drying blood, broken by Fowler's first assault.

"I told you," the doctor cried, "I don't know what you're talking about. I don't have a bank down here. I don't have a signature loan. Someone must have stolen my identity!"

"That's not possible. The credit line is being paid down, a few thousand dollars at a time. Nobody other than you would have any motivation to pay down that loan, Dr. Sandridge. It *has* to be you."

"It's a set-up. I'm innocent!"

"Then explain how you launder money for the Sybillene Cartel, hmm? If you're innocent, you'd be helping us now. You took a three-hundred-thousand-dollar loan from First American Bank. Where is that money?

"I don't have any money. I didn't take a loan."

"Who did you give the money to?"

"Nobody. I never had it."

The night went like this for another two hours. It was like juicing a turnip. Lots of effort for very little juice.

Sandridge was exhausted, sore, and very scared.

380

44

False Flag

THE reports of horrifying medical side effects began appearing three days later. People were getting sick, and some were dying. The reports came in from the emergency rooms of ten cities, and these reports were much more convincing than they had been before. Although Naked Emperor users could see through the earlier lies that SEA had planted with their media associates—claims that Sybillene was dangerous, addictive, and deadly—these new stories were real, and verifiable.

Over a few days, dozens of Naked Emperor users died of biochemical asphyxiation—complete failure at the cellular level. The media touted it as a horrible and unpredictable side effect of the drug. Hundreds of others suffered symptoms of respiratory failure after taking Naked Emperor. Coughing, wheezing, mucus filling their lungs, as if they had inhaled a highly corrosive agent. Which, in fact, they had. To the population, Naked Emperor was no longer harmless, no longer risk-free.

If they were lucky, new users of Naked Emperor simply had a strange rush, a bad rash, or no effect at all.

The SEA spread lies that Sybillene itself acted like cyanide, and the more people used it, the higher the risk of death. They spread the word that it could and often did kill on the first use, just as their predecessors had done for crack cocaine. They spread the word that whoever manufactured it had allowed it to be contaminated with various toxins. The same sort of rumors that the government and its many sycophants had used to discredit marijuana, LSD, and psychedelics in general were used to discredit Sybillene.

They spread stories of dire injury, like they did about bathtub gin during the prohibition of alcohol. A lie was most effective when seasoned with some elements of truth. Squeezed between laws and the police, the people became as malleable as a ball of Silly Putty.

Taking Naked Emperor had become akin to playing Russian roulette, not just in the mind of the public—a mind that can change with a well-crafted news report—but in seeming fact. The public had no way of knowing whether a canister of Naked Emperor was real or counterfeit.

And then four school shootings occurred over a week, all in the Northeast corridor of the United States, where Naked Emperor use was most prevalent. The SEA blamed the shootings on the use of Naked Emperor. But, oddly, the perpetrators neither committed suicide nor were captured ... or even identified. Manifestos left at the scenes of these horrors claimed the shooters belonged to a secret club of teenagers who used Naked Emperor to identify the evil of the schools. These manifestos promised more would come. No one knew who wrote them. Apparently there was something about Naked Emperor that made the kids who shot up the schools clever enough to vanish without a trace, without a single witness left alive. The media speculated extensively, with complete confidence and no data whatsoever.

The National Rifle Association immediately lined up with the SEA in assigning blame to Sybillene.

*   *   *

"It's falling apart, Alpha. We have plenty of supply from this last shipment, but I don't think we can sell it. They've executed a gambit; I don't have an effective countermove. This could well be the end of the game."

Alpha had taken the train up from Washington to Penn Station in Manhattan. Today, Alpha would meet Uncle Maurice. "Fighting the government isn't always smart, Paladin. In fact, it's looking suicidal. We all gonna end up in the federal pen, or more likely, just dead. Sorry."

"Trench warfare. We lost our supply chain. We lost some good people. I was naïve not to anticipate how far they might go. Sybillene has the potential to overthrow the way the world works. It should have been obvious they'd stop at nothing."

Alpha rubbed his hand across his smooth scalp. "Another thing that you won't wanna hear: the money flow may be getting compromised too. They figuring out some of the money-moving system you came up with."

"Yeah?"

"I saw in the paper this AM. They found the body of Dr. James Sandridge, squashed into pieces and all over the highway. Police're saying it was suicide."

Charles's head slumped forward. He sighed, and closed his eyes.

Charles had thought he was fighting this class of rent seekers with scientific credentials by using against them the system they had been milking. Their MD credentials and fat NIH grants ensured easy bank credit. Identity theft was easy. Diplomas, Social Security numbers, work records, addresses, and the doctors' excellent credit scores were all a matter of public record. Banks were happy to loan to doctors; they were excellent credit risks.

That money would have been easy to steal. But, apart from being against his personal code, the object of the exercise wasn't just self-enrichment. This effort was purely for the purpose of ensuring that the feds could not follow the money from the street dealers who sold his version of Viagra. All the money that the small dealers took in went to pay the credit lines. All the money was being paid back, ahead of schedule. If anything, these doctors' credit scores were being improved, and they were entirely oblivious to the whole thing. It wasn't supposed to harm these physician-scientists. They certainly weren't supposed to die.

Alpha said, "Didn't you say no one sucking the government's tit is innocent? I understand why you picked the doctors you did in order to get the cash moving. They're not innocent, Paladin. They may not be the ideal targets, but they part of the machine."

"True, my friend, I did say that. But that doesn't mean Sandridge deserved to die; the penalty here is way out of proportion to the crime."

"Don't forget, you didn't kill him."

"If I hadn't used his name, he'd be alive now." Charles held the weight of his head upon his hands, his elbows resting on his knees.

"You didn't kill him, Paladin!"

"Yeah ... well, unintended consequences are a bitch. But who *did* kill him?"

"If it wasn't suicide, then it was SEA. The Fat Man was right. SEA has been killing our men, counterfeiting our drug, and trying to follow our money. SEA killed Sandridge. They must've followed the dealer who pays down that loan. I bet SEA set up the school shootings. Dawg, you know Sybillene don't do that way. It's the SEA. Fowler and his state-trooper goons."

"I haven't met Fowler, but I've seen him. He's everything I detest."

"Me too, Paladin. Me too. It's all SEA, Paladin!"

"Governments put their own survival above anything. It's why almost every country in the world has secret police."

Alpha said, "Including us now."

Charles's teeth clamped shut. The notes of Prokofiev streamed through his mind, the music danced as colors in his eyes. Red, black, angry.

Some people were beyond reform. An active liability to everything they touched. He'd have to work out the moral implications, but it seemed pretty clear that some people just needed killing.

But he couldn't just kill Fowler without *knowing*. Vigilante justice was one thing, but the vigilante had to be much more than just sure of himself. Before going after evil, a moral vigilante actually had to *be right*. It was why vigilantes had a bad name; many acted on emotion alone. In a way, Fowler himself was acting as a vigilante, just under cover of the law. In the drug war, *the law* had unjustly killed and imprisoned myriads—by intent, or by accident.

His racing thoughts were interrupted only because they approached the restaurant where Maurice, for his first expedition out of his home in months, would feast. They entered and easily found the great man.

"Hi, there." Charles protected his uncle's identity as the single most important promise he had ever made.

"Well, m'boy. Shit's hitting the fan, I see."

"Yeah. It appears this is the end game, and checkmate is imminent. This may be my last time dining in a fine establishment for a while."

"They'll be casting a wide net soon."

Charles nodded. But then he scanned the restaurant, not yet resigned to the new reality that his life might change for the worse at any moment. He might as well enjoy dinner. "This is Alpha. Alpha, this is Maurice. You won't ever hear another name."

"Sit down, sit down. Alpha, I hear I need to get to know you. Charles is worried he might be forcibly decommissioned. Rightfully so." He turned to Charles. "I'm sorry, kid. You did good, but they did better. You're going to close up shop?"

"Mostly closed up already. You've got to know when to fold 'em. We'll salvage what we can, and make sure we're not caught in the dragnet." Charles looked at Alpha. Alpha nodded.

Maurice said, "Maybe you can keep the Viagra thing going."

"Others will. But I won't be able to. Donald Debocher is onto me now. He knows they're related."

"Yeah, but where is *he?*"

"What do you mean?"

"News trickling out of Gondwana."

"Something other than the fact that the United Nations blew up my facility and killed our people?"

"Not public yet. But it appears that two Americans—two government special agents, a male and a female—were kidnapped. Word is that a secret society is involved."

"Debocher?"

"Yes. He was one of them."

Tristana might not know yet.

"And the woman? Is it Sabina Heidel?"

"In the flesh. You know she's been working for Paul Samuels?"

"Samuels? The president of the New York Fed? *That* Samuels?"

"The very same. She likes to run with the big dogs. I seriously doubt he'll just let his agent disappear into the boondocks and drive on like nothing happened. She's a wicked and talented vixen, and he's going to want her back."

"And so will her father."

"Oh, that's right. Ted Lichen. He has pull far beyond the IRS now. But not as much as Paul Samuels. Samuels has influence, if not control, over most any government resource he wants. He not only has the ear of Cooligan, he has him by the balls. A president is just hired help, whether he knows it or not. Samuels and his associates aren't just billionaires. They control trillions of dollars, and I mean that literally. They're completely wired with every head of state, all the top generals, agency heads, corporate CEOs, and media moguls. I wouldn't envy anybody that Paul Samuels gets in his sights."

"I'm in his sights, aren't I?"

"Yes, you are. Naked Emperor probably got his attention before you were even aware that it existed. He's that good. He would have known

Naked Emperor was a risk to him and the whole financial system, the same way you knew it. Once he saw what Naked Emperor could do, you never had a chance. He probably had Sabina Heidel in at FDA and DEA within a day, to make sure everything went as he needed it to."

"I knew the establishment would line up against us. But I never gave them credit for as much competence as they've shown."

"Neither have you given them credit for being as genuinely nasty as they are, Charles."

"I started to as soon as Sabina showed up at Visioryme. But I never took seriously the possibility that they'd do anything other than try to shut us down and put us in jail."

"You're still young, kid. Still naïve. It's one thing to be smart. It's another thing to learn to think like a criminal, so you can anticipate their next move. You need more practice being a criminal."

Alpha chuckled. "That's wha' I keep telling him. He's not experienced."

Maurice nodded. "We'll have to take him to school, Alpha, you and I." He turned back to Charles. "I'll check into it, but I bet the SEA is Samuels's creature. All that power SEA has been given? Likely Samuels, pushing the right buttons.

"Once you were in Paul Samuels's sights, it was just a matter of counting the moves until checkmate. He's brilliant. He and Sabina are criminal sociopaths, and very smart ones. They're more Deep State than the intelligence community. Only the smartest and most ruthless sociopaths make it to the level of these … people. Count yourself lucky to have done as well as you did."

"I did well. They did better. What did that one president say? I *misunderestimated* them. I'm going to have to improve my skills, if I'm going to play on the same field with people like that."

"I'll give you a tip: don't ever play on their field."

"Yeah, but what if they're playing on mine, Maurice?"

"Then you find another field. Or maybe blow the field up. What are you going to do, Charles?"

Charles stayed quiet for a long time.

Finally, he said, "I'm going to have dinner."

The three men enjoyed the fine dining that Maurice paid for with a stack of crisp new bills. During the evening, Maurice gained some confidence in Alpha. The two might have to work together, if Charles was out of the picture.

*   *   *

Charles had a long "to do" list.

Right now, he needed to make sure his friends and colleagues were out of harm's way. Collateral damage rained down upon those close to a subject of a manhunt, as had happened to his friends and colleagues eight years ago after Smolderhof's mining fraud in Gondwana. Time to clean up loose ends, and for everybody to make themselves scarce.

Charles processed his anger, allowed his mind to settle, and dropped into meditation, separating himself from the world.

Alpha sat next to him in the back of a black limousine as they headed south to D.C. He pressed the button to close the partition so as to provide some privacy from the hired chauffeur. He watched Charles for twenty minutes, without saying a word.

Charles returned to the present. "OK. Look, Alpha, you need to keep running the business. Sell Fiagara. Help people control their cholesterol and lower their blood pressure. That business can keep going."

Alpha smiled sympathetically. "And Naked Emperor?"

"It's dead for now. We can't win that one. It's not just the government that's lined up against us there. It's the entire world establishment—the financial system, the religious establishment, the media, doctors. Even the NRA."

"I been working these streets a long time, Paladin. Ain't no improving the human condition."

"According to Einstein, after hydrogen, stupidity is the most common thing in the universe. But Naked Emperor isn't gone forever, Alpha. It just has to go into hibernation. For a long while, I fear."

Alpha nodded. "OK, so I get to run the Viagra and semilegal drug operations."

"Let's make a new deal. I won't be the wholesaler anymore."

"Why not? Where you going?"

Charles ignored the question for the moment. "I get five percent royalty off top-line revenue for having built the system. But you're the man now. After I do what I need to do, you'll be in fine shape. It'll be like at the beginning. The cops who aren't on the take will appreciate your help keeping the dealers occupied. You'll be back outside of the SEA's and DEA's range of concern. Save my share. You'll hear from me at some point."

"What about you?"

"They know who I am. I'm a danger to them, but also to you now. And they'll need to have some political closure for Naked Emperor. They need to eliminate Naked Emperor's drug lord. If I stick around, they're gonna find me."

"Run, man. Go to Africa."

Charles couldn't just run. There was something else he had to do.

"There are thousands of canisters of poisonous counterfeit Sybillene still out there. The people who've bought those canisters won't believe the government stories; they know that SEA has lied to them all along. The problem is that, this time, they're telling the truth. We're living in Bizarro World. People need to know that those canisters are deadly. It's not just a question of more people dying, but the *best* people dying. The people who *want* to take Sybillene are exactly the ones we most want to see alive, and exactly who SEA and Paul Samuels want dead."

Alpha looked at him expectantly.

Charles shook his head. "I have to do whatever it takes to get the word out. There's no choice. What I have to do may end up getting *me* dead."

"Ahh, man."

"I have to discredit Seth Fowler, in a way that's going to stick."

"*Dis*-credit Seth Fowler!" Alpha looked partly amused. "That better be your word for capping that cat!"

"It wasn't what I was thinking."

Charles's phone rang. He didn't recognize the number, which was as it should be. At this point, no one should use their own phone to call him.

It was Tristana. He hoped she'd heard about her husband.

"Tristana, hi."

"Hi, Charles. I'm just checking with you. I haven't heard from Rainbow in a few days. Is she OK?"

"Hold on, Tristana." Charles's heart dropped into his belly. He looked at Alpha with no effort to conceal concern. "Has Rainbow been with you for the last couple of days?"

Alpha shook his head slowly, while suspicion and fear began to grow on his face.

Charles turned back to the phone. "No, Tristana. Neither Alpha nor I have heard from her. How long's it been?"

"Um. Since Monday morning, I think. There's usually something from her. Not this time."

"You've tried her cell?"

"Straight to voice mail. Charles, I'm worried about her."

Charles looked into Alpha's eyes. "Yeah, we are too. We'll find her. And she'll be fine, OK?"

His words could not calm her apprehension. And now he would add to it.

"Have you heard from Donald?"

"Not in a week."

"He's in Gondwana. And he's missing."

"Missing?"

"Possibly kidnapped." He added more, perhaps in an effort to mitigate any misplaced feelings of guilt Tristana might have. "He and Sabina Heidel, both. They were traveling together."

Tristana, like so many people, could become ice cold when she needed to.

"His kidnappers best not count on me to pay any ransom. Donald Debocher can rot in hell. Now you go find Rainbow, Charles. Find her."

*   *   *

Rainbow sat on a hard metal chair, her hands restrained behind her back by a zip tie, shoulders pulled back. Everything in her body either ached or burned. But mostly, she was frightened out of her wits.

She'd been scared before, more times than she could remember. She'd learned not to show it. But this time, she knew her fear must be visible to the man who appeared every few hours. How could he not notice?

To Rainbow's sore and heavy eyes, the man who appeared in her cell, for it seemed a cell, embodied evil. He didn't care that she sat there in pain. He didn't care that she was parched, so dry that her tongue stuck to the back of her teeth when she had, so briefly, fallen asleep. He didn't care that she needed to go to the bathroom so badly that she could now hardly breathe. This man, who had introduced himself as Seth Fowler, was devoid of feelings.

"I'm thirsty. I need the bathroom," she croaked. Tears would have dripped down her face had she sufficient water in her body. Instead, her eyes felt as though she had walked through a sandstorm.

Her pleas to Fowler received only nasty rejections. She now knew antagonism was the only response to expect from him.

So when Fowler's response this time proved different, she felt hope. Yet all he had said was "I need information."

To Rainbow, it sounded like an invitation, or even an offer. Maybe there was a long-shot possibility that he'd grant her base biological needs. When you're simultaneously dying of thirst and about to wet your pants, priorities change. Lower brain functions displace the higher ones. Maslow's hierarchy would put rationality way below thirst, hunger, pain, and misery, regardless of the long-term cost. It's the same hardwired component of the reptilian brain that gets co-opted by addictions: to food, to sex, to drugs.

The fact Fowler responded with something other than an outright denial, or a smack with a rolled-up magazine, filled Rainbow with unexpected optimism. She found herself warming to the man. Whereas earlier, she had dreaded his voice, the sound of his boots scuffing the floor, and the cologne he wore, now she was glad he had entered the room. Hope does strange things to a desperate mind.

There was a chance.

She reflected back on the last three days.

They may have been watching the spot for weeks, or longer. Since Roberta had disappeared—hopefully running off to Texas or Montana with her boyfriend as she had long planned—Rainbow had avoided this drop-off site, just in case Roberta had moved on to worse pastures instead of better ones.

The space beside the FedEx box, where a handful of other packages that couldn't fit through the slot awaited their daily three o'clock pickup, provided fine cover for an occasional drop-off of Viagra and Naked Emperor. With this method, the worst thing that could happen was a failed pickup—FedEx would find a box addressed to a nonexistent person in Albuquerque, and without proper payment. The box would be set aside somewhere at FedEx headquarters. The drug would be wasted, but it was cheap. The safety of the system would be preserved.

This time, however, safety failed. As Rainbow placed her box among the others, a man had approached, with package in hand, apparently to do the same for a legitimate shipment.

The man placed his own box on the floor, and then blocked Rainbow's egress, both with his bulk and with his badge. The badge had a snake molded onto it. Rainbow tried to push by, but he threw her against a wall. Within a minute, she was cuffed and searched, her weapons—a knife and a small .25-caliber pistol—both taken. Minutes later she was in the agent's car, and twenty minutes after that, she had landed in this room, where she had been for two days, with one, and only one, trip to a bathroom.

Rainbow knew what had distinguished her from others who innocently placed their boxes into FedEx's trust. The man hadn't picked up on her hair or clothes, now more conservative than in months past, but on her gloves. Gloves protected the box from fingerprints, adding an important layer of protection. Since the creation of SEA, precautions seemed wise. But this time, it backfired. In the warmth of the early autumn, the gloves marked her.

She was proud of one thing. As always, just in case she was caught, she had hidden her cell phone before her rounds. Doing so provided a layer of protection for those who might panic when her absence was noted: Alpha, Epsilon, Charles, Tristana.

Water. She needed it. She begged for it. And a bathroom. It was all she wanted in the world.

And this man, Fowler, gave her hope.

*　　*　　*

"They got her," Charles said, looking at the floor of Xander's apartment. "Somehow they got her."

Charles sat by the kitchen table. Tristana stood next to Alpha by the balcony door.

"SEA, Fowler's goons," Charles added.

Tristana said, "We don't know that."

Alpha put a hand on Tristana's arm. "It happened, Tristana. We don't know exactly what happened. We don't know *how* it happened. Or where she is for sure. And we don't know what to do about it yet. But we'll figure it out."

Tristana choked on a sob. She had always disliked Fowler, but now she hated him.

"Look, honey. Most of our folks picked up for Naked Emperor get their day in court. Sometimes it takes a while, but they do."

"But some never do. Isn't that right?"

"Some never do, Tristana. But that's not my Rainbow. She a survivor. And we're not gonna sit idly by. We'll take care of this, girl."

"I'll call Fowler. Or I'll call Kate. Kate's his wife."

"It's a thought," Charles said. "But we have to think through the implications."

Tristana shouted back, "The implications are that I tell Fowler to let Rainbow go!"

Alpha reached out a hand and placed it on Tristana's shoulder. It served to comfort her a bit. But he couldn't hide that he was, like her, seething. "Would a man like Fowler do what you ask, Tristana?"

She tried to control her fury. She tried to think. What would Fowler do? He'd deny it, of course. He wouldn't tell Kate he had a kid locked up. He didn't have to admit anything to anybody about Rainbow or anyone else.

Charles spoke in a low tone, looking again at the floor. "Asking Fowler for anything just strengthens his hand. And it won't help us get Rainbow back. No. I've got to come forward. They don't want Rainbow. They don't want the people they're locking up. They want *me*." He looked at Tristana. "I'm going to need you to do me a favor."

He explained what he needed.

When he was through, and when she had failed to convince him to think of something else, anything else, Tristana tried to recover by looking out over the river, but she couldn't focus.

Stephan was dead, along with other friends at Visioryme: killed by the United Nations. Her drug, her baby, banned and now blamed for illness and death in numerous cities. Her trust in herself and her reputation in pharmaceutical development would never recover. Rainbow was missing, and likely in some nameless prison.

And now Charles was about to embark on a suicide mission in a probably futile attempt at damage control.

He hadn't caused the damage. He hadn't created Sybillene, or Naked Emperor. He hadn't destroyed her marriage or kidnapped her husband. He hadn't killed Stephan. He hadn't closed down Visioryme. He hadn't murdered schoolchildren. He hadn't supplied a poisoned counterfeit drug to an innocent population.

And he hadn't allowed Rainbow to be captured.

Charles had done *nothing* wrong. Yet he was the catalyst for so much of what had ended up wrong.

She thought she might love him, but wished she had never met him.

45

Who Needs Killing?

ALBERT Peale could help address a deadly predicament. But he wasn't allowed out of New York.

Tristana rode a train to New York City to meet him.

She walked through the door to the coffee shop rendezvous and picked out Peale almost as fast as he found her.

"Mr. Peale, thank you for meeting with me."

"It's a pleasure, Ms. Debocher. You're a hero to many." He guided her to a booth in the corner, where no one would bother them.

She didn't feel anything like a hero. She felt like a failure. She felt frightened. She felt that imprisonment was her future. Still, she tried to maintain an even temper. "You started the ball rolling, Mr. Peale. *You* should be the hero. You named Naked Emperor, after all."

"I wonder how long we heroes will be staying out of prison. Or alive. Heroes often wind up dead."

"Maybe not long, Mr. Peale. The guy who runs SEA—Fowler—is a horrible man. I knew him for a while, some years back."

"I sympathize with you then. The guy's not going to let his baby die just because Sybillene disappears. They claim those school shootings and other murders were done by Sybillene users. It's a perfect excuse to go after anyone who acts, or talks—or even thinks—like they might have once used Naked Emperor. They've turned this into a crisis. And like that schmuck in Chicago said, you *can't let a good crisis go to waste*."

"They'll watch *you* for sure."

"They're already whacking at me. IRS audits. Searches of my apartment when I'm away. Police surveillance. Tapping my phones—not just the NSA-type stuff everybody gets, but a warm body paying attention. So much for freedom of the press. It's easy for them. I'm a convicted felon on probation! I'm surprised they haven't just shipped me back to the can without telling anyone. They could, any day. It's almost as if they're toying with me, playing some kind of psychological game. Maybe they're trying to push me over the edge. Maybe they have other plans. Some kind of PR coup."

"Or maybe they're looking to get something on your contacts…"

"Yeah, that could be. These SEA people are evil. It's not like they were recruited from ads on pizza boxes like the TSA. It's like they select these guys based on their character. Or lack of it."

"You may not know the half of it, Mr. Peale."

"I expect you wanted to meet to tell me the other half. I'll be honest with you, Ms. Debocher. I've been *advised* not to publish anything more about Naked Emperor."

"Who advised you?"

"Goons in cheap suits dragged me to Fowler."

"Fowler threatened you?"

"Not even remotely, and that's the most powerful threat of all. They lectured me on the greater good. This whole country is turning into a giant Milgram experiment."

She looked at Peale. "We need a favor."

"I'm listening."

"We've found counterfeit Sybillene, and lots of it."

"It's what's making people sick."

Tristana asked, "You knew this already?"

"Sure. I enhance regularly now. It makes seeing stuff like that a lot easier."

"Enhance?"

"Yeah. You know. I keep some Naked Emperor around where the goons don't know to look. I use it when studying material. I *enhance*. Lots of people do."

"Enhance. I guess that's a new term?"

"Not *that* new. I heard it from someone who heard it from someone who claimed some judges enhance before complicated decisions."

"Aren't you worried about getting counterfeit Naked Emperor?"

"Old supply. I haven't bought any since the counterfeit stuff came out. So, what do you want me to do?"

"It's not going to be easy. I want you to publish some incomplete truth. I'm going to *tell* you the whole truth, but then I'm going to ask that you not reveal the part that you will most want to reveal."

"That's a lot to ask, Ms. Debocher. If I were interested in writing what other people told me to, I'd be rich, famous, and working for the 'Washington Post.'"

"If we didn't think you were special, we wouldn't have come to you."

"Who is *we?*"

"Charles Knight and I."

"Nice young man. So, what's the big news that you don't want me to include?"

"The counterfeit Sybillene was made by the SEA, and they're the ones putting it on the street. SEA put vanadium chloride and cyanide in those canisters, the ones that are killing so many people."

Peale stood up, knocking his half-filled coffee cup on the floor with a thud. "Jesus H. Christ! Not even those assholes would do that."

"You're wrong. They can and did."

Peale shook his head, eyes closed, face taut.

"It's happened before."

Peale declared, "Yeah, in Nazi Germany, in Stalin's Russia! During the Spanish Inquisition. But it's happening *here?*"

"Mr. Peale, this country isn't what it used to be. To them, it's for the *greater good*."

"Can we really be so foolish, Miss Debocher?" He thought for a minute. "Yes, we can."

They sat in silence for a time.

Peale looked up. "I assume you got proof."

"That doesn't matter. Remember, that's the part we don't want you to mention."

"What *do* you want me to mention?"

Tristana replied, "Our first job is to warn people. I can't stand by and watch mass murder."

"That's what you want me to do? Warn people? The best way to do that is to tell the whole truth."

"No. The people we're up against have way too much power with the media. If we tell too much of the truth, the first thing that'll happen is that we'll be painted as wacky conspiracy theorists, the ones with tin-foil hats. We won't be able to make this stick to SEA. We don't have sufficiently convincing evidence. People just won't buy it. It's not just that they already don't believe most of the media; they don't know *who* to believe. So they'll keep taking the fake drug in an effort to perceive the truth. And they'll keep dying."

He replied, "What's the second thing that's going to happen?"

Tristana sadly shook her head. "They'll wait until nobody is thinking of you, and then they'll disappear you. Charles thinks the SEA is becoming the most powerful agency of the U.S. government. He thinks that its powers will be used to create a real secret police. Thought police. Fingermen in the real world. If you accuse SEA, you'll be disposed of, Mr. Peale, and have accomplished nothing. We have to get enough of the truth out there to protect the people. That's our priority. If we do this right, the people will listen to you. They'll listen to me. They'll listen to Charles. We all have a role."

"Charles Knight is a folk hero. Not everywhere, but he is with smart people. Like Timothy Leary was to many in my generation."

"Yes, well, he couldn't care less about being a celebrity."

"That may be the only thing that will keep him alive…"

"Charles is going to ask everyone to stop using Naked Emperor, for their own protection, because the supply has been irredeemably corrupted."

Peale shook his head. "The school shootings on top of all the deaths haven't gotten people to stop using it. People truly *like* your drug, Ms. Debocher. Despite all the propaganda, all the manipulations, the severity of the punishments, the school shootings, and now poisoning the supply. It doesn't seem to matter; people will use Naked Emperor. It's not because they're addicts, feeling sick in withdrawal. *It's because they value the truth so much that they are willing to risk their lives!*"

Tristana said, "It makes me feel like Eve, offering everybody the forbidden fruit."

"Yes, Tristana. You planted the Tree of Knowledge of Good and Evil in our garden. And your customers want to eat from it. Even under threat of death by God himself."

"Or rather the SEA. Mr. Peale, that's exactly our fear. The people who will still use Naked Emperor, despite the media storm against it, are the very people SEA *wants* to kill. Any Sybillene out there could be poisoned.

397

Charles says we've been checkmated. I think we folk heroes of Naked Emperor—you, Charles, Tim McBride, me—*we* need to be the trusted information source for the people. Or else they won't believe, and a lot of them will die."

"They'll want more of the *real* Naked Emperor, you know."

"Well, for a while, there won't be any more real Naked Emperor. A U.N. air strike at our facility in Gondwana killed almost all the people involved in making it."

"*You've* been the ones making it, then, ever since Visioryme was shut down?"

"Yes."

"Well, I won't release *that* information, at least."

"But you need to. Charles wants you to. All the blame is to go on Charles Knight. That's how he wants it."

There was no other way. Charles would risk a lifetime in prison, or worse, to save the people who were now in danger ... endangered by the evil of their own government.

*　*　*

Charles had to assume Rainbow was still alive, because there was no acceptable alternative. He wracked his brain for a way to neutralize Seth Fowler and rescue her.

It seemed completely hopeless, but he had the kernel of an idea. He started making calls, the most important one first.

Charles wasn't sure how to ask for what he sought, or even exactly what he needed. TJ could make no promises, but Charles was confident TJ could reach anyone and accomplish almost anything in Gondwana. Connections and family relationships counted far more there than in the U.S.

Charles had to assume TJ's success, also because there were no alternatives. He had no backup plan. Which is a mistake even under the best of conditions.

It was as if he were playing poker with a short stack, and an unsuited 2-7 for a hand. Dark thoughts consumed him, more so than at any other time of his life. Much of the nation stood ready to rip out his throat. The whole of the established system—cultural, religious, social, and political—

had allied with the spin power of the media against Naked Emperor, and against him.

In contrast, Fowler had become a media hero, the handsome point man working for the safety and security of the nation to destroy the drug that threatened them all.

"When are they going to come for you, Paladin?" Alpha asked.

"Soon."

Alpha's eyes reflected the concern of the true friend he'd become. Charles knew his real name now, as Alpha knew Charles's. But the names didn't matter. Loyalty, mutual respect, their effectiveness as a team to accomplish their common aims, their willingness—which became eagerness—to help each other, were far more important than names. It trumped any differences in race, culture, and experience.

He sat in Alpha's new home, a renovated townhouse in D.C.'s Shaw area. Once the home of an upper middle class white family, then used for decades as a flop house by ghetto blacks, and now on its way up again. Spacious, classy, but modest enough not to attract undue attention.

Charles was no Sydney Carton, although it was quite possible that he would now suffer a similar fate, perhaps not by guillotine, but by bullet to the head. He might be trading his life for the lives of many others, as had Carton. If he had to die, it wouldn't be out of altruism, but because he felt he had, in a way, created the problem. So he had to accept responsibility for it.

Was it even possible to stop psychopaths like Seth Fowler or Paul Samuels from killing, controlling, manipulating, and destroying? He thought not. *Short of becoming an assassin.*

The insane mob mentality of the French Revolution hadn't yet taken control in the U.S.—although the situation could easily devolve into that. But the country was unstable and degraded enough that it was possible for a few criminals at the top of the pyramid to infect the whole country. Would Germany have turned bad in the 1930s without Hitler? Would the Soviet gulags of the 1950s have existed without Stalin? Would the disastrous Chinese Great Proletarian Cultural Revolution of the 1960s have existed without Mao? History was full of similar questions.

And so it occurred to Charles, as it had occurred to others before him: If he took out the really bad apples, would it make a meaningful difference?

And, perhaps more important, should he? Perhaps an assassin could be an effective agent of good.

No one was killing the sociopaths, or even calling them out. In fact, most of the country thought they were heroes.

Most likely the story would end with *Charles* dead, or perhaps imprisoned in one of their un-named dungeons somewhere.

Charles had so far avoided the psychological prison most Americans now lived in. He would not abide a lifetime of physical prison.

He saw a picture of himself on the television screen. Alpha tossed him the remote, and he turned up the volume.

The network news anchor spewed out what the teleprompter told her to say. Charles snorted in amusement. The very same anchor regularly ridiculed the U.S. president for doing exactly the same thing.

"Charles Knight—the promoter of Naked Emperor—thought to be a hero in the eyes of some, but in reality an associate of the Mexican drug cartels, has been knocked off his pedestal. According to newspaper editor Albert Peale, the man who gave Naked Emperor its name, Charles Knight has asked all people to stop using his drug, as even he admits that it has proven too dangerous."

The screen cut to a shot of *Albert Peale, Journalist—New York City*. A viewer could assume that what followed was the truth according to Peale. But since he was never permitted to speak on camera, the discerning mind might question the provenance of the story that emerged. Of course, the report was completely unfavorable to Charles, and only faintly resembled reality. It was like most news stories on television: packaged infotainment and *agitprop*.

The meteorologist sitting at the desk alongside the anchor served as a sort of sidekick, the comic relief spicing up the anchor's recitation. But now he effected a serious face, reflecting the gravity of the matter. "My, my," he said. "You know that Naked Emperor is bad when the drug lord selling it begs everyone to stop using his poison."

The anchor replied, "Yes, Jim. It just goes to show how important the Food and Drug Administration is, protecting us for all these years. You know, the men and women of the FDA are really the unsung heroes here."

"I have to agree, Jane. Although let's not forget the boys from the SEA. It's hard to believe that some people want Charles Knight to run for president. I agree with SEA. I think he needs to be in prison."

"With the manhunt for him now, he'll be behind bars soon. Should we give him some credit for finally speaking up, though?"

Charles turned off the television before the blow-dried and braindead television personalities could deny him even that empty credit. He tossed the remote on the sofa next to him.

"I've never felt so powerless, Alpha."

Alpha, a pragmatist at heart, replied, "So how we gonna kill 'em?"

Charles didn't like killing, but he knew he *could* kill in self-defense. Or to protect an innocent victim, although that was a slippery slope, requiring exquisitely careful consideration.

He needed help thinking this out. So he asked, "Kill exactly whom?"

Alpha answered from the kitchen, reaching into his refrigerator. "Anyone who's been part of this. Anyone who had a hand in hurtin' our girl."

"Even that horrible news anchor?"

His voice came back muffled. "I know what you're sayin'. That's up to you, Paladin. They in it up to their necks too."

"It's not right to kill people just because they're stupid, Alpha."

Alpha handed him a bottle of beer. "True dat. But don't let stupid be an excuse for evil either, dawg. I wasn't thinking of them news-losers. They just bit players. But we gotta put Seth Fowler on ice."

"I know."

Charles had been here before, deciding whether to kill an evil being or let it continue to exist and wreak havoc. Killing another human required dehumanizing him. Then you weren't killing a person, you were just killing "the enemy" or "a threat." On the other hand, when it came to killing active, proven sociopaths, dehumanizing took less effort, for they fully dehumanized themselves.

"I don't think Fowler is the type to surround himself with guards. He sees himself as a tough guy. He's making himself into a national hero. And he's not a target of drug cartels, so he doesn't feel threatened."

"But he needs to be a target of *our* little cartel, Paladin! Let's stop talking about it. Say we go find out how easy it is to take him out."

Charles exhaled. Behind Fowler were others. An unlimited supply of creatures like him were building blocks in the pyramid of government power. Knocking the top of the pyramid off just made room for the next guy.

They were like sharks' teeth; you pulled one out only to find a dozen more in back of it. And then, behind them all, stood men like Paul Samuels. How many would have to be taken out before their system would collapse?

"All right. Can you get the Alphabet Men to watch Fowler for a few days? See what more we can learn. I'll do my homework. Maybe the solution to the Fowlers of the world is to do just as you say."

"Yeah. Kill 'em until they dead. We got your back, Paladin. You stay down for the next couple of days. Can't have them finding you first."

*　*　*

Paul Samuels walked into Seth Fowler's office in a rush.

"Thank you for seeing me, Mr. Fowler."

Fowler had no idea who this man was until a few minutes before his arrival. To him, the president of a bank meant a nerd in a suit, albeit a nerd with influence. The president of the New York Fed, as a source of much of the government's money, had power. It would be wise to know the man. And then have his staff get to know *about* the man, as well. SEA should develop a thick and incriminating dossier on every important person.

"What can I do for you, Mr. Samuels?"

"Sabina Heidel. What do you know?"

"What is your interest?" Fowler guessed at it, but wrongly.

"Ms. Heidel has worked with me for several years. She is a highly valued asset to the Federal Reserve Bank."

Fowler had no recollection that Sabina had worked for the Fed.

"As part of the president's government-efficiency program?"

"Effectively yes, Agent Fowler."

"It's *Director* Fowler, actually."

"Of course."

By means of hints and suggestions, Paul Samuels made it clear that Sabina was accustomed to circulating with powerful men. The commissioner of the IRS was her father, for god's sake. And Vice Chairman Samuels was her direct boss. From what he gleaned, she even used to date the president of the United States. Maybe she still did.

But none of that made much difference. Fowler had both little hope and little concern that Sabina Heidel would be recovered from the clutches of the secret society that had kidnapped her in Gondwana. How do you find, much less rescue, someone who's been carried off into the jungle of an obscure, backward country? He would miss her presence. He would miss her skin, her scent, her body. But he had to admit it would be safest for him if Sabina was permanently silenced. He couldn't quite tell Samuels that, of course.

The U.S.-government intelligence agencies knew little to nothing about the activities of the secret societies. Fowler heard that, once captured, rarely did anyone escape. If Sabina were alive, she'd be held captive far out in the bush, never again to be seen by a civilized man. Even a full invasion force of U.N. peacekeepers wouldn't find her. They'd be tramping around the jungle for months, constantly misdirected by the natives. Although, from what Fowler heard, just such a U.N. force was already arriving in Gondwana to search for her, door-to-door, with no regard for anything but the mission. For a time, the people of Gondwana would be treated like the people of Kabul or Baghdad. And they still would never find her.

"I'm sorry about this whole situation, Mr. Samuels. We're doing everything we know to do." Which wasn't much.

"And I'm grateful, Director Fowler. I'm pulling every string I have. She's very important."

Fowler had never seen a man so near to spontaneous human combustion as Paul Samuels. All that money, all the power he wielded, and yet the man would lose to some uneducated and impoverished spear chuckers in an African wasteland—men who'd never heard of him and likely wouldn't care if they had.

Fowler didn't give the other kidnap victim, Debocher, his old neighbor, much thought. Whereas he could see Sabina serving some diabolical use, Debocher would serve little purpose for the secret societies. Perhaps his death would assuage the anger of some weather god. Maybe they'd eat him. He imagined natives dancing around, bones in their noses, as Debocher was cooked in a big iron pot. Good riddance. Debocher had been both a nuisance and a menace. And no more valuable to him than any other sniveling spy inside FDA.

He'd already lined up a new source for FDA insider-investment tips.

*   *   *

Fowler had a meeting at the White House later that morning, to brief the chief of staff on the successful campaign against Naked Emperor.

He had to wait outside of Stafford's office for an hour. As he became more powerful, it became harder for him to suppress his anger at the slight.

"Sorry, Seth. I was with the president." Stafford strode briskly through his office door, removed his suit coat, and laid it over his chair.

Fowler followed. "No problem." A file should be put together on Stafford as well. Was he a drug user? A child molester? A wife beater? Who knew what bad habits he'd picked up swimming in the D.C. cesspool for so many years.

"What's the situation with Charles Knight?"

"He's hiding out, waiting to get arrested," Fowler replied. "We'll find him soon enough. I intend to grind him to dust."

Stafford nodded slowly before replying, "We don't think that's a good idea, Seth."

"What? Why not?"

"If it goes to trial, he might be found innocent."

"But he confessed."

"Indirectly, to a journalist. The attorney general says that confession won't stand up."

Fowler leaned forward. "But he's a danger to everything we stand for. I want Knight in prison, or dead." Knight's note had taunted him at the port in Baltimore, and Fowler could not allow that to stand.

"Fowler, let me make this clear. Knight's *not* important. It's *you* who's important. *SEA is important.* While Congress and the media have been distracted with fears of Sybillene, we've accomplished what we never thought possible."

"What do you mean?"

"I mean that there's never been an agency with the powers of SEA. It should be able to trump the FBI or the CIA, and it's small and personal enough that we can direct it. Those big agencies are so entrenched that they have lives of their own. The paranoids and conspiracy theorists are actually more right than they know. The CIA, the FBI—and for that matter the NSA, DEA, ATF—they actually *are* out of control. They generate their own incomes, they have their own private armed forces, and they don't have to come begging for money or disclose their black ops. We can't be sure that they're even working for us anymore.

"The Naked Emperor crisis has led to the creation of what this country needs to survive the trying times ahead. The SEA now has more official *legal power* than any of them, but it's small enough—and we'll maintain the kind of personal relationship—that we can keep it under control, and useful. So you see, the enforcement precedents that SEA has established can't be risked for your vendetta against one man. If we're going to get Knight into prison, it needs to be done without a trial."

"So you'd prefer him dead?"

Stafford shook his head slowly. "I don't want him to have a trial. But I don't want SEA seen leading the charge against Charles Knight either. We're not interested in making him into a martyr."

"Oh, come on, Stafford! You can't let the guy skate!"

"Don't forget that FDA approved the drug in the first place. Look, Seth. The guy came forward and basically took responsibility for the whole thing, including all the deaths, including the school shootings. A lot of people think he's a hero, trying to save lives. And plenty of them still believe in Naked Emperor. Sure, a lot more are calling for his head on a platter. But we're not interested in making this into another O.J. Simpson trial. We've accomplished the mission; SEA is here, and it's ours. We don't need people asking all the whys and wherefores. Let the dust settle. Let our position consolidate."

Fowler had to let that all sink in for a minute.

Stafford continued. "Our friendly news anchors are, for the first time in years, holding hands with the Republicans for chrissake! Everyone is standing together to support SEA and all your good work."

Fowler thought about it. Indeed the pro-gun lobby blamed Naked Emperor for the school shootings, while the gun *control* lobby also blamed Naked Emperor for creating the psychological conditions that *led* to the school shootings. The Baptists blamed Naked Emperor for destroying family values. Hell, the pope himself lambasted Naked Emperor as a modern black plague, a scourge on the faithful. It was something almost everybody could agree on.

"You see it, don't you, Seth? This is an opportunity we must not squander. We can't have this thing turn into a circus. It's too early to exhume bodies, parse evidence, and examine the SEA's powers in the judicial system. We need to let its powers mature, like a good scotch. So we want him quiet and suppressed as fast as possible; the news cycle will drive on, and people will forget about him. They'll just have a vague memory that there was a huge danger, but due to their government's quick and efficient action it was averted, and normal life can go on."

Fowler considered. He wanted Knight dead. And he wanted SEA strong. He wanted *both.*

Stafford spoke again, with his voice softer. "We're going to control this case very carefully. The attorney general is taking it from here."

Fowler ground his jaw, making no effort to hide his feelings. All he said in words, however, was a deliberate "Just let me know what you want me to do."

Stafford replied almost off-handedly. "We think, at this point, it's best if you stay out of the Knight affair entirely. We want you to focus your efforts on cementing SEA's position in a post-Sybillene world. Never let a good crisis go to waste, huh? SEA is far too valuable an asset to endanger. It's still just a toddler. We're thinking about how to use SEA going forward. I'd like you to think on this as well, and report back to me in two days how you recommend carrying SEA forward into this new era we've opened up. For the moment, the plan is to declare victory, and drive on."

And with that, Stafford turned to other matters, and Fowler was dismissed.

*   *   *

Fowler marched out of the White House barely in control of his rising fury. Stay away from Knight? Really?

Stafford's reasoned arguments meant nothing. Leave Knight to the attorney general? Was the man serious? Was Stafford that dimwitted?

Knight needed to go down hard, Stafford be damned. Fowler could come up with so many reasons to justify Knight's death. But he didn't require even a single justification beyond his own instinct that *he* was better off with Knight dead.

Like the president himself, Stafford would be out of the White House someday. But Fowler intended to stay in power for much longer. Soon, if he could stay in control of SEA, Fowler would be giving orders to Stafford and anyone else he wanted. *Soon* could not come soon enough.

Fowler's energy rose as he left the White House grounds, walking out through the southeast gate. His pulse pumped in his ears, the blood a hammer drill in his head. He knew what was happening. It had been too long. It was one thing running the killer elite agency. But he needed to stay in tune personally. And he missed his playmate.

He crossed the street to the Willard Intercontinental, almost adjacent to the White House, where he had spent so many afternoons with Sabina Heidel. The opulent hotel served as a transient palace for the powerful, and for those who strived to be powerful.

He was livid, and he didn't care who saw it. The doorman picked up on the fury and moved to inject himself between Fowler and the hotel lobby, but Fowler showed him his SEA badge and flipped the man a middle finger. Fowler possessed power equivalent to the Stasi of East Germany, the Gestapo, the Untouchables, or Stalin's secret police. He had the power to do whatever he wanted. Who would challenge him?

He was on a mission to get to the bar, and one of the high-end prostitutes that, with fat tips to the bartender and hotel security, used the place as an informal office.

The young woman that found him twenty minutes later possessed a splendid smile and enticing physique. The oldest male and female occupations—the mercenary and the prostitute—usually worked under assumed names. Her nom de guerre was China.

He and China stayed together all night, in a room up high overlooking the White House, and made a date to repeat the mutually beneficial transaction. He tipped her handsomely before booking the same suite for two days later. Next time, she'd be waiting for him in the room.

Sex was almost as satisfying as violence.

Fowler paid China well enough, sure, but it was another man, one whom she had known since childhood, who had paid her even more.

46

Getting to Know You...

FROM one of many burner phones he now possessed, Charles made the call he had avoided for far too long. He would have to keep it short to avoid tracking. They were almost certainly monitoring his father's phone.

"Dad, it's not the way it sounds, I promise you."

Charles's father, a widower for more than fifteen years, was a flag-waving patriot supporting the United States in the naïve and unexamined belief that it was still America. He said, "Pshaw." And then he said it again, as if it were a real word.

Charles's father neither looked nor acted much like Charles. Nor could the smile always on Charles's face be considered a genetic gift from the senior Mr. Knight. There had been a slight distance between the two men even before his mother had died, and certainly after. His father was so unlike his mother, whose love to this day, long after her death, influenced the way Charles related to people in general. Her love had flowed profound and constant, whereas his father's was aloof and irregular.

Seven years out of the country had not drawn them closer.

Neither of his parents had the whole answer. A love provided with no demand for return, or an unrequited love, or a love that persisted no matter what infraction and betrayal occurred, was a love that risked moral hazard, that risked abuse. Conversely, a love that required some regular payment was little more than emotional prostitution. The latter was his father's style. Charles could have used—at this most trying moment of his life—some of his mother's manner of love instead.

"Charles, I told you to be careful."

"You always told me that, Dad."

"Why don't you listen?"

"I do listen."

"Yeah, but you ignore my advice."

"I don't ignore it. I just don't always follow it. I've always wanted an exotic, adventurous life. I knew there'd be some risks…"

Charles carefully did not say he strove for a *good* life, for fear of implying that his father's life was not good. In fact, his father was a good man who had provided solid guidance throughout his childhood—he was always a good influence. And not all fathers were. Like Peale, his father still edited a small, perpetually struggling newspaper. It was never much of a business, and it had gotten even worse since the Internet took hold. But he stuck with it because it kept him immersed in his town.

He was a little like Peale that way. Decent and honest. But he held to a morality based on authority. That narrowed his thinking. He rarely left his small town in Montana, and that isolated him from outside ideas. But, on the bright side, it kept him far away, physically and psychologically, from the parasites and fetor permeating Washington, D.C. He always blamed its troubles on the *other* political party.

"What happens next, son?"

"I've been laying low for a few days. And I may need to be out of touch for a while."

"That's nothing new. Where are you going this time? Antarctica?"

"I'll let you know my plans as soon as I can."

"If they catch you, you'll go to prison."

"I know that."

There was a long pause on the phone, during which time Charles wondered how the man could tolerate his son being not just a jailbird, but a notorious enemy of the state. Perhaps it was easier than having his son on the street, dealing drugs, which was how he thought of Charles now.

"Charles, you be careful."

"This time I will, Dad."

"I love you, son."

It sounded flat.

Maybe his father felt compelled to mention his love only when faced with unbearable loss, as when his mother lay on her deathbed. His expression of love marked the end of a chapter, not the beginning of one. It was no way to love, Charles thought, as his father hung up the phone.

* * *

It had taken Charles an hour to work his way through the New York Fed's bureaucracy to get through to Paul Samuels's secretary, and more time before he could connect with the man himself. To get past the secretary, he had to drop names. His own name, and that of Sabina Heidel. They were sufficient. Paul Samuels responded.

"Mr. Samuels," Charles said through the phone, "I believe that you and I have been at odds for many months now."

"Have we, Mr. Knight?"

"Oh yes. Of course we have. We might as well admit that, so we can move on to shared interests."

"And what shared interests are those?"

Charles had to play it cool with the man. Mr. Samuels needed to understand that this would be a level playing field, a situation Samuels wasn't used to.

"Sir, we each have something important to us, in the custody of an enemy."

"Oh, I see. Should I assume you're involved in the kidnapping of Ms. Heidel?"

"I imagine it would be a relief to you if I *were* involved. But I'm not. However, my sources concur with yours. The male secret society in Gondwana has her. It's unlikely the U.S. or the United Nations will be able to get her back. But that doesn't mean she's irretrievable."

"No? You believe *you* have influence?"

"It's possible. You have influence over matters that I care about, and I have influence over matters of interest to you. Perhaps neither can make any guarantees..."

Samuels angrily interrupted. "Then why are we talking?"

"Because *no one* can make guarantees when dealing with secret societies or corrupt bureaucracies, Mr. Samuels. However, with some effort, each of us has a reasonable chance of getting what the other wants."

"I presume you're seeking something non-monetary, then."

"I have no interest in your counterfeit dollars, Mr. Samuels."

"Of course. You would be more interested in gold."

"In this case, I'll insist on something even more valuable than gold."

Samuels replied, "And what might that be?"

"My needs are simple and cost you little."

"I don't see myself trusting a drug dealer."

"Oh, Mr. Samuels, I'm not a drug dealer. A whole new agency has been formed just to hunt me down. I think that entitles me to the moniker of drug *lord*. Don't you agree?"

"Amusing, Mr. Knight. But we have serious issues in front of us. How do you propose to establish the necessary trust?"

"I don't. I expect that you influenced the creation of the SEA, partly because you wanted to eliminate one of the most valuable aids ever developed in the cause of human liberty: truth. You've set up what amounts to a secret police force. And, by the way, destroyed my company and killed my friends. You're a criminal, Mr. Samuels. And I'm your sworn enemy. So there can be no trust."

"I see. Without trust, how can we accomplish our mutual aims?"

Charles replied. "Through consequences, of course. You do your part, and I'll do mine. If I don't deliver my end of the bargain, I expect you'll have something extra nasty in store for me. No one in government is going to want a long jury trial, I'm sure, for reasons we're both aware of."

"And if I fail at my end, a similar fate awaits me?"

"Well, fair is fair."

"But Mr. Knight, *you* are the criminal, not me."

"Let's dispense with that foolishness. In addition to what I've already mentioned, you run the largest counterfeiting operation in world history. Probably the biggest crime of all. You needn't be so modest about your credentials."

"I'd best learn what you expect of me, Mr. Knight."

And so Charles provided his list. He didn't ask for much. He had no confidence that Samuels would value Sabina sufficiently to trade much of value. Maybe, at this point, Samuels saw her as a rusted-out junker that wouldn't start and needed tires. Can't expect much in a trade.

But he had no concerns about Samuels's ability to hold up his end of the bargain. If he wanted to.

Samuels agreed to Charles's terms.

Whether TJ could arrange Sabina's release, however, remained in serious doubt. Charles never imagined that he, of all people, would be rooting for Sabina Heidel's escape from captivity.

*　　*　　*

Sabina Heidel was wrapped in swaddling clothes and sleeping in a manger. Of course there was absolutely nothing Christ-like about her. The cows, pigs, goats, and donkeys that once fed in the little barn had long since been eaten to feed the soldiers and rebels who fought during the Gondwanan civil wars. If any large animals escaped, they were eaten by the families who owned them to avoid starvation. Only a few farms near the coast had begun to repopulate the country with newly imported livestock.

Here, far out in the middle of nowhere, what little still remained from more civilized days had been absorbed back into the jungle. The wood of the ancient manger had rotted over the decades, but remained solid enough to firmly hold the straps that kept her captive.

She had no idea where she was, nor any clue as to how long she'd been there. Sunlight trickled through holes in the thatched roof over her head, but then so did rain. The drugs, the fitful sleep, and the regular application of a bag over her head made it impossible to keep any track of time. The drugs left her nauseated and vertiginous. She knew she couldn't trust her own mind; she might never be able to think clearly again. She lay confused, angry, lost, and scared.

She had not once seen a woman during her vaguely alert periods. Always men. And that horrifying creature that stared at her, if it could be called staring. Almost as wide as it was tall, the living haystack stood wrapped in layers of cloth, with a place where a face evidently belonged, yet no face was there. Ancient leather scraps, or ancient swaths of human skin, outlined where a thick neck might be on the creature. The thing had no place outside of a horror movie directed by a man with a very sick mind. Occasionally she had sufficient wits about her to realize that a human stood within the diabolical outfit.

Other times, she assumed she was in hell.

She thought it rained less and less with each period of wakefulness. The rainy season was ending. What did that mean? She didn't know. Weeks perhaps. She could not recount how many strange ceremonies they had immersed her in. Strapped to a board, immobile, covered with dead palm

412

fronds, with teenage boys dancing around, frequently exposing their transitioning manhood to her, doing what teenage boys throughout the world do to stimulate themselves, and doing it with no regard to privacy. But she hadn't been raped, at least not while she was aware.

Sometimes she returned to consciousness to find that she had been bathed and wrapped in a clean swath of cloth. She felt grateful to whoever performed this service, but her consciousness was so fleeting that she had no idea what service she had performed in return, if any.

She ate the food they placed in her mouth. She chewed the bland paste and swallowed it, followed by water.

She awoke this time to find a man holding her right hand. Her left hand was still strapped to the manger's wooden support beam. She turned her head to look into eyes that, to her mind, seemed to show sympathy.

She was lucid enough, for a moment, to feel disgusted with herself. How could she have been captured by these savages?

She sought no mercy. She sought no display of kindness. She didn't have the consistent cognitive function to seek to escape.

But here were those eyes. They belonged to a more mature man, not one of the boys that populated the place. The haystack devil stood in the corner, maybe facing her, she couldn't tell.

"Ms. Heidel," the man said.

The tenor of his voice seemed familiar. She had talked to this man before, hadn't she? Yes, she had. While stuporous. She remembered something faintly. He had asked her questions.

She jerked upright then, so fast that the thick leather strap that restrained her wrenched back her shoulder. Her mind came fully alert now, and she remembered that this man had interrogated her. And under the influence of the drugs, she had answered him.

"What have I told you?"

The Gondwanan man was handsome, with a rounded belly and the earliest touches of gray hair at his temples. He replied, "What we needed to know. The truth. The number of canisters of fake Naked Emperor you have released on the market. And why you did so. And about the killing of schoolchildren, orchestrated by you…"

She experienced a flash of terror, but replaced it immediately with defiance, and a slight smile.

The man continued, "… and carried out by a man whose name you kindly provided."

Her momentary pride faded.

"Where's Donald?" she asked.

"Mr. Debocher is no concern of yours now."

"And Tip Harding? The embassy is going to call out all hell on you people."

"The man from the embassy is well. The Poro have no use for him. Unlike you."

"Who are you?"

"I am just a man."

She gazed at him, and ingrained his face in her memory. "Why are you here?"

"I have been coming each day to make sure that you don't cause harm to any of the boys here."

"Me? Harm *them*?"

"Yes. These boys are blameless. They'll be here for many months, some for years. They are becoming adults here in this place. We hope that they will become good men. You, however, are evil. Evil spreads as does a plague. I come to make sure you are kept incoherent, so your words and ideas and actions don't infect my people."

"Why don't you just kill me then?"

"Is that what you wish?"

"Yes." She spat her answer at him.

"You don't get what you want, Ms. Heidel. At least not now. For several reasons, I desire you to be kept alive. For the moment, you are serving a ritual purpose that provides for the needs of the young men here. Depending on events outside of your control, it is possible that your service in these rituals may last for many years and influence many men. Your life may become an ongoing sacrifice, and these men will use your spirit as a conduit to the dead who have preceded us. Perhaps for the first time in your life you will be doing something of value."

"I'll be rescued. Someone will tell the outside world that there's a white woman here."

"Oh, the taboo against anyone doing so is *very* powerful. I assure you that what you hope for is … is quite impossible."

"Then I'll commit suicide."

"That would be a fitting end to a woman who has killed so many. But we will keep you alive, at least in a way..."

"Fuck you."

"I do have one more question. A confirmation really. Your honest response will be met with a reward you would not expect."

She sat quietly.

"Who would have killed Dr. James Sandridge?"

She was alert enough that she would never answer such a question.

"Well then, I'll be back small-small. Your memory will, I'm sure, improve."

The man let go of her hand, turned to the straw devil and spoke incoherently. And then he stepped out.

Sabina had never cried in sadness, as far as she could recall. Crying served only as an occasional tool of control. In her current situation, crying would serve no purpose.

Instead, while still lucid, she would plot her escape and revenge.

But before she could engage her brain in that pursuit, the drugs she had swallowed, mixed as they were in the starchy paste and eaten half in sleep, reached her brain. She watched the faceless straw devil smile without either a mouth or eyes, and then she drifted back into a state of nightmares and nonexistence.

*　　*　　*

Xander Winn kept his condominium overlooking the Potomac for reasons beyond convenience and inertia. The first was that it kept appreciating in value as the money spigot poured full blast over Washington, D.C. The second was that, barring nuclear calamity, Washington was likely to be the one city in the United States that would thrive—even, or especially, during an economic collapse. Washington was Rome. As the outlands fell, this capital would stay secure. At least until all its domains had been leached of value. Only then would the proles revolt, either before or after the barbarians breached the walls.

He could have rented out the elegant apartment. With its superb panorama of D.C. and the Potomac, some lobbyist would have paid top dollar. But Xander had no need to do so. He needed a place to hang the artwork he'd accumulated in the U.S. over the years. He had other properties—in

Europe, South America, and Asia—but this one was convenient for the few times a year he had business here in Mordor. Or was it Trantor? D.C. could pass as the product of either Tolkien's or Asimov's imagination. During this past year's absence, the place had also served as Charles's part-time home.

Xander sat on his balcony in the cool, dimming light of autumn, winter just knocking at the city's door.

He heard a key in the door. Xander's eyes closed, and a smile of contentment appeared on his tanned face. He rose from his perch and stood to greet the young man he had not seen in almost a year, and then only briefly.

A bold handshake, a broad smile, and an extra squeeze on his shoulder indicated their mutual fondness.

Charles held several paper bags of Chinese food and a six-pack of Negro Modelo.

"I probably would have welcomed you even without the food and beer, kid."

"I was hungry. Figured you might be too."

"We could have gone out."

Charles said, "It's hard to eat in a restaurant while wearing a hoodie. At the moment, I don't go anywhere without my hoodie. And billed cap. And usually dark glasses. And that's what this scruffy beard is about."

"That's right. The cameras are everywhere. I hear they can program them to look for people wearing a certain color, people of a certain height, people with distinctive gaits. God knows what else. The hoodie isn't sufficient. You should stay off the street."

"I do. With rare exceptions. I do get hungry though."

"Well, you've got me here now, kid. So, time for you to stay in place. Do people know you've been living here? They could snitch."

"I've kept a low profile; mostly been at Alpha's place. I don't want your neighbors to know you're harboring a drug lord."

Xander popped the tops off a couple of bottles, and set out plates and utensils on his old wooden dining table. It looked like it had been crafted from an ancient barn door. Because, indeed, it had been. Xander not only liked the way it looked, but liked the fact any further damage would just add to its character. The two men dug into the food as if it were a last meal, perhaps because it might be.

"What's on your mind, Charles?"

Charles chewed on a too-large piece of dumpling and then swallowed.

"Remember when we decided to kill that raging maniac in Gondwana? I was just a kid, but I knew it was the right thing to do."

Xander replied solemnly. "I remember everyone I've had to take out, Charles. And I regret some. But not JohnJohn. I've never regretted that."

"I found another one of those types."

"I have a feeling you're talking about Seth Fowler, right?"

"Exactly. He's got a young friend of mine, a kid really, on ice."

"Killing him won't help with that."

"He's murdered hundreds of people with the fake Sybillene that he put out on the streets, and thousands more are sick. Some are permanently disabled."

"This was all done intentionally?"

"Yes."

"You sure?"

"Yes. And the school shootings too. They were all staged."

"Based on what information?"

"TJ heard it straight from the lips of Sabina Heidel."

Xander exhaled deeply, leaned back in his chair.

"What can I do to help, Charles?"

"Well, for one thing, I'm going to need to borrow a rifle."

47

Praetorians

CHARLES and Xander talked through much of the night. It should have been just a pleasant evening for two men with a lot in common, not least some dangerous adventures. But theirs was a business conversation focused on how best to kill a high government official. And an ethical discussion of whether doing so was right.

"When I was young, my uncle asked me what it meant to live a good life."

"I know," Xander replied. "So what's your answer?"

"I'm still working on it."

"When you figure it out, kid, let me know. I'm thirty years older than you, and I'm still looking for that answer."

"I was hoping you'd have figured it out and could save me some time..."

"A lot of people have put their answers in books over the last few thousand years. Lots of answers. But I don't know anybody has *The Answer*. If I thought I had *The Answer*, I'd tell you. But maybe I'd be wrong. And if I were, you might go off in the wrong direction. So I wouldn't be doing you a favor. Anyway, it's more of a process than a destination. There are many paths up the mountain. I'm afraid most people are too lazy or distracted to even look for one."

"Yeah, that's what my uncle would say."

"He's a good man."

"It's time to go."

Xander drove his '68 Mustang, rocking and reveling in the automotive dinosaur's character as they accelerated.

"Remember, I'm a wanted man, Xander." Charles pushed his feet against the floorboard. "Let's not give the cops any cause to look at us."

Xander let the car slow down, while now moving just slightly faster than the traffic stream.

They made some strange purchases that morning. They found a seedy thrift shop run by a church in a poor neighborhood, from which they acquired old wool clothing that hadn't yet been dry-cleaned for resale. Perfect. At a grocery store, Xander bought some canned meat and a toothbrush. They stopped by a hardware store where Xander bought a whole-body Tyvek outfit, the kind used by painters to protect their clothes. They put it all together in a single large suitcase. Then, Xander rented a car using one of the many false identification cards he kept on hand. He covered the license plates with a light-refracting plastic surface that was reasonably competent at confounding digital cameras. They left Xander's Mustang in an underground lot and drove into D.C.

Fifteen blocks from the Willard Intercontinental Hotel, Xander pulled into an alley. Charles removed a tall suitcase from the trunk. The disassembled rifle fit neatly inside it. He sat down on the ground. Xander accelerated out of the alley and disappeared.

Charles, dressed in one of the thrift-store coats, appeared homeless. He sat on the pavement next to an odiferous dumpster, for hours, and tried to read. This ought to prove his loyalty to Xander, for he did this purely to diminish the possibility of the ubiquitous street cameras connecting the visiting Dutchman's face with a homeless bum that would soon be a *person of interest* in the investigation of a major crime. Was it overkill? Maybe. But he had to protect Xander.

When the time came, he applied false eyebrows bushy enough to distract an observer from noting any other facial feature. It was a simple disguise, but effective. He covered his head and as much of his face as possible with a scarf and large sunglasses, adopted a slouch, and began the long trek, just another bum, rolling the case behind him. He cut through side alleys, seeming to wander aimlessly behind buildings and dodging, as often as possible, the numerous security cameras that would be examined in exquisite detail after the fact. Although the exertion helped warm him up after sitting for so long, the chill of the late fall helped avert sweat that might cause his

419

extra-furry eyebrows to become cockeyed. Hunching over throughout all this time caused his back to complain.

Just before he entered the Willard he improved his appearance by changing into a respectable overcoat and standing erect. He transformed from a bum to a harried businessman in two simple steps accomplished on the fly, thus averting any unwelcome attention from the doorman. He headed to the elevators.

The suite on the top floor overlooked the Treasury Department and the South Lawn of the White House. He went straight up to the room, donned latex gloves outside the door, and knocked. No answer. Good. Behind a fire extinguisher he found the keycard, exactly where China had promised to put it. It opened the door, and he slid inside.

He stripped out of his clothes while standing in the shower, and placed them in a plastic bag. He then showered thoroughly to remove skin flakes with a bristle brush, and then drip-dried before slathering himself with skin moisturizer. He let the shower run for an extra half an hour. He wrapped himself in his Tyvek suit, leaving only his face exposed. He removed the old clothing from the suitcase, and shook the nasty decades-old dust and human skin flakes that had accumulated on them around the hotel room and bathroom. The dust slowly settled into the carpet and bed clothes. After opening the window about four inches, he sat on his suitcase and read another book. He had a long wait ahead.

*　　*　　*

Dick Stafford sat at his desk in the West Wing with his eyes closed, awaiting the next barrage of disasters that would manage to get past his secretary and walk through his door. He had aged three years for each year in this office. While the president had been just the vice president, he had had little to do, leaving him plenty of time to plot. But now, as chief of staff to the president of the United States, there was hardly time to breathe, never mind time for plotting. He made decisions on the fly, usually based on pure expedience. Right and wrong barely entered his conscious thoughts anymore. In fact, it was increasingly hard to tell the difference. Or care what difference it made. If there really was a difference to start with. As in the jungle, life in the White House consisted of trying to survive another day.

How did it get this way? Why was he always putting out fires?

The answer, he logically thought, was that he had no time to *prevent* the fires.

But there was another answer, lingering in his subconscious, barely visible under layers of defense, self-deception, foolhardiness, and brainwashing: he had spent his political career dodging anything inconvenient. If it didn't fit, it couldn't be true. If he'd taken just ten puffs of Sybillene he might have seen the truth that, to avoid having to put out all those fires, one should stop *lighting the fires* in the first place.

Under the debris that buried this truth, however, Stafford possessed an excellent intellect. It was why the president had kept him close all these years. His was a powerful mind that could see how to put out fires, dodge the bullets, or kick the can down the road. All valuable skills in D.C.

Just as capital accumulation was essential to create material wealth, power accumulation was essential to what Stafford valued. Stafford had power now, but only through the medium of the president's ear. He'd fed off his friend's political charisma all the way into the White House. He was brighter, more capable, and more discerning than his boss, but he lacked his friend's charm. Until recently, there had never been an opportunity to detach from his friend and be something other than a sidekick, an also-ran in the game of life. But now, a light, in the form of the SEA, appeared far up the tunnel, and it beckoned him. It was a place where electability didn't matter.

Stafford opened his eyes and took a breath. His mind would soon be distracted by the next unpredicted fire.

His secretary ushered in Seth Fowler.

"Seth, thanks for making the effort. We won't need the president today."

Fowler said, "You might want to reserve judgment on that."

"Fair enough," Stafford replied. But he had no plans whatsoever to involve the president. "What do you have for me? What are your thoughts about how we best leverage the … momentum … SEA has built?"

"I have an idea."

"Go ahead and sit down, Seth. I'm sure we're on the same wavelength." He didn't like the man, or think he was particularly smart. But he recognized Seth had some talents and that they shared a similar worldview—and, disturbingly, that the man had become quite powerful in his own right in recent months.

Fowler sat opposite him and stared, too intently and for too long, before he said, "We're successful with SEA because we know that to succeed, one has to do whatever is necessary. That's always seemed obvious to me."

Stafford listened.

Fowler continued, "A modern government needs to do whatever is necessary. There are too many dangers in the world, too many threats. We can't afford anachronistic laws that limit our options and effectiveness."

Stafford felt no need to interrupt. There were some who might raise legal, historical, or philosophical objections to these views, but they were an insignificant minority at this point. What Fowler said was just common sense.

"We need to run a tighter ship. The president is the head of this nation. He's the CEO of the greatest country in the world. Our position is fading because the people have become lazy and uncooperative. We've got to be disciplined and united."

Stafford looked at Fowler with concealed amusement. The muscular man in front of him had no idea about the financial structures that really controlled things. Or the shaky foundation everything rested on. No matter. Fowler was a useful idiot. Even a necessary idiot.

"So what's the role of SEA, Fowler?"

"The SEA should remain the SEA."

Stafford frowned.

Fowler explained. "I mean, we keep the name SEA. It's focused. It's limited. It declares on its face that our authority is over Sybillene. With actual Sybillene out of the picture soon, few will pay attention to us. And we can go about our work unnoticed. That is, until we want to be paid attention to."

Stafford liked where this was going, but he chose to counter by saying, "Congress may pay attention less too. SEA might lose funding."

"Don't count on that. They'll need us for whenever Sybillene raises its head. Any Naked Emperor anywhere is sufficient to scare Congress. And I'm sure we can raise that specter in the news conveniently before Congress sets budgets. We have the muscle, and judicious use of our emergency powers will keep any politicians who might buck the trend in line. My people have started to put together dossiers on select members of Congress. And some other prominent people as well."

Stafford picked up on the subtle change in expression that Fowler no doubt intended to reveal. With a barely perceptible lilt and a slant of a cheek muscle, Fowler made it clear that he had a file on Stafford.

Fowler continued without missing a beat. "I have some ideas on how to get some self-funding as well, like the CIA has done for decades. And I anticipate that my people will have time to work on this. If anyone opposes us, well, we'll tear the rug out from under them. Congress will get the message."

"Just like Hoover?"

Fowler smiled. "Like Hoover on steroids."

Stafford prodded. "Of course the same methods can be used to keep the Supreme Court in line too."

Fowler nodded. "Only used for the greater good."

"Of course."

"We've been given a very deep tool chest. SEA could do a lot of good behind the scenes with the powers we've been granted. SEA can become the president's discretionary force. The way I see it, we'll function inside this country like the CIA functions outside. We'll identify and eliminate threats to the authority of the president of the United States. We'll be doing what no one else can."

"Yes … a praetorian guard."

Augustus, the first Roman emperor, maintained the appearance of normalcy by creating a pretense that the old republic remained intact. He didn't want to appear as a dictator—that's why Caesar was assassinated, after all—but rather as first among equals. He also needed a cohesive, powerful group under his direct control while he consolidated power. The praetorian guards were necessary to make sure everyone cooperated. Controlling the praetorians, however, was like keeping a pet tiger.

Fowler nodded knowingly. "Absolutely loyal to the president. And with essentially no limitations. SEA will quietly, unobtrusively protect and serve the country and the president. For as long as he remains the president."

Something in Stafford's traditional middle class upbringing triggered some queasiness at Fowler's suggestion. However, he also knew this was the direction things *had* to go, if the nation were to survive. At least in anything like its current form. This was just the next step in evolution, as had happened in Rome. Paul Samuels would favor it. The Federal Reserve's high-wire balancing act would someday fail, perhaps soon, and decades of economic distortions would come unglued in a massive depression. What

Fowler recommended now would soon be necessary to stay in front of the coming political and social firestorm.

Wealth was increasingly concentrated in the hands of the politically connected. And although they'd also become wealthy, politicians had to remain in the good graces of those in whom wealth was concentrated. It was the same in the days of Rome. Whenever in history wealth wasn't supported by sufficient power, bloody revolution ensued. That was just human nature and envy at work, and they had to be beaten back by whatever means necessary. As the system became more unstable, more force would be needed to keep it together. The powers of SEA were a necessary part of the arsenal. Inevitable.

Good and bad, right and wrong, moral or immoral—none of that mattered. It didn't matter what party held power. The future of the country would follow the dictates of historical necessity.

"Seth, you're a like-minded thinker. Let me incubate this. We have some of our own ideas too. We'll get together again in a few days to discuss a workable synthesis."

It was good to be the closest advisor to the king, but better to be the closest advisor to an emperor. And of course a praetorian guard would be needed to secure the position. The SEA could help maintain and expand the components of the status quo that benefited Stafford. As long as it persisted, he would attain more power, more wealth. For Stafford, it had become the meaning of life.

Stafford's own idea for the future of the SEA was quite similar to Fowler's. However, it made no sense to leave Fowler in charge; the praetorian commander usually assassinated the emperor and his court, and assumed the throne himself.

So he, not Fowler, had better be the commander.

Unfortunately, Seth Fowler had modeled himself as a new J. Edgar Hoover. Successfully pushing him aside without destructive blowback would require exquisite caution.

* * *

Fowler walked down the steps of the White House's eastern entrance into a freezing rain, moving quickly. He rounded the corner and looked up toward the top floor of the Willard Intercontinental, one block away. In one of those rooms, China awaited him. Perhaps China would become a regular and replace Sabina. His clothes started to soak through, but he wouldn't be wearing them for long, and there should be plenty of time for them to dry.

He had the impression that Stafford would work against him. In what way, he didn't know. It was more of a gut feeling than anything that Stafford had said. Something in his mannerism, his tone. It wasn't right. He wasn't being offered the full support that he deserved.

If Stafford got in his way, Fowler would need to employ all the tools in his arsenal, and many of the methods he had learned over the years, and, he had to admit, more recently, through Sabina's mentoring. His tools came with no rules limiting their use, other than the mandate to use them to accomplish whatever aim he saw fit.

Yes, SEA was a great tool for the United States to use against the whiners, the traitors, and the politically unreliable types who infested the country. But it also would serve well in the defeat of Dick Stafford, Chris Cooligan, and anyone else who might obstruct him.

His pace quickened and he stood more erect. The future was his to take. And he would take it.

He was just about to cross 15th Street when his phone buzzed in his pocket. He answered.

*   *   *

"Hello, Fowler."

"Who is this?"

"Charles Knight." Charles spoke with composure that he didn't feel.

The rain fell hard enough that no one would want to stand still. Nonetheless Fowler stopped in his tracks. Charles watched from Fowler's own hotel room window as Fowler stood on the other side of the street below, cell phone to his ear.

"Mr. Knight."

"Yes, it's me, Fowler. In the flesh, as they say."

"Excuse me for not being sure of that. I'll hold off on judgment."

"I wish that was truly in your nature."

"Enough chitchat. I presume you're calling from a secure location, on a disposable phone. So what's on your mind?"

A garbage truck carrying a commercial-sized green metal dumpster on its rear forks made a racket as it came barreling down 15th Street. It would pass by Fowler in a moment. Charles could hear the truck better than he could hear the man on the other end of the phone.

"I have no proposition for you, Fowler. I just wanted you to stand still for a moment. It makes my job easier."

It came to Fowler a second too late.

In that moment, his body crumpled to the pavement, blood streaming from his twisted neck, forming a winding rivulet on the wet sidewalk until a red river found its way into a storm drain.

Seth Fowler thus pumped his life blood into a gutter, which flowed into a sewer, and on into the Potomac.

*　　*　　*

One shot. One kill.

Xander had taught him that.

The rifle's screw-on suppressor significantly reduced its report. Contrary to the impression the public gets from movies, a suppressor doesn't truly silence most guns loaded with anything larger than a .22 rimfire. Certainly not a rifle with enough punch to get a serious job done. But today the sound of the shot just might go unnoticed. To be heard, its report had to compete with pounding rain, the traffic, and especially the clamor of a trash truck.

Charles had planned for the hotel room to be found. Investigators would be on the scene, and over time might reasonably triangulate the path of the bullet, fired from so close, just across the street. Neighboring guests might have heard the muffled gunshot, if anyone were yet in those rooms. Soon, the investigators would find that the SEA—indeed, Fowler himself— had secured a hotel room that fit within the range of the shooter's predicted position. Regardless, they'd search every room on this side of the hotel as a standard operating procedure.

Authorities solved very few of the many murders in Washington, even though they had plenty of technology available. In a routine homicide, resources couldn't be spared to go through thousands of hours of video camera footage in an attempt to track every person caught on film who might have approached or left the murder scene. But when the head of the SEA is killed just after departing the White House, every scrap of DNA and all the available footage would be viewed, processed, correlated, and tied together.

426

Although he'd done everything possible to minimize his DNA signature in the room, he was glad that Xander had recommended camouflaging what did come off of him. Thus all the nasty accumulated skin flakes from old people's old clothes.

Charles had the window closed and his suppressed rifle disassembled and back in the suitcase before anyone even noticed Fowler on the ground, the rain soaking his warm dead body.

He knew where the hotel CCTV cameras were located. He took a necessary calculated risk, looked up and down the hall, and walked into the adjacent stairwell. There, he stripped off his painting attire, stuffed it into the suitcase, changed latex gloves for leather, reapplied his thick eyebrows, put on a brimmed hat, and donned an overcoat and raised its collar. He descended two flights before taking the elevator to the lobby. He exited from the far side of the hotel and walked east toward Union Station at a reasonable clip, the suitcase in tow. It was a long walk in the freezing rain. With video cameras on all the streets recording almost everything, the suitcase would be relatively easy to pick out and track. But that would be in retrospect, only later, as the investigation into Fowler's death ensued.

At Union Station his trail would be lost. In a busy but unsurveilled hallway previously scouted by Xander, he covered his suitcase in duct tape, radically altering its appearance. Hundreds of people walked by while he did this, but no one paid any heed. He looked like a frustrated man fixing up a ripped zipper on his baggage before boarding a train. He changed his coat and hat, and then turned back to come in the way he had entered, out into the world of video cameras, to the ticketing desk, where he bought himself a ticket on the next train to anywhere. With cash.

Thirty minutes later, when the northbound train next stopped, he exited the train and called Xander for a lift back.

It was an enormous amount of effort to avoid being caught, considering that he knew he would, in a few days, be locked in a cell.

But he wouldn't be in a cell for the crime he actually committed: the killing of Seth Fowler.

*   *   *

Sabina emerged through the brown fog of a persistent nightmare. Monsters, naked youths, hatred, and abominations coursed through her confused mind. She felt mud, dirt, grass beneath her. And rain. Fear. Shaking horror. She could take no more. And then she slipped back down through her levels of consciousness, arriving back into that corner of hell from which she had come.

Later, when she came back up through the mists again, she felt pain. In her stomach, everywhere. She vomited time and time again. When finally she finished, she rose slowly to her knees. Scrub and bamboo surrounded her. Clarity gradually returned, with an incessant pounding in her head.

She vomited again, but this time it alleviated her pain. She lay back down and fell into a fitful sleep, and when she awoke her mind seemed clearer. She examined herself. Blood and mud covered her fingers, which cried out in pain when she touched anything. Otherwise, all seemed intact. Except...

She had no fingernails. And she had no hair.

She ran her hands over her scalp. Smooth.

Her pained fingers felt no eyebrows. And, no eyelashes either. She'd heard about female circumcision in Africa. Anxiety streamed through her then. A bright-blue African dress, long and rough, covered her. She shrieked in agony as her bloody fingertips grasped at the rough fabric and pulled it up above her thighs so she might examine herself. No hair. Not even there.

But no injury either.

She squeezed her eyes closed, and then opened them again. She breathed until her heart rate settled some. Slowly, she rose to her feet. Flat sandals protected her soles. She was grateful for that. But her toes had suffered the same procedure as her fingers. Toenails removed to the quick, congealed blood covering all.

She heard road noise. A passing car. And a rooster. Sounds of children. She pushed through the bush, cutting her arms on palm fronds and broken bamboo. It didn't hurt as much as the astonishing shocks that shot up from her feet with each step. In a few yards, she came out into the clear, and looked over a small village of concrete houses with corrugated-zinc roofs.

She stumbled to the nearest house.

In ten minutes, she had borrowed a cell phone. She suffered exquisite pain, one number at a time, as she dialed Paul Samuels.

Sabina Heidel was free from a nightmare few had ever escaped.

And then, for the first time in her memory, she cried.

48

A Good Deed Unpunished

THE courthouse was filled to capacity as guards paraded Charles Knight toward his seat on the left, designated for those presumed guilty. There would be no trial. He was here simply to plead to an offense sufficient to make the government happy.

While awaiting trial, the attorney general had threatened him with a series of criminal indictments that would have had him locked up for the rest of his life. He'd even had a visit from Dick Stafford, the president's very own chief of staff.

"Mr. Knight," Stafford had said. "We haven't met. But I remember you. We let you go free eight years ago when we should have indicted you for insider trading."

Charles did not feel particularly talkative after sitting in a cell for four days.

"The attorney general is going to offer you a deal. I suggest you take it."

Charles replied, "Somehow, I don't think it's going to be a fair deal. *Whatever happened to justice?*"

"Justice is meted out at the discretion of the victors. And you, Mr. Knight, are not the victor."

Charles looked into Stafford's eyes. Cold intelligence emanated from them. *Was this man soulless? Or was he just a bureaucratic machine, trying to get through his week?* "Am I just the next fire for you to put out, Stafford?"

"The fire you started is already out. I'm here to help make sure it doesn't reignite."

"What are you proposing?"

"From what I understand, you take your freedom seriously."

"Wouldn't anyone with any self-respect?"

"Yet you walked into the FBI headquarters and turned yourself in."

Charles didn't reply.

"Why?"

"SEA has been killing people. That's why. I want to exercise my right to a speedy trial. I'm going to take the stand."

"Yes, yes. Speedy trial. You know there is no definition of that anymore, right?"

"My lawyer goes public today about SEA's creation of the toxic counterfeit Sybillene. That will be enough to get the ball rolling. It should cause quite a scandal."

"They won't believe your lawyer."

"They won't believe you either."

"Well, that's partly your fault." Stafford flared his nostrils, a faint bit of anger emerging.

"I hope so," Charles replied. "I'll ask again. What are you offering?"

"Seth Fowler is dead."

"Yes."

"Donald Debocher is probably dead. And between you and me, I don't think their loss is worth mourning. If there have been any excesses at SEA, or with Visioryme, and I don't admit there have been, well, these are the people responsible for it."

Charles again chose to say nothing.

"Right now there is a power vacuum at SEA. I'm about to fill that vacuum. The first thing that will happen is that SEA will release information as to how to distinguish the real Naked Emperor—your drug—from the poisoned canisters."

Charles exhaled.

"But SEA will only do this, Mr. Knight, if you assist us."

"You're going to let people die unless I go quietly into the night?"

Stafford shrugged. "We want you to leave it to us to clean up this toxic Naked Emperor mess. Without interference, without inflammatory statements from your lawyer. No one wants any more people dying."

Charles stared at him. "I don't like hypocrites."

"We're on the same team, you and I. We both want to end these unnecessary deaths."

Charles said, "So I tell my lawyer to keep SEA's involvement in Naked Emperor a secret. We keep it secret that Sabina Heidel—an employee of the Federal Reserve and special assistant to the president—hired a man to murder children in four schools. And if I do that, you will let me go free?"

Stafford laughed. "Free? No. Of course you can't go free. Don't you know there are mobs—virtual ones on the Internet, anyway—clamoring to string you up? To half the country—Democrats, Republicans, whoever— you're a demon, a drug lord, an assassin of hundreds of innocent people, a veritable terrorist. In their minds, you're one step below the Antichrist. If we let you go, Mr. Knight, that might start a different sort of revolution than what Naked Emperor might have triggered. So, no, we aren't letting you go. Not entirely."

"You're promising you will go full out to make people aware of the toxic counterfeit?"

"Obviously I cannot put that in writing, but we will." Stafford nodded.

Charles tried to believe him. But it was logical. They needed the whole scandal to die, and then to claim a victory obtained by the hands of vigilant and dedicated public servants.

"Will you dismantle the SEA?"

"What happens with SEA isn't your concern, Mr. Knight. It has its own destiny. It will have new leadership, obviously. And I can assure you that I will be watching it closely."

"Somehow, that doesn't console me."

"In exchange for your cooperation, we will allow you to throw yourself on the mercy of the court."

"I don't expect much mercy."

"Just between you and me, and never to be repeated, the judge for your case has been carefully selected. We've instructed the judge to sentence you to twenty years. Maybe you'll be out in fourteen, with good behavior of course. Good, quiet behavior."

That was a hell of a lot of life to lose.

Charles prompted, "Every news station in the country, all those networks you control, every one of them gets the story about how to identify the toxic Naked Emperor, and they get that story tonight, right?"

"I can make that happen."

"Stop the killing, Stafford."

"I'm interested in a quiet, docile country. That's incompatible with a lot of mayhem. So, yes."

"Then I'll agree."

Bureaucracy rarely moves fast. Except when the leaders make urgency clear and personal. The leaders wanted the news cycle to roll off of Charles Knight and Naked Emperor and onto something positive, like some new legislation, or the most recent Hollywood divorces. So the process moved extremely fast, and Charles found himself in court for his sentencing in a week. They would put him away in a nice quiet place until he was fifty.

*　*　*

So Charles trudged into the courtroom in prison garb and manacles, for he had refused to wear a suit.

He scanned the audience. In the very back row, notepad in hand, sat Albert Peale and his probation officer, Tony Sciberra. Xander Winn rounded out the row, looking on with an expression more of pride than concern. Charles was about to turn forward when he saw Tristana and Alpha and, sitting between them, Rainbow.

Charles breathed a sigh of relief. Although pale and weak and with fading bruises still on her face, Rainbow was alive and free.

Rainbow smiled and waved.

Check one off for Paul Samuels. So far, he'd held up his end of the bargain. Clearly not from any sense of honor. No doubt it just didn't matter to Samuels if Rainbow lived or died. There was no cost to him in letting her live.

The bailiff ordered all to rise upon the judge's arrival.

"Hear ye, hear ye, hear ye. The United States District Court for the District of Columbia is now open. The Honorable Warren Thomason, presiding."

Charles tried not to smile.

The silver-haired judge whom Charles had met over a year ago in a checkout line at Walmart jostled with his black robe as he took his seat. Judge Thomason looked out over the packed courtroom and then focused his eyes on the defendant. He imperceptibly smiled at the man who every month supplied his son with the medication needed for his muscular dystrophy.

Check off another for Paul Samuels. Charles would never underestimate the power that the Federal Reserve held over the system.

Charles masked his recognition of the judge but allowed a quick smile of his own, and then averted his gaze while the reporters and audience watched him with intense curiosity.

The prosecutor had been told, actually commanded in no uncertain terms by the attorney general himself, that a twenty-year sentence was what the president wanted for Knight. No more, and no less. He'd also been counseled not to allow this case to come to full trial by means of any last-minute legal tricks.

As part of the deal, Charles was only required to plead to possession. With the new laws passed by Congress, that would be enough.

Charles would plead nolo contendere to two counts of possession of Sybillene. The mandatory punishment for possession was severe, at ten years per count. The fact that he had no prior convictions was no justification for leniency in Sybillene-related cases.

As Judge Thomason spoke, Charles could hear the man's empathy. But no one else could. To everyone else, the voice was insistent and direct.

"You have no counsel, Mr. Knight. Do you understand that you have the right to legal counsel?"

Some right that was! Stafford had made it clear that if Charles retained legal representation, government efforts to publicize the toxic counterfeit Naked Emperor would stagnate. Charles's waiver of his right to counsel would lead to fewer people dying at the hands of government. And so he replied, "Yes, your honor."

A giant parasite had latched onto him. He felt it deep in his chest.

"Do you understand the charges brought against you?"

"I do, sir." He understood them far better than the prosecutor did. He saw his liberty circling down a dark vortex.

"Is it your decision," Thomason said, "not to have a jury, and to plead nolo contendere, which is tantamount to a guilty plea, pursuant to a plea agreement?"

Charles replied, "It is, your honor."

"And that you will therefore be convicted of the charges brought against you, and that your sentencing will be immediate?"

"Yes, your honor."

Was it a law of physics that government destroys liberty the way a black hole consumes everything, including light?

"We note that there will likely be no appeal from this case. Do you understand?"

"Yes, your honor." Charles had fallen inside the event horizon of that black hole.

"Then the prosecution may proceed."

And the prosecution did so. With a no-contest plea, the tiniest scintilla of evidence would be enough to convict. They had that scintilla, although not much more.

Charles sat still. He barely heard the words that came from the government attorney. Why bother to listen?

It was all formality at this point. In the end, Charles stood, and Judge Thomason declared him guilty.

Judge Thomason then proceeded to pronounce his sentence, also predetermined by an unjust system.

The judge said these words: "Charles Knight, after contemplating all the facts and considering all the circumstances, this court hereby sentences you to twenty years' incarceration in a federal penitentiary."

Chaos arose in the courtroom as the crowd cried out in anger, a few because his punishment seemed too little, but most because it was far too long.

All Charles heard was their anger. All he felt was the years fall away from his life. He even then began planning his escape, a hope to keep himself alive while his most treasured asset—his freedom—was stolen. He felt no anger himself, but rather shock, a deep loss. He looked up at Judge Thomason, his eyes expressing the emotions that roiled within him.

Charles could see in the judge the anger that he himself now lacked. It was the same contained fury he had seen in the man's eyes in Walmart—a contempt for the pharmaceutical and medical-insurance industries and their cronies in the FDA. A hatred for the system that preyed upon his son.

Voices filled the room behind him as every person expressed disapproval.

Thomason's lips quivered. Charles frowned, curious.

It seemed the judge was not done.

Charles watched Judge Thomason as he added, almost inaudibly over the courtroom noise, "Twenty years. *Nineteen and a half years suspended.*"

The gavel fell hard.

Charles absorbed the judge's words first. After all, it mattered to him more than anyone. His mind raced. He flashed a smile. Then a frown, and then a smile again, as Judge Thomason's words washed away his momentary and useless self-pity.

Word of the suspension of ninety-eight percent of the sentence sped like lightning as the uproar of angst behind him turned into a thunderous celebration of the folk hero and admiration of the judge. The courtroom, packed with Charles's supporters, cheered. The blindsided prosecutor sat still in shock.

Charles felt a surge of warmth through his body. Seemingly he was not quite so universally despised as he had, in his darker moments, imagined.

Judge Thomason was now ready to retire.

Charles would be processed into the federal prison system for a term of six months, slightly less actually, given time already served and good behavior. Before the bailiff led him on the perp walk out the door leading to prison, Charles turned to the back and smiled at everyone there. Everyone in the courtroom stood, applauding and cheering.

He lived an exotic and adventurous life. His next adventure would involve six months in prison. Six months was enough time to gain some experience. But not enough to pick up too many bad habits. Hadn't Edmund Dantés—the Count of Mount Cristo—served harder time, and come out stronger as a result? Perhaps upon his release, Charles too might find a fortune in treasure and craft his own type of revenge.

He could handle anything for six months. His penitentiary accommodations would be better than the best hotel in Djennetown, Gondwana, that was for sure.

Charles, dressed in orange, handcuffed and with leg irons, smiled.

Life could be much, much worse.

Epilogue

SIX months later, the dry season had passed, and raindrops the size of golf balls fell on Djennetown for most hours of the day, every day. The inhabitants stayed off the streets. Little work got done—at least by people.

But work of another kind continued. The work was performed by torrents of rain hammering the pile of rubble at the top of TJ's father's mountain, where Charles's Sybillene factory had once stood. The facility had been the hope for an economic rebirth in the impoverished county. Now, through the actions of the U.N. and the U.S., it lay in ruins. It wasn't the first time they'd destroyed some backward country, while selling themselves as saviors.

The rain first washed shattered fragments of wood down the slope; soggy decaying patches of plaster from the destroyed buildings went next. Over the subsequent days and weeks and months, the rain would work its way through the larger pieces of wreckage, carrying dirt and muck down and through the fractures and holes.

The bombs dropped by the French carrier-borne jets had blown away tons of detritus, as well as the innocent people who worked there. Then the Hammer missiles had fractured the earth to a depth of fifty feet and more. The first five feet of rock had been utterly pulverized, and the rain would start its work on that material next. But nature moves slowly. It would take two years of the rainy season's incessant pounding for erosion to clear those five feet of pulverized material off the mountain top.

In a small shallow filled with water, no more than a puddle really, lay a human skull. It had been placed there carefully, silently, by a devil—or was it a man dressed as a devil?—after completion of very secret and extensive ceremonies that took place far out in the bush. That skull was the most substantial remainder—there were other pieces here and there—of the creature once known as Donald Debocher. The traditions of the secret society held that this skull would forever keep evil away from the top of this mountain.

Five feet under the skull, below the rubble chewed up by the bombs, lay what TJ's father had always claimed was there, waiting for two hundred million years to see the light of day. It had sent out its tendrils back then, little veins of itself that reached for miles. Acid ground waters had leached some of it away over the eons, grain by grain. Some of its molecules now lay in riverbeds, or even in the sandstones formed from beaches at the edge of a primordial sea. But the great mass of it remained in this mountain.

It was what had first drawn Charles Knight to Gondwana in another lifetime, eight years before.

A few more years of Mother Nature's rains—a millisecond in geological time—would remove the rest of the debris covering an exposed vein of visible and very rich gold. Light would once again reflect off of its forever-unchanging sheen.

It had long been hidden. Fifty inches wide, and plunging hundreds of feet down, it curved around the entire peak of the mountain before heading off to its origins.

It would someday, very soon in geologic terms, be recognized as the largest and richest vein of gold that would ever be discovered.

And Charles Knight owned it all.

About the Authors

DOUG Casey spends most of his time in Argentina and Uruguay, with frequent visits to the U.S., Canada, and various dysfunctional hellholes.

JOHN Hunt, MD, is a pediatrician, pulmonologist, allergist, immunologist, and former academic who resigned his tenure at a major university and stopped practicing because the insane had taken over the asylum. Now he keeps himself occupied trying to slay Leviathan.

Keep an eye out for Charles Knight's return, in Book 3 of the High Ground series: *Assassin*.